CW01652309

Daughter [illegible] ar

Annie Marks was born in Twickenham in 1947 and developed her taste for history at an early age by being lucky enough to attend primary school within Hampton Court Palace, where history lessons were quite simply walking in the corridors and State apartments. Later she went on to boarding school and after leaving at eighteen, first visited America for some months, and then worked at a wide variety of jobs from secretary to theatre dresser to a custodian in a stately home. In 1970 she moved to the Isle of Wight, but her spiritual home is the West Country, particularly the moors of Devon and Cornwall, where she plans to retire. She is married and has two grown-up sons.

Daughter of Tremar

Annie Marks

Pan Books

Daughter of Tremar first published 2000 by Robert Hale Limited

This edition published 2001 by Pan Books
an imprint of Pan Macmillan Ltd
Pan Macmillan, 20 New Wharf Road, London N1 9RR
Basingstoke and Oxford
Associated companies throughout the world
www.panmacmillan.com

ISBN 330 39891 1

Copyright © Annie Marks 2001

The right of Annie Marks to be identified as the author
of this work has been asserted by her in accordance with
the Copyright, Designs and Patents Act 1988.

All rights reserved. No part of this publication may be
reproduced, stored in or introduced into a retrieval system, or
transmitted, in any form, or by any means (electronic, mechanical,
photocopying, recording or otherwise) without the prior written
permission of the publisher. Any person who does any unauthorized
act in relation to this publication may be liable to criminal
prosecution and civil claims for damages.

1 3 5 7 9 8 6 4 2

A CIP catalogue record for this book is available from
the British Library.

Typeset by Derek Doyle & Associates, Liverpool
Printed and bound in Great Britain by
Mackays of Chatham plc, Chatham, Kent

This book is sold subject to the condition that it should not,
by way of trade or otherwise, be lent, re-sold, hired-out,
or other wise circulated without the publisher's prior consent
in any form of binding or cover other than that in which
it is published and without a similar condition including this
condition being imposed on the subsequent purchaser.

Chapter 1

The old lady sat bolt upright in bed, watching the doctor who stood politely before her, with shrewd, bright eyes. She wore a white nightgown with a pink bed jacket, a small, white cap over her sparse grey hair, and with her pointed, papery-skinned face and wary watchfulness, resembled nothing so much as an indignant bird.

Oliver had never met her before. He'd been warned more than once during these first few months in his new practice that the old girl who lived at the manor was extremely eccentric, but had told himself confidently that as a member of the new breed of young, modern doctors, a dotty old Victorian relic would be no great challenge. Now, as he actually stood beside her bed, clad in spotless flannels and sports jacket and trying to exude an air of confidence, he was forced to admit that it was more of a sham than he was comfortable with.

Politely, he waited for her to open the conversation, it was her bedroom, after all. Perversely she made him wait as she scrutinized him uncomfortably.

Finally she said, with what sounded like a faint air of disapproval, 'So, you're the new doctor I've heard so much about. You're very young, aren't you? I assume that's why you're improperly dressed. I hope you're truthful.'

'I hope I am too,' Oliver replied, somewhat surprised. 'I'm very pleased to make your acquaintance, Lady Florence.'

'You are not here to make my acquaintance, Dr Crompton,' she retorted cuttingly, 'you are here to diagnose my illness. Your predecessor, Dr Raynor, was old and irritatingly bound by class consciousness – although he did at least wear a suit! I want nothing more from you than an honest assessment of my trouble and an estimate of my life expectancy. Please don't fawn over me and kindly don't broadcast my business about the village.'

Oliver Crompton blushed hotly. He couldn't remember ever having been quite so rudely snubbed and decided, savagely, that everything he had been told about this eccentric old female from Tremar was quite true, She was a first class bitch!

'You will get, Lady Florence,' he said in a voice as stiff as her back, 'absolute professionalism from me at all times. I am not remotely interested in the social standing of any of my patients and I most certainly do not discuss their business with other people.'

'And,' she added with a highly amused little smile, 'you keep your temper admirably, young man. Tested and found not to be wanting. Good. I shall not need to be rude to you again. Forgive me but I'm old and it's not easy to trust the young on first acquaintance any more, things were so different in my day . . . still, to business then.' She wriggled down the bed on to her back and lay looking up at him. 'Prod about if you please and do your worst.'

The draughty bedroom in which the doctor and the old woman were suddenly intimately close smelt strongly of lavender. The furniture was big and dark, but quite evidently good, and though in places the wallpaper was not just tired, but peeling off, the pictures that hung about the walls were exquisite. The air of neglect quite obviously had nothing to do with lack of money.

Tremar was a compact manor-house, small in comparison to some of the grand houses in Cornwall, but very old. Some parts of it dated back to the fifteenth century and there had been Drakes living there since long before the Civil War. They were a very old Cornish family, and had owned the best part of the surrounding countryside for centuries, though the walled area that comprised the house and formal grounds was really not that extensive, and there was no great park.

Over the centuries it had seen many changes, and the village of Polwean had come into being because of the manor, even though it was now no part of it. Once there had been a flour mill, blacksmith's forge, wheelwright and carpenter's shops and a flourishing quay with lime kilns. Now the estate comprised seven tenanted farms, the two inns in the village, acres of woodland and two large sawmills just outside Bodmin, along with various other diverse interests.

Somehow, through all the years since the grateful reversal of their fortunes at the end of the Commonwealth – Tremar had always been fiercely loyal to the Monarchy – the one thing no Drake had ever seemed inclined to do was pull down the manor and build something twenty times the size, and so apart from the dower-house, which was a later addition, it remained distinctly cosy. There had been no black sheep in the family either, and the last of the line, Sir George, Lady Florence's late husband, had been as careful with money as the rest, so the old lady was extremely wealthy and could have fully staffed the house if she had chosen to, though clearly she did not.

An elderly, poor-sighted female who appeared to be a single, lonely companion had admitted him to Tremar and led him up a carpeted wooden staircase to her employer's room. Everywhere he had seen was predominantly panelled with good pictures and some massive Chinese porcelain vases. In the hall a huge grandfather clock ticked into the musty silence with musical softness and closed doors had faced him in all directions. Closed doors that he thought had probably been closed for years.

What light there was in the hall and landing had come from tightly closed, smallish windows, through which he had caught glimpses of the dower which stood at a sharp right angle to the house, and appeared to be completely deserted now. Also he had seen tiny fragments of the formal gardens, lawns appearing to need attention, and an old stone fountain which almost certainly didn't work any more, and away towards the sea, an ancient orchard just beginning to bud with spring.

Spring! However long had it been since anything like spring had crept into this house? Surely time had stood still here for years. But why, he wondered?

Now he bent over his elderly patient, tenderly fingering the ominous looking growth in the lower part of her thin, withered stomach. It was well on in development and firmly ensconced with undoubtedly deep-seated roots. He knew what it meant and had a decided idea she knew as well, but what was it she feared, pain or death?

'Are you in pain?' he asked.

'As a matter of fact, yes,' she replied. 'Is there anything that can be done?'

He looked at her, she was watching him shrewdly. There was no point, he decided, in being evasive. not even much point in trying to be kind, considering how capable she was of extreme rudeness. He plumped for brutal honesty.

'I could arrange for you to go into hospital in Bodmin,' he said, 'but

I can't promise they'll do anything. I doubt very much that the tumour is operable. On the other hand I can care for you here, but you'll need a professional nurse.'

'Please arrange that,' she replied immediately. 'I shall not leave my home and I should infinitely prefer your care to that of a lot of strangers with whom I have nothing in common and in whom I have very little faith. How long will I live, Dr Crompton?'

'I have no idea, Lady Florence,' he replied truthfully. 'Maybe a month, maybe six. I can only promise that when you need me I will be here for you.'

With great care he covered her skinny body with her night-gown and lifted her into a sitting position, propping her against her pillows. In silence she gazed at nothing in particular, seeming to brood, as the heavy air of the bedroom echoed with her wheezy breathing, then her painfully thin, parchment-dry hands moved jerkily upwards and rubbed her face with a faint scratchiness.

Oh dear no, he thought, you are no part of the coming spring. This is 1938 but you're lost miles back in time somewhere. I'm told you lost your son in the war and they mutter darkly about a daughter but they never actually say anything. What are your secrets, Lady Florence Drake, I wonder?

Abruptly, as if in answer, she turned her eyes towards him swiftly.

'Were you in the army during the war?' she asked.

He shook his head.

'I was only fifteen in 1918, but I suppose I would have gone, if it hadn't ended when it did. I remember those dreadful mornings at school when the headmaster read out the names of the fallen and the missing – so many were names I knew.'

'My son, Alexander, died at Ypres,' she murmured. 'The cream of this village died in France, you know. Twenty-seven fine young men went from here and only three ever came home. They went away in their prime, with pride in their hearts – and died face down in the mud! Dear God, what a waste, what a dreadful, dreadful waste . . . and now there's talk of another war with Germany, against this man Hitler. Doesn't anyone ever learn. . . ?'

She tailed off again into silence and Oliver glanced surreptitiously at his watch. In half an hour it would be time for evening surgery so he must make a move.

'Lady Florence,' he said gently, 'I'll call again tomorrow morning, if I may, after I've arranged a nurse for you. But in the meantime I'll give you an injection to help the pain and make you sleep.'

He opened his bag and drew out a syringe, half filling it from a small bottle of clear liquid and then squeezing out a few drops into the air. As he bent to unbutton the sleeve of her night-gown, however, she abruptly yanked her arm away.

'No!' she said in a tone quite different from anything he had heard so far. 'I'm afraid I can't allow you to drug me into insensibility. I wish I could, but I daren't. I have a dreadful confession to make and just at this moment I find the prospect of meeting my Maker quite terrifying. If I go off into a world of morphine-induced insensibility I fear that I'll never have the courage to come back and the terrible wrong I did will never be righted. Dr Crompton, will you hear my confession please?'

Oliver glanced at her warily out of the corner of his eye.

'Lady Florence,' he murmured, 'if you need to confess, surely a priest would meet your needs better than I can. I'm a doctor, not a man of God.'

'Yes, but this is a confession someone could do something about, if it's not too late,' she replied. 'I couldn't ask Dr Raynor, he didn't think we were wrong – but you're young and the young think differently, don't they. . . ?'

She closed her eyes and he saw her slip back into some long ago memory – but not for a moment could he have realized the suffering she found there.

She was again, for the ten thousandth time, downstairs in the hallway, with the front door standing open and the sun streaming in, touching everything with gold – and the shadow cast by the abominable carriage on the drive. White to the lips, she fumbled with the string of pearls across her firmly upholstered bosom as the beautiful girl, with the sun in her chestnut hair, gazed at her, half crazed with terror.

'Mamma, don't let him do this to me! Don't let them take me!'

And they dragged her away; hauled her through the front door as she screamed in panic . . . and the carriage wheels crunched across the gravel drive; and the grandfather clock ticked on and on; and he banged the door shut behind them. . . .

'Oh God,' whispered the old lady. 'What did I do? How many times have I asked myself?'

Oliver sat down on the edge of the bed, mentally abandoning his evening surgery. Sophie, his wife, would smooth it over for him. She had a number of stock-in-trade phrases for waiting patients and she was actually quite good at it. He gazed at the dying old lady with her little cap covering her faded hair and her sharp old face and wondered what on earth she could ever have done that was so dreadful. The quintessential Victorian, tight-lipped, proper, proud and haughty, surely as emotionally tightly corseted as she must once have been physically, to cram herself into those extraordinary Edwardian dresses he remembered from childhood.

'Lady Florence,' he murmured, 'I will do whatever I can to help you, it's part of my job. And please be assured I shan't breathe a word of our conversation beyond these four walls.'

'Oh you will,' she replied, 'I promise you will. You'll have to eventually.'

It was dark, inky black by the time Oliver returned to his wife and two children in Lamplighter House, the large, remarkably draughty dwelling that was both the surgery and the doctor's residence in the village. One of six smart houses situated along the left-hand edge of the green, it had a neat front garden and steps up to the front door. Inside the hall, which was flagged and cold, the surgery was on the right and the waiting-room on the left, the windows of each room looking out across the green to the twelfth-century church and the Drake Arms, the much more salubrious of the two village pubs.

Polwean was at the bigger end of Cornish villages with both a farming and a fishing community. It had a butcher's shop, a grocer and greengrocer, and a post office and general store, but the narrow little streets of tiny dwellings seemed to be packed in between this show-piece of the green with its six classy houses, church and pub, and the harbour with its fleet of very small, inshore fishing-boats and its rough and ready local pub, whose doors opened straight on to the harbour slipway and whose regulars were close, and suspicious of strangers.

Tremar lay on the outskirts of the village, on the sea side but nestling in the downs with a glorious walk through the formal grounds, the orchard and a copse of predominantly pine-trees, to the bay. There the coastal path led steeply around the headland, coming eventually to the harbour. The bay had been private once, but now walkers came and went from it regularly and many strained to see Tremar through the trees, but it was visible only in glimpses from the cliff path, and then mostly only in winter when the trees were bare.

And all alone there, stopped in time, the old lady of Tremar had lived; a widow for the past five years, a guilt-ridden, emotionally numbed, obedient creature for eighteen years before that. Of course the villagers knew what the Drakes had done – those who had lived there before the war – but presumably they didn't know why, because Oliver had been the resident doctor for five months now and many of the inhabitants had been eager enough to gossip to him about Lady Florence, but not one had ever mentioned her secret.

Quietly Oliver let himself into his house and crossed the darkened hall to the back rooms, those inhabited by himself and his family. The high-ceilinged, one time long drawing-room, with french windows out into the back garden, was full of Sophie and his children and abysmally untidy as always. Shabby, and in need of fresh paint because the fire smoked when the wind was in the east, there were toys strewn wildly about the threadbare carpet. The bricks from Edward's push-along cart were spilled anywhere, Alice's dolls and teddies were ranged along the front of the grate, wrapped in makeshift bandages and covered with teacloths, and half a dozen books had been knocked over and then forgotten. To add to this mess, Sophie had apparently made an effort to do a spot of dressmaking at sometime during the day but had got nowhere with it, leaving the pieces draped about the armchairs, and, as it had rained during the afternoon, one corner of the room was swathed in damp washing, slung carelessly across the wooden clothes-horse.

The children ran to him joyfully, Alice, at five years old with her shiny dark hair in plaits and her cheeks pink from the fire, Edward, at eighteen months lurching unsteadily on his sturdy little legs, his blond hair untidy, his jaw thrust out forcefully. Oliver swept them up in his arms and kissed them.

Sophie smiled. 'So what was Tremar like then?' she asked. 'And is the old lady as dotty as they say?' Rather vaguely she began to clear a chair for him, pushing her straggly blond hair behind her ears as she did so. 'Do tell.'

'Well I will, when I can sit down,' he replied coldly. 'Dear God, don't you ever tidy up, this place is like a pigsty!'

His wife, thin, nervous and generally careworn looked shamefaced.

'I do try,' she said unhappily, 'but it's been pouring with rain so I can't let them go out to play. They haven't got anywhere else but in here. And really, does it matter? No one sees this room.'

'Except me,' he observed and took the glass of sherry she handed him without saying thank you.

Oliver was an ambitious young doctor, with his sights set on Harley Street one day. At the time he had fallen in love with Sophie she had been delicately pretty and vulnerable enough to arouse the protective male instinct within him and he had chosen not to notice her obvious shortcomings. They had been married expensively, for they were both from good families, and she had floated down the aisle amid white lace and red roses, looking like an illustration from *Vogue* magazine. But sadly that was where they should both have left it.

Seven years later, in a not terribly lucrative country practice, hundreds of miles from their original homes in Sussex and burdened with two fast-growing, expensive children, Sophie's heavenly inconsequence, which had so charmed him once, now drove him up the wall. Her glaring inabilities as a housewife, even with a lady from the village coming in each morning to clean, wash and iron, were a source of deep irritation and her generally untidy appearance annoyed him. Certainly the villagers seemed to like her; she was always polite and he supposed she looked vulnerable to them, but nowadays he found her very wearisome.

'Were there many at evening surgery?' he enquired, not for a moment thinking to apologize for not being there.

'Just three,' she replied, beginning to gather up Edward's bricks and toss them into their little wooden cart. 'I said you'd been unavoidably delayed and they said they'd come back in the morning. So why were you so long at Tremar – or don't you want to tell me?'

Alice had wriggled off her father's knee after her cuddle and returned to her doll hospital in front of the fire. Oliver watched her dark, silky head bent over her charges and thought about what Lady Florence Drake had told him.

After a minute he said, slowly, 'Have I ever shown you Blackridge Asylum, Sophie?'

She frowned at him.

'What, that awful place on the edge of the moors that looks as if it ought to have "Abandon Hope All Ye Who Enter Here" written above the door?' she asked. 'God, it lives in my nightmares, that place. We drove past it once and you pointed it out to me, and I remember thinking I'd rather die than ever have to be sent there.'

'Well, Lady Florence Drake has a daughter who's been incarcerated there for going on twenty-four years,' he murmured. 'She was committed in 1915 and has never seen the light of day since.'

Sophie Crompton winced and Oliver saw her reach out a thin hand very quickly and touch Alice's shiny hair with her fingers.

'And I did hear,' she said sadly, 'that she lost her son in France in 1916. How awful for the poor old girl, to have lost her son and be left with nothing but a mentally deficient daughter. Life can be so unfair sometimes.'

Oliver gazed bleakly into the fire as a log shifted and sent an army of orange sparks marching up the back of the chimney wall. After a moment of silence he heard himself say in a flat voice, 'Actually it isn't as simple as that. You see when Julia Drake was packed off to Blackridge in 1915 she was seventeen years old, and the only thing wrong with her was that she was pregnant. She must have had a very brief affair; she had only left her boarding-school in the July of 1914, and the old girl doesn't know who her lover was. It seems no one took the trouble to find out. Anyway, whoever he was, one supposes he went off to war along with all the others in 1914 and never came back. Certainly no one returned searching for her when it was all over. Sir George was outraged when his daughter's condition was discovered and in his rage he had her packed off to Blackridge and refused ever to see her or talk about her again. Morally unstable he called it.'

'And she was perfectly sane?' Sophie whispered in horror.

He nodded.

'That would appear to be the case, yes. She was summarily disinherited, of course, which left Sir Charles as the last in a centuries-old line, but that doesn't appear to have mattered to him, Tremar has been rotting away every since, whilst, presumably, Julia Drake has been rotting in Blackridge.'

'And Lady Florence did nothing?'

Sophie sounded both amazed and indignant. Oliver shook his head sadly.

'My dear,' he said, 'it wasn't quite the same in those days, it wasn't considered all that out of the way to commit a girl who had disgraced herself, so the authorities at Blackridge would never have questioned Sir George's actions, and Lady Florence comes from a generation of women who never dreamed of questioning their husbands. Alexander Drake died at Ypres as did most of the lost generation of young men from here. They were heroes. There was a terrible sense of loss in such a small community and as far as I can gather the word went about the village that Julia had become unbalanced because of the loss of her dear brother and so many others of her generation. The fact that she'd been carted off long before they died just seemed to get lost in the general upheaval of the time.'

'But when it was over,' Sophie persisted, 'when everyone had calmed down, why didn't someone go and get her back? She most certainly wasn't still pregnant by then, and she could simply have slipped back into her old life as if nothing but a touch of brain fever had ever happened, couldn't she?'

He pursed his lips sadly.

'It seems not. Lady Florence has only seen her once since she was dragged away from Tremar all those years ago. She went to see her in 1918, to tell her her brother had been killed, and Sir George was furious. He beat her and then dragged her to the family Bible and made her swear, with her hand on it, that she would never go to Blackridge again. "We have no daughter!" he apparently shouted, "And you will not speak or even think about her again. She is as dead to us as Alexander and like Alexander she will never return to this house!" And that was it, there was no communication ever again.'

Sophie stared at her daughter, sitting on the rug before the fire in her little red and green kilt and warm red jumper, nursing a doll in her arms and lost in her own little world of fantasy. She would die to protect Alice; kill to prevent her ever being taken away. It was unbelievable – and outrageous!

'And what is it the old girl wants now, then?' she enquired bitterly. 'Is she lonely stuck up there in her manor house all by herself: Has she decided her daughter might be belatedly useful?'

'Oh dear, no,' Oliver replied, shaking his head, 'all she wants is an assessment of the girl's condition, at the moment anyway. Besides, she wouldn't have time to re-establish a bond between them even if she wanted to, she's far too ill. She has asked me to go to Blackridge, decide Julia's state of health and report back so that she might have a chance to consider her future. And anyway, I doubt there is any possible way Julia could ever be freed; let's face it, after all this time she can't possibly be sane any longer.'

'She can't be a girl, either, Oliver,' Sophie murmured. 'She's over forty now.'

Chapter 2

On the morning Oliver set off for Blackridge Asylum, Annie Paynter climbed over the crumbling wall into the grounds of Tremar, glanced furtively around for signs of activity, and seeing no one, slipped cautiously down to the house. Hiding behind the long-dead stone fountain she gazed keenly up at the manor with its lichened walls, and the dower with its roof collapsing in its need of repair. Poor Tremar, soon it would be empty, for word in the village was that the old lady was dying, and of course her daughter was mad and shut up in Blackridge.

Annie Paynter was fourteen and actually very pretty, though it was hard to see it through the dirt. She had a mass of red curly hair, green eyes and freckled skin, but through general neglect and ill-use she was very small for her age, and always hungry.

The youngest child of a local farmer she had older, much bigger twin brothers who worked all hours on the farm, a father who regularly got drunk and beat her and a mother who loved her well enough, but lived in terror of her father. Since her father owned his farm and he and her brothers were not tenants or farm labourers dependent on a landlord for their money, their share of food was rather better than it might have been. But nevertheless, her father's excessive drinking and gambling resulted in considerable shortages, and because he hadn't wanted her in the first place and then she had had the bad grace to turn out to be a girl, she was brutalized and neglected. When she did sit down with them at the family table, she was given next to nothing to eat. During the day if she was at home and he wasn't, her mother would feed her and give her love, but such was her fear of her father that she went home as little as she could.

Most of her life was spent roaming about the countryside. She hadn't attended school since she was eleven years old, but she was a familiar figure in the village, where, since she was popularly believed to be 'eleven pence ha'penny in the shilling', she was often in receipt of charitable handouts of food.

Annie encouraged the impression that she wasn't quite right in the head; it paid dividends and kept her from starving. Actually she was very clever, so clever in fact that she had outgrown the local school at eleven and begun then to foster the idea that she was stupid.

She had been due at eleven to move into the senior end of the school, but Annie was dirty, ragged and didn't smell very nice, which made her a target for the other children and this had served to make her quick with her fists. In class she had a tendency to be disruptive, so when she wasn't there life was much more peaceful, and a succession of teachers had discovered that threatening Annie with the cane, or even caning her, made little difference; she was so brutalized at home she couldn't be cowed by any threat of pain. So she had been allowed to stay away unreported for almost four years now, and since she was thought to be unteachable, it followed that it didn't matter if she didn't learn anything.

But Annie was quite teachable, she was, in fact, ambitious and greedy for knowledge. For some months she had searched around for a source of education and then she had happened upon the library at Tremar.

Tremar was inhabited now only by the old lady, who was bedridden, and her faithful companion, a Miss Higgins, who was ancient and poor-sighted. There was a woman from the village who went up each morning to clean and another who did the washing and ironing once a week, but Annie knew their times and the routines they followed perfectly.

By chance she had discovered that the lock on the french windows which led to the library was old and weak and extremely easy to pick. What was luckier still was that the library was actually in the dower, a sort of joining room between the two parts of the house, and as the rest of the dower was completely deserted, no one ever went there. Avoiding Miss Higgins was easy, and so a couple of times a week Annie let herself into the house, chose a book, returned the one she had previously borrowed and slipped away to read.

Slowly and methodically she was working her way along the shelves and a world of excitement was opening up for her as she went. She discovered E.M. Forster, Jonathan Swift, Jane Austen and the Brontës, J. Meade Falkner, Arthur Conan Doyle, Charles Dickens and many others. She swallowed up fabulous adventure stories about sailors, diamonds, little people and Sherlock Holmes, and curled up tightly in her little bed at night, she dreamed. As soon as she was old enough to leave home she was going to seek her fortune.

Sadly for Annie, however, her father still belonged to an age where a life in service was considered acceptable for a girl, and it was still possible to find well-to-do families who would take a girl and train her. Just such a family, with a sizeable estate some way out of Falmouth, had expressed an interest in Annie and were expecting her in January when she turned fifteen. Lady Florence Drake had made the arrangements before she had become too ill to care; it had been thoughtlessly undertaken and she had long since forgotten about it. Annie had been condemned by a greedy father and a distracted old lady, and all but the barest minimum of the money she would be earning was to be paid to her father until she came of age.

She was a commodity and she had been sold.

In the meantime she had just a few short weeks before the old lady finally died and the library was no longer accessible to discover how to run away from home and make her fortune, and there were still so many books to read.

It was significant that it had never occurred to her that some of the books in the Tremar library might be worth a lot of money. She was not a natural thief, in fact the only thing she had ever stolen in her life was food, and that mostly fruit from other people's trees, but she was desperate to escape from the hell of her grinding existence.

There was another born-and-bred inhabitant of Polwean desperate to escape from hers, too, but as yet they knew nothing about each other.

Julia Drake, sitting in the sewing-room of the largest building within the complex that was Blackridge Asylum, gazed absently through the barred window at the world beyond which had not touched her at all for twenty-three years now. A long time ago – thousands of years maybe – she had yearned for freedom; dreamed of it night and day; asked, begged, sobbed and screamed, and been rebuffed every time. Eventually, to preserve her sanity – though God knew what for – she had stopped dreaming, and thrust her memories of Tremar down so far that they never surfaced any more. She had learned to live at Blackridge with the same absence of hope as everyone else and after a while it had become a fairly painless existence.

Around her in this sewing-room were many women with assorted handicaps, both physical and mental, some of whom she thought actually might well have as clear an understanding of reality as she did, though she had never yet met another inmate like her, who had no handicap of any kind whatsoever. They made dresses; blue, heavy cotton things which those patients with no clothes of their own wore. They made other things too, items that went out of Blackridge and were sold. She had become quite an accomplished needlewoman over the years.

Blackridge had many workshops in the complex, male patients made shoes and furniture and other items that went out for sale. There was also a flourishing laundry. Male patients were never seen by the female patients except occasionally in the grounds. The only men they ever saw these days were the doctors. Julia slept in a huge dormitory at the top of her building which permanently smelt of urine. The roof arched sharply, increasing the volume of noise and there was no such thing as privacy. Even taking a bath there was no privacy.

Sometimes it was hard to remember now how she had come here in the beginning; it was a nightmare from the past. She had no real memory of her family any more, not of their faces, just a choking hatred when recall surfaced briefly and was thrust down again. She had only a hazy memory of many of the years she had spent there, too, for after the first terrible five years she had begun to close down her mind; in those days there had been no other escape.

In the early years of Blackridge the regime had been savage. Patients had been regularly brutalized and abused; kicked and punched for making a noise or soiling themselves. Not long after her arrival she had been punished twice for being disruptive and the memories of that were quite clear, though she never allowed herself to dwell on them. Dragged into the freezing, rat-infested basement of the building, to an empty, vaulted room with a soakaway drain in the middle of the stone floor, she had been stripped naked by a number of male orderlies, hosed down with icy water and left there for hours until, half-dead with cold, she had been dragged back to her dormitory. It had taken her almost a month to recover from that ordeal.

The second time she had been whipped as well, flayed as she lay helpless on the floor, and she had very nearly died from that. She had never allowed herself to earn a third basement punishment, but there were some who had. Some had never come back, either, but no one had seemed to notice, or care.

Then, ten years ago a new regime had come into being and now things were much more bearable. Now it was possible to smile sometimes and almost be happy, on a very superficial level. A matron, a Miss Ilona Vincent, had been put in overall charge of the female patients. A good woman with a very strong character, Miss Vincent had very quickly changed the system to put a stop to the abuses. The women never saw male orderlies any longer, which meant the sporadic rapes had stopped as well. The nurses and female orderlies were now encouraged to be patient and kind, and reported savagery towards an inmate was rewarded by dismissal. Kindness and understanding were the rules, a recognition of the fact that even the inmates of a mental hospital were entitled to their dignity – but from Julia's point of view it was too late.

Though Miss Vincent had made a determined effort, personally, to rehabilitate her, she was not responsive beyond the level of basic politeness. She and her one friend, Minnie, lived their lives around the flowers they found in the gardens and what they could expect for lunch each day. As far as Julia could see there was nothing beyond the walls of Blackridge but a deaf, uncaring world and though she obediently performed tasks in the office for Miss Vincent most days, and listened to the radio whilst she was doing them, she was truly not interested.

The world turned, revolved, people were rich for a while and then poor. Events passed by and it simply didn't matter. She accepted the books Miss Vincent lent her and read them mechanically, and she slept without even giving herself the escape of dreams any more.

Ilona Vincent was becoming frustrated and angry. She was losing Julia Drake and she knew it, but there didn't seem to be anybody in the world apart from her who cared. So she had been overwhelmingly delighted when Dr Oliver Crompton had telephoned her and asked if he might visit.

Now, as Julia and Minnie sat in the window of the sewing-room, stitching asylum dresses which stained their fingers blue with the dye, the sun shone through the window on to their faces and was warm. Another spring was on its way. Another season.

Such was their level of consciousness that they gazed without interest at the handsome, beautifully dressed young man who had parked his car on the drive and was scrunching across the gravel towards the reception area on the ground floor of their building. He would have to climb the ten stone steps to reach the big wooden door and then he would be inside their hell on earth.

Minnie was several levels of intelligence lower than Julia, a shapeless drudge beaten so badly by her father as a child that her brain had been permanently damaged. She lived her life in a constant state of nervousness and she clung to Julia with a passion. They had met only days after Julia's arrival all those years ago, and Minnie had seemed to imprint on her in a strange sort of way. For a while, in her pain and fear, Julia hadn't wanted the encumbrance of this sad, rather lame, clumsy girl. She had actually yelled at her to go away. But when she had awoken after her second basement punishment, raw and agonized and unable to walk, Minnie had been sitting by her bed. She had gone on faithfully sitting beside her bed for the next six weeks and after that she had become the most important thing in Julia's life.

The young man disappeared from view below them and they stopped watching him and looked briefly at each other.

'We'll go for a walk in the gardens after lunch, Minnie,' Julia said. 'I've got to go to the office for a while this afternoon, but there'll be plenty of time for a walk first.'

Minnie gazed at her lovingly.

'There'll be snowdrops soon, won't there, Julia?' she asked in her earnest, childish way. 'Snowdrops are white.'

Julia smiled.

'There are snowdrops already,' she replied softly, 'there'll be daffodils soon. And daffodils are. . . ?'

'Yellow?'

'That's right, yellow. Well done. You're getting really good at your flowers, you know.'

It had taken twenty years for Minnie to know that daffodils were yellow, but she knew that snowdrops were white and roses were red – and she didn't remember a time before Blackridge. She didn't even now remember a time before Miss Vincent, when they had lived in such fear. Ironically, Julia was happy for her, but if she was honest, slightly envious.

Suddenly a nurse came into the sewing-room, scanned the faces and then came across to the window-seat.

'Matron wants you, Julia,' she said, 'you have a visitor.'

Julia regarded her with dull, bored eyes.

'I don't have visitors,' she replied, and the nurse put a hand on her shoulder.

'Well you've got one now,' she said firmly, 'come on, it'll be a nice change.'

Minnie stared at Julia in terror and Julia touched her face softly with her fingers.

'Don't panic,' she smiled, 'I'll be back in a minute. Remember it's pie for lunch today and we like pie, don't we? Then this afternoon we'll have our walk, all right?' and obediently she followed the nurse out of the room.

Oliver, with his smart clothes and polished shoes had been quite unprepared for the nightmare that was Blackridge. Dreadful, peeling whitewashed corridors, a terrible smell of boiled cabbage, urine and general hopelessness, and the noise! The noise seemed to bounce off the walls and assault him with vicious spite.

The woman who walked beside him was small and tightly uniformed. She had a rather sharp face and gave the impression that she stood for no nonsense, but she had made a particular point of meeting him at the front door and introducing herself as the matron, and she seemed to be oddly grateful for his visit.

As they stepped smartly along endless corridors that seemed to be sucking them into the terrible heart of this place, a nurse wheeling a patient in a wheelchair passed them and Oliver stared in horror. Bent and twisted, toothless, blind, and with only tufts of grey hair on an otherwise bald head, the woman in the wheelchair screeched and dribbled.

Ilona Vincent touched his arm swiftly and when he looked at her her face seemed almost contemptuous.

'You have no experience of anything like this, do you, Dr Crompton?' she asked. 'Well there are places like this all over the country, full of such unfortunate human beings who are carefully hidden from sight. They are the dregs, the unwanted. They have to go somewhere, because if they didn't the people outside are so prejudiced and fearful they would suffer even more. Here at Blackridge we do our best to look after them, but I assure you, they are not all like that!'

'And Julia Drake?' he asked, slightly shakily.

She raised her eyebrows.

'Julia Drake is not at all like that,' she snapped, 'but I shan't say any more. If you are anything like a doctor you will see for yourself the situation with Julia. At least I hope you will. Although if you'll take my advice you won't waste time asking irrelevant questions to try and establish her level of understanding. Here you are, this is the visitors' room, I'll leave you to it.'

The room in which he found himself was small and bare but for a crucifix on the wall and a small, high window. There was a table with two chairs, and a light bulb hanging from the ceiling – and it did nothing to ease his sense of dread. He felt frightened and claustrophobic as he stood there, waiting for his first sight of the birdlike Lady Florence Drake's only daughter, and he felt he knew one thing for certain anyhow. Whatever it was the matron wished him to see in Julia Drake, it could not be any measure of sanity after twenty-three years of this! Angrily he wondered what he was going to tell the old girl, fighting with his better nature because to tell her the truth would be spiteful, but she really didn't deserve a placatory lie. Then there was a sound outside in the corridor and he seemed to freeze on the spot.

Abruptly the door opened and Julia Drake came in.

She wore a shapeless blue smock of some heavy material, grey socks and sandals and an ancient brown cardigan. Her hair, which was of the finest chestnut colour, was cut raggedly about the line of her jaw and her hands were rough and stained with blue dye.

But through it all she carried her tall, lean body with the greatest dignity. She faced Oliver with faintly dark-circled eyes in a pasty-skinned face but with her head held proudly high and he was astonished. For though she didn't look at him directly he knew immediately that there was no lack of understanding. What was more, she was beautiful, Extremely beautiful. Not doll-like and pretty as he thought Lady Florence had probably been in her youth, but classically breathtaking, with an impression that the passing years had enhanced rather than detracted from her exquisite face.

'Miss Drake,' he said, automatically extending his hand, 'my name is Oliver Crompton, I'm the doctor in Polwean. Won't you please sit down.'

She shook his hand firmly and then with remarkable grace sat on one of the wooden chairs, folding her hands in her lap, and finally raising her eyes to look directly at him. But though the eyes were fully comprehending there was no question in them. It was obvious she expected to be given a piece of information and sent away again, nothing more. That this young man of the world might desire a few moments of her company was way beyond her understanding now.

She simply looked bored.

'Miss Drake . . .' he began again, and the deep brown, beautiful eyes were like dark pools of colour, for her eyes hadn't faded like her skin.

She watched him with complete detachment, just watched and waited and his little speech dried on his lips.

He opened his mouth, closed it again, licked his lips and finally said, 'Look, may I call you Julia?'

'Of course you may,' she replied in faint surprise, 'everyone else does.'

He licked his lips again, she really made him feel astonishingly uncomfortable. Don't waste time asking irrelevant questions, the matron had said. Well it seemed to be fairly obvious what that had meant, but he had to be sure. He decided to plough straight in.

'Julia, I've actually come to see you at the request of your mother,' he said. 'She's anxious to know how you are.'

Even as he said it he realized just how absurd it sounded, and her reaction left him in no doubt. Her head snapped sharply upwards and she stared at him in complete silence, a silence distressingly long enough for him to fully absorb the dark circles under her eyes, the whiteness of her lips and the increasingly bitter sneer creeping across her face.

It left him in no doubt of anything,

In a tone of utter disbelief she finally whispered, '*My mother is anxious to know how I am!* My mother, Dr Crompton, hasn't been to visit me, or enquired after me since October twenty-third, 1918. She came to tell me that my brother had been killed in France, three years previously, and when I cried and begged to be allowed to go home with her . . . when I cried . . .' abruptly she lowered her eyes as if she couldn't bear him to see her expression. 'When I begged on my *knees*, she ran out of here without a word. That was twenty years ago and she's never been near me since! So what is it she is anxious to know now, whether I've finally had the grace to go insane? I'm afraid you'll have to tell her no!'

Oliver gazed at her, speechless with shock, and his emotions were so strong, his rage so powerful, he found he actually couldn't breathe properly. She was *sane*! Perfectly sane. Sane to the extent that she could remember, to the day, exactly when she had last seen anybody she knew, and she had existed for twenty-three years in this place surrounded by insanity, suffering God knew what indignities! How could the old lady have been a party to this? To hell with the girl being pregnant; they could have sent her away until the child was born, couldn't they? God, it was easy enough in those days, especially, for the well off. An 'educational trip', and no one any the wiser when after a few months the girl came home. *No one* deserved to be punished like this! And punished for what? For falling in love with a young man who gave his life for his country in a foreign battlefield a few months later!

'Oh God,' he whispered, mostly to himself, 'I'm so sorry. . . .'

She looked at him blankly.

'Sorry?' she echoed. 'For what?'

He wiped his hand across his mouth. He was furious and he was appalled, both at Florence Drake and himself. Hadn't Sophie said she couldn't still be sane, after all this time? And hadn't he confidently agreed? Well they were wrong. Monstrously wrong. And he should have known better.

And he was frighteningly out of his depth.

'Julia,' he said uncomfortably, 'your mother is dying, that's why she's asked about you, She has a tumour in her stomach, it's completely inoperable, and frankly I doubt whether she'll live more than another six weeks at most.'

There was another long silence as she seemed to carefully weigh up what he had said, then without any expression, either in her face or her voice, she observed, 'And for that you are sorry? Am I supposed to be sorry too? Is that why you're here?'

Well he'd walked right into that one. Hating it he battled on.

'She did ask about you,' he murmured lamely, 'have you no message for her?'

Julia's lip curled contemptuously.

'Oh, certainly I have a message for her,' she replied with quiet venom, 'I hope she dies in agony and rots in hell! And what about my father? How does he feel about my mother's illness? No doubt he considers her to be thoroughly selfish and inconsiderate. Sympathy never was his strong suit.'

'Your father!' Oliver exclaimed in surprise. 'Julia, your father's been dead for five years, Did nobody ever tell you?'

It was a cruel betrayal, blurted out thoughtlessly in surprise. In the moments that followed he saw with dreadful clarity what it really meant as her face crumpled with bewilderment and despair. He saw her body sag with defeat and a stream of bright, wet tears trickle down her cheeks. Silently he gave her his handkerchief and after pressing it to her face in what was obviously a desperate attempt to control her emotions, she finally broke down and sobbed into it as if her heart would break.

At last, when eventually she could speak, she whispered, 'She said I couldn't go home because he wouldn't have me back, but she didn't want me either, did she? Five years. Any time in the last five years she could have come for me, but not a word.'

Oliver abruptly knelt on the floor in front of her and took her hands, holding them tightly as if he could squeeze the pain away. Lady Florence Drake had said perhaps they had been wrong to do what they'd done – it wasn't wrong, it was criminal. Julia was a dreadful victim, cheated of her rightful life, bewildered by her treatment, and worst of all, betrayed by the people whose role in life should have been to cherish her – and Oliver was desperate to ease her pain a little.

'She was frightened, Julia,' he murmured. 'Terrified. It had been *so* long.'

She nodded, her face congested with tears.

'I was terrified too,' she replied thickly, 'when they brought me here. I was seventeen years old and six months pregnant. I'd managed to hide it until then but at six months I was way before my time. The shock started my pains and my baby was born *two days* later, but in all that time there wasn't a single word of comfort from anyone. They just let me lie on the table and scream until I was exhausted, and all I was ever offered was a drink of water! When she was finally born I heard the doctor say, "It's a girl, but it's dead," and the nurse in attendance, who'd threatened to slap me if I didn't stop making so much noise, replied, "Good, no arrangements to be made then," and she scooped up my baby and wrapped her carelessly in some old rags. I suppose they just dug a hole out there in the asylum cemetery and dropped her into it. I tried to find her often in the beginning, but there's no marker for her.'

'And you've lived with the memory of that all these years?' he murmured.

To his great surprise she uttered an entirely mirthless little laugh at that and glanced at him with bitter reproach. In some ill-defined way she abruptly withdrew from him too. She seemed to put distance between them though neither of them moved. She built wall between them, he thought.

'Oh no, Doctor,' she answered, 'you clearly do not understand how it works here. If I'd allowed myself the luxury of memory all these years I really would have gone insane by now. I haven't even thought about my child, or my home and family, for as long as I can remember. Oh yes, in the beginning I did. After my baby was born I was certain they'd come back for me and I waited desperately, kicking against the authorities, until I was so severely punished I almost died. When still no one came I finally understood I'd been abandoned and I had two choices. Remember and go mad, forget and stay sane – and for some reason I chose to stay sane. Now I live on the lowest emotional level I can manage. I care whether I'm too hot or too cold; I guard my dry mattress, because I'm one of only a handful who don't wet the bed, and lunch is the highlight of the day. I take great care of Minnie, because she loves me and she isn't strong enough to look after herself, and I'm grateful to Matron for putting an end to the worst of the suffering here, but the coming of spring means summer is next and then autumn and then winter. In summer it's hot here and in winter it's cold. And half-way through the winter another year begins – but it doesn't mean a thing.'

Oliver stared at her for a moment then impulsively kissed her two hands which he still held in his.

'Julia, would you like to go home?' he asked earnestly, and this time she laughed outright, removing her hands from his and carefully wiping her face with his handkerchief before solemnly handing it back to him.

'Matron should have told you, Doctor,' she replied, 'you're not supposed to make promises you can't keep, it's bad for morale. Thank you for notifying me about my parents – but please don't trouble to come and tell me when my mother dies, I'm really not interested.'

She was leaving, finishing the interview and walking away as remotely as if he had been a picture on the wall in an art gallery and she had merely paused to glance at him in passing. She stood up with a sort of detached elegance and turned to the door.

'Julia, I'd like to come and see you again, if I may,' he called after her and she turned back briefly.

'That would be nice,' she said. 'You're only the second visitor I've ever had. One day, in a few months' time, if you happen to be passing, but please don't make any particular effort. Goodbye now.'

The door swung shut slowly behind her. Oliver was alone.

He stood quite still for a moment as memories of the last half-hour swilled about in his head like a stormy sea. Eventually he pressed the button on the wall near the door marked 'Matron' and the sharp-faced, uniformed woman who had brought him to this awful room came almost immediately.

'Where's Julia?' she demanded.

'She left,' Oliver replied, 'I think she'd said all she had to say to me. Why didn't you tell me she was perfectly sane and lucid? It wasn't fair.'

'Because I didn't want to prejudice you,' she retorted and then blew out a little sigh of undisguised glee, 'So you've confirmed it, she's perfectly normal and she has absolutely no place here. Now you must do something about it.'

'Me!' Oliver exclaimed. 'Look, I'm a country doctor, I don't know anything about places like this. You've got psychiatrists, why doesn't she see one of them?'

Ilona Vincent bit her lip.

'Dr Crompton,' she said slowly, 'let me walk with you to the front door, and I'll try and explain.'

They began once again to traverse the soulless corridors with their peeling white walls, uniformly placed, indistinguishable doors and endless dark floors, and once again Oliver was assailed by the awful stink and endless, echoing noise.

'Do you think this is a place for the sane and normal?' she enquired of him conversationally as she sensed his distaste. 'Do you think this is a place where a lovely, highly intelligent woman, who has committed no crime that I can readily see, should grow old and die? I hope you don't.'

'Well, no,' he replied carefully, 'of course I don't, but I simply cannot see what you expect me to do. I was merely sent here by Julia's mother to assess her condition, that's all, she never asked me to bring her home.'

The matron smiled.

'No, of course she didn't,' she said quietly, 'and even if she had I'm not sure I would have allowed that, but the fact is she *wants* to know. She could have gone to her grave without telling anyone about Julia and then, probably, at some time someone would have told you the old lady had a daft daughter shut up in Blackridge. You'd have taken that at face value, you'd never have come to see her, or even phoned to ask about her, but it seems to me that in her rather pathetic way the woman is, albeit rather late, trying to make amends. You have to go home and tell her that Julia is perfectly sane and must be released. You have to tell her you'll kick up a proper shindig if she doesn't do as she's told, and she must do it *now*!'

Oliver uttered a mirthless little chuckle and abruptly saw the huge front door, closed and locked before him at the end of the corridor. It seemed to bring him up short suddenly.

'Look, do you know Lady Florence Drake?' he enquired uncomfortably, and Ilona Vincent shook her head. 'Well believe me, she's not the kind of woman you threaten,' he observed, 'she's a vicious old bird and she's dying!'

'Then she *must* be threatened,' the matron said firmly, 'and very quickly, before she has a chance to die. I don't believe she had anything to do with this in the beginning, you know, I think she was born of a generation who obeyed their husbands' wishes without question, and that Julia's father, not her mother, was responsible for Julia's punishment. Julia never sees a doctor here, Dr Crompton, because there isn't any point. When I first came here I was so appalled that I actually tried to get in touch with the family with a view to explaining to them that they'd made some dreadful mistake. I was ten years younger and somewhat naïve in those days and I was dumbfounded when I received a letter from the family's solicitors politely telling me that Sir George wanted no communication with me about his daughter and if it was more money I wanted, would I notify them of the required sum. Not, I hasten to add, that I think Cruikshank and Scattergood are party to the conspiracy, old Mr Cruikshank seems like a nice old boy, but they pay Blackridge's account every six months and that's all they're detailed to do.'

Whilst she was talking she had unlocked the front door and abruptly the sun streamed in, warming their faces. The sky above them was china blue and the air smelt fresh with the promise of spring. Oliver thought about the colour of Julia's skin – evidently 'outside' was not somewhere she had access to very often.

'Does everybody pay to be here, Matron?' he asked and she glanced at him ironically.

'Dr Crompton,' she observed patiently, as if he was being particularly obtuse, 'this is a hospital for the – quote – "deserving poor". Most of the patients have no families at all, those who have wear their own clothes and often receive treats. A small minority are paid for, but not particularly handsomely. The amount the hospital receives for Julia Drake is enormous in proportion, and out of it she receives nothing, no books, no clothes, nothing. It was an arrangement made by her father in 1915 and it has *never* been changed. We are being handsomely paid merely to make her suffer! She told me once about Tremar, somewhat reluctantly, so I climbed the cliffs behind it to look down on it – since I'm not in a position to march up to the front door. It has the appearance of great luxury, like a beautiful fairy-tale, from up there.'

Oliver shrugged sadly.

'Not any more,' he replied, 'it's being allowed to fall into ruin, but for all that the old lady is worth a fortune, and she seems to be allowing it to collapse as an act of contrition. She tells me Sir George disinherited Julia at the time she was committed, so Lord knows who pays once she's dead, but it sounds as if all that has been very well taken care of, doesn't it really? So what do I do when I get back to the village then?'

Without really knowing why, he had suddenly committed himself, and he saw the sharp features of the matron soften as she offered him a charming smile.

'So you will help then,' she murmured, reaching for his hand to shake it. 'Thank you. I don't know what I'd have done if you'd gone away without saying you would. Well, for a start I shall need some letters from the old lady saying that she wants her daughter home and admitting they were wrong to send her away in the beginning. After that Julia must be reinstated, so that Tremar comes to her when her mother dies and then I shall require an independent assessment of her condition from you. Armed with all that the hospital board won't be able to ignore her any longer and they certainly won't want to keep her here if there's no more money coming in.'

'And then she goes home to her mother?' Oliver enquired.

Ilona Vincent sneered.

'Not likely! *Then* she goes to Truro, to stay with a retired psychiatrist friend of mine and his wife. He's a marvellous man, worked tirelessly with the worst cases of shell-shock at the end of the war. Once he has rehabilitated her – and her wretched, undeserving mother has died – she can go home to Tremar, and I shall know that for once in my life, I've made a difference.' Abruptly she smiled at him and added, 'and so will you, Dr Crompton, believe me, I doubt you'll ever do as much for anyone else in your whole career, however hard you try.'

Oliver glanced back into the gloomy corridor and thought again of Julia, but this time, for no particular reason, he recalled her beauty. Twenty-four years ago she had looked with those beautiful brown eyes upon a young man who was getting ready to go off to war. That exquisite face had softened for him and she had touched him with love – it wasn't surprising he hadn't been able to resist her. And for that she had been punished with unbelievable savagery.

'I'll see Lady Florence this afternoon, Miss Vincent,' he promised, and for a final time she gripped his hand.

'Bless you,' she murmured, 'I shall look forward to hearing from you.'

Up in the sewing-room Julia and Minnie watched Oliver crunch away across the gravel, to his car.

'What did he want, Julia?' Minnie asked. 'Is he going to take you away?'

Julia smiled at her gently.

'Of course he's not going to take me away,' she replied, 'by tomorrow he won't even remember he met me – Oh, but . . .' she paused as in her mind's eye she saw the cliffs towering above the sparkling sea and heard herring-gulls crying on the wind, 'it would have been nice to see Tremar,' she whispered to herself, 'just once more.'

Angrily she pushed down the memory. It didn't do to remember, made you go mad!

'We'll see if we can find some daffodils after lunch, Minnie,' she said gently.

Chapter 3

Oliver had been right about Lady Florence Drake, she was no part of the coming summer, she died early in May in the thick, dim, airlessness of her sickroom, when the air outside was sweet with the scent of bluebells and a fresh breeze blew in from the sea.

In her final hours she hardly seemed to breathe at all as she drifted towards death. The only sound in the room was the quiet snuffling of the pathetic little Miss Higgins, weeping at her mistress's bedside – and that, which was the only true expression of mourning at her parting, the old lady didn't seem to notice. Only once she opened her eyes, and she looked up at Oliver.

'You promise Julia's safe?' she whispered and he touched her cold, thin, hand reassuringly.

'Safe and happy, Lady Florence,' he replied. 'She's living in Truro with a doctor who is helping her to adjust. She was at Blackridge a long time, remember, it isn't easy to come out into the world again after so many years.'

The old lady uttered a whispering sigh and closed her eyes again.

'I wish I could have seen her, just once,' she murmured and Oliver looked at her sharp old face rather sadly.

You could have, he thought. You had five years. You could have got to know her, learned to love her again. Still, no point in that now, I suppose.

'It's better this way,' he whispered, 'better for her not to have seen you when you were so ill. She remembers you very fondly, you know.'

'And she has forgiven me? You promise me that?'

'I promise,' he lied. 'Truly, I promise.'

In his mind's eye he saw Julia's face, her lip curled with disdain.

'Come and see her before she dies? And say what, for God's sake? She can go to hell for all I care: join my father there, they'll be company for each other! Oh, give her my love, Oliver, if it makes you feel more comfortable, but just remember when you're doing it that it was your idea, nothing to do with me.'

Lady Florence's brown-spotted, bony hands convulsed suddenly against the obscenely distended mass of her cancer-riddled stomach and a small moan escaped her lips. Oliver filled a syringe with morphine for the last time and some hours later, as dawn began to pale in the eastern sky, she slid silently into death.

She had not spoken again.

Rising from the chair beside the bed he gazed down at her for the last time. She seemed in a strange way to be taking an era with her as she went. Beautiful women in magnificent, fussy dresses, men in frock-coats and top-hats, bawdy, slightly *risqué* music-hall songs; all those carefree, halcyon days before mud, blood and trench-feet. The world had grown up a bit with the coming of the war; she at least would not have to wait to see if it was going to grow up a bit more with the coming of a second one. Her vanished, innocent youth was as dead as she was.

Oliver left the body to the last tender ministrations of her faithful companion and slipped out of Tremar into the fresh early morning.

One week later, on the morning the ancient glass, horse-drawn hearse came to take the old lady on her final journey to the family vault in the church, Annie Paynter shinned up one of the big beech-trees at the front of the manor and lay along a branch, looking down with interest.

The two undertaker's assistants stood on the drive below her. When you got close to them they smelt of cigarettes and mothballs and one of them, the young one who was still only an apprentice, had a particularly foul mouth. Annie knew him quite well because he hung around a lot with her twin brothers and she'd heard them swearing like troupers together. She knew the horses too, big gentle creatures who lived in a field on the edge of her father's land. She stole apples for them in the autumn and liked to feel their hot breath on her face and smell their warm, horsy smell. She'd been told that in Truro and other big cities like that they had motorized hearses nowadays; great long, sleek cars probably as big as the doctor's car – though she couldn't imagine how you got a coffin in the back of one of them, despite its size.

With the old lady dead, Tremar was going to be shut up for a few weeks she'd heard, and then – it was the talk of the village – the mad daughter from Blackridge was coming home! Her father had got very drunk and shouted and yelled about it. Hammered on that the doctor wasn't fit to be called a doctor if all he could think about was getting mad people let out of Blackridge to terrorize the village, and he wouldn't be getting any business from the Paynters!

She'd smiled at that, because if it came down to it there wasn't anybody else except Dr Crompton, and anyway, the Paynters had no money for doctors, they had no money for anything. However, keeping a sharp eye on the proceedings, she'd noticed that her mother was very quiet – even uncomfortable – about the subject of Julia Drake, and that had seemed to make her father even angrier.

Now as the coffin was carried out of Tremar and slid carefully into the back of the hearse, Annie watched Dr Crompton lead the ancient and sobbing Miss Higgins to his car and then pack her meagre possessions into the boot. Miss Higgins was going to live with her sister in Torpoint apparently, there was to be no one except Julia Drake living at Tremar from June onwards.

Julia Drake the mad woman from Blackridge . . . Annie saw the hearse and the doctor's car off the premises and slid down the tree, dodging around the back of the house, heading for the library.

In the village a good number of locals had gathered around the entrance to the church to see the final exit of Lady Florence Drake. Most were merely curious, but some, those who considered themselves a cut above the rest, were ranged in the church pews for the service, clad in their best sombre black, rubbing shoulders with the very small number of the old lady's relations who had turned up.

Lady Florence Drake had sprung from another of Cornwall's aristocratic families and had spent her childhood in a vast Georgian mansion several times larger than Tremar. But her marriage to George Drake, twelfth baronet and heir to Tremar, had been very well received by her family and for a while, after Sir George had died, Tremar had actually been willed back to her family. Now, of course, the rightful heir was to take possession in June, and consequently only a surviving brother and sister, three nieces and two nephews had turned up for the funeral.

But no one except Miss Higgins, actually mourned her parting.

Less than an hour later, when Lady Florence had been duly dispatched to lie beside her husband in the cold, stale-smelling family vault, Oliver joined Miss Higgins beside a memorial in the west corner of the church and they stood either side of it, gazing down upon it.

In pure white marble, with his face smooth and beautiful and his eyes closed in death, lay a full-length effigy of Alexander Drake, clad in his officer's uniform, his marble hands folded on his marble breast. It had been lovingly and meticulously, carved, from his curly hair down to the nails in the soles of his boots – and it must have cost a fortune. It stood on a three-foot high polished Italian-marble plinth which bore a lengthy inscription in gold lettering. Detailed were Alexander's dates of birth and death, his grieving parents, his education and his noble departure from this life in the service of his country, with the information that he lay in a grave in France, surrounded by those of his regiment who had died with him. The whole thing was beautiful and, so Oliver was given to understand, quite a visiting point for sightseers.

But from what he had been told, Alexander Drake had never lain this comely in death. The spit of machine-gun bullets that had taken his young life had, apparently, sliced off his right leg and ripped open his stomach so that as he fell his bright, blood-red intestines spilled out and brown glutinous mud seeped in. In his last few seconds of life he had screamed in agony, choking on his own blood.

Mud, blood and filth replaced by white marble.

Death sanitized.

Miss Higgins, who had withheld her floral tribute at the door of the vault, now laid it lovingly upon the breast of the statue.

'You must remember Alexander?' Oliver murmured.

Her poor old myopic eyes were bright with tears and her lips trembled.

'He was a lovely boy,' she replied, 'the apple of his mother's eye. It was such a waste, such a terrible waste. . . .'

'And Julia?' Oliver asked. 'I assume you are one of the very few people in this village who actually knows why Julia was shut up in Blackridge in 1915? That her father had her declared insane because she was pregnant?'

Abruptly he saw the faded blue eyes harden and the lips become thin and uncompromising.

'You shouldn't lay all the blame for that at the master and mistress's door, you know,' she answered defensively. 'I'm not saying Julia wasn't a charming girl, she was, and I'm sure I never had cause to question her manners, but she was wilful, and that sort of wilful leads to trouble in the end. Well it certainly did with her, anyway.'

'Wilful!' Oliver echoed, quite unable to keep the irony out of his voice. 'Twenty-three-and-a-half years in an insane asylum is some punishment for being wilful! If you're interested she isn't very wilful any longer.'

Miss Higgins peered at him through her pebble glasses, withdrawing a step or two as she did so.

'Dr Crompton,' she said primly, 'it isn't our place to question the master and mistress's business and I have no intention of doing so. For your information Julia never told her parents who the father of the child was, and it could have been anyone. In fact, whoever it was you can be sure he would have been most unsuitable because there wasn't anybody in this village nearly good enough to marry a Drake! Almost certainly she disgraced herself with a village boy, and the summer before her coming out. Who would have wanted her after that, I'd like to know. Well, not wishing to be uncharitable, I hope she'll be happy at Tremar now and I hope she'll take the proper care of it. That I wish things might have ended differently is neither here nor there.'

How differently, I wonder, he thought, gazing at the wall above the head of the statue. Would it have been tidier if she had died in childbirth, alone in that place, in terrible pain? Would there then have been another expensive memorial here, possibly a classy marble plaque with the words 'dearly beloved daughter' on it somewhere and nothing to say why she died at seventeen. The tragic Drakes, their beautiful children cut down in their prime.

Unable to hide his scorn he watched the faithful old 'Higgie's' back as she shuffled out of the church into the sunshine.

Not so easy to sanitize what had been done to Julia, was it? he thought.

Julia had been released from Blackridge less than a month after Oliver had first found her there. Twenty-three-and-a-half years imprisoned in an asylum for the insane and she was released without question in days. It certainly gave some question to the system, Oliver thought.

When he had reported back to Lady Florence after his visit, mindful that Miss Vincent had said the old lady must be bullied if necessary, he had found her only, too anxious to do whatever she could to get her daughter released. He hadn't even had to insist, let alone bully her. Within hours she had produced half a dozen beautifully worded, if slightly shaky, letters demanding the release of her daughter and admitting that she had been quite unjustly committed in the first place. Then she had telephoned the solicitors, ordered a new will to be drawn up in Julia's favour and instructed them to cease all payments to Blackridge Asylum immediately.

For the couple of days all this activity had taken, Oliver had been amazed to see the fanatical enthusiasm with which the old lady had accomplished the task. Sick as she was, it was obvious her guilt was far more painful than any cancer could be, and it had begun to become apparent to him that she was fully expecting Julia to come straight home to Tremar.

It had been quite moving, even disturbing to watch the light die in the faded blue eyes as he had told her Julia was to go to Truro for a period of convalescence.

'I suppose, if I had thought about it, I should have known it would be like this,' she had murmured in a slightly tremulous voice, 'but I had so hoped Julia might want to come back to Tremar.'

'And she does,' Oliver had promised firmly, 'of course she does. She just needs a little help first, Lady Florence. You see, you'll have her home by the summer.'

Home by the summer! Julia had made it abundantly clear that she would not set foot in Tremar until after her mother was dead and buried.

Going on for a quarter of a century of dreadful, wrongful imprisonment and suddenly Julia was to go free. Naturally Oliver had expected her to be full of gratitude, but her departure hadn't been like that at all and each time he thought about it it haunted him, for it highlighted again his own inadequacy of understanding.

Julia might not have been happy at Blackridge but it was all she had known for more than half her lifetime; and Julia was the only thing Minnie had in the world.

Minnie howled and sobbed as she was taken away from her friend. Her pain was so tangible that he could still feel it when he let himself listen to her suffering in his head. The dreadful noise of her shoes scrabbling on the stone floor as she frantically wriggled and fought to escape the tight grip of the two nurses who were detailed to remove her, firmly, but as gently as they could. The terrible echoing sound of her voice wailing, '*Julia! No! No! No!*'

Julia stood in the echoing reception area, dressed in the brown suit and cream coloured georgette blouse he had bought for her, and fought to hold on to Minnie for a few seconds longer, her face contorted with pain.

'I'll come back for you!' she promised fiercely. 'Wait for me, darling, and before winter I'll be back. I swear I will.'

Minnie's reply, if there was one, was incoherent and as they were finally obliged to carry her away she screamed over and over again, the sound fading with their departing footsteps.

Tears were streaming down Julia's face.

'Why can't I take her?' she demanded. '*Why*? She'd be safe with me, you know she would. I thought you were my friend, I thought you understood!'

Miss Vincent took her hands firmly, squeezing them in her own.

'Give yourself time,' she begged gently. 'I'll look after Minnie, I promise, and when you're settled and comfortable in your new life, we'll set about approaching the hospital board together, But it *will* have to be done that way, Julia, she has nobody to write and demand her release like your mother has done for you, and she *is* handicapped, she isn't like you. She'd never cope on her own on the outside, and you must be settled and adjusted before you take her on, otherwise she'll suffer, and I'm certain you don't want that.'

Julia choked back a sob, scrubbing away her tears with the palms of her hands and staring at the now empty corridor. She looked so bewildered and confused that just for a dreadful moment Oliver thought she was going to refuse to leave.

In a terribly bleak, lonely voice she said, 'We've never been without each other, not since a few days after I came here. I was still bleeding from the loss of my baby and she just – latched on to me. When I was so ill after those two basement punishments she sat by my bed day after day for months, even when they punished her she still came back. We were so young then, no more than children, and she could still remember what had been done to her. She'd had her legs and arms broken, that's why she's so lame, and when he was drunk her father used to throw her against a wall . . . Oh, God, don't let her go to bed without somebody to comfort her tonight, please! And you will let me visit her, won't you?'

Miss Vincent smiled gently.

'Of course you can visit her, but not for a few weeks, all right? Be fair to her Julia, please. When you come back from Truro, then you can come and see her, she'll have calmed down by then. Now go along with Dr Crompton there's a good girl, don't keep him waiting any longer please.'

Julia turned and went down the front steps to the car, but her back radiated resistance and she kept turning her head to look behind her. Eventually Oliver handed her into the passenger seat and closed the door firmly.

'She won't want to come back here once she's been away for a few weeks,' he observed, smiling a confident goodbye to the matron, 'of course she won't.'

To his surprise the woman returned his look scornfully.

'I wouldn't be too sure of that, Dr Crompton,' she replied, 'and please don't forget that she's been deprived of her rights for nearly a quarter of a century now. If she wants to see Minnie when she's living at Tremar I trust you'll see to it that it is made possible for her to do so, as often as she likes. Goodbye, for now.'

Ilona Vincent's elderly psychiatrist friend in Truro had welcomed Julia into his house with great kindness, and for her it was like starting from scratch. It had been more than half her life since she had slept alone, since she had had a room of her own, since she had had the freedom of choice to make a single decision for herself. In this man's gentle care she was given her first opportunity to turn her mind back to the real world beyond Blackridge, and at the same time learn a few of the skills she would require to live her own life again.

Freedom had equalled all the dreams she had never dared to dream at Blackridge, but was in many ways bewildering and at times quite frightening. In twenty-three-and-a-half years at Blackridge her world had not only shrunk, but effectively stood still. All she had seen since entering the place in 1915 had been the grounds and the five uniform red-brick buildings that surrounded the great clock-tower centrepiece of the hospital. The grounds were pleasant enough, with flower beds and lawns, but they were enclosed within a stout brick wall. From some of the upstairs windows it was possible to catch glimpses of the moors through the bars, but they were distant, unchanging views and she had ceased to notice them at all after a few years.

Meanwhile the world had rolled on.

There had been the roaring twenties, the general strike and the stock market crash, the dreadful depression, the death of King George V, and, shockingly, the abdication of Edward VIII for love of a divorcee! She had actually known about those last three, since Ilona Vincent had been dragging her back into the real world again when they happened, but all the while she had expected to be a resident of Blackridge until she died, what went on in the real world hadn't interested her much, It had seemed remote and frankly unimportant and nothing much more than inherent good manners, learned in childhood, had stopped her ever saying so to the good woman who was so busily trying to rebuild her life for her. Now she was discovering that all these things – particularly the lingering depression and the German chancellor, Hitler – were crucial, and life on the outside was governed by the fears about what was coming next. Everyone was gearing up for war again.

The doctor and his wife had a wireless in their front room, from which they listened to world news, literally almost as it was happening. The wireless she was already used to. Much, much more startling was the other very popular pastime, this thing called the cinema, where fabulous talking pictures were followed by newsreel pictures, so everyone could see, and become chillingly familiar with, the funny-looking little German with his lanky hair and boot-brush moustache.

To everyone around her this cinema was an everyday experience, but what was extraordinary for her was that it was quite acceptable to go to these splendid picture palaces with a young man – and sit in the dark holding hands! And women wore red lipstick now and painted their nails and bobbed their hair – and smoked, in public!

Oh, Lord, how life had moved on.

During these weeks of fantastic new experiences the handsome Oliver Crompton was a regular visitor and it was apparently not at all out of the way that he took her out in his car and bought her intimate presents, such as stockings. It was seemingly unremarkable, too, that he accompanied her on shopping expeditions, choosing beautiful clothes for her at exclusive dress shops, and lunching her regularly at expensive little restaurants.

Julia had rarely eaten in restaurants. Before her imprisonment in Blackridge she had been too young to dine out and had only ever eaten lunch in hotel dining-rooms on rare jaunts out of Cornwall with her parents. Taking Alexander to school was one occasion which stuck out in her mind. Alexander had been educated at Eton after his formative years, and at the beginning of his first term they had stayed for a week at a hotel in Windsor whilst such things as he might require were purchased for him.

She had seen the castle there, where King George and Queen Mary lived when they were not in London; she had been eleven years old and it had all seemed fantastically romantic. But eating at table with her mother and father had been not so much a pleasure as a ritual filled with pitfalls for the unwary. For a start she had never to been allowed to choose what she ate, speak, other than to say thank you, or to leave anything. Her first lunch out with Oliver was strained and nerve-racking, she felt clumsy and awkward, but he was so patient that by the end she had relaxed sufficiently to actually quite enjoy herself.

Afterwards he had bought her some face powder and a lipstick at the perfume counter of an exclusive store and at the same time purchased, and had gift wrapped, a bottle of perfume which she had found by her place at the breakfast table the next morning. It was like being in a fairy tale, she decided.

It wasn't so surprising, really, that she thought she was developing quite a crush on him, though it never occurred to her to tell him so. It never occurred to her either that he might be falling in love with her. He was a married man with two children. She'd seen photographs of them, a little girl with shiny dark hair and a blond, plump, baby son. She was in no way yearning for him, she was really just enjoying the little *frisson* of excitement she experienced when she opened the front door and found him on the doorstep, but she was rather pleased that he would be just down the road when she finally came home to Tremar – and once or twice she did just allow herself a little fantasy of a stolen kiss in the orchard perhaps, some day. . . .

For Oliver it was very different. Oliver was so blindly in love that once Lady Florence had died he was in danger of neglecting his practice, he spent so much time in Truro. He knew he must rush Julia back to Tremar as soon as he could. Remote from Sophie and even from his beloved children, he carefully organized a thorough spring-clean of Tremar so that it should be perfect, arranged daily servants for her as requested, and gardening staff.

He told anyone who asked, particularly Sophie who was growing very unhappy, that after twenty-three-and-a-half years of wrongful imprisonment, it was vitally important everything was exactly right for Julia's return. In reality he was so completely consumed by his passion that he simply couldn't concentrate on anything else – and his fantasies were excessive and outrageous.

And so as the day in June approached when Julia should return home, Oliver dreamed his absurd dreams and Julia bought practical clothes: jodhpurs, some rather daring slacks like she'd seen American stars wearing on the films, a couple of hacking-jackets and boots. For Tremar was calling to her fiercely now and she dreamed of walking on the cliffs with the wind tugging at her hair, and sitting safe and cosy by the fire on cold winter nights as furious gales beat upon the windows, and growing old in her beloved home with Minnie by her side.

Chapter 4

She finally came home to Polwean on a brilliant June afternoon after she had been away for almost a quarter of a century. Oliver's car rounded the last bend in the road between the tall hedges that would suddenly swing away to reveal the centrepiece of the village, and Julia squeezed her eyes shut and pressed her arms against her chest.

She could hardly breathe. She was terrified to look and yet she wanted to see it all.

The village in which she had grown up, her whole, tiny world of childhood, the scene of her last sight of her beloved brother – and of the brilliant, red-headed, green-eyed, godlike boy whose hands had touched her young, beautiful body in that last summer, and never touched another before they had stiffened in premature death like so many others . . . the very last, familiar sight she had briefly glimpsed as they took her away to her living hell.

She breathed fast, drawing up her courage and at last she opened her eyes and looked, and it was slipping and sliding absurdly in her vision. She was crying! Blinking rapidly she looked again and a thousand emotions crowded in on her as each familiar memory pushed itself up to be reintroduced.

So changed and yet, so immediately familiar. . . .

'Would you like to get out?' Oliver asked. 'Julia?'

He might have asked the question two or three times, it was hard to say, so lost in the tide of her emotions was she. It was just after lunchtime, with the sun slanting down on the church and the ivy-covered pub with its long, low, slate roof. The houses on the opposite side, which included Oliver's, were bright white with dark roofs, and the grass between them a lush, summer green. But the trees on the green were so big now from how she remembered them, and the colours so bright and everything so different, and yet – the same.

Slowly Julia stepped down from the car and bending for a moment ran her hand through the grass thoughtfully, then straightened up and just gazed.

'The Drake Arms,' she murmured eventually, 'I never thought I'd see it again.' A small, slightly ironic smile touched her lips and she added, 'I suppose you know it belongs to me?'

Oliver nodded.

'I had heard it was part of the estate. Would you like to go in for a drink now?'

To his surprise she chuckled and gave him an old-fashioned look.

'Oliver, I've never been into a pub in my life!' she retorted. 'It would never have occured to me to go into the Drake Arms when I – and certainly I never went near The Smugglers.'

'The one on the slipway down in the harbour you mean?' he said. 'I heard that belongs to the estate as well, am I right?'

'Oh,yes,' she uttered a little snort of laughter. 'Stuffed full of the biggest rogues in the district every night – or it always used to be. There was more skulduggery went on in there than anywhere within a twenty-mile radius so I was told. Or perhaps it's been made respectable now?'

'I think not. I've never had cause to go in there myself but I understand it's always where any trouble is to be found. Do you intend to clean it up?'

She smiled at him, narrowing her eyes a little against the bright sunlight. She really was, he thought, a stunningly beautiful woman, her chestnut hair now so professionally cut and styled, her skin pink and healthy from her newly acquired outdoor life.

'I don't intend to interfere in anything,' she replied. 'All I want is a quiet life at Tremar with my possessions around me and perhaps a couple of dogs for company. Our family solicitor, Mr Cruikshank, telephoned me in Truro, yesterday – that's the new, "young" Mr Cruikshank, his father was the one you spoke to, he's just retired – well anyway, he's going to organize an estate manager for me who will simply call on me when he needs to. I can't think of anything more perfect.'

To Oliver, whose fierce ambition was the driving force in his life, this sounded absurdly negative, and not in keeping with the 'Rhine maiden' persona he had dreamed up for her at all.

'Surely,' he exclaimed, 'you must want more than that? After all you've been through!'

The look she gave him was faintly withering, but he didn't notice. In fact Julia had been touched by a feeling of irritability towards him a couple of times in the past few days, a new sensation that she had found slightly bewildering, but the fact was, Oliver was extraordinarily self-centred. He saw everything in terms of how it affected him, and she had an idea he was expecting to be allowed to make her decisions for her now she was home. Well if that was the case, he was destined for disappointment.

'Exactly,' she replied, 'after all I've been through. I want the things that you take for granted in life, Oliver. The choice of what time to go to bed or get up, the incalculable delights of choosing what I want to eat, all those little, simple things.'

'And nothing more?'

'Yes, I want Minnie – and I mean to have her.'

If Oliver had intended to reply to that he didn't get a chance, for unbeknown to him, his beautiful little Alice had been standing at the gate of Lamplighter House for the last five minutes, saying, 'Daddy, Daddy, Daddy,' and getting no reply.

Now the gate had opened and Alice, in company with her mother and her little brother, was striding purposefully across the green towards him.

'*Daddy*!' she cried, and slid her hand into his, making him jump galvanically.

Sophie, her fly-away hair hanging untidily about her head, her face rather pale and almost pinched, stood with Edward perched on her narrow hip. She was a harassed mother, willowy-thin and tired-looking, facing the tall, lean, exquisitely manicured beauty of Julia – having never been party to the grey, hopeless drab she had been not so many weeks ago – and she managed an extraordinarily friendly smile of welcome.

'Miss Drake,' she said, 'I'm Sophie, Oliver's wife. I'm so pleased to meet you.'

For a few seconds Julia looked completely nonplussed, then mustering her dignity with a considerable effort she smiled as well and offered her hand.

'Mrs Crompton,' she replied, 'how nice to meet you too, I've heard so much about you and your lovely children.' She chucked Edward under the chin as he offered her an unrelenting, wide-eyed stare. 'A fine boy,' she murmured. 'Oliver has proudly shown me his photos, and Alice,' she touched the child's head softly, 'with your beautiful, shiny hair.'

Sophie said, 'This must all be very strange for you still. Please, if there is anything you want, don't hesitate to phone, will you?'

'Am I on the phone then?' Julia asked, bewildered, and then laughed softly. 'I suppose I must be. Mrs Crompton, Oliver has been so kind and so generous to me in the last months – well, let's face it, I wouldn't be here at all, but for him. If there's any way I can repay his kindness . . . I mean, if you'd like to bring the children to play at Tremar, or perhaps you'd care to use the bay; it's lovely and safe for little ones and quite private. . . .'

She tailed off, embarrassed, feeling inadequate and uncomfortable. Gently, and with her special charm, Sophie came to the rescue.

'We'd love to,' she said, 'thank you very much, that would be wonderful, a real treat for the children. Come on Alice, Daddy wants to take Miss Drake home now.' She looked at Oliver – and saw how he looked at Julia. She felt hot tears spring to her eyes and blinked them back hastily, then she said slightly nervously, 'Will you be back for evening surgery, dear, or do you want me to tell anyone who comes that you'll see them in the morning?'

'Oh, he'll be back for surgery, I promise,' Julia replied warmly. 'He's given me far too much of his time already and I have no intention of keeping him from his work, or causing you any more trouble. Besides, I've got twenty-three years to catch up on at Tremar and I mean to do lots of it tonight, all by myself.'

Her words came straight from the heart. She had no idea at all of the mixed emotions they generated in the other two. She would learn of Oliver's love and Sophie's jealousy in the coming weeks and she would learn to experience fierce emotions of her own again, but now as she looked at their carefully controlled faces she didn't wonder why they seemed to stand so far apart, or why they studiously didn't look at each other, she just thought Sophie was pretty, if a little untidy, and the children – were children, and she had no experience or understanding of children so they made her feel faintly uncomfortable.

She was anxious to go on to Tremar.

She stood on the threshold, staring through the open door at the familiar, oak-panelled hall. The sun was at the back of the house now, because it was afternoon, and perhaps it was just as well, for the sun had streamed in through the open front door as the men from Blackridge had come to take her away and her mother had stood there, white to the lips, silent and staring. . . .

The hall was empty now.

The first sight of her home for more than half her life, during which time a generation of young men had been wiped out in a futile war and a new way of life had emerged. Tremar had been full of servants when she left, now she had chosen to live there alone.

In Truro there had been new things to learn every day, a new world to watch with wonder. Now, as she stepped into Tremar, everything seemed to come to an abrupt stop. Nothing had changed at all. All the dark, polished furniture she remembered stood in exactly the same places, the big old grandfather clock, lazily ticking away the years, slow and gentle and strangely comforting. She shivered slightly, although it was warm, and took a deep breath as the familiar smells of polish and old wood mingled in her nostrils. It was all *exactly* the same.

Deliberately then, and apparently unaware of Oliver's presence, she marched across the hall to the far end and threw open the double doors into the drawing-room.

The sun streamed in from the gardens beyond.

'Oh, Tremar . . .' she whispered, 'Oh, dear God . . .' and two tears trickled down her cheeks.

Oliver had never seen the drawing-room. Although he had organized the army of cleaning ladies from the village in the previous weeks he had not actually been to Tremar himself since leaving with Miss Higgins on the day of Lady Florence's funeral, and then the place had been mostly closed up. It came as a slight shock to him to realize he had actually seen virtually nothing of the place; it wouldn't have been so difficult to have taken at least a cursory interest, but every moment of his spare time had been occupied with Julia, not her house. Now he gazed around him with keen interest and was fascinated by what he saw.

It was a huge, elegant room, extremely well appointed and comfortably furnished with beautiful, obviously very expensive furniture, but it was very much early Victorian. Although the outside of Tremar had remained virtually unchanged for hundreds of years, each succeeding baronet had reworked the inside, fiddling with it to suit the fashions of the day. All except Julia's father. He had barely changed anything at all, and in a quarter of a century nothing had been moved, either – much to Julia's obvious discomfort.

On the floor was an enormous Persian carpet and the curtains on the big windows were of floor-length red velvet with deep Victorian pelmets. A couple of breathtaking paintings adorned the walls, both wonderful seascapes, and above the fireplace hung a huge, gilt mirror, with family portraits, two deep, one above each other on either side. On the Italian-marble mantelpiece were two exquisite bronzes and a porcelain-and-ormolu clock which ticked at least twice as fast as the grandfather in the hall and tinkled out the hours prettily.

All this was Julia's inheritance. All this she had grown up with and played in, safe and secure in her well-ordered life. And it was a million miles from the stinking, peeling, barren wasteland that was Blackridge.

In silence they absorbed the understated opulence, thinking their very different thoughts. Oliver had come from a comfortable, middle-class home, one where there had been enough money for a reasonably good quality public-school education, but nothing like this. A small part of him, probably almost an unconscious part, was envious, even with his unforgettable memories of Julia at Blackridge.

Julia had been betrayed by this.

For this and all it stood for, the class consciousness, the deep-seated feelings of superiority, her father had sacrificed her. Hard-faced he had watched his beloved daughter dragged from her home and never spoken about her again, because his position in life had mattered more than his affection.

Slowly and thoughtfully, Julia took up a silver photograph frame from the top of the grand piano and gazed at the slightly grainy sepia photo within it. Alexander Drake in his uniform, smooth and handsome, photographed for his mother before going to France.

'My brother,' she murmured.

'There's a full-length, marble effigy of him in the north aisle of the church,' Oliver said then, 'lying in his uniform with his head on a pillow and his hands folded on his chest.'

Julia smiled grimly.

'There would be,' she replied. 'Sandro died a hero. It is exactly what my father would have done, and believed he was right to spend a fortune doing it, when I wasn't even getting enough to eat.'

Oliver frowned at her.

'Did your father not like you?' he asked and she carefully put down the photograph.

'He loved me. He loved us both. He was proud to have a son and a daughter, only his son died bravely, without a stain on his character, whilst his daughter proved herself to be unacceptably lacking in self-control. I very much doubt Sandro died a virgin – in fact I know he didn't – but boys are lucky, they don't get pregnant.'

'But I can't believe,' Oliver persisted, 'that they could have lavished such affection and so much money on remembering their dead son, when they had a perfectly healthy, living daughter whom they had chosen to shut away.'

'Well I don't know why you can't believe it,' she observed, 'you knew my mother, even if it was only slightly – that should have taught you something about my family.'

Abruptly she went to the french windows and after fiddling with the catch for a moment or two, threw them open and stepped out on to the terrace which had a weathered stone parapet and a single flight of steps in the middle, and sported a small but long-dead stone fountain with a plump lead boy in the centre, his arms around a fantastical fish from whose mouth the water had once spouted. The little boy was sad and stained now and growing green stuff on his head and shoulders, whilst the contents of the fountain basin were unspeakable.

'It used to play when I was a child,' she whispered, gazing at the little grey boy and his fish. 'It's funny what you remember, you know. I used to dream about him at Blackridge – why him, I wonder? And now he's sad and neglected like I was.'

Running away from the foot of the terrace the now overgrown but once obviously splendid formal grounds were bathed in summer sunshine, nestling as they did between the downs. Great trees fringed the edge of the estate, funnelling away towards the bay, and between them could be seen snatches of an ancient wall. A beautiful cedar grew below the terrace, with dark, overhanging branches, and beyond the lawns the orchard was leafy and fresh. An ancient summer-house, beautifully designed but obviously crumbling away, was visible to the right. Once there had been tennis-courts and a cricket-pitch, but now the formal lawns, edged with high, thick, shady hedges, needed mowing rather badly.

With her back to the stone parapet, Julia gazed first at the house and then at the dower, running away at right angles, the only bit of it clearly visible being the room on the end, which was the library. From this side of the house the dower roof could be seen to be in a shocking state. She looked for a very long time, shading her eyes against the brightness of the day and then she smiled.

'Oh, Lord,' she observed cheerfully, 'that looks as if it's going to be an expensive job, that roof. And the fountain needs a thorough overhaul if I'm going to get it working again. Obviously I need an estate manager rather quickly, don't I? Oh, thank the Lord, Papa was a good, honest, deep-down Drake and never spent a penny more than he had to on anything, otherwise heaven knows where the money would come from for all the repairs. As it is Mr Cruikshank assures me I'm very rich – and I shall spend the Drake fortune exactly how I choose!'

Oliver was astonished at her matter-of-factness. She might have been away on a six-month trip in Europe, so casually and calmly had she dropped back into her old life.

'Miss Higgins,' he murmured, gazing at the library's french windows, 'maintained that during the last couple of years of your mother's life the library was either haunted, or someone was getting in and out of the house that way. She said she was always finding the doors unlocked.'

'You mean she kept forgetting to lock them,' Julia retorted. 'Oh, come on, Oliver, Higgie was my mother's personal maid and she was old when I was a child. By now she must be the Ancient of Days.'

'Well certainly nothing ever seemed to be missing,' he agreed lamely and fell silent for a moment, gazing intently at the collapsing roof. Eventually he asked, 'How was the dower ever allowed to fall into that sort of decay? I mean, your father was hardly short of money.'

Julia smiled; it was a bitter-sweet smile of fond memory and cruel betrayal.

'The dower was falling into disuse when Sandro and I were children,' she said slowly. 'We had our nursery in there, and the schoolroom, but the bedrooms were hardly used because the plumbing left much to be desired. When guests came to stay they stayed with us in the house – there are dozens of bedrooms – and anyway, people only came for weekends by then.

She paused, rocking slightly against the stone parapet as Oliver tried to imagine the rich and beautiful people who must have come here to Tremar for weekend parties before the war. Handsome young men, exquisite ladies, slipping out perhaps to enjoy a brief, secret tryst by the fountain, or at the summer-house.

'What *should* have happened of course,' Julia continued, abruptly dragging him back from his reverie, 'was that Sandro, in the proper scheme of things, found himself a suitable girl to marry and Papa replumbed, redecorated and refurnished the dower, to present to them as a wedding present. What *did* happen, however, we all know and I imagine Papa left it to rot quietly away as a sort of penance for Sandro's untimely death.' She paused and then added with a bitter laugh, 'Better to spend thousands erecting some great marble effigy than be practical and repair the house. That definitely would have been their way of thinking. After all, when they knew Sandro was dead they also knew the Drake line was finally at an end, didn't they?'

Oliver stared at her.

'No! They had you.'

'No, Oliver, they didn't.'

He turned swiftly and rested his elbows on the parapet, gazing intently at the grounds, at the weeds in the flower beds and the briars round the summer-house, at the unloved beauty left to lie forgotten. Just like they had left their unloved beauty to lie forgotten all those years at Blackridge.

'I'll never understand,' he said quietly.

'And I'll never forgive,' she replied. 'But,' her voice suddenly became crisp and efficient, 'standing here wallowing will get me nowhere. Firstly I'd like you to tell me what domestic arrangements you've made for me and then I'd like you to go home to your surgery and leave me to my memories. I long to be alone here, Oliver, truly I do and whilst I'm really not ungrateful for everything you've done for me, just at this moment I desire solitude more than anything in the world. If that's selfish of me I'm sorry and I'm sure you'll forgive me.'

He glanced at her doubtfully for a moment, then smiled.

'Well,' he said, 'Mrs Collins from the village will come Monday to Friday eight-thirty to four-thirty and Saturday till lunchtime. She's your cook-housekeeper. She'll organize all your deliveries, you know, bread and so on, and leave dinner in the oven for you each evening. Damn good cook too; patient of mine who brings wonderful cakes for the children. She's seen the house and she seems to think that with the amount of it you're likely to be using at the moment, she can manage on her own, but if she can't she'll speak to you about hiring a girl. Monday and Tuesday mornings she'll bring her cousin, who will wash and iron for you, but Saturday afternoon until Monday morning, I'm afraid you'll be all by yourself.

Julia uttered an ecstatic sigh.

'Lovely!' she exclaimed, and saw him frown.

'Well that's all very fine,' he replied, 'but you still have to eat at weekends.'

'Which I'm sure you'll find I can manage on my own, as you've provided all those lovely – what did you call them – labour-saving devices, whatever they are,' she retorted with more than a touch of irony in her voice. 'I shall have to go to the kitchens and familiarize myself with domestic appliances, shan't I? But they are discreet, aren't they, these servants of yours? They won't broadcast my business around the village?'

'They don't know you,' he replied. 'Oh, they know the basic circumstances of your return home – everyone in the village knows that, though it would appear not many people actually know why you were sent away to begin with – but they don't gossip. Mrs Collins and her husband came to live in Polwean in 1926. He and his cousin run the blacksmith's – and they've struggled during the depression, I can tell you. Anyway, she should be good at her job; apparently she's spent half her life in service, but I wish you'd have just one live-in servant. I'd feel much happier.'

'No,' she said firmly. 'Absolutely not. For almost twenty-four years the only place I've been able to be alone is inside my head. I understand loneliness, I suffered terrible spiritual loneliness in Blackridge, but all the time, wherever I went, there were *people*, breathing my air and filling my space. Tonight there will be no one but me and I can drift from room to room haunting the place like an unhappy ghost if I choose! So, go home and don't worry about me. In fact, be glad for me.'

Oliver sighed.

'All right,' he said, 'if that's what you want, fair enough. Still, may I call in after my rounds tomorrow, just to see how you've enjoyed your first night home?'

She smiled fondly and touched his hand – and his heart turned a somersault in his chest.

'I shall look forward to seeing you,' she promised. 'Now let me walk you to your car.'

As he turned his car in the drive he was aware of her watching him from the front door and his mind spun away in a glorious fantasy. Julia as his wife, her beauty and aristocratic bearing such an asset to his Harley Street practice. She raised her hand to wave him goodbye and there was something of the imperiousness of her mother in the gesture. Already she was fully at home in Tremar; as at home as if she had never been away. She would adjust with just such ease and grace to any new surroundings and she would be perfect. She was all he had ever wanted in life.

He had missed a valuable lesson in that imperious wave.

Julia was at home. In the hour since she had arrived she had begun to sink her roots deep back into the beloved soil of Tremar and already her plans were made.

'You are mine, Tremar,' she whispered, as the grandfather clock ticked lazily in the hall, and the shadows lengthened in the garden, 'and I shall never leave you again. As soon as I can I shall have Minnie to live here with me and together we shall grow old in your peace and tranquillity. And with Minnie I shall share a grave in the churchyard, just across from the family vault, so that for eternity I shall be a thorn in your side, Papa. You may have rejected me in life but in death and for as many centuries as the church and the graves remain, everyone who cares to read about it will know and despise you for it!'

Chapter 5

The evening shadows were beginning to lengthen as Annie Paynter scurried down the worn path to the crumbling wall around Tremar, found the usual very broken bit and clambered over it into the estate.

She hadn't known until the middle of the afternoon that the mad woman was coming back today and she still had two books to return to the library. Then one of her brothers had nabbed her and set her to work collecting the eggs – and that had taken ages, like it always did, because the stupid hens laid all over the place in the barn – and here it was, late, and she still had the books, clutched tightly in a canvas bag in her grubby hand.

Cautiously she peered round the bole of a tree. The terrace was deserted, but the french windows were open, so obviously the woman was in there somewhere. Well, she'd just have to risk it and hope she could be in and out quick enough to avoid detection. With great care she began to snake down through the long grass towards the house.

Julia had flung open the windows in her mother's bedroom and allowed the salty fresh air to swim headily about her as she unpacked all her beautiful new clothes. Oliver had chosen this room for her and had arranged for it to be thoroughly cleaned and changed around, but with the heavy velvet curtains opened wide and sunshine streaming in, its shabbiness was sadly evident. It was also depressingly familiar; just exactly as she remembered it as a child, only scuffed and peeling now and not remotely like that wonderful Aladdin's cave she recalled from the past, when her mother's jewellery had hung about the gilt dressing-table mirror and the air had been heavy with delicious and expensive perfume.

It really seemed as if with her departure to Blackridge and her brother's demise in France everything in Tremar had come to an abrupt halt: like Sleeping Beauty's castle, she thought fancifully.

And now was coming the awakening.

In the days to come, when she felt a bit more emotionally secure, she would venture into her old room, and Alexander's, and then into the dower. Would their school-books still be there, and the maps of the world with all the pink areas that signified the British Empire? All packed up and abandoned to the spiders. How would that feel? To allow herself the luxury of remembering again after so many years of forcing herself to forget.

Her unpacking done, she prepared to go downstairs again and thought she might venture below stairs and explore the kitchens. Oliver said tea had been left for her and all this fresh air was making her quite hungry. A few sandwiches and a slice of cake wouldn't go amiss now, and would be all the nicer because she could choose to have it when she liked and eat it where she liked.

Leaving the room she caught up her mother's wedding-ring from the glass tray on the dressing-table and slipped it on to her finger. The rest of the jewellery must be somewhere, she supposed – not that she was likely to want to wear any of it. But she did remember it, particularly the pearls. Her mother had been wearing those pearls, fingering them on that last morning . . . fingering them and staring. . . .

She would sell the pearls. They would probably fetch a lot of money.

The kitchens were exactly as she remembered them cavernous and white with the meat hooks still in the ceiling, the vast black range and huge fireplace in the back kitchen, and the enormous glass-fronted wooden cabinets on the walls in the room with the long, scrubbed table, where the staff had taken their meals.

Red tiles on the floors, dusty glass and china in the cabinets, piles of cooking pots; it all smelt old and unused now, with an underlying scent of disinfectant, and sat terribly at odds with the new touches, the huge white bulk of the refrigerator and the electric oven – extraordinary items that they were! So much needed doing to sweep it all away with its memories. Perhaps whatever a modern kitchen was nowadays could be fitted in its place? She decided she would give that some thought.

Finally there was the door to the scullery where the big porcelain sinks stood and the copper and the mangle had been housed in the old days, and that bit she decided she couldn't face quite yet. That bit which had been so hot and steamy and smelt strongly of washing soap on Mondays . . . back then . . . the safe days.

Shivering slightly with the memory she put out her hands towards the range, finding that thankfully someone had seen fit to light it since she didn't think she could possibly have managed the newfangled electric stove. So at least she could have some tea later on.

After that she very cautiously opened the new refrigerator door to inspect the food she had been told had been left in there for her. The cold seemed to rush out at her, touching her face, and to her amazement all the plates and the huge jug of milk on the shelves inside were icy to the touch, but the food had a wonderfully crisp appearance to it, as if it had been newly made. Lord alive, progress was a remarkable thing!

Fish-paste sandwiches by the looks of it, and some very nice-looking scones, and four pieces of lovely, moist-looking sponge cake: chocolate and, possibly, lemon. Well that would be more than enough to last her till morning, she decided, carrying the plates to the table. Oliver had told her Mrs Collins would make breakfast for her in the morning – Oliver was obviously quite unaware that after twenty-three-and-a-half years in Blackridge, eight-thirty in the morning was half-way through the day for her.

Annie was beside the cedar tree, plucking up courage for a final dash to the terrace when Julia emerged from the house, and in terror she shinned up the tree like a monkey and lay flat along one of the overhanging branches, desperately trying to quieten her breathing.

Julia sat on the edge of the old fountain and narrowed her eyes against the golden brightness of the evening sun as it cast long shadows across the garden. Above, in the blue sky that was already subtly darkening towards nightfall, a herring-gull screamed and floated on the warm air and a faint breeze gently rustled the leaves in the orchard. Slowly and without any real thought she drew off the gold wedding-ring and held it up between her thumb and finger, squinting at the sun through it, smiling contentedly. Later, when the sky was navy-blue and night was creeping in she would walk through the orchard to the bay. She would stand on the beach and watch the tiny waves lapping softly against the sand, and come back in the dark. . . .

Annie was almost directly above her now, gazing down at her with keen interest. To her frank, child's eye this 'madwoman' looked quite disappointingly normal, not remotely like Mr Rochester's terrifyingly dangerous wife at all. In fact she wondered if it wouldn't be better to just hand her the books and walk away, but she thought she'd hang on for a little bit longer, just to see if anything exciting happened.

She was just deciding to stay up the tree until it got dark and then, if the woman was still on the terrace, drop the books beside her and scarper as quickly as possible, when there was an abrupt crack like a gun shot and the branch on which she lay dropped about four inches.

With a sharp scream of fright she let go of the canvas bag and the two books fell, slap, slap, at Julia's feet. For a second time the branch cracked and Annie slid off it, hung for a second by her fingers and then dropped on to the terrace and fell backwards on to her bottom with a yell of pain.

Julia, jumping galvanically with surprise, jerked her arm sideways and the ring flew into the air, somersaulted two or three times, and landed on the scummy, green surface of the fountain.

A second later it was gone.

For what seemed like an age, but was no more than a heartbeat, nothing moved at all. The woman and the child stared at each other in fright and astonishment, then Julia clutched her hands to her chest and drew a shuddering breath and Annie was on her feet in terror and tearing off her dreadful, old, brown cardigan, preparing to plunge her arm deep into the noisome green water of the fountain to retrieve the ring.

'I'm sorry! I'm sorry!' she cried in panic. 'I'll get it! I never meant no harm, honest!'

'Er . . . no,' Julia stammered, still breathless with shock, but appalled at the idea of anyone slopping about in that fountain, 'no, leave it!' but Annie's fingers were hovering above the fetid muck.

'I promise it ent lost!' she squealed, I promise it ent,' and she squashed her skinny body against the stone basin of the fountain, rocking forwards to get her feet off the ground and give her more reach. If she went in head first she would choke to death in seconds – and what a way to die.

'*No*!' Julia exclaimed loudly, taking a step towards her with the idea of grabbing hold of her. 'Come away from there this instant. Listen, if you put your arm in there I won't let you have any cake, and that's a promise.'

There was nothing she could have promised that would have been more effective. Annie let her arm hang motionless above the slime and slowly her feet came back down on to the terrace.

'Cake?' She said cautiously. 'What sort a cake?'

'Chocolate – and lemon, by the looks of it.'

'And I can have some?'

'If you stay out of that fountain you can. If you don't you'll probably drown, so you won't be able to have any anyway.'

Julia bent and gathered up the two books at her feet examining them carefully. Fortunately they were none the worse for their hasty journey down from the tree, which was just as well, for they were very old, valuable, leather-bound books, and instantly recognizable.

'Hullo, these are mine!' she observed. 'Were you stealing them?'

Annie planted herself before her, pulled herself up to her full height and put her hands on her hips indignantly. A skinny, starved-looking waif with a shock of unruly red hair that was full of straw from the barn, flashing green eyes, a filthy face and an awful old summer dress coming undone at the waist and hanging limply and unevenly about her stick-thin legs.

'No I weren't stealing them!' she declared furiously in her thick Cornish accent. 'I ent never stolen nothing from you. I was reading them if you must know and now I come to put them back.'

'*Reading* them?' Julia echoed, studying the titles. 'You want me to believe you've read these?' She was seriously unconvinced. 'How old are you?'

'Fourteen. I's fifteen between Christmas and New Year.'

'And you've read these? Well you won't mind telling me what they're about then?'

To Julia's complete amazement Annie sat down beside her on the edge of the fountain and began, excitedly, to tell her the story of each of the books. She smelt of farmyard and dirty child and she had scraped knees and grimy fingernails. She also, Julia noted, had some nasty bruises which didn't look to have been acquired in the usual tomboy way a fourteen-year-old might acquire bruises, but she was so animated as she told her tales, so caught up in the wonder of them that somehow the dirt and the smell seemed to fade away and leave just a pair of bright excited eyes and a tumble of beautiful hair.

'My word, you really have read them,' Julia whispered eventually, 'and enjoyed reading them, too. Amazing. I remember a girl who lived near here once and who was reading beyond her years . . . when we were children. She was at the village school, and nobody understood how bright she was. I wonder what happened to her. Well, you won't know, will you. Do you go to school?'

'Not much,' Annie replied truthfully. 'Only enough to keep my pa from beating me. It don't matter though, 'cos most people in this village thinks I'm simple. I'm a charity case, I've heard them say so.'

'But you're not simple, are you?' Julia said. 'Not remotely simple.'

Annie grinned at her cheerfully and Julia, though not Annie, suddenly found herself astonished. It was as if they had known each other for years, so calm and unselfconscious was their conversation. It felt good somehow; comfortable. She should have been furious that this scruffy urchin had been helping herself to the contents of the library, but instead she felt delightfully companionable.

'I ent simple, and you ent no madwoman,' replied the child with innocent frankness. 'Leastways you'm not mad like I thinks of mad. You don't hammer about the place setting fire to everything, like Mr Rochester's wife.'

Julia gave her a sideways look.

'I see,' she observed. 'So you've read *Jane Eyre* as well. My copy? Yes of course, silly of me to ask. Oh, good God, now I understand, you're the ghost that spooked Miss Higgins, while my mother was still alive. Just how long have you been breaking in and out of the library?'

'About two years,' Annie admitted, having the grace to look slightly uncomfortable. 'Well there ent no books in my house, and there ent no books to speak of in school, neither. It were easy. The old lady – I mean your mother – well she never come downstairs hardly for months, and that Miss Higgins, well she were half blind. Look, I never damaged any of the books, I was ever so careful, and I never took one without returning it. You can go and look if you like.'

Julia stood up.

'I suggest we both go and look,' she said. 'Then you can show me exactly what you've read.'

The library smelt of polished wood and old books. It had an air of calm and, for both the woman and the child, a feeling of promise. Julia had read very few books in the last twenty-three years, only those Miss Vincent had brought for her which had not really been much to her taste. She had been brought up with the freedom of this library and suddenly she had it again. Annie simply wanted to devour knowledge as a starving man devours a loaf of bread.

At Julia's invitation she went swiftly along the shelves, touching the books she had read in the past two years, picking out her favourites, her eyes alive with pleasure. Julia watched and listened, becoming slowly but steadily aware that this dirty, scruffy object who had fallen out of her tree was in fact a rare gift. The child was brilliant; clever way beyond her years. She had not just absorbed the novels on offer but studied geography, history, and basic science. She had even, she said, tried a bit of Latin, because lots of the books with animals and birds and plants in them had Latin names, but she hadn't got very far with it because she had no idea of the correct pronunciation.

'I can teach you that,' Julia said, 'if you want to learn.'

'Can you?' Annie replied, gazing hopefully at her. 'Can you teach me all the things I want to know?'

Somewhat taken aback Julia gave a little shrug.

'Well,' she said cautiously, 'I'll teach you what I know, certainly. You evidently come up here most evenings to raid the library, so I'll give you lessons if you like, and then perhaps, at the end of the summer if you're still keen, we could sort out a school for you. One where you could go daily and actually learn something. I went to a boarding-school not far from here, St Margaret's Academy, near Bodmin. Maybe Oliver could help. He must know what schools are available round here. Come on, lets go and have that cake now, and talk about it.'

As they crossed the terrace together Annie suddenly said sadly, 'Course it'll only be till Christmas. Come January I got to go to work. Pa says he's found me a place in Falmouth as a kitchen maid; I'll be cleaning boots and things and washing up at a big house. Will they let me read, d'you think?'

Julia suddenly fetched up in horror as cold fingers of reality touched her and scratched at her suffering. This child was to be put away, just as she had been put away all those years ago. It wasn't the same, of course, and a life as a kitchen maid was a big step above the life at Blackridge, but it amounted to the same thing. No choice and no hope.

'You can't be a kitchen maid!' she exclaimed. 'You've got to go to school. A mind like yours can't be wasted cleaning boots for heaven's sake!'

They had reached the kitchen and Annie's gaze alighted upon the plates of sandwiches and cakes. Her stomach was so empty that she actually felt her lips become wet with anticipation and for the moment all thoughts of learning were gone from her head. It seemed as if she heard Julia's voice from far off suddenly and was barely able to concentrate on what she was saying. She could think of nothing but the food, and she couldn't wait any longer. She took a sandwich and stuffed it into her mouth.

Julia stared. The child was starving! A village the size of Polwean, where pretty well everyone knew everyone else and there was a starving child in their midst. It was outrageous.

'Who are you?' she demanded. 'Where do you come from?'

Annie was singularly involved in the food, almost light-headed with the delight of it and thrusting it down so fast that her stomach was protesting, but it didn't stop her. It left no time for an answer, however.

Julia said again, 'Look, please will you tell me your name; apart from anything else, I must speak to your father about your schooling. I will not have you bundled off into a life of service. It's absurd! And furthermore,' she added, gazing at the rapidly disappearing sandwiches, 'I'd like to speak to him about your lack of care. When did anyone last feed you, for pity's sake?'

Eventually, with that blissful, settling feeling of a full stomach; with the delight of having food inside her for the first time for nigh on twenty-four hours, Annie paused and perused the rest of the spread with choice, rather than need and at the same time considered Julia's anxious questions.

Abruptly she looked up and smiled. It was a beautiful smile and it gave Julia a painful jolt, for it reminded her quite brutally of someone she had known years ago.

Coming home to Tremar was proving to be a waterfall of memories and emotions and she knew she shouldn't be surprised that faces from the past should suddenly thrust themselves up at unexpected moments – but it was ironical that this underfed child should remind her of this someone in particular, this someone whom she had not dared to think of for so many, many years.

Annie answered her question then, and almost floored her.

'I'm Annie Paynter,' she exclaimed cheerfully, 'and I comes from Rectory Farm. Sorry, I forgot, you ent bin here before have you? Everyone else knows who I am. Please can I have some cake now?'

She didn't wait for a reply, but immersed herself immediately in the ecstasy of chocolate cake with butter-icing on the top, without looking again at Julia. She was completely unaware, therefore, of the look of frozen shock on Julia's face as her heart jolted so violently in her chest she was obliged to clutch the edge of the table to stop herself falling down.

The room seemed to dip and sway uncomfortably and her mouth was unpleasantly dry.

'What did you say?' she whispered eventually. Annie *Paynter*?'

Annie nodded disinterestedly.

'Umm,' she said, carefully licking the icing from the top of the sponge. 'This is ever such good cake.'

Julia's hands were shaking almost uncontrollably. She murmured, '*Annie Paynter*,' and her eyes searched the child's face desperately. 'What's your father's name, Annie?'

Annie looked up.

'Arthur,' she replied.

'And how old is he?'

Now the child looked astonished.

'How old is he?' she repeated, and then shrugged. 'Well, I dunno – about your age I suppose. No, bit older p'raps – well I dunno 'cos my pa drinks, see, so he don't look the same as other people.'

'And beats you when he's drunk,' Julia whispered, touching a bruise on the child's dirty face with a trembling finger. 'I don't believe it – I can't – I was told your father was killed in the war.'

'I didn't know you knew him,' Annie said, adding, with childish frankness, 'I wish he had of bin . . . killed in the war, I mean. You look ever so pale, are you all right?'

Julia perched on the edge of the table. She was very shocked and there was a pain deep inside her that seemed to tear at her insides, but twenty-three years at Blackridge had taught her iron self-control, at least. She would need to think deeply about what this child had just told her, and at the moment she only wanted answers to her questions.

'Could be I'm hungry,' she observed, 'not that it'll do me any good, since you've eaten all my food. Annie, are you like your father, to look at?'

Annie shrugged her shoulders.

'I s'pose,' she answered. 'Well he'm got red hair anyway – or leastways he did have. He'm all grey and weird looking now. Here, I got to go home in a minute, I has to get in the house when I know he's in The Smugglers, that way I don't get knocked about too often. I'm sorry I ate all your tea.'

'Forget it, I'm not really bothered,' Julia replied with a little grin, knowing she wouldn't have been able to force a morsel of food between her lips just at the moment, so churned up were her insides. 'You will come back tomorrow, won't you? Oliver tells me the housekeeper will be leaving dinner in the oven each night, so perhaps we could share it? Annie, who's your mother?'

Annie frowned, wriggling her bottom on the kitchen chair.

'Why d'you want to know about my family?' she asked suspiciously. 'You ent going to report me for not going t'school are you? I don't want t'go to school down there, they got nothing to teach me, and the boys are horrible to me.'

Julia rubbed her face with her hands, knowing she was still shaking and wondering if she was going to cry. *His* child! *His* daughter! He was supposed to be dead, had been dead in her mind for more than twenty years and here before her sat the product of his union with another woman; a child he quite obviously cruelly abused. But dear God, if he really wasn't dead, then the pain of what he had done to her was unbearable – unspeakable.

'I'm not going to report you to anybody,' she retorted. 'But I am going to feed you, and teach you all the things you want to know, that's a promise! Come on, I'll see you to the door, you're not earning yourself another beating on my behalf, for sure.'

'The door,' Annie echoed. 'I don't use the door. I goes over the wall, up the back.'

Julia chuckled and was astonished that even with the unexpected news she had just received, she could be amused. Two months ago she had been a hopeless prisoner in a place from which there was no escape. Twenty-four hours ago she had been in Truro, now here she was in the home she had never expected to see again in her life, with an extraordinary, clever, dirty, bruised but cheerful child whose name had unleashed a waterfall of emotions within her, and she could laugh!

I must be hysterical, she thought and abruptly cupped the child's face in her hands fondly.

'Well I'd better walk "up the back" with you then, hadn't I?' she said. 'So that I can see for myself where it is you regularly trespass on my property.'

The garden smelt rich and heady with summer as, in the darkening air, they went together across the formal lawns, past the collapsing summer-house, towards the orchard. The tennis-courts were high with weeds now, the box-hedges thick with brambles. Everywhere had a neglected air and yet, to both of them, it was not remotely sad. For Annie it was just the way the countryside was, she didn't really notice it at all. For Julia it was Sleeping Beauty's castle again, stopped in time with the bramble wood grown up around it obliterating the memories of long ago. But it was never going back to the way it had been, she had already made up her mind about that.

In a clump of trees, mostly oak and beech that had been allowed to grow out of control too close to the wall, roots and branches had carelessly tossed aside man's handiwork and the wall was a pile of rubble requiring no more than a careful step out into the field beyond. It was all part of the estate still, but around the edge of the field was a public footpath, one of many that criss-crossed the estate avoiding only the formal gardens.

Cows grazed in the field, big and black against the darkening sky and snorting gently as their soft mouths cropped the grass.

'Where do you go from here?' Julia asked Annie, now barely visible under the trees.

The child pointed across the green slope beyond.

'That way takes me to a stile at back of the Drake Arms,' she replied, 'and then I take a short-cut across your land. Apparently it's not a footpath but everybody uses it; have done for years, my pa says. He was whining about what you might do now you'm home the other day, and my ma said he should watch out; that him and his mates might get a bit of a shock.'

Julia looked at her slightly cynically.

'I see,' she said. 'So everyone pleases themselves at my expense these days, do they? Well, we'll see about that later. Annie, please tell me, who is your mother?'

'Gladys,' replied the child, picking her way carefully across the broken wall in her dreadful old boots and managing to tear her dress a bit more in the process. 'She goes quiet when your name comes up, you know, and sometimes she looks proper frightened, but she loves reading all your books. I bin sharing them with her when Pa isn't around. I hope you don't mind.'

Julia drew a deep breath and pressed her lips together thoughtfully.

'Yes, it all fits,' she muttered, mostly to herself. 'All of it, even down to you. Go on then, run home and take care, and I'll see you tomorrow.'

Annie looked back at her in the darkening, warm-smelling evening. She seemed to study her with great care and as their eyes held each other's gaze for some seconds she suddenly offered a huge grin.

'D'you know something,' she said with wonderful child's frankness, 'you'm proper disappointing for a madwoman, you ent done nothing exciting at all. Good-night then!'

Julia returned the grin and her heart wrenched so painfully in her chest that she actually uttered a tiny little noise.

'Good-night,' she replied softly, and through a flood of silent, private tears, watched the child until she was out of sight.

Eventually she wiped her face with great determination and came out from under the trees, but she didn't go back towards the house, she picked her way through the darkening orchard, and then through a squeaky iron gate into the pine copse beyond. The scent in amongst the pine-trees was strong in the warm, summer air and with it came the salty freshness of the sea, blowing on the breeze. Small noises all around her in the dark trees were quite unalarming as she passed across a spongy carpet of pine-needles, and when she came to the wall again, to the bolted wooden door in it that led out into the bay, she touched it with trembling fingers for some seconds before trying to open it. Just touched it and could hardly breathe for the fullness of her heart.

In the end the door took some opening; obviously it had been shut for a considerably long time and both its lock and its hinges were stubbornly rusty. But eventually, grumbling to itself, it swung open and she was a matter of feet from the water's edge.

She stepped down from the path on to the beach.

Flat, yellow sand; small, brown rocks; gentle, lapping waves – and surrounded on either side by steeply rising cliffs.

The moon was growing bright now in a still not completely dark sky. High cloud was streaked black against navy with a sprinkling of white stars. Everywhere was still silent and empty. *No people.* The first time for more than half her lifetime that she had been alone.

Over to her left, nestling under the cliff, was a long, low boathouse and it was to this final destination that her footsteps now took her. Even in the darkness she could see it was derelict; the big rowing-boat they had kept in there as children was long gone. The door was missing now and the windows completely devoid of glass, but Julia stepped up on to its rotting deck and stood, just inside the door, leaning against one of the thick, wooden poles that had once supported a large storage shelf high up in the roof. And she stood there, gazing into the far corner of the room, where once there had been a pile of rugs and cushions for the boat, and in the darkness, across the bitter, wasted years, she saw them.

Two young, beautiful people, barely more than children, their bodies gleaming in the moonlight, entwined in love. The girl was firm and athletic with a hard, flat stomach. She could row from one side of the bay to the other faster than the boys on a good day. She had small, sharp breasts and long, firm limbs; chestnut hair that tumbled about her face in rich profusion; deep brown eyes. Beside her, on the deck, lay her brown taffeta skirt and white lace blouse, her cotton lawn drawers and white stockings – and with them, the boy's clothes. His best suit and shirt; rough, cheap material and heavy linen; his boots thick-soled and heavy. Farm labourer's boots.

But naked he was a god, his body strong with muscled arms and a bronzed chest, his hair auburn and curly, his eyes green, his mouth full of strong, white teeth.

He said, 'I love you, Julia,' in his Cornish brogue, and the salty freshness of the sea, the sharp scent of the pine copse, the promise of life, blew across them in the summer darkness.

Julia rested her back against the pole and slid down so that she crouched on her haunches, still gazing into the empty corner of the boathouse where those young, virgin children had come together and without shame shared the delights of their bodies.

Annie Paynter was fourteen with beautiful red hair and green eyes.

'Would our daughter have looked like that, if she'd lived?' she asked out loud of the young man who had lain with the girl in the corner of the boathouse in the summer of 1914. 'Would she, Arthur? And would you have come for me, if she'd lived? You betrayed me . . . I can't believe it. Of *everything*, that's the worst. You've known all these years where I was and you did nothing. You did *nothing*!'

And this time she sobbed out loud with the breaking of her heart.

Chapter 6

When Oliver arrived at Tremar the following morning he was admitted by Mrs Collins, who was obviously delighting in her new-found importance as housekeeper. She swept him grandly into the house, her ample bosom swathed in a sparkling white apron, and offered him coffee.

'Miss Drake was up and out afore I arrived,' she said, 'said she took an early-morning stroll down to the bay. Every scrap of the food I left last evening was gone. Any'ow, I made her breakfast and now I believe she's out in the stables.'

'How did she seem?' Oliver asked and the woman gave him a conspiratorial look.

'Well, if you ask me,' she replied, 'she hadn't not but passed a restless night. And there's something fair heavy on her mind – though it ent my business to ask, of course. You go and find her, Doctor, and I'll make some coffee while you're gone.'

'All right, thanks, Mrs Collins,' he said and set off round the side of the house.

The stables, a collection of low, semi-derelict outbuildings, had not been used as stables for many years. Sir George had kept a car in them for a short while, but not long enough for them to be properly converted to a garage, and now they lay empty, devoid of everything but dust.

Julia was standing in the middle of the wooden floor, directly in a shaft of sunlight that had forced its way through a grimy window high up in the wall; dust motes danced about her in profusion. She wore a pair of slacks and a hacking-jacket and she looked splendid with her chestnut hair shining in the sunshine. It would never have occurred to Oliver to permit Sophie to wear trousers, yet the fact that Julia was obviously making some sort of statement and that it was almost certainly a fierce statement of ownership was lost to him completely. His heart simply leapt with desire in his chest.

'Oh, hullo,' she said, in what seemed to him a rather weary voice. 'How are you this morning?'

'I'm perfectly fine,' he replied. 'The point is how are you? How was your first night alone in your beautiful home?'

'Very good,' she answered in a manner that suggested it had been far from very good. 'I didn't sleep very well, but I suppose that was to be expected. So much silence, after so many years of noise.'

'The silence kept you awake?'

'Well, no, actually, but something did. Do you have time to stay and have coffee?'

'I have the rest of the day for you, if you would like it,' he said, pushing the look of angry suspicion on Sophie's face quickly from his mind. 'Nothing booked until evening surgery. So what plans do you have in mind for here, then, a car perhaps, or a horse?'

He had moved to stand beside her, gazing with her at the empty stalls and dusty wooden floor of the stable and was visited by a delightful fantasy of her proudly riding into the village on a glistening, expensive steed as the inhabitants respectfully doffed their caps.

To his surprise she laughed.

'Just chickens, Oliver,' she said.

To Oliver – to whom snobbery was such an important part of life – the idea of her keeping chickens was not at all suitable. He stared at her in astonishment, which made her purse her lips somewhat abruptly.

'Chickens!' he exclaimed. 'Whatever for?'

'Because,' she replied, turning from him quite sharply towards the door, 'in twenty-three-and-a-half years in Blackridge I never once had a boiled egg, and I love boiled eggs with a passion. Besides, everyone seems to think there's going to be a war, so to do my bit I shall keep chickens.'

Oliver watched her back as she walked away. She had snubbed him and he was hurt, but somehow there was more than that. It was as if between saying goodbye to her yesterday afternoon and arriving this morning something had happened which had destroyed the glory of her home-coming.

And obviously she wasn't going to tell him about it.

They sat on the edge of the fountain drinking their coffee, making small talk and listening to the birds singing in the trees and the gulls calling mournfully overhead, but it was not the relaxed affair it ought to have been. When it was finished Julia stood up and brushed her trousers briskly with her hands, as if she was anxious to get on. Or anxious not to sit and give herself time to think by doing nothing? he wondered.

'I want you to take me to Blackridge this morning, please, Oliver,' she said. 'I bought some clothes for Minnie when I was living in Truro and I should like to take them to her today.'

Oliver didn't answer immediately, but his heart sank. He didn't want her to go to Blackridge again, he didn't want her to think about it any more. Minnie would have forgotten all about her by now, he was sure, and anyway even if she hadn't what good did it do to stir up her memories? He wanted to tell her he didn't think it would be fair to Minnie, since realistically there was no escape from Blackridge for her, but fortunately for him he lacked the courage.

The hostility in her eyes as the silence between them lengthened became almost tangible.

'Don't worry about it then,' she snapped, 'I'll get the taxi. Mrs Collins tells me her husband runs a taxi service in the village as well as working in the forge, so I'll try it, it'll be a new experience for me. Apparently you just ring the blacksmith's and request the taxi and he comes as soon as he can.'

Oliver pressed his lips together sharply.

'No, of course I'll take you, if you want to go,' he said quickly, climbing to his feet. 'I just want you to be absolutely sure you're strong enough, that's all.'

She turned slightly and gave him a mocking look out of the corners of her eyes. It said it all.

'Strong enough for what?' she enquired. 'Do you think my poor, female sensibilities are going to be shocked by what we find there? Well I'm sure you've got a bottle of smelling salts, if it all proves too much for me. Excuse me whilst I go and put a skirt on, better not begin my triumphant return home by shocking the good people in this village out of their senses, eh?'

Oliver wondered if he wouldn't be wiser not to open his mouth again this morning.

His car was warm and smelt of leather. Julia settled herself comfortably in the front seat beside him and leaned back, letting the sun streaming in through the windscreen warm her face. On the back seat were a couple of brightly coloured, stiff, paper carrier-bags bearing the names of stores in Truro; four simple summer dresses which she had lovingly chosen for Minnie. And Oliver was forced to admit that Ilona Vincent had been right: parted from Minnie, Julia was not going to forget her. Though whether Minnie would remember Julia remained to be seen.

As the car reached the edge of the village they passed the entrance to a dirt-track which wound away out of sight and sported a peeling, mud-spattered sign that read, 'Rectory Farm'. Oliver saw Julia's hands suddenly clench in her lap and glanced at her face, but her expression was unreadable.

'You didn't by any chance have a visit from a half-witted child called Annie Paynter last evening, did you?' he asked, thinking to play detective. 'I meant to warn you about her, but I forgot. That's where she comes from, Rectory Farm, and a dirtier hovel it would be hard to find.'

After a moment, which seemed to him to be strangely tense, she replied, 'As a matter of fact I did have a visit from Annie, yes, though I don't know why you should ask.'

'Well, mainly,' he said, 'because she had the run of your grounds for years when your mother was alive. Frankly, there wasn't anyone to chase her away and I think perhaps she felt safe there. The children in the village bully her mercilessly. Anyway, Tremar was most often where she was to be found, and she's such a creature of habit I don't suppose anything's changed now. I'll have a word with the Paynters, ask them to keep her away.'

'You'll do nothing of the sort!' Julia snarled and then bit her lip quickly. 'I'm sorry,' she murmured. 'It's just that, well, in case you haven't noticed, Oliver, the child is covered in bruises and for obvious reasons I have a vested interest in saving her from any more ill-treatment. Anyway, what makes you say she's half-witted?'

Oliver smiled as the car purred along summer-rich Cornish lanes towards the moors where the views glimpsed through gaps in the hedge were breathtaking.

'Julia, the child's simple,' he said, 'everyone knows that. If you had a conversation with her you must have realized it immediately.'

There was a pause then, as Julia gazed out of the window. For some minutes she seemed to be deep in thought, then, abruptly, she turned to look at him and her eyes were definitely haunted. Had poor little

Annie's plight so touched her then, he wondered, feeling warm towards her.

'Oliver, will you tell me what you know about Annie's family?' she said. 'Her father, Arthur Paynter, is he about my age?'

He nodded.

'He is indeed – and a more unpleasant man it would be hard to find. Arthur, so I'm told, was one of only three young men from Polwean who came back from France in 1918, and he seems to have been trying to drown his memories in the bottle ever since. He's foul-mouthed, cruel to his family and a lousy farmer. He has twin sons of eighteen who are more brawn than brain, poor little Annie who's fourteen, I think, and a wife whom no one sees much, but who I understand lives in a permanent state of exhaustion and fear.'

'Are the twins called Jed and Jethro?' Julia asked and he nodded again. 'Then his wife *is* the Gladys whom I used to . . .' She paused and counted briefly on her fingers. 'Huh, he didn't waste any time marrying her when he got home, did he?'

For a moment Oliver gaped at her as if she had just brought off a remarkable sleight of hand, then, remembering, he blushed slightly and muttered, 'Sorry . . . I forgot. Now you tell me what you know.'

She smiled sadly, it was a remote smile and her face betrayed how bitter-sweet were her memories.

'Gladys Penhaligan had twin brothers, Jed and Jethro,' she said slowly. 'They and Arthur Paynter were best friends from babyhood almost. The three musketeers they were known as; always together no matter what. But they were thick as thieves with my brother Sandro, always trooping up to the back door to ask if he could play – much to Papa's disgust. And then when everyone was too old to play any more they'd take him fishing or shooting, or meet him in The Smugglers for a drink when they could, even when he was at Oxford. In that last summer before the war the four of them were together all the time. I remember. . . .'

For a long time no sound could be heard in the car but the gentle hum of the engine. Julia sat with her head bent, staring into her lap, lost in her memories.

'Was it a good summer?' Oliver asked softly at last and she jerked up and smiled at him quickly – and he knew what she was remembering. But of course her young man had been lost with the others.

'Annie's not simple, you know, Oliver,' she said slowly. 'She's not remotely simple, in fact she's extremely bright. She's Gladys

Penhaligan's daughter and Gladys was a very clever child. When we were young, the village school was run by a single, middle-aged lady and she came up to Tremar to speak to my mother about Gladys. She hoped that a place might be found for her to continue her education beyond twelve – but of course it wasn't. Gladys was what she was, a local fisherman's daughter; her future was written in stone. By the time she was Annie's age she was mending nets and gutting fish. And in the end, true to form, she finished up married to a farmhand.'

Oliver glanced at her sideways.

'Well, Arthur Paynter's hardly a farmhand,' he observed, 'but I know what you mean, of course.'

'Not a farmhand?' she said. 'Of course he's a farmhand. What else would you call him? Oh, a tenant farmer I suppose, yes, well, all right then.'

'He isn't a tenant farmer either,' he replied. 'He owns Rectory Farm, and in the last – what – eight or nine years I suppose, he's had a dreadful struggle, so they say. People in the village claim it wouldn't be in half such a mess if it was still owned by—' Abruptly he stopped, realizing what he had said. 'Oh, Lord, of course, it belonged to the estate, didn't it? You didn't know your parents gave it to him when he came back from France?'

Her expression said it all. Savage, mocking bitterness.

'I didn't know he'd *come* back from France until last night,' she answered simply. 'And no, I didn't know my parents had given him Rectory Farm. Yet again a fine example of their generosity, wouldn't you say? A vastly expensive marble memorial for Sandro, a great chunk of the estate for Arthur, and for me? Not even a simple piece of clothing I could call my own, or a book, or some bread to fill my empty belly. Nothing but pain and suffering for me!' A stream of bright, wet tears had begun to trickle down her cheeks, reminding Oliver suddenly of that first ever interview he had had with her when he had first encountered her in this place. 'Dear God, what a gracious and generous lord of the manor Sir George Drake was, wasn't he?' She spat. 'What a fine, upstanding citizen!'

They were just reaching the gates of Blackridge. For some moments the large Victorian clock-tower that was the famous Blackridge landmark had been visible and Oliver wondered whether it was that which seemed to be making her so agitated. He turned right, braked smoothly and the car purred to a halt outside the black, iron gates. Silently, as last time, he handed her his handkerchief.

'How fitting!' she observed with a sneer, scrubbing furiously at her face with the handkerchief and reaching for the door handle. 'Would you like me to get out and open the madhouse gates, Oliver?'

Very softly he laid his hand on her knee and felt her almost rigid beneath his touch. Was it being back here, he wondered, or had Annie Paynter somehow conveyed something to her that had thrown her into such agony, for certainly he had never seen her like this before. On the contrary, he, and the elderly psychiatrist with whom she had lived in Truro, had both been astonished by the way she could apparently dismiss at will anything from her mind that she chose not to remember.

'Julia,' he murmured, 'ever since I first saw you this morning you seem to have been in a turmoil. Tell me, did Annie do or say something to you last night that brought this on, because if she did then she really should be encouraged to stay away.'

She turned her head towards him so sharply, that for a moment he actually thought she was going to either slap his face or scream at him, then, abruptly, she seemed to sag and he watched her twist his handkerchief in her fingers.

Finally she looked at him.

'I'm sorry, Oliver,' she said, 'but you simply don't understand what this is like for me – and I can't explain it, because it isn't as I expected. I'd never thought about going home when I was here, not really, I'd never dared to in case I opened the floodgates and swept my sanity away with the memories. Now I have Tremar back, my estate, the village – but Polwean is trapped in the past, the same as I am and I keep stumbling over it. Let me see Minnie now, please, she's all I have in my life that I can call familiar any more. Let me be for the moment and don't push me, please.'

He smiled and for a rare moment he saw her for what she was and not what his fantasies wanted her to be. It was not destined to last; Oliver's fierce desires were much too strong for that, but at least for a moment he could touch her with understanding.

'I'm sorry too,' he said quietly. 'It's bound to be a strain for you and I haven't allowed for it, have I? Nevertheless, whatever you might think about Annie Paynter, she's a very strange child and you mustn't let her upset you. Now you promise you won't?'

Julia laughed softly and he watched her as she turned down the sun visor to check her face in the little mirror on the back.

'I assure you, Oliver,' she replied, taking control again, 'strange, I'm quite used to. I lived with it for twenty-three years. Annie is the last person who is going to upset me. On the contrary, Annie may prove to be my salvation in the end. Ready then?'

'How are you, Julia?' Miss Vincent asked, smiling and touching her fondly. 'You look splendid.'

They were standing on the vast stone doorstep and behind her Julia could see into the echoing corridor that led into the depths of hell beyond it. She could smell it, too, and no longer used to the smell, recoiled from it. She didn't want to go in, not for anything in the world did she want to go in.

'I couldn't be better thank you, Matron,' she replied, dragging her eyes unwillingly away. 'I've bought some dresses for Minnie. May she have them?'

The woman with the sharp face and severe uniform smiled and Oliver wondered why he had thought her so hard, the first time he had seen her. He recognized her now for the compassionate woman she was, and was about to learn that there was much thought in her compassion, as well.

'I should be delighted if Minnie finally had some dresses of her own,' she said, 'and before you ask I promise I will personally see to it that they remain specifically her property. We'll sew name tabs in them and she can wash and iron them herself, it will do her good, be a valuable lesson to learn. You can see her alone, too, if you like, I'm sure Dr Crompton will be happy to go with me and have a cup of coffee.'

'I – don't want to go – in,' Julia suddenly whispered, and the woman touched her again, with great gentleness.

'Of course you don't,' she replied. 'Minnie should be here in a moment and you can go to your favourite spot in the garden together. Dr Crompton can come and find you when he's ready to leave.'

Minnie came like a child who had just been given the thing in the world she most wanted above all else. She hurtled down the corridor shouting, 'Julia! Julia!' and flung herself out through the front door into Julia's arms.

Oliver and Ilona Vincent stood and watched in silence as Minnie sobbed and gabbled and Julia hugged her in delight, but in their minds, the doctor and the matron were miles and miles apart. Oliver didn't like to see Julia cuddling Minnie, it didn't fit with his fantasy. He wanted her to turn her back and forget. He watched them walk away like a couple of schoolgirls, their arms about each other, their eyes alight with pleasure and as he turned to face the woman he realized that his expression of distaste must be glowing on his face like a sky-sign.

She shook her head very slightly.

'I thought you might have grown to understand by now, Dr Crompton,' she remarked. 'Are you in love with her?'

'I'm a married man with two children,' he replied sharply, wondering if she was perceptive enough to recognize that he had avoided the question. 'I just don't think that in the long run regular visits back here are what Julia needs. She's taking confident strides into real life now and she must be encouraged to look forwards, not backwards. She needs to put this behind her and forget it.'

The woman stood back, allowing him to pass in front of her into the corridor, into that dreadful stink and the noise.

'No one any longer has the right to try and force Julia to do, or be anything she doesn't want, Doctor,' she said quietly. 'She has earned the right to live her life exactly how she pleases.' She opened the door to her office and showed him in politely and as she closed the door behind them she added, 'I have tentatively spoken to the hospital board on the subject of Minnie eventually going to live at Tremar with Julia. There was remarkably little opposition to it, as a matter of fact.'

Oliver turned to stare at her and he knew immediately that she had seen through his evasive answer.

'Don't make her any promises yet, I beg of you!' he exclaimed, furious as the words simply came tumbling out of his mouth.

She smiled, but her face was very sharp.

'If you are a married man with two children, Dr Crompton,' she observed, 'I can't see what possible difference it could make to you if Minnie goes to live with Julia or not. I'll order some coffee, shall I?'

Out in the summer sunshine, in a sheltered spot on the edge of the graveyard behind the wooden hut where the tools were kept, Minnie and Julia sat on a couple of straddle stones that had been there for as long as they could remember – though for certain no one had ever built a barn in that particular corner. Julia took the four dresses out of their bags and watched Minnie's faded eyes light up with delight.

'For you, Minnie,' she said and yanked her out of her dreadful, blue sack-dress, throwing it on to the ground.

She supposed she'd never noticed before, in the years they'd been living there together, the greyness of Minnie's skin, the sagging of her wizened breasts and belly, the raggedness of the scratchy woollen underwear they were issued with. She didn't actually know how old Minnie was, but she found the sight of the flaccid skin a shock and the unhealthy, stale smell of the body unpleasant.

Was I like this? she wondered. I suppose I must have been and I never noticed.

'Which one would you like to put on first?' she asked, and Minnie chose the dress with the brightest colours. 'And they're yours to keep, my love,' Julia whispered, buttoning her into the dress and fixing the belt approximately where Minnie's waist might have been. 'Matron's going to make sure of it. There. You look beautiful, you know, really beautiful!'

Minnie danced around clumsily in her dress for a moment and then abruptly sank down on to the grass beside her beloved Julia and pressed her head against her knee. Julia touched her thoughtfully and for a long time they were silent in each other's company, listening to the sounds of the summer.

Eventually Julia whispered, 'Can I tell you a secret, Minnie? And if I tell you, will you promise never to tell anyone else?'

'Of course I will, Julia,' Minnie replied earnestly, gazing up with her dull, confused eyes. 'What comes after summer?'

'Autumn,' Julia murmured softly, cupping the poor, half-witted face fondly in her hands. 'Minnie, he's still alive, the man who was responsible for putting me in here. I thought he was dead. I thought he'd died with my brother at Ypres but he didn't. He came home after the war and he married someone else. He never came for me . . . all those years and he never even came to see me . . . and when he took my virginity on the floor in the boathouse, he said he loved me.'

Minnie gazed at her like a loving spaniel. She didn't understand, but it really didn't matter.

'Don't leave me again, Julia,' she begged and Julia kissed her swiftly.

'I must today, darling,' she replied, 'but winter comes after autumn and before winter is out you will be living with me at Tremar, I promise. Be strong for me and wait, I have a score to settle first, but we shall have Tremar, you and I. And I think Annie will have a place there, too.'

Minnie didn't ask about Annie and Julia didn't furnish her with the information.

'I don't like it here without you, Julia,' she said plaintively.

'No, but you'll love it at Tremar,' Julia answered. 'You've just got to hang on here for a little while longer. I tell you what, I'll come and see you every week from now on and now you've got your dresses, I'll take you out to tea sometimes, if you like. Would you like that?'

Minnie gave her a simple little smile.

'Yes, Julia,' she replied obediently. 'What's going out to tea?'

'I suppose it doesn't hurt to make Minnie such promises,' Oliver said thoughtlessly as they drove away from Blackridge an hour later, 'she isn't likely to remember them, is she?'

When she looked at Oliver, Julia still experienced a certain desire for him, though she had not yet examined it too closely in her mind. She had wondered, briefly, if she wanted him to notice her and touch her simply because nobody else had done so for so many years. She wore beautiful clothes now and smelt of perfume. She wore make-up, and her hair was stylishly cut, and he was younger than her and extremely handsome – but when he made remarks like that she was intensely aware of his insensitivity.

She had no idea at all of how he felt about her and certainly whilst she was in Truro she had enjoyed her little daydreams about a romance with him. But she had Tremar back now and she had found Annie. More than that, the stunning piece of information Annie had innocently handed out the previous evening had abruptly seemed to make her immediate future quite full enough – though she was not ready, yet, to encourage him to stay away.

'Would you feel uncomfortable taking Minnie to a teashop, then?' she enquired of him, gazing out of the car window as they left the ruggedness of the moors behind and came back towards the softer greenness of Polwean. 'If I'm allowed to take her out to tea I expect Matron will see to it that she's been bathed. Tell me, Oliver, did I smell like that? That first time, when you came to tell me about my mother, did I smell stale like that?'

There were times when her blunt questions embarrassed him considerably, and this was one of them. Yes, she *had* smelt awful. He remembered it quite well.

'I don't think I noticed,' he replied not very convincingly, and saw a ghost of a smile on her lips. 'I really just remember being so shocked at finding you perfectly sane.'

'And ugly, and pasty and very smelly. Dear God, Oliver, I *lived* there for twenty-three-and-a-half years and Minnie smelt awful to me today.

Well she won't smell awful any more once she's living with me at Tremar.'

They were on the outskirts of the town now, only about three miles to go to Polwean.

He said, 'I wish you'd think a bit more about that, Julia. Minnie isn't like you and if you take her to live with you at Tremar she'll – well, she'll be a burden, which is not what you need after so many years of suffering. You need your freedom now.'

Julia turned and looked at him and if he'd had any idea of pursuing the subject her look very clearly advised him not to.

'There used to be a particularly good haberdashery in this town when I was young,' she said. 'Minter's it was called, I seem to remember. I wonder if you could find it for me now, Oliver, I'd like to get some material before I go home. I'm not going to buy Annie any dresses, I'm going to teach her to make her own, that'll be much more useful for her.'

'Julia, you are not a charity!' he exclaimed angrily and she smiled. It was a very cold, cutting smile, but very controlled.

'No more I am,' she replied sweetly, 'and you most definitely aren't, are you, Oliver?'

Annie came creeping over the terrace at almost six-thirty. Julia was sitting on the edge of the fountain sipping a sherry, and she had just begun to accept the fact that the child wasn't coming after all. It made her feel sad. She had been looking forward to another encounter with this offspring of the union between Arthur and Gladys. When she saw Annie lying almost flat on the steps and peering nervously round the corner she watched her in astonishment for a few seconds – and then raised the glass to her in a toast.

'I thought you'd abandoned me,' she observed, 'why are you so late?'

'I didn't know whether you really meant it,' Annie replied honestly. 'Most people don't want me anywhere near them. I'm stupid, an' I smell.'

'You could do with a bath, that's true,' Julia said, equally honestly, 'but you're not stupid, and the bath can be dealt with quite easily. I've got a surprise for you, would you like to come and look?'

Annie's little face was vulnerable as she gazed at Julia. It was painful; in a way, Julia thought, it reminded her of Minnie, except that Annie was young and beautiful, but the look was the same. Nervous uncertainty. Only people used to being hurt could look quite like that.

'Come on,' she said, and taking Annie's hand, led her through the drawing-room and up the stairs.

Annie gazed about her in amazement as her boots scuffed on the carpets, hanging back as she took it all in. The housekeeper's workroom, in the days when there had been a resident housekeeper at Tremar, was on the top floor near the servants' bedrooms and contained huge linen cupboards, long trestle tables and a sewing-machine. Beside the sewing-machine now were half a dozen lengths of brightly coloured, crisp cotton and three different patterns.

'Which of those materials do you like the best?' Julia asked, pushing Annie gently towards the machine. Annie pointed to one immediately. 'And which of the patterns?'

Now Annie looked at her with open alarm.

'Look,' she whispered, 'I don' 'ave no sewing skills, an' if you was wantin' me to dressmake for you in return for your teachin' me, well I can't. . . .'

'Oh, Annie,' Julia whispered, cupping her face softly, 'I don't want you to dressmake for me, I'm going to teach you how to do it for yourself. Those patterns and materials are for you! I thought we could make a start tonight, after supper, and then tomorrow, if Oliver's not too busy, we could go into the nearby town and buy you some shoes.'

Annie's mouth hung slightly open as she stared at the gifts that were on offer. Annie had never been given anything in her life other than food and she was overwhelmed. Then Julia saw her brow furrow and abruptly her green eyes filled with tears.

'I can't go home in new clothes,' she whispered bleakly, 'my pa'd have them off me afore I got upstairs, and I wouldn't never see them again.' She sniffed and wiped her nose with the back of her hand. 'It's ever so nice of you, but – I can't.'

'Oh yes you can,' Julia said fiercely, taking the child into her arms. 'Look, Annie, according to you you don't go to school and you stay out of your home as much as you can, right? Then I suggest you come up here first thing in the morning, have a bath and put your new clothes on and then you can stay here all day and change back to go home at night. I'd really like us to be friends, you know. I need a friend, I don't know anybody here now and already I find I'm a bit lonely. Tremar's frightfully big to rattle about in all by yourself!'

Annie hugged her. She smelt frightful and Julia thought she knew why the other children in the village bullied her; she was an easy target, dirty and unkempt as she was. But she was so sensitive, so beautiful – how could it be possible that Arthur Paynter and Gladys Penhaligan were her parents? How had they changed, for God's sake, that this lovely child was so dirty and neglected? Gladys, sweet little Gladys, and the godlike Arthur.

Suddenly Annie looked up into her face and there was honest-to-God fear in her bright green eyes.

'When my pa got home from The Smugglers last night,' she murmured, 'he were so drunk he couldn't hardly stand up. It woke me up and I went on the landing to listen. They started to row, Ma and Pa. Ma said, "She's back, Arthur, she come back to Tremar today, and unless she's changed out a all recognition first thing she'm going t'do, she'm going to come looking fer *you,* because you *bleddy* owe her!" And then he said, "She comes round here, woman, and I'll bleddy see her off with my feckin' shotgun!" And I think, well, I think they was talking about *you*!'

Julia nodded.

'Yes, I'm afraid they were,' she replied quietly, and then, kissing the child, smiled warmly. 'But it's nothing for you to worry about, what happens between you and me has nothing to do with anything else. Come on, bath-time and then we'll go and have, something to eat. And Annie, maybe it would be better if you didn't tell anyone you were coming up here regularly, not for the time being, all right?'

'Well Ma won't mind, she's good to me, Ma is, but I ent going to be telling my pa, anyway,' Annie assured her.

Chapter 7

The days of June began to march onwards and life seemed to fall into a remarkably set pattern for Julia very quickly. Suddenly she had been back at Tremar for three weeks! For twenty-three-and-a-half years it had been as if she had lived in some sort of prolonged, terrible dream and when she had eventually woken up everything had been strangely unchanged – and yet entirely different. There had been only dirt roads in Polwean in 1915, and there had been more shops when she was a child. Yet of the shops that were left, two were, astonishingly, still run by the same people. They were much older now, just as she was, but they were still there.

It would have been nice, she thought wryly, to have known how it felt to Sleeping Beauty after a hundred years of sleep – or maybe she had been too busy with her handsome prince to notice.

She had a handsome prince of sorts, too. Well, he was handsome anyway, and he was always finding excuses to be at Tremar, only he happened to already have a wife and two small children – and besides, she had rather more to think about just at the moment. Her solicitor was already interviewing prospective estate managers for her, so he told her on the phone, and he seemed as anxious as she was to start getting Tremar back into shape.

'My father did speak several times about it to your father, Miss Drake,' he told her diffidently, 'but he really seemed extraordinarily reluctant to repair the dower and would never tell Father why. Father tried to explain to him that if the roof collapsed the damage to the rest of the house would be appalling, but he virtually told him to mind his own business. And then after he died, your mother just wasn't interested.'

'My father was allowing Tremar to rot away as a fitting memorial to my dead brother, Mr Cruikshank,' Julia replied, struggling to keep the irony out of her voice. 'He had no heir, so it no longer mattered what happened to the house.'

'But he had . . .' his voice tailed away abruptly and Julia fancied she could see the look on his face: a mixture of embarrassment at his *faux pas* and relief that she couldn't see him.

'Yes, I know,' she agreed. 'But I was disinherited in 1915, remember; Tremar was willed elsewhere. I would still be at Blackridge if my mother hadn't remembered I was still alive just before she died – and Dr Crompton hadn't happened to be young and forward thinking, and absolutely determined I should get my rightful inheritance back. Tell me, Mr Cruikshank, did you know I existed?'

She heard him cough uncomfortably at the other end of the line. He was young, too, older than Oliver, but still their generation. He had taken over the business from his father, who had in his turn taken over from *his* father, but 'young' Mr Cruikshank was a very different proposition from young Dr Crompton. When he had called on her in Truro she had found it hard to believe that anyone could be so relatively young and still so Victorian. Left to him she would never have escaped from Blackridge – he would never have considered it necessary to see her. He would have taken her reported mental state at face value and that would have been the end of it.

Nevertheless, for all that she was quite happy to have him as her solicitor. She had been quick enough to recognize that no one would ever put anything over on Mr Cruikshank.

'Well, yes of course I did,' he replied truthfully in answer to her question. 'Father told me that you were – er – a patient at Blackridge, we were detailed to send the six-monthly cheques to the place for your keep . . . but of course he didn't know the circumstances. Not the truth, you understand. Father wouldn't have been a party to such a thing, well, you know. . . .'

Julia smiled and when she spoke her voice was warm.

'Mr Cruikshank, you don't need to make excuses, really you don't,' she said. 'My father was to blame for what happened to me and my mother compounded the felony, there was no blame to be laid at anybody else's door, and as I know your father is still alive perhaps you'd be good enough to tell him I said so. I remember your father when I was a child, he was a very kind man.'

'He'll be very pleased to receive your greeting I'm sure, Miss Drake,' the precise voice at the other end of the telephone said. 'Now is there anything else I can do for you whilst we're talking?'

Julia looked up: across the lawn at the back of the house, in her scuffed boots and scruffy dress, came Annie Paynter, her red hair shining in the sunlight.

'As a matter of fact there is,' she said quietly. 'I wonder if you'd look into the circumstances of Rectory Farm for me, Mr Cruikshank. I'm told it was given as a gift to one Arthur Paynter in about 1919. I should very much like to know, please, how much land he was given and any other agreements that were made with him – and as soon as possible, please, if it's not too much trouble. Oh, and he beats his daughter, too, which I find *most* distasteful. Let me know what the law says I can do about it, if I find it necessary, would you?'

She was replacing the receiver as Annie kicked off her boots and came through the french windows, barefoot, and smiling cheerfully.

Julia watched her with warm affection as she threw herself down into an armchair showing long, firm child's legs, brown from so much exposure to the sun, and as they gazed happily at each other, Julia realized that Annie was somehow like manna from heaven; an extra treat, in a way, and one that was turning out to be comfortingly constant.

It was more than possible, she realized, that after the initial euphoria of returning home had worn off, she would have found the vast emptiness of Tremar, the loneliness of being friendless and virtually unknown in the village now, hard to bear. Mrs Collins kept strictly to her domain in the house and made it obvious that she did not wish to be regarded as a friend, but Annie came first thing in the morning now and cheerfully stayed all day, and for hours she and Julia would sew dresses together, study Latin verbs and happily chatter.

Julia was teaching the child the habit of taking a bath regularly and feeding her on good, wholesome food. In the three weeks she had known her, she had bought her two pairs of new shoes, they had made four summer dresses for her so far, and looked through some magazines to see what was going to be fashionable for the autumn, though to Julia's growing anger, Annie went through a grim ritual of changing back into her dreadful old clothes before she went home each evening, because of the fear of her father.

Actually, the shock of discovering whose child she was had faded now, settled into place in a way, but it was beginning to become obvious to Julia that Arthur was going out of his way to avoid her. Well that was all right, let him avoid her if he chose, he couldn't do it for ever. Eventually, one day, he would have to face her.

And eventually one day, she was deciding, albeit as yet fairly vaguely, he would have to pay for what he'd done to her. Exactly how was in no way clear at the moment, but it really didn't matter. She had all the time in the world. Twenty-three-and-a-half years of imprisonment surrounded by the feeble minded, by the dribbling, incontinent, vague-eyed wrecks of humanity whom nobody wanted had taught her to be patient. And revenge after all this time would be so much the sweeter.

Arthur Paynter had once or twice thought, in those moments between being pleasantly warm with drink and being blind drunk, that it would probably be all right if he could make sure none of his family ever went near Tremar. After all, he was no longer a tenant farmer of the estate, there was no need for him ever to run into Julia Drake unless he was careless. She wasn't a prisoner in her old manor house like she had been at Blackridge, but unless she planned to actually knock on the door of Rectory Farm and demand to see him, the only other place he was regularly to be found was in The Smugglers, and she definitely wouldn't go looking for him there.

And even if she did confront him, what could she say? He'd been given the official version of her disappearance on his return from the war: that she'd gone mad with grief at the loss of her brother and so many others. And that's what he would tell her.

He'd known the truth, of course, but even if he hadn't he wouldn't have believed, any more than anyone else, that the Drakes, with their money and their class, would have shut their daughter up in Blackridge. But it was the official story and it was what he had been told.

Occasionally, in his bleaker moments of sobriety, he remembered back to that summer before the war. It might as well have been somebody else's life for all the reality it held for him now, a world of make-believe before the relentless pounding of the guns, the mud, the stench and the bits of human being scattered about. Jed and Jethro Penhaligan, Alexander Drake and himself, and then, one glorious June afternoon on her return from her boarding-school, Julia Drake.

Alexander was at Oxford and Arthur and the Penhaligan twins had half expected him to spurn the friendship of the locals when he came back for his long leave, but Alexander had always liked the company of the three musketeers and he never seemed to change, no matter how long he was away from Polwean. Julia was a couple of years younger than the others and in the past they'd not bothered with her much, other than to dump the twins' little sister, Gladys on her, but he remembered her particularly in the bay, on that first afternoon of her holidays – and he thought he couldn't understand why he'd never noticed her before.

She'd climbed the cliffs for a dare, wearing a pair of her brother's cricket flannels, and then tossed a couple of handfuls of stones down at them. She'd demanded to know if they were going to fight and then she'd climbed down and stood before him, with those hypnotic eyes, and called him Aramis, the clever one. He hadn't known anything about *The Three Musketeers*, he hadn't got the reading skills for a book like that, but, Oh, God, he'd wanted to be the clever one, for Julia.

In the end he'd gone back to the boathouse with her whilst she changed and Alexander had called after him, 'Don't let her lead you astray!'

What had Alexander meant by that? Not, Arthur felt certain all these years later, the sort of 'astray' to which they had eventually fallen prey.

He remembered as clearly as Julia did, those extraordinary moments in the corner of the boathouse, naked amid the blankets and cushions. The war had been snapping at their heels by then, close enough for them to know there was no escape from it, it really was coming. Three times they had made love. Three times, always with that slight underlying fear that someone might walk in on them – perhaps that was what had made it so exciting.

He remembered quite clearly her beautiful, firm body, the fragrance of her skin; he remembered, too, that they had not seemed to fumble uncomfortably in their virgin states but been as real lovers, urgent and receptive. She had certainly not seemed to feel any pain – as he had been told virgins did – though she had bled a little and had showed him her virgin blood in triumph. But she had not wept, or cried out loud, or been difficult to penetrate. She had sighed with pleasure and wrapped him in her long legs – and he had felt like a god as he possessed her.

Under the circumstances it had been just as well, he realized, that he had resisted the urge to run round the village telling everybody!

It was Gladys who had told him why Julia had been locked up in Blackridge – and Gladys was the only person in the village who knew and had always known that Julia's seducer had been Arthur. Gladys had told him in a letter, long before they got married. So he had known the truth perfectly well when Sir George and Lady Florence had welcomed him home from the war; had thrown a garden party at Tremar to honour the three miserable heroes on their return from hell; and had begun to draw up the legal papers to make Rectory Farm and Swallows Wood his property.

'Because,' Sir George said stiffly, 'we are told that you, very bravely, carried Alexander in from no man's land when he was wounded and saved his life.'

That was right, he had done just that – and for what? Less than six months later, still bandaged from his original wound in the leg, Alexander Drake had been cut to pieces – and Arthur couldn't have carried him back that time, even if he'd wanted to. He could never have picked all the bits of him up. Alexander Drake was just one of the reasons Arthur Paynter preferred to look at life through the befuddled eyes of a drunk. Julia Drake was another.

Just over three weeks after Julia Drake's sudden, absurd return from Blackridge – where she should have had the decency to go mad – Arthur caught his daughter, Annie, wandering through the slum kitchen of their farmhouse one morning, and grabbed her arm painfully, swinging her round to face him.

Annie always looked satisfyingly frightened when her father attacked her, so did Gladys. Jed and Jethro, who were in many ways much like their long-deceased uncles, were much too big to pick on any more, and much too useful. Arthur had long since ceased to be even remotely competent as a farmer; Jed and Jethro were quite good at it. It was only thanks to them that there was any money at all any more. They worked very professionally in Swallows Wood each year, cutting and stacking timber, replanting and thinning. The rest of the time they worked with the dairy herd, grew adequate feed in the fields, tended the horses and laboured astonishingly long hours, and thanks to them there was food on the table. But the fact was they were hardly more than children themselves – and if there was going to be another war now, which everyone seemed to think there was, they would probably go to the front, like their uncles, to fight. And like their uncles, they probably wouldn't come back.

Held painfully in her father's vicelike grip, with only the tips of her toes touching the floor, Annie gazed up into his drink-sodden face and smelt his soured breath.

'When the old witch up at Tremar were alive,' he whispered viciously, 'you used to go up there. I knows you did. D'you go there now, do you?

Is that where you gets to every day?'

'Why would I want to go to Tremar, Pa?' Annie bleated in terror, 'There'm nothing for me at Tremar.'

'No, there ent! ' Arthur agreed. 'And you keep away from the place, or I'll flay the bleddy hide off yer! Now get out a ma sight, you dirty, skinny runt!'

As he swung her away from him he caught her a savage smack across her face, sending her sprawling across the stone floor, thwacking her knees and elbows painfully as she landed. For a moment Annie lay panting on the greasy, dog-smelling tiles, then, with a terrified glance at her father, she hauled herself to her feet and scuttled out into the yard.

She rubbed the bits that smarted for a few moments, then slopping in her ill-fitting boots through the general muck, pushed her way cautiously into the barn. Inside it smelt of straw and chickens. It was usually full of cats, but most of the farm cats were virtually feral and spent their lives happily ratting in there.

Mostly the dogs would go in there to whelp, too, and according to what was born the puppies would either be sold as soon as they were weaned, or put down. Puppies sired by a stray dog in the village were unnecessary mouths to feed, only those sired by one of the two farm dogs were allowed to live. Jed and Jethro each had a pure-bred male Border collie to whom they were very attached; the bitches numbered four, and they only kept their places on the farm because they were good working-dogs.

Annie knew there was a litter of puppies almost ready to leave their mother in a corner of the barn. They were penned up with her and there were six of them. Jed and Jethro already had takers for most of them, they would fetch a good price and they would be going within days. Two of them, Annie decided sourly, as one of her knees oozed a small stream of blood down her leg and her ear burned very painfully from her father's callous blow, were going to go right now! Yesterday Julia had said she would like a couple of dogs and as far as Annie was concerned she owed Julia a present.

Gwenan, the mother of the pups, was not the nicest of the farm dogs by any means. Mostly she was given a fairly wide berth and the boys only kept her because she was so good at her job, but no one had ever bothered to notice that all the dogs, even the risky-tempered ones, were perfectly placid with Annie. In some strange way it was as if they recognized her plight. Now, as she approached the pen, Gwenan bared her teeth briefly and then began to wag her tail as the squeaking puppies leapt clumsily in Annie's direction.

Annie climbed into the pen and selected her two favourites, a lively male and a particularly pretty female, while Gwenan watched her without even bothering to stand up. Annie put some straw into the bottom of an old box, dropped the puppies in, closed the lid and grasping the box staggered out into the yard. Gwenan went back to sleep.

In the sun-filled yard Annie glanced about her slightly nervously. She knew Jed and Jethro were down in Swallows Wood and she hoped by now her father had gone to join them. It was a long walk up the lane from the farm to the road and then a considerable walk to Tremar. The box was heavy and an awkward shape to carry, but up at Tremar, in the top room, there were two more lengths of material and a choice of patterns waiting by the sewing-machine. There were two new pairs of shoes as well, white leather sandals and the smartest pair of black shoes she had ever seen, and as far as Annie was concerned, helping herself to two of Gwenan's puppies from the barn in return for these luxuries was a fair price to pay.

She was half-way across the green, plodding along under the weight of the box, which wobbled dangerously about as the puppies wriggled nervously inside, when she ran into Sophie Crompton and her children, Pretty Sophie – the posh bitch – as her father called her. Annie had noticed long ago that Sophie always seemed to pull Alice and Edward close to her when they ran into each other. It was an advantage and Annie always played it. Sophie gave her food quite often, sometimes very tasty food, and if she didn't feel inclined to let Alice and Edward get too close, well that was fine with Annie, she didn't want to play with them anyway. She didn't have a lot of time for small children.

Sophie was pushing Edward in a push-chair and Alice was walking beside her, good as gold.

Sophie said, 'Annie? What on earth have you got there?' and Annie put the box down on the grass carefully.

'Some puppies,' she replied.

Sophie frowned.

'In a box?'

'They're my puppies!'

'Yes dear, but where are you taking them?'

Annie opened her eyes wide and gave Sophie what she hoped was a suitably stupid look.

'They'm heavy,' she said, 'they don't like it in this box.'

As if on cue the lid of the box shot upwards and a rather nervous black and white furry head appeared. The puppy had boot-button eyes and a quivering pink tongue. It panted as it took in its surroundings for a few seconds, appeared to be contemplating making a run for it and Annie snatched it up in her arms quickly and then sat on the box firmly to stop the other puppy escaping.

Alice took a couple of steps forward and Annie saw Sophie's hand come out protectively. Ignoring her she very carefully pushed the puppy towards Alice to be stroked, and Alice gazed up at her mother as she stroked it lovingly.

'Annie, where are you taking the puppies, dear?' Sophie asked slowly, bending towards her, 'because they look a little flustered,' and abruptly they both saw Oliver's car round the bend in the lane and come smoothly down into the village, sliding to a halt outside Lamplighter House. His timing couldn't have been better, Annie thought, in fact it was just what she had been hoping for.

He climbed out and came across to them. Smart Oliver in his spotless flannels and beautiful jacket. He spoke gently to his children, kissing them fondly. Annie couldn't remember if her father had ever kissed her in her life, but she thought not.

'Annie?' he said and she squatted on the grass, looking up at him.

'You going to Tremar?' she enquired.

He frowned.

'Well yes, I was just going to pop in for a few moments,' he replied, 'why?'

No one in Polwean ever guarded their facial expressions in front of Annie, no one ever considered they needed to and in consequence Annie knew a lot more about the people who lived in her village than almost anyone else. She saw now the look on Sophie Crompton's face. She saw the pain and anger. She saw Oliver's eyes turn in the direction of Tremar and she saw Sophie's fists clench quickly. She had already seen, a number of times, the look in Oliver's eyes when he looked at Julia, but she had also seen what he failed to see. Julia's look was very different when she looked at him.

'Julia wants some puppies,' she observed, 'but this box is heavy. Will you take it in your car?'

Puppies! In his beautiful car! This was not Oliver's idyllic view of country life. He didn't mind fields full of lowing cows or farmyards full of livestock, but he had no desire to mingle with them. He patted the occasional dog, but had never wanted to own one and one of the things about Polwean that irritated him most of all was that his shoes were regularly covered in farmyard muck. Oliver longed to return to the city.

'Well it wouldn't hurt you to give her a lift,' Sophie pointed out when the silence had become embarrassing. 'Since you say you're going up to the manor anyway. Put a rug on the back seat if you're worried about your upholstery.'

Her tone was resentful, almost tearful; Oliver looked furiously down at Annie who continued to squat on the grass, smiling up at him, then he turned swiftly away.

'All right,' he said, 'I'll give you a lift, of course I will, but I will get a rug if you don't mind. That box doesn't leak or anything, does it?'

'It's got puppies in it,' Annie replied at her most stupid. 'Puppies don't leak.'

Sophie sniggered and Oliver looked very angry indeed.

'Oh yes they bloody well do,' he muttered. 'Leak, chew and get under people's feet! Stay there with that box and wait for me.'

Annie grinned and congratulated herself on making him angry, but then Annie had a vested interest in making Oliver angry. She had never had a friend before; Julia was a new and wonderful experience for her. In her child's mind, which though clever beyond its years was not experienced in anything other than indifference and violence, she recognized that Oliver viewed her as a rival. Oliver wanted Julia, but Oliver already had Sophie, Alice and Edward. Annie had no one, so as far as she was concerned her claim to Julia was a more valid one than his.

Mrs Collins opened the front door of Tremar to them. She looked, as always, importantly delighted to see Oliver on the doorstep, but like everyone else in the village, she scowled at Annie.

'What you want Annie Paynter?' she enquired. 'I'm not sure the mistress is free to see you, just now.'

'You ask her!' Annie retorted rudely, but Oliver left her standing on the doorstep as he stepped into the house and the door was closed in her face. She sat on the step beside her box and waited and within two minutes the door was opened again, this time by Julia.

'Hullo,' she said, smiling. 'You don't have to wait out here, you know, you can come in whenever you like.'

'Not according to them,' Annie replied. '*She* says you didn't have time to see me. I got you some puppies, like you said you wanted, they's in return for my new shoes an' dresses.'

Julia squatted on her haunches beside the box and opened it carefully. She had simply mentioned in passing to the child the day before that she fancied a couple of dogs and she certainly had not expected to receive a box full of them as a result. She had an idea that good puppies were expensive and one look at these two told her they were very good. They squirmed out at her excitedly as the sun penetrated their dark box and Julia was pleased to see that at least they were weaned, though she had nothing to feed them on.

'Annie, they're gorgeous!' she exclaimed. 'Did you ask your father if you could have them?'

'No, 'course I didn't,' Annie replied cheerfully, 'he wouldn't a let me; fact he'll throw a fit when he finds they'm gone! He says he'll flay the hide off me if he catches me coming up here to see you. He *really* doesn't like you, does he? Why is that?'

Julia tightened her lips and glanced away. It was very quick, but Annie didn't miss it. When she looked back she was smiling.

'He hasn't seen or spoken to me for more than twenty years,' she answered simply, 'so I can't imagine. Perhaps he thinks I'll infect you with something. Listen, can I keep these two in the house?'

'Well I wouldn't,' Annie said, 'they'm never been in a house. Why don't I take them into the stables with the chickens for now and then when you got beds for them and things, we'll train them to come in the house?'

'Sounds good to me.' Julia smiled and they carried a puppy each round the side of the house towards the stables.

She left Annie sitting on a bed of fresh straw in the stables playing with the puppies, as some of her newly acquired chickens clucked and scratched about on the insect-littered floor. Back in the house she looked into the kitchen where Mrs Collins was making supper.

Mrs Collins seemed to leave a huge amount of food when she went home each night. Every morning when she arrived every scrap of it was gone, but she never remarked upon it. Julia sometimes wondered if she put it down to the fact that Julia had gone without for so many years that she was making up for lost time now, or whether perhaps she and Mr Collins were used to eating such quantities themselves and didn't think it odd at all. It didn't occur to Julia, or to Annie, who shared the food with her every evening, that both of them had abnormally small appetites, since neither of them had been fed properly for best part of their lives.

'Mrs Collins,' she said, struggling to keep her voice light, 'I thought you understood, Annie Paynter is free to come and go from Tremar as she likes. I'm teaching her to sew and read and so on, it's good for both of us.'

The housekeeper's huge, white, sparkling bosom swelled ominously and Julia sensed her disapproval.

''Course, I don't know the relationships in this village like others do,' she observed stiffly. 'She's some kin of yours, is she, Miss Drake?'

Julia shook her head.

'No kin, just an unfortunate child who needs a friend.'

'You do know she's a thief?'

'Is she? Has she stolen from you at some time?'

'Well, no, but I knows people who say she'm thieved from them. Things gone missing: blame Annie Paynter, that's what they say.'

Julia swallowed to quell her anger.

'Sometimes, perhaps we're all a bit quick to judge, don't you think?' she murmured. 'I mean, I was incarcerated in Blackridge Asylum for twenty-three years and I think I'm perfectly sane. You don't seem to be afraid of working for me, so I assume you think I'm perfectly sane too? You understand my meaning, Mrs Collins?'

Not trusting herself to wait for an answer she smiled and left the kitchen, finding Oliver waiting for her in the hall. She smiled at him too and walked away towards the open french windows and the broken fountain, knowing he would follow her. Her back radiated hostility, but Oliver chose not to notice.

'She may not gossip,' she remarked coldly, without looking at him, 'but she certainly makes judgements, your chosen housekeeper. She, like you, is certain Annie is an unsuitable visitor for me. Strange, when I had no visitors at all for twenty-three years – apart from my mother who called to see me *once* – now for some reason you think you should have a say in who is, and is not, allowed to take up my time. You don't like me visiting Minnie, either, do you, so what would you have me do to pass the time, Oliver, join some suitable ladies church-group, knitting gloves for the needy?'

'I didn't say you shouldn't let Annie visit you!' Oliver retorted indignantly. 'I only said you aren't a charity, Julia. And Mrs Collins is right, that child is a thief, anyone in the village will tell you that. Good God, she's been taking your books for the last two years or more, on your own admission.'

'*Borrowing* my books!' she shouted furiously, 'She has never stolen anything from Tremar, Oliver, not a damn thing! She is an ill-used, remarkably clever, starved, resilient child and her father brutalizes her. All I want is to make her life a little more bearable. Dear God, if you weren't so middle-class and had the smallest understanding of suffering you wouldn't be so quick to condemn.'

Oliver tightened his lips sharply at the jibe. It was cheap and it hurt.

'An understanding of suffering is not your exclusive prerogative, Julia,' he said eventually. 'I do see how much Annie suffers at the hands of her father, I just maybe don't see the genius you claim to see shining out of her eyes. You know, every time I come here you snap and snarl at me and you seem to think I condemn everything you want to do, but I don't. I take you to see Minnie, don't I? I take you every week to see her. I took you to buy Annie's shoes. I do what I can for you, but you seem to have lost sight of me altogether. I'm just a chap with a car and as much free time as you require. What happened to the friendship we had in Truro?'

She stood still with her back to him, feeling angry and resentful. To a great extent it was true what he said, she did use him as a free taxi-service most of the time and she did abuse him, but he got under her defences.

She was not at all prepared for what happened next and her reaction to it shook her considerably.

He suddenly put his hands on her shoulders and drew her against him until their bodies were intimately close. She could feel his breath on her neck, the pressure of his fingers, the warmth of his body, and though her instincts told her to move, she stood quite still; then she actually leaned back against him.

'You're shaking,' he whispered and she drew her breath sharply, putting her hands up to her face.

'Because I can't make you understand,' she replied. 'Because – I can't tell you what I want to tell you . . . Oh, Oliver, I'm sorry, I don't mean to snap at you all the time, and I don't mean to use you, either. I'm not kind to you, I know I'm not and I have no right after all you've done for me.'

His fingers began to massage her shoulders, it was a very soft, gentle movement and abruptly her body became sharply sexually aware of him. She wanted to turn and kiss him so badly that she found herself licking her lips, and her breasts tingled with the desire for him to touch her. When his lips were suddenly pressed against the back of her neck she hissed her breath softly and felt the hair rise on her scalp – and this time she took a firm step away from him.

'What time do you send Annie home in the evening?' she heard him ask very softly. 'Because we need to talk, Julia, alone.'

She went to the stone parapet and leaned on it, not looking at him but taking care to keep some space between them.

'I don't think that's what either of us needs at the moment, Oliver,' she replied carefully, 'to complicate things like that. I've got my new estate manager coming to see me for the first time tomorrow and, well. . . .'

'Well what?' he enquired, as she tailed off lamely. 'Julia, you know we want each other, that's why you snap at me so often, I'm sure, and that's why I come here every single day. But I never find you alone, do I? So what time do you send Annie home?'

'At about eight-thirty,' she murmured reluctantly. 'It takes her half an hour to walk back to Rectory Farm from here and she has to be sure of not finding her father at home when she gets there. That way, as far as I can gather, she gets at least a few minutes love and attention from her poor mother.'

'Then I shall come back tonight at about eight forty-five and we shall spend some time together, like we used to do in Truro before you came home,' he said. 'I think you owe me that.'

At last she turned to look at him and her eyes were almost pleading.

'Oliver,' she whispered, 'I loved – someone, in 1914, and I gave myself to him because he told me he loved me. It cost me twenty-three years of my life.'

'And giving yourself to me will not cost you anything like that, I promise,' he replied softly, touching her cheek with his fingers. 'I shan't even ask you to give yourself to me at all if you don't want to, but I think you owe me the truth and you haven't been truthful with me up to now.' She opened her mouth to speak and he put his fingers against her lips. 'Shush, no more until this evening. We'll walk down to the boathouse together, because that was where it happened, wasn't it?'

'What happened there?' asked a small, resentful voice behind them. 'There ent nothing in the boathouse now, 'cept spiders and rotten planks. I know. I bin there.'

Julia's face broke into a gentle smile and she put her arm around Annie fondly.

'That's right, there isn't,' she replied cheerfully, 'and we have some sewing to do and then some Latin translations – and you're going to have a bath before lunch, young lady. Don't let us keep you, Oliver, if you're busy.'

Oliver wore an entirely unreadable expression on his face as he watched them, but he smiled as he turned to leave.

'Until later then,' he murmured and crossed into the beautiful drawing-room. 'I'll see myself out.'

As Annie watched his retreating back she suddenly turned her green eyes upon Julia and her expression was instantly readable. She was triumphant.

'You know that Sophie,' she observed, 'that he's married to? She'm proper jealous of you and that's a fact. Shall I go and have my bath first?'

Chapter 8

The meal that appeared on the table at Rectory Farm at six o'clock that evening was fried cod, potatoes and cabbage. Arthur Paynter looked at it in disgust and then glared at his wife.

'Is this the best you can manage?' he demanded. 'Fried bleddy cod again! I'm sick of fish, Gladys!'

'Be grateful,' Gladys Paynter replied sourly. 'We'd not have that if your drinking mate Tom Pennard hadn't given it me, I've had nothing from you for long enough, in case you hadn't remembered! By the way, he says he won money off you in The Smugglers the other night. We haven't got money to gamble Arthur.'

'Mind yer own bleddy business, woman,' her husband retorted warningly. 'If I wants a game of cards with me mates, I'll have one. All right? And where's that runt Annie? She'm not been here supper-time for weeks now. Just where does she go, Gladys, I'm bleddy certain you knows?'

Gladys Paynter was positive she knew too, and the thought terrified her, because it hurt to see Arthur bully the child like he did. She glanced nervously at her husband and was relieved when one of the twins broke into the conversation.

'What the hell do it matter where she goes, Pa?' Jethro asked, tearing himself off a hunk of bread with his big, rough hands. 'Ent no food for her here anyway, you hardly lets her have any, do you? So let her get it somewhere else. Some soft bugger's feeding her, they must be.'

His brother chuckled and also tore himself off a piece of bread.

'You got to hand it to her,' he observed, 'I've even seen her get food off the butcher's wife, and she'm by no means the most generous woman you ever met.'

They were as alike as two peas in a pod, their sons, both large, but not bad-looking boys. Ghostly touches of their long-dead uncles revealed themselves to their mother occasionally, and when they did it tore at her heart. She too remembered those halcyon days before the war, when she had loved her brothers – and admired the handsome, sunny Arthur from afar. Somehow it had all been so clear cut then. She had known she was cleverer than the rest of them, but the knowledge that one day she would be Arthur's wife had compensated her in a way. Girls didn't have careers, well, local fishermen's daughters didn't, anyway, but she would be proud to be the power behind Arthur's throne one day.

When he'd gone off in his uniform, with her brothers and the sparkling Alexander Drake, he'd been a god to her. Then the ruined Julia Drake had been dragged away to Blackridge and the years after that had been one nightmare after another. Jed and Jethro dead; Alexander cut to pieces; Julia suffering God knew what; and then, at last, the hero's return. Some hero! The years between 1914 and 1918 had completely destroyed Arthur Paynter. The handsome, curly-haired boy who had gone away to fight came home an embittered man, old before his time and with a developing taste for the drink.

Gladys had married him because she had always blindly loved him, but she'd never been able to forget what he'd done with Julia. It wasn't easy to be anybody's second choice. It hadn't been easy, either, to sit back and let him ignore it. She had liked Julia very much indeed, in fact as far as they were able to be they had been friends. But having secretly ruined their daughter, he'd taken the farm and the land from the Drakes and continued to accept all the hand-outs that had come his way over the years – and frankly he damned well deserved the retribution she knew he feared could well be coming now! Although for all that she was at a loss to know just how Julia could really do them any damage.

Arthur scowled up from his plate of fried cod and the look that passed between him and his wife was understood only by them.

'If I find,' he muttered, 'that she'm up at Tremar, I swear to God I'll thrash her to death, Gladys! So next time you sees her, you tell her that.'

'Well she'm not likely to be coming to no harm up at Tremar, Pa,' Jethro Paynter observed cheerfully. 'In fact I should think she'm quite a bit madder than Miss Drake, by what I's heard.'

Arthur rounded on him furiously.

'Ent no business of yours!' he snarled. 'And you mind that, boy!'

The boys exchanged baffled looks and shrugged, then Jed, swallowing a mouthful of food, put his knife and fork down and said, 'By the by, two of Gwenan's pups has gone from the barn. They bin sold already? I thought they weren't going till next week.'

'*What!*' his brother exclaimed, half rising from the table. 'I ent shifted no pups! Pa?'

'Don't look at me,' Arthur retorted, 'They'm not my bleddy dogs, are they? You'm left a bleddy gap in the pen I'll bet, and the buggers have got out. Well we'd better get out there and look, I s'pose, afore they disappears altogether.'

But they never did find the missing puppies although they searched until it was getting dark. At just before nine o'clock the three of them, Arthur Paynter and his two strapping sons, trailed disconsolately down the lane towards the harbour and The Smugglers Inn. The loss of the puppies was a financial blow – and in the pub they bought whisky chasers with money they could ill afford to waste.

In the back kitchen at Tremar, in a snug bed made from two old blankets, the puppies curled in together whimpering a little, finding themselves bewildered by the loss of their mother and their brothers and sisters, but at least comforted by the warmth of each other. Julia had given them milk to drink and Oliver was bringing some chicken from the village so that they would have breakfast in the morning.

Annie, who knew all about rearing puppies, had directed operations and felt extremely important. She also knew that if her father ever found out what had happened to the puppies, which almost certainly had been missed by now, he would most certainly carry out his threat and beat her terribly, and just before she left to go home, as she took off her lovely new sandals and slid her feet back into her horrible old boots, her nerve failed. She looked up at Julia.

'Please,' she said carefully, 'would you not say they puppies come from me, if anyone asks, and can you ask Doctor not to tell either?'

Julia widened her eyes in alarm and put her hands on the child's shoulders.

'You stole them!' she exclaimed. 'Annie, you silly girl. I only took them because I thought nobody wanted them. I thought your damned father was planning to drown them or something. Are you going to get into trouble if anyone connects them with you?'

Annie nodded.

'But I wanted to give you something!' she said passionately. 'You give me shoes and dresses and food, I didn't have nothing to give you . . . only Jethro were going to sell them, and they fetches a good price, his puppies do.'

For a moment the woman and the child regarded each other steadily, then Julia snatched her in her arms and hugged her fiercely – and as she stroked all the mass of red hair back from Annie's face she saw, for the first time, the child's bruised and slightly swollen ear where Arthur had struck her so viciously earlier in the day.

'Did he do this to you?' she whispered. 'Your father, did he do this?'

Annie silently nodded. There were five nasty little bruises on her upper arm, too, which Julia angrily realized she hadn't noticed. Bruises from savage, cruel fingers.

Annie had so many bruises on her body that even when she was clean and naked after a bath she was always covered in little scratches and black marks. Certainly some of them resulted from her lifestyle. Shinning up and down trees, climbing walls and getting in and out of places where she had no business being didn't help to keep her skinny little body unmarked, but far too many of them were blatant signs of violence, and too many new ones kept appearing. Something had got to be done, Julia knew, but she also knew she was treading a very fine line: too much fuss and she was likely to lose Annie altogether.

'If anyone asks,' she said coldly, 'I bought those puppies and paid a fair price for them, and if your father doesn't believe it, tell him to come up here and ask me himself. Annie,' abruptly she hugged the child again, in terror, 'he won't hurt you again when you get home, will he? Promise me you'll be all right.'

Annie smiled at her.

'He'll be in The Smugglers by now,' she replied cheerfully, 'and if he don't find out about the puppies I won't come to no harm, I promise. Ma protects me as much as she can.' Spontaneously she kissed Julia on the cheek. It was a fierce kiss, hard and passionate and for long after she had gone Julia could still feel it. 'I love you!' she declared without embarrassment. 'I ent never had anyone to love before, 'cept Ma, and I like having you,' and with that statement she set off across the garden towards the broken wall.

Sophie Crompton came downstairs from putting Edward to bed and stood in the huge, untidy living-room gazing resentfully at her husband. She was particularly untidy this evening, Oliver thought, with her corn-coloured hair hanging about her face in straggly wisps, her cheeks pale, and dark circles under her eyes. She looked harassed and tired and Oliver should have had some compassion for her, but his mind was wholly occupied with Julia – and Sophie knew it. She knew he was lying to her, but she lacked the courage to face him with it.

'I don't understand,' she said, her voice edged with tears. 'I didn't even know you *had* a patient over at Loxley Cross, let alone that she was so ill you felt obliged to go out there at this time of night and sit with her! Why can't her husband telephone, or something, if he needs you?'

'Because they haven't got a phone, Sophie,' he replied patiently. 'They're tenant farmers, they can't afford the luxury of a telephone. Good Lord, you ought to have worked that out by now, we've been here long enough.'

'Precisely!' she retorted. 'And in all the time we've been here the only patient you've ever been to sit with at night, apart from women delivering babies, was the old lady from Tremar. If they can't afford a phone, I'm certain they can't afford you going out there to sit for hours, so where are you really going, Oliver? Why don't you tell me the truth?'

'I'm going to Loxley Cross, Sophie,' he replied coldly, 'and I'm going now and if you're going to start doubting me every time I have to go out and do my job, well I think we might well have to seriously consider our relationship. Good-night!'

She was crying as he left the house; he could hear her, but he could feel nothing else but unreasonable anger. He got in his car and swung away round the green towards Tremar and as he drove up the drive under the beautiful evening sky, he felt such a sense of elation that he was able to dismiss his wife from his mind as simply as if she had never existed. He was calm, he was going to see Julia and he was heady with excitement.

He went round the side of the house and came quietly to the terrace. Julia was sitting alone on the edge of the dead fountain and as he watched her, before she spotted him, he saw a look of ineffable sadness on her face. She was gazing pensively into her lap, picking absently at one of her thumb-nails, her heavy, chestnut hair falling forwards to frame her face, and she was very beautiful.

It was typical of Oliver that he didn't wonder at the look on her face. He never really allowed himself to think too hard about what Julia's memories might be; he had even managed, to a large extent, to dismiss from his mind the picture of her the first time he had seen her. The hopelessness in her eyes, the bitterness – they were of the past and the change in her was so extraordinary that it never occurred to him she would not be able to change like that again, to suit him.

Oliver's hopes and dreams for Julia were unrealistic and pregnant with disappointment, just as, a few years ago now, his hopes for the delicately pretty Sophie had been. He had tried pretty and helpless and found he didn't much care for it, now he thought he wanted a Rhine maiden – but Julia wouldn't be able to match his fantasy, any more than Sophie had been able to do.

Now, though, he simply wanted to possess her.

He had stood for some seconds watching her before she suddenly became aware of him and her head snapped up abruptly. She smiled. It was a slow, gentle, confident smile.

'Right on time, Oliver,' she said and stood up. 'Can I offer you a drink?'

'Maybe when we come back,' he replied. 'First I want a walk in the garden with you.'

'A romantic stroll at dusk with a handsome man,' she observed with the merest touch of humour, 'what more could I ask? My word, my world's changed a bit in the last few months hasn't it? So where would you like to stroll to, Oliver?'

He knew she was laughing at him, but hidebound as he was by class consciousness it wouldn't have occurred to him to protest. It made her weary of him. In the normal course of events, without her nightmare past, she would have dismissed him with the same crisp authority her mother had always employed, but Julia had her own agenda, and for the moment Oliver would fill it nicely.

They crossed the formal lawns and passed through the orchard, which smelled fresh in the darkening summer night. For a moment she paused and looked up into the leafy branches above her head.

'It looks like it'll be a good crop this year,' she observed. 'I suppose you don't know what happens to the Tremar harvest? I only ask because – well, frankly, you do seem to know most things.'

'Well, so I'm told,' he replied slowly, 'the Paynter twins have been collecting the apples for the last few years. When Home Farm began to run down and your father was unwell and didn't seem to care any more, the apples rotted on the trees one year. The following year the tenants plus the Paynter twins were told that if they cared to pick them, they could have them. That happened for a couple of years and then most of the tenants stopped bothering as well, so now the Paynters get the lot, except for the token share Tremar takes.'

Julia continued to gaze up into the apple-tree for a moment, then turning her eyes upon Oliver she smiled, but only with her lips, there was no smile in her eyes.

'All roads to everywhere seem to lead to Rectory Farm, don't they?' she remarked lightly. 'And no doubt despite the hand-outs, the twins poach on my land regularly too. Maybe it's just as well I'm getting an estate manager tomorrow, I think I need to establish a few boundaries, don't you?'

Oliver shrugged his shoulders.

'What, a few rabbits?' he said. 'I thought rabbits were supposed to be a pest.'

Julia nodded.

'Umm, but they're my rabbits. You need to be a landowner to understand, Oliver dear.' Abruptly she saw his face and realized she had touched a nerve. 'Sorry,' she said cheerfully. 'And who am I to talk about being a landowner, a refugee from Blackridge! Come on, we need to hurry if we're going to reach the bay before it's too dark to see anything.'

Seeing the boathouse, bare and decayed and yet so peaceful in the dying moments of a beautiful day was no longer a shock to Julia, she had been here a number of times already in the three weeks she had been home. That initial bitter-sweet memory was stored away again now and was no longer choking. For some moments she and Oliver stood and looked at it and then, to Oliver's astonishment, she kicked off her shoes and, raising her skirt without the slightest appearance of modesty or embarrassment, undid her stockings, rolling them down and sliding them over her feet. A few seconds later she was splashing in the water, stirring up the sand with her toes. She threw out her arms and, laughing happily, turned a couple of circles, the water splashing up around her and dampening the hem of her skirt.

Oliver watched her in fascination as his emotions threatened to overflow.

'Don't you want to paddle?' she asked him, grinning at him in such a way that he felt himself blushing. 'Years ago, when I was at school, I could row across this bay faster than Sandro or the three musketeers, you know. I could climb that cliff, too. At least I think it was years ago, I suppose it might have been in another life. Here, Oliver,' she came to the very edge of the water where tiny waves lapped lazily against the damp sand, and held out her hands to him, 'if you want to come here and risk those beautiful shoes, you can kiss me if you like.'

They were beautiful shoes and not for another woman in the world would he have risked them getting covered in sea-water, but for her he came immediately and took her proffered hands, pulling her gently towards him. Then she was in his arms and their lips were hungry for each other and he was drowning in his overwhelming delight of her.

They kissed for a long time, their tongues touching and exploring, their mouths damp and delicious, At last, panting slightly, they parted and at once Oliver's fingers were at her throat, fumbling with the buttons of her dress.

Abruptly and sharply she said, 'No!' and he drew back as if he had been burned.

'But I thought. . . .' he whispered, and she walked deliberately away from him.

'Not here, Oliver,' she replied, 'absolutely not here. This place belongs to someone else: a girl who was full of hope and love and who died at Blackridge, along with her child, whilst the great war was slaughtering the cream of this country's manhood. This place belongs to her and one of those young men. You and I can't have it, I'm sorry!'

She was standing with her back to him, gazing at the boathouse which was barely visible in the dark now. Deep in its dark depths, across the wasted years she heard the girl utter a tiny cry of pleasure and sigh as her long, firm body relaxed against the muscular hardness of her young Adonis.

'Oh, dear God,' she murmured and Oliver's lips touched the back of her neck, drawing her back to the present.

'All right, not here,' he said softly, 'I understand that, but please, Julia, tell me who he was. Please do that. Please tell me about him.'

Very slowly she turned to face him. In what was now almost the dark of night he could just see her face and a small, cynical smile playing about the corners of her mouth.

'Tell you about him,' she echoed. 'Surely I don't need to do that, you know who he was. Haven't you guessed yet? You must have done.'

She never forgot what he said next. It pigeon-holed him instantly and for Julia he would never escape again. They were worlds apart and they might physically touch, but they would never ever touch and understand. She suddenly saw him for what he was, as she realized her mother must have done, and she understood, too, why her mother had chosen him to come to Blackridge. Oliver yearned to be what she was. He yearned for her social standing in life and he had no concept at all of the pain she had suffered because of it.

'Was it your brother, Alexander?' he asked, and she stared at him in blank astonishment as the water lapped against the sand and the silence of the night settled like a blanket around them.

'*Sandro*?' she whispered eventually. 'Oliver, what sort of family do you think we were? Sandro! My God, do you think that was why my father had me locked in lunatic asylum, because I had carnal knowledge of my *brother*! Oh, dear Lord, I ought to slap you for that!'

'Well who else of your class was there likely to be around here?' he replied, looking baffled. 'You were at boarding-school, weren't you? Who else did you know?'

She yanked herself away from him furiously.

'Do you think that my damned class somehow precludes me from contact with anyone else?' she almost exploded. 'What do you think we were, dwellers in some bloody ivory tower! I'm not a fairy-tale princess, you idiot! My God, my father might *just* have had the right to lock me up for being morally unsound if I'd been bedding down with my brother, but you've missed the point. He didn't *care* who I'd bedded down with. He wouldn't have cared if it had been the Prince of Wales! His inflated idea of his own importance, of his *class superiority* was all that mattered to him! My lover, for your information, Oliver, was one of the three musketeers. The one who came home!'

There was a long, highly charged silence. They stood close together in the darkness and he could hear her breath coming hard and angry. He thought she might be crying, but he couldn't see. He searched through his mind for her previous references to the three musketeers and abruptly he knew who she was talking about.

As he said the name his voice was appalled

'*Arthur Paynter*!'

Julia turned and walked away from him. She gathered up her stockings and tucked them into the pocket of her dress and wriggled her damp, sandy, bare feet into her shoes. Then, to Oliver's surprise, she came back for him. She took his hand and began to walk with him back towards the gate in the wall, towards the very dark, sharply scented pine-trees, towards the orchard and the formal lawns, and the faintly lit terrace of Tremar. She said not a single word, though it took them a long time to pick their way home in the dark, but she held his hand the whole way.

Finally, back beside the fountain, with the french windows open and warm light from the drawing-room spilling out into the darkness she raised her face and looked at him.

'Do you want to kiss me again?' she asked quietly. 'Or have I put you off for life.'

He didn't reply, but was very fast to snatch her into his arms, and for some moments they stood entwined in the warm night air, then they sat down side by side on the edge of the fountain and he seemed to be bursting with questions, but still remained tensely silent.

Julia glanced at him sideways.

'Please do talk about it, Oliver,' she said, 'you very obviously want to.'

He took a long, deep breath and at last he looked at her. 'You let a man like Arthur Paynter rob you of your virtue?' he said in amazement. 'Arthur Paynter! I want to understand, Julia, but I simply don't. The man's an ugly, drunken wreck.'

She smiled.

'I don't know what Arthur looks like now,' she replied. 'He's doing such a good job of keeping out of my way that he's about the only person in the village I haven't seen, but think of Annie, Oliver. Think of those wide green eyes and all that red curly hair. She's a beautiful child and she takes completely after her father. He was a farmhand with big boots and rough hands and coarse clothes. He could barely read and he wasn't all that bright, but he was godlike. His face was exquisite. He had the most beautiful, strong body imaginable, and because he went stripped to the waist in the fields when no one was looking, he was golden brown, despite being a redhead. When he touched me his fingers scratched my skin . . . and it was wonderful. . . .'

Oh, God, her body tingled at the memory, making her draw her breath sharply. Hastily she pushed it from her mind.

'But you could never have hoped to marry him, surely?' Oliver said, assuming her quick, sharp intake of breath was for him and drawing her head down on to his shoulder. 'I mean, even if he hadn't made you pregnant and there hadn't been a war, your father would never have agreed to that.'

She shrugged lightly.

'Oh, no. I was going to London for the Season the following year. Arthur and I made love because the war was coming. I think.'

'You think?'

'Well, somehow that summer was so unreal. They all knew they would be in uniform by the autumn and we were so thrown together in those last weeks, struggling to stave off the inevitable. I really did think I loved him with a grand passion, you know – in fact I *did* love him with a grand passion, he was my first love and don't they say your first love is always your strongest?'

'Do they?' Oliver murmured, moving to look at her. 'Perhaps so.' He suddenly raised his hand and very delicately touched her face with his finger, tracing the line of her features. His hands were soft and sensitive. Doctor's hands. 'I assume your father never knew who your despoiler was?' he said. 'Well he can't have done. I can't imagine he would have rewarded him with a farm and other assorted perks on his return from France if he had.'

'Which is exactly the point, Oliver,' she replied quietly. 'My father didn't *want* to know. He didn't *care*. On the morning he was told of my pregnancy, which was the only time he ever spoke about it and which was two days before he had me removed to Blackridge, he didn't even ask me if there was a chance for me to marry the man in question. He spoke to me as if I was something dangerously infectious; an appalling infestation that needed to be removed from the house as quickly as possible. And because he was my father, and up until then I had been the apple of his eye, I simply didn't recognize his rejection. I wish I had, I could still have run away at that point.'

'And gone where?' he asked.

She stood up and for a moment her eyes strayed across the dark lawns, then she smiled bitterly.

'I'd have sooner had my child in a ditch like a gypsy than in that place,' she answered. 'Shall we go in now?'

She lay naked for him on the big, wide bed in the room where he had last seen her birdlike mother fading into death. She lay on her back, watching him without embarrassment as he undressed, and she was a truly splendid sight. Long-limbed, narrow-hipped, lean and firm with dark-tipped breasts, she was remarkable for a woman of forty. Oliver wanted her so badly it blotted out everything else in his life.

'You're so beautiful,' he whispered, coming to the bed and gazing down at her. 'You really are truly beautiful, Julia. Even that first time I saw you I was arrested by your bearing, you were like a queen in that place, you know.'

She smiled, a smile touched with faint cynicism.

'Years of not having enough to eat and scrubbing floors,' she replied cheerfully. 'It tones up the muscles a treat – and I do take after my father, he was tall and lean too, at least he was when I knew him. Goodness knows what he was like when he was old. What was my mother like?'

'Like an indignant bird,' he answered truthfully and she sniggered.

'I thought she was majestic when I was a child,' she said, 'it just shows you, doesn't it? Ah well . . .' she raised her arms to accept him as he prepared to lay his body down with her and abruptly he saw a thin, white scar on her belly. Pausing he reached out and touched it very softly with his finger and at the same moment he saw her eyes cloud with pain.

'What?' he asked softly.

'One of the first things they took from me,' she whispered. 'My ability to bear children. They sterilized me. It was crude and painful and I was desperately ill afterwards, but you see, I was subhuman, like all the other inmates in that place, I had forfeited my right to give birth to a child I could hold in my arms and love—'

'Oh Julia,' he whispered, and she kissed him quickly.

'Forget it,' she replied. 'Love me, Oliver.'

He was a remarkable lover, gentle and considerate and very skilled. Julia could make no real comparisons; her only other lover had been her godlike farmboy a quarter of a century ago and then her body had been young and urgent. In the interim there had been other men she chose not to think about, men who had used her body when they thought no one was looking, hastily pushing her up against the wall. Now, surely, this was what, fleetingly, she had dreamed about. The handsome, beautifully dressed, exquisitely perfumed Oliver Crompton. He raised her to remarkable physical heights – yet in that moment, at that first encounter, she learned one thing for sure. No matter how good he could make her body feel, she didn't love him and she never would.

If I was kind, she thought, gazing at his dark head on the pillow beside her as they lay quiescent, all passion spent, I would send you home to your Sophie. If I wasn't bitter and resentful I wouldn't do this – but I want your love for the moment. I *want* you to find me beautiful and treat me like a queen and in the end I shall probably want to hurt you. So what does that say about me, I wonder, and do I care? No. I don't think I do!

Abruptly she rolled away from him and sat up, swinging her legs over the side of the bed. She sat for some seconds, gazing at nothing in particular in the very muted light from the bedside lamps, and was suddenly aware of his fingers on her back. She felt them move as if tracing lines and then he sat up quickly.

'Those are scars!' he exclaimed in astonishment. 'Good God, you've been *whipped*. Who on earth did that to you?'

She closed her eyes and she could see – and smell – the great, cavernous basement room at Blackridge, so dimly lit that its corners vanished into blackness. She could feel the penetrating cold of the wet concrete floor, the ache of her freezing limbs; and then – Dear God – the *agony* of the whip across her back. A male orderly held her down, with his boot on the back of her neck, and though her whole body contracted with the pain, she was completely unable to protect herself. They called her an idiot and made reference to whipping dogs to train them, and they cut her back to bleeding ribbons.

'Have the marks really lasted all these years?' she said lightly, turning her head slightly to look at Oliver. 'I wouldn't know, I've never seen my back.'

'But who did it to you?' he asked in horror, and she chuckled.

'I'm not sure this is the moment to talk about the special delights of Blackridge in the early days,' she replied. 'If you want chapter and verse sometime, well come and ask me over tea, or something.'

She heard him utter a little sound of disgust in his throat and then she felt his hand moving softly across her back, as if trying to stroke away the horror.

He began, 'But I thought the place was supposed to be . . .' and tailed off into a sort of faintly confused silence, as she turned to face him, kneeling on the bed, smiling.

'I don't think you thought about the place at all,' she replied, 'until my mother sent you there, and since then you haven't been able to stop thinking about what you found when you got there. It is a palace in comparison to what it was in 1915 and Miss Vincent is a saintly guardian angel, believe me. Do you know, Oliver, it's nearly midnight? Hadn't you better be going home soon? You're not staying here all night, if that's what you wanted; Mrs Collins gets here far too early for that and I'm not going to be branded again by the people in this village.'

'I promise to be gone long before Mrs Collins arrives,' he said as he bent his head again to her breasts, touching one of her hard, dark nipples with his tongue.

Julia gasped and gazing down at his dark head against her pale skin, raised her hand and touched his silky hair lightly with her fingers.

'Maybe once more then, before you go,' she whispered and rolled on to the bed beside him, abandoning herself to the irresistible urge of his touch, rising with him in breathtaking pleasure.

At last she arched her body and cried out as she climaxed, and then sank down, revelling in the delight of this handsome man who wanted *her* – not just any female who was sufficiently in control of her body-waste not to be too unappealing even for a quick poke. . . .

But they were the darkest secrets, the ones she thought she probably would never even be able to tell him. They were locked deep inside her and they hurt when they surfaced.

They were the secrets that made her burn in her heart for revenge.

It was just after two when Oliver slid into bed beside Sophie. She made a little moaning sound and turned away from him, as if slightly disturbed in her sleep and resettling, but in fact she was very much awake. He had undressed in the dark, but he hadn't washed, only pulled on his pyjamas, and he smelt of the outdoors.

He also smelt of perfume. And sex.

Chapter 9

It was only just past eight-thirty when someone knocked on the front door of Tremar the next morning. Early for anyone, Julia thought, and certainly much too early for Oliver.

She was sitting on the floor in the drawing-room, thinking about Oliver's love-making of the previous night, waiting for breakfast and playing with the puppies, and when Mrs Collins knocked and entered to announce the visitor, she was still quite obviously bristling with silent disapproval. Annie's puppies had made more mess than anyone would have thought two puppies could make on the back kitchen floor during the night.

'Mr Matthew Logan,' Mrs Collins said stiffly and Julia scrambled quickly to her feet.

In the doorway was a huge, benign-looking, bear of a man. He had wavy, sandy hair and a bushy beard, he stood well over six feet tall and he wore tall leather boots, a green corduroy jacket and a rich plaid across his shoulder. In his hand he carried an enormous stick and as he stood on the Persian carpet, a hugely incongruous figure, he was like something from a story-book.

'Miss Drake,' he said in a deep voice with a lovely Scottish lilt, 'I have been appointed as your new estate manager by "young" Mr Cruikshank of Cruikshank and Scattergood in Bodmin. I shall endeavour to give satisfaction to the best of my ability and I am ready to receive my orders.'

He was so formal that Julia only just avoided laughing, but there was something so unaccountably gentle and warm about him shining through the formality, that she found herself instantly drawn to him. 'Young' Mr Cruikshank, as he was obviously known by everyone, was evidently more perceptive than even she had given him credit for.

'Please, Mr Logan,' she replied, offering her hand, 'do take a seat. Mrs Collins, I wonder if we might have some coffee please? Oh, and some toast too, if you could manage it, I don't know about Mr Logan, but I'm starving.'

In the weeks she had been back at Tremar, Julia had fallen, without thought, into her parents' way with staff. If, at the beginning, Mrs Collins had thought she might be able to bully her into doing things in some different way to her chosen one, she had learned better by now. Julia knew exactly how she wanted Tremar run, precisely what place in its life was allotted to its housekeeper, and, to the letter, who was welcome and where they were to be received when they came.

Annie came and went now like a duchess when she could get away with it even despite the fact that she refused to use the front door – and she was permitted to sit on the furniture when she chose and run about the house as she pleased. The fact that Mrs Collins disapproved was entirely beside the point and though Julia, like her mother, was never rude, she also left no one in any doubt about her wishes.

So Mrs Collins obediently went away to make some coffee and Matt Logan chose himself an armchair and sat in it. Almost as if by instinct he swept up one of the puppies and held it, wriggling, in one of his enormous hands, examining it carefully.

'Good, strong wee thing,' he observed. 'Have you begun to train them?'

'Well I only got them yesterday,' Julia replied and watched him carefully return the puppy to the floor.

'Never too soon, if you'll pardon my saying so,' he said, and she grinned.

'I don't mind you saying so at all. You can train them for me if you want.'

'Aye, but then they'll be my dogs, not yours – by which I mean they'll be obedient to me rather than to you.'

She shrugged.

'Well I'd better get out there and start this morning then, hadn't I?' she said. 'Mr Cruikshank didn't tell me you were from Scotland, Mr Logan. You're a long way from home.'

He was very still as he sat in the chair, she noticed. He didn't appear to be remotely nervous or uncomfortable, he was like a great, placid giant and she liked him enormously.

'I came away from Scotland some years back,' he replied, 'and I have no desire to return. The west of England suits me very nicely, your winters are much more gentle than the ones I remember from childhood. Not that that has anything to do with why I would prefer to be away from Scotland, of course, but I'm happy to say the Cornish have received me well enough and I've enjoyed my time here so far.'

Julia smiled at him warmly.

'Then let's hope you'll enjoy your time at Tremar, Mr Logan,' she said. 'After we've had some coffee we'll do a short tour and have a look at the things I think need doing first.'

Mrs Collins had an entirely unreadable expression on her face when she carried in a tray of toast and coffee some moments later. Julia felt certain she didn't approve of the concept of the mistress drinking coffee with the staff and had she been invited to join them, she would certainly have refused – but then, as Julia wryly thought to herself, she was, after all, Oliver's choice of servant and if there was proof needed of like attracting like, her inherent, uncomfortable snobbery was precisely like his. Rigidly hidebound by class distinction. Evidently, she decided with some relief, this was not the case with 'young' Mr Cruikshank.

She and Matt Logan enjoyed breakfast and half an hour of pleasant small talk during which time he complimented her on the elegance of the drawing-room, and then, putting away their coffee cups, they rose and went out towards the terrace.

At the french windows he paused and looked back for a moment, studying the room carefully with his deep blue eyes.

'You must find great peace in this room,' he observed. 'Have you changed it much since you were a child? I think you must have done to suit it so exactly to your needs.'

Julia felt quite absurdly pleased at the compliment he had paid her – if it was a compliment. She said, 'Yes, I have changed it, completely, I wanted contentment, not memories so I moved everything around until it was perfect. I've moved pretty much everything in every room since I came home. I even moved the grandfather clock in the hall and it's still ticking madly, despite the fact that Mrs Collins swore it would never go again if I disturbed it!'

He chuckled.

'I saw it had been moved,' he said. 'The wallpaper where it stood before is very much unfaded, and clock-shaped.'

Julia burst out laughing and was suddenly sharply aware of his eyes on her. She wondered if she ought to be embarrassed and decided she wasn't and in consequence his next remark did not faze her in the least.

'You are very beautiful when you laugh,' he murmured, and turning his eyes away from her immediately, crossed the terrace to the fountain and stood beside it, gazing across the grounds towards the orchard and the pine copse. 'Perhaps,' he continued after a moment, 'it's because you have had few opportunities to laugh in the past. I think I should tell you now that Mr Cruikshank told me of your years in the asylum, that was why he chose me for the job, because I, too, have spent time in an asylum for the insane.'

'Good Lord!' she exclaimed softly and was gazing up at him with deep interest when the puppies, finding freedom, scuttled across the terrace towards the steps, yapping happily. Instantly he snapped at them with the authority of a man skilled in the art of dog training and to her surprise they came back.

'I think perhaps you'd better have them, Mr Logan,' she said. 'Take them with you when you go, you are, after all, the estate manager here, so it stands to reason the dogs should be yours. My father's manager always had dogs; English setters, I remember. Perhaps we could share them?' She stopped, and for a long time she gazed at the green scum on the fountain as he stood beside her and the puppies skirmished at his feet. Then she asked very quietly, 'Why did they lock you away?'

He continued to gaze across the estate, narrowing his eyes.

'Because I killed a man,' he replied.

Julia sat on the edge of the fountain, where she had sat so often in the past three weeks with Oliver Oliver! She hadn't even thought about him for an hour or so now and last night they had been lovers for most of the night. Life was very disorientating in the outside world.

'And they didn't hang you?' she observed. 'You were lucky.'

A ghost of a smile crossed his face.

'It doesn't make you afraid of me, then?' he asked, and she shrugged.

'I've spent the last twenty-three-and-a-half years in an insane asylum. Does that make you afraid of me?'

'No, but then according to Mr Cruikshank, you didnae do anything. I killed someone.'

'With good reason I imagine, well, with extenuating circumstances anyway. Would you like to tell me about it?'

He sat beside her on the edge of the fountain and they both began to gaze, with interest, at the dower roof. An instant later they were talking about the repairs that needed doing and the speed with which they were required. She talked about builders and he about estimates and they discussed the fountain. They knew they would come back to the other conversation and as if by tacit agreement they knew when it would be. They were neither of them surprised, or taken off-guard when they switched back to it as abruptly as they had left it.

'I was one of the relatively few who came back unscathed from France in 1918,' he said, 'and I went home to Scotland because it was where my family were. My father managed the estate of an earl, one of the would-be kings of Scotland; it had been a fine place in which to grow up in those days before we knew what trench warfare was. Anyway, I'd no been home long when I went on a trip for him and whilst I was away I had occasion to visit a brothel on the outskirts of Glasgow. There was a man there; foul-mouthed and filthy, you ken well the kind – too weak to fight in a war, but happy to bully women, He slashed a wee tart's face with a knife, cut right through her cheek into her mouth and ruined her looks. She was sobbing and fainting with loss of blood but he wouldnae let her go to the hospital because he said he'd not had what he'd paid for! I broke his neck.'

Julia frowned.

'That still doesn't tell me why they didn't hang you,' she murmured and heard him utter a small, mirthless chuckle.

'The fiscal declared I was one of those damaged by my experience in France,' he replied simply. 'Fact was, I think, he didnae want to hang me for ridding the world of a louse! They sent me to an institution where I was supposedly given some treatment and after five years, they let me out. I left Scotland then and have never been back. I've seen that place on the moors where you were held, it's a dark and unwelcoming place to be sure.

'You should see inside,' she muttered and abruptly stood up. Her face was soft as she looked at him and she smiled very gently. 'I'm *so* glad Mr Cruikshank employed you, Mr Logan,' she said warmly, 'you were an inspired choice and I truly hope you'll be very happy here. Please don't hesitate to let me know if you have any complaints about anything, will you?'

'Well, so far I have none,' he assured her. 'I ken fine the farmhouse at Home Farm. I arrived yesterday evening and after I'd put my bags in I thought I'd just familiarize myself with the territory a bit, so I already know I have plenty of work to be getting along with. Did you know the farm seems to have been abandoned some years ago, most of the land is either fallow or being used – without payment – by your tenants for various purposes?'

'No I didn't know,' she replied, frowning. 'My father's been dead five years or more now, of course, and Mother doesn't seem to have done anything at all after he died, though I believe there was someone living at Home Farm until a year or so ago. When I was a child, Mr Logan, Home Farm kept us supplied with meat, milk, fruit and fresh vegetables for most of the year – can it be revived?'

He nodded, his eyes twinkling with what seemed to be delight at the prospect of so large and long a task.

'Oh, aye,' he said, 'but it'll take a while. In the meantime there are a couple of matters a bit more urgent, I think. Perhaps you would be good enough to give me a key to the dower, I shall need to inspect the inside before I hire roofers and builders.'

Julia gazed at the collapsing roof.

The dower – it hurt her heart – so many memories of Sandro in the dower. . . .

'I've not been into the dower since I came home, you know,' she suddenly said, almost by way of a confession at her own weakness. 'When you want to go let me know, I'll go with you.'

They were looking at each other and smiling as Oliver came round the corner of the house and climbed the steps up onto the terrace. Both their heads turned swiftly towards him as he appeared and his gut tightened with jealousy. He had no idea who the man was, but he had not missed the intimate smile on Julia's face and in consequence he was foolishly unguarded in his actions.

He walked swiftly up to her, put his arm around her shoulders and kissed her. The instant he'd done it he wished he hadn't – on more than one count. Standing in the drawing-room removing the empty coffee cups was Mrs Collins, and she had seen quite well what he did.

Julia's face looked as if it had been cut from a piece of rock.

'Good-morning, Oliver,' she said icily, 'please, do let me introduce you. Mr Logan, Oliver Crompton, our village doctor, Oliver, this is Matthew Logan, my new estate manager.'

The two men greeted each other politely and Matt immediately gathered up both the puppies and his great stick.

'I'll no take up any more of your time, Miss Drake,' he said with a smile. 'I'll be getting these two back to Home Farm and then, if you don't mind, the first thing I'll do is walk the estate, and introduce myself to some of your tenants. Best they know right away where they come if they want anything; stop them wandering up here mithering you. Will you be wanting anything else from me this morning?'

'No, but this afternoon we'll tackle the dower, I think,' she replied, returning his smile. 'Strike while the iron's hot. Thank you, Mr Logan,' and she made a point of watching him until he disappeared around the side of the house and vanished from view.

Then she turned her attention to Oliver.

'What the hell do you think you're doing?' she enquired furiously. 'Do you plan to run it up the flagpole for everyone to see, or don't you think you can spread the word fast enough so you'll give Mrs Collins an opportunity to help you on your way!'

'I'm sorry,' he muttered. 'But seeing you there with that great grizzly bear—'

'He is *not* a grizzly bear and seeing me there, *what*?'

'I was jealous.'

'Well you have no right to be! I'm not your property, Oliver. You are a married man with two children. I warn you, if you *ever* touch me in public like that again I'll bar you from Tremar!'

Oliver stared at her in astonishment.

'Why are you so upset?' he asked eventually. 'I only gave you a little kiss, and I did promise you in the beginning that Mrs Collins doesn't gossip. I think perhaps you have a guilty conscience and that's why you're so angry with me.'

'Oliver,' she replied sourly, folding her arms tightly about herself as if she was suddenly cold, 'I have a fear of discovery that you can never imagine, and never understand, either. And if you wish to continue being my lover you will please be good enough to consider my feelings on the subject! You might consider your wife's while you're about it, too,' she added spitefully.

She saw his eyes widen with the shock she might have expected if she'd struck him, and it occurred to her that to him that was exactly what she'd done.

For some seconds he stared at her in astonishment, then he murmured very quietly, 'That was cheap, Julia,' and a tense silence hung painfully between them.

Finally, in some discomfort, she muttered, 'Yes, well, all right I apologize, but isn't it bad enough that you're being unfaithful to her, do you really need to rub her nose in it? I know I'm the other woman, Oliver, but I've met your Sophie, she's a sweet and pretty girl, I can't believe you don't care if the whole village starts talking about you and me; whispers behind her back when she goes in and out of the shops, it's so cruel!'

Oliver pursed his lips.

'And what are you trying to do now?' he enquired. 'Ease your own conscience? She'll have to know eventually, Julia. I didn't make love to you last night just because you were there, you know. I love you. I love you more than anything in the world and I intend that one day you shall be my wife.'

'And I think you're going much too fast,' she replied. 'Why can't you just enjoy what we've got at the moment? Why must you make plans? All right, you're welcome to come again tonight if you want to, you made me feel wonderful and you know you did, but please, just think about it. I've spent more than half my life in a dreadful kind of limbo, I'm flustered and bewildered at the moment. Have some patience, I beg you.'

A breeze blew across the terrace from the sea and ruffled their hair as they stood, gazing at each other. It made Julia shiver, seemed to blow across her heart in some indefinable way. She knew that if she really had a conscience she would send him away now and never share the delights of her body with him again, for it was not just little Sophie Crompton who was going to suffer in the end: he was as well. But last night she knew she had held him captive, she had been clean, sweet-smelling, beautiful and desirable, and she wasn't strong enough yet to give that up. So many years of being a drab, of not even being spoken to by most people because she wasn't expected to be capable of an answer – it was hard not to want to be queen for longer than a day now. Impossible.

'Nine o'clock then?' he asked quietly, and she nodded.

'But, we will be careful,' she replied, 'and we will be discreet. You've got to promise me that, all right?'

'I promise,' he said and touched her hand briefly. 'I must go now, I'm supposed to be doing my rounds, but I'll see you later, my love. Have fun with your grizzly bear this afternoon.'

More than you know, she thought as she watched him leave, because with him I don't have to pretend, but it's all pretend with you, isn't it, Oliver, and it isn't ever going to be anything else. Well, I hope your wretched Mrs Collins is really as discreet as you say, because if she isn't rumour in the village is going to be rife in twenty-four hours from now.

It was going to take much less than twenty-four hours and it didn't come from Mrs Collins.

*

It started in the butcher's shop, where the butcher, who was one of the long-term inhabitants of Polwean and perfectly well remembered Alexander and Julia Drake from before the war, had a long-standing arrangement with a disreputable old poacher who went by the name of Tolly Tranter. Tranter stank to high heaven, had a mouthful of rotting teeth and used the foulest language in the district, but could be relied upon to supply good game – most of it poached from the Tremar estate.

Keeping well down wind of his brief visitor, the butcher cast a practised eye over the spoils and opened his till to pay suitable recompense.

'And another thing,' drawled the filthy Tranter, pocketing the money and then wrapping himself in his untouchable raincoat, 'you'm never going a guess who I seed a-coming out of Tremar, at two in the fekin' morning? Only bleddy high and mighty Doctor! Two in the feckin' mornin'! And the mad bitch from Blackridge ent sick, you can be sure of that.'

'What, walking?' the butcher enquired.

'Never bleddy walking,' retorted Tranter. 'Sliding down the road in that posh car.' He uttered a guffaw of laughter, filling the shop with a gale of foul-smelling breath. 'I seen her, you know. Good, handsome bitch for all she'm mad. Bet high and mighty Doctor's enjoying a good bedding down with that, and no mistake!'

Mid-morning there were four women in the village shop. Miss Penrose and Miss Hewlett, who ran the shop, and two ladies from the village – and they were deliciously immersed in the one topic of conversation.

'Oh, that poor little Mrs Crompton,' said Miss Hewlett, a spiteful spinster with a curious habit of squeezing her lips together, like a baby making sucking motions with its mouth. 'She told me this morning he had to sit with a woman over at Loxley Cross last night.'

Miss Penrose, far and away the more poisonous of the two, sneered.

'Well of course,' she observed primly, 'those of us who've bin in this village all our lives knows right well why Julia Drake was sent to Blackridge in 1915. And it didn't have nothing to do with her fretting for her brother, whatever they says. She were pregnant! And I'm afraid morals like that ent never going to change, whatever you say.'

And five minutes later the other two women, who hadn't been in the village all their lives and had never seen Julia Drake either, went home to get their husbands' dinners, bursting with their news.

Arthur Paynter was told at just after twelve o'clock. He met one of the fishermen on the narrow road coming up from the harbour and they fell into conversation, and Arthur devoured the rumour greedily.

As Gladys Paynter turned from her greasy kitchen range ten minutes later when he came in for his lunch, she saw that he was smiling. But it was not a pleasant smile. It was a smile of triumph and he slapped his hand on the kitchen table.

'I've just come by a bit of news, Gladys!' he declared gleefully. 'You'm never going to believe this, but I'm told Julia Drake's already climbing between the sheets with that bleddy doctor what got her out of Blackridge. Five bleddy minutes she'm bin home and she's at it again! She'm got the morals of an alley cat that bitch has.'

Gladys turned away quickly and gazed down into her big pot of stew . . . 'But you shouldn't a done it, Julia! God, what *was* you thinking of!' The words echoed down to her across the years.

They had stood together on the cliff above Tremar, Julia Drake in her beautiful russet-coloured skirt and coat and crisp, white, broderie anglaise blouse, and Gladys in torn, striped cotton that smelt of fish. It had been October, Julia's seventeenth birthday, and Gladys had given her a piece of pink rock-crystal, polished by the sea – and never seen her again from that day onwards.

It had torn Gladys's heart with jealousy: Julia pregnant by Arthur, and blissfully unaware of the fact that Gladys loved him too, but it had seemed, somehow, such a terrible omen. When the four young men, the musketeers and their D'Artagnan had gone off to war in August they had talked about being home for Christmas. On that bitter, windy October morning everyone had known that the war wouldn't be over by Christmas – but somehow it had seemed so much more terrible; the boys gone, Julia ruined. Gladys had feared at that moment that the joy of their youth had been abruptly snatched away from them and they would never get it back. She had been quite right.

Nothing had ever been the same again.

But the Lord only knew she had prayed for Julia, over the years. Every single day she had prayed for Julia.

Now, in her grimy kitchen she stirred her stew with a long wooden spoon and clattered the lid back on the saucepan.

'Who told you Julia's sleeping with the doctor, Arthur?' she enquired coldly.

He chuckled.

'It's all over the bleddy village.'

'And you couldn't wait to believe it, right?'

'She was a tart, Gladys! She was a hot little bitch who couldn't wait to take her drawers off. And you knows it.'

Gladys rounded on him furiously. She was forty now and her always slightly pudgy face had lost its smooth roundness a long time ago. She was plain, with saggy skin, small eyes, roughened hands and a thick waist. She was tired, hopeless and frightened of the man she was married to. She loved her twin sons with a passion and adored and desperately feared for her cruelly brutalized little daughter, because her father hated her so much, and hurt her so often. She was dissatisfied with her unfulfilled life, frustrated and most of the time miserable, but she had always known that whatever her suffering might be, it was nothing in comparison to Julia Drake's and because, somehow, that last, extraordinary summer had bound them inextricably together there had not been a single day when she hadn't thought about Julia at least once.

He had ruined Julia! This man who had dared to come home alone in 1918, married her, beaten and abused her and turned her into a shapeless drudge. *He* had been responsible for Julia's monstrous suffering, and now, because he was such a coward, he was terrified to face her but only too willing to believe any foul village gossip about her which came his way.

'She was a beautiful girl who gave you her most valuable possession, because she loved you!' she retorted passionately. 'And one day, Arthur Paynter, God is going to punish you for what you done to Julia. Now get out a my kitchen, afore I throw something at you.'

He laughed nastily. '*God*?' he scoffed and watched her turn away from him swiftly.

'Well *someone* will,' she whispered under her breath. '*Someone* will!'

Chapter 10

The next time Julia saw Matt Logan he was coming across the formal lawns with a furiously wriggling, protesting Annie in his grasp. For a moment she watched sharply, alert for any sign of savagery towards the child, then as she saw that he actually held Annie only very lightly and there was a look of definite amusement on his face, she sat on the stone parapet and watched with interest as they fought their way up the terrace steps.

'Pardon me, Miss Drake,' he said as, still holding Annie by the arm, he stood before his employer, 'but I caught this wee lassie climbing over the wall into the estate and, well, ye cannae be too careful. I though mebbe she had a mind to be stealing from you.'

Julia shook with silent laughter as Annie yanked her arm free and glared at him like an indignant, ruffled bird.

'You get off me!' she snorted furiously at him. 'I'm allowed to come here when I like!'

'Is that a fact, missy,' he retorted placidly. 'Well mebbe we should consult the owner about that. Mebbe she recognizes you for the scurrilous villain you are and I should be warned about you. Did you think about that?'

Abruptly Julia's laughter burst out of her and to Annie's inexpressible rage she rocked backwards and forwards, holding her sides. The look on Matt Logan's face was a picture: his beard quivered with mirth and for some moments they were both speechless, then Julia wiped her eyes with her fingers and stood up.

'Oh, I'm sorry!' she exclaimed, still highly amused. 'This, Mr Logan, is Annie Paynter, and I assure you she doesn't steal from me – unless you count robbing my library blind. Anyhow, yes, she is allowed to come here whenever she likes, but she refuses to use the front door. She looks like a scruffy urchin because she's always climbing trees and crawling into places she's got no business being in, but I'm struggling to teach her to be a lady, and an hour from now, when you see her at her books, you won't believe she's the same person.'

'So that's told *you*!' Annie declared gazing up at Matt with her hands firmly planted on her hips and very delicately he reached out with one finger and touched her on the nose.

'I'll be watching for you, missy,' he said, scrutinizing her with merry blue eyes. 'And if you don't learn to use the front door, well I might have to set the dogs on you.'

Annie grinned cheerfully.

'What, they puppies?' she said. 'They're my puppies, I stole them off me brother so as I could give them to Julia. They'm good, strong puppies, ent they?'

Matt Logan frowned at her slightly.

'You know about dogs?' he asked, and she shrugged.

'Well I lived on a farm all me life and we've always had proper bred dogs. My brothers destroys any puppies that comes of some stray dog getting at one of the bitches. I know them two is good 'cos I picked the best of the litter.'

Julia saw him incline his head slightly and she realized that he was impressed with Annie. It made her feel good. For some completely unfathomable reason she very much wanted them to like each other and this appeared to be a promising start.

'Aye,' he observed, 'Well you certainly picked well, lassie. So tell me, if you're always shinning up trees and getting yourself into wee places you shouldnae be, you must know pretty much all that goes on in this village?'

'I might,' Annie replied cautiously. 'Who are you, anyway? Gamekeeper?'

'Estate manager,' he said.

She nodded.

'Oh, right. There were one of they when the old lady was alive, but we never worried about him,' she admitted frankly, and then, to Julia's astonishment, slewed her eyes sideways to look at him and added, 'I can tell you who the local poachers are, p'raps, for a price.'

Julia gaped at her.

'*Annie*!' she exclaimed, but Matt held up his hand quickly.

'Nay, she's right,' he said, 'a fair price for fair information. She doesnae take from you without payment, hence the puppies. So what do you fancy, lassie, money?'

They both saw a tiny flame of alarm spring up in Annie's eyes at the mention of money and she seemed to wriggle nervously.

'I don't want money,' she replied swiftly. 'If my pa ever heard I'd bin spending money anywhere he'd tan my hide off! He wouldn't have it that I hadn't stole it for a start and anyway, *all* money that comes into our house has to go through him first. No thanks, not money.'

Julia frowned and put her hand out to the child protectively, a gesture that Matt Logan didn't miss.

'Well mebbe I could pay you in kind then,' he suggested. 'A favour for a favour? We can store it up if you like and I can owe you. Nice to be able to call in a favour at sometime, at least I always think so.'

'You could help my pa drown hisself when he comes out The Smugglers blind drunk one night if you like,' Annie observed bitterly, and Julia and Matt exchanged quick glances: the glances, she realized, of two like-minded people who recognized a dilemma between them and were both noting the information.

She said, 'Annie, run inside now and have your bath, get yourself into one of your dresses and then we'll have some lunch. And for Lord's sake clean the bath after you, Mrs Collins grumbles all the time about the way you leave the bathroom. Mr Logan and I have to spend an hour or so in the dower this afternoon, so I'll set you some work.'

'And I'll come back at two,' Matt said, bowing politely and stepping backwards, instantly allowing them space. Julia and Annie watched him as he went back down towards the formal lawns.

'I like him,' Annie observed innocently, 'he's nice. I like him much better'n the doctor.'

They crossed the terrace together and went into the house. Julia had her arm round Annie's shoulder and they were idling, like a couple of school pals might.

'But he just hauled you up before me as a potential thief,' she pointed out. 'And now you like him? That was quick.'

'He don't disapprove of me,' said the extraordinary child cheerfully. 'The other one do, the doctor. They'm talking about you and the doctor all over the village, Julia, I heard my pa saying so to my ma just now, afore I come out; that's why I'm late, 'cos he come in when I weren't expecting him, and I had to wait for him to go in the barn afore I could get through the kitchen.'

Julia felt a jolt of alarm in her chest and stared at Annie sharply.

'What are they saying?' she demanded, and Annie shrugged.

'I don't 'zactly know,' she answered, 'but my ma got very upset. She shouted at pa and she don't never usually do that. What's more my pa didn't thump her like he usually does.' She suddenly turned her green eyes fully upon Julia in a wide stare. 'My pa's scared of you,' she said. 'I didn't think he was scared of anything, but he's bleddy scared of you!'

Julia hadn't managed to pluck up the courage to go into the dower since her return home. There were three entrances, an outside front door, a door through the library on the ground floor and a connecting door on the first-floor landing. Each time she had approached one of them she had funked it, and now, forced to go in with Matt, she briefly wondered if she was going to funk it again.

She had settled Annie in the library with some books, and Matt was beside her as she searched through her bunch for the correct key. Finally finding it she reached out to slide it into the lock and saw to her horror that her hands were trembling quite violently. With extraordinary tact he took the keys from her gently and pressed the one she had been fumbling with neatly into the lock.

'Yes, you're right,' he observed, behaving exactly as if she had been simply having some trouble with it, 'It's very hard to turn. Happen the mechanism needs oiling. I'll see to it in a day or two,' and he stepped aside to allow her to enter before him.

On the other side of the library was a huge, unfurnished sitting-room with dirty windows and peeling wallpaper. Everywhere there was an overwhelming smell of damp and decay and a dreadful mess of cobwebs, mouse-droppings, dust and other assorted nasty items. For Matt Logan it was an exploratory trip, and not a moment too soon as far as he could see, for this whole section of the manor was in imminent danger of collapse, unless he was much mistaken, which obviously accounted for the rather musty smell in the library, although that room was lovingly dusted and cared for.

For Julia, however, it was a journey into a painful, dead past and she was in emotional turmoil. But the giant Scottish bear who walked beside her along evil-smelling passages and into long, long-deserted rooms, was astonishingly gentle. He stood back at the door to each room, allowing her as long as she required to gaze into it before he spoke.

At the moment they walked into the old schoolroom Julia stumbled and he very gently took her arm to steady her. In wordless despair she gazed at the mouldering tables and chairs; the school-books neatly stacked on the bookcase shelves and black with damp and cobwebs; the globe, filthy, but in its usual place; and the selection of maps of the world – as it was at the turn of the century – still rolled and stacked in an umbrella stand.

She touched one of them and it instantly turned to dust.

'How appropriate,' she whispered bitterly.

They had been educated up to the ages of eleven and thirteen respectively in this schoolroom and then gone away to boarding-school. They'd had a dry, spidery tutor who was very boring, and a French mistress who scared them rigid. They'd looked down from the window and longed for escape so many times, in a distant world that was now long forgotten. In the safe days. And all through that time Alexander had been fiercely loyal to his three friends. Even after he had left home and gone to Eton, when the twins and Arthur had been leaving school with barely the basics in numeracy and literacy and facing lives of hard work in the open air, the friendships had remained deep and mutually respectful.

Maybe Alexander had known all along that when he came to die the deep affection of his three chums would mean so much more than his class superiority.

'Sandro could speak French, you know,' she murmured, mostly to herself, walking across the schoolroom to the window and gazing down. 'I wonder if it mattered, when he was bleeding to death in the mud? I don't suppose so, do you? And I wonder if he would have ever forgiven his friend for what he did to me. Sandro had a very keen sense of fair play, and he expected nothing less from his lifelong companions. How hard, isn't it, to discover that even those we love sometimes have feet of clay?'

'It's very hard,' Matt Logan replied quietly, dragging her back to the present with a sharp jolt. 'And a painful lesson we all learn at sometime in our adult lives.'

She blinked at him in confusion for a second and then felt herself blush hotly. She hardly knew this man, had only met him a few hours ago, and she was baring her soul to him. Julia wasn't used to such familiarity.

'I'm so sorry,' she said briskly, 'you must think I'm quite mad, and you won't have the slightest idea what I'm bleating on about either. Do forgive me.'

'I ken fine what you're talking about,' he answered very gently. 'Mr Cruikshank told me exactly the circumstances of your incarceration. You were pregnant, and I understand now that it was one of your brother's friends who made you pregnant. Mebbe, I wonder, if things had been different, if, although your brother didn't return, his friend had done so, perhaps he would, after all, have fulfilled your brother's expectations of him. The war tore so many families apart in my estimation.'

Julia smiled at him bitterly and turned swiftly away from the schoolroom and its memories.

'But you see, Mr Logan,' she whispered, 'he *did* return. He was the only one who came back, but he never made any attempt to help me. He married someone else and conveniently forgot about me. He has children by his wife; our child died, and now that I'm back he avoids me at all costs, but, I understand, is happy to spread malicious rumours about me. He went out into no man's land in the face of sniper fire to carry my brother back, six months before he was finally killed, but he left me to rot for twenty-three years in Blackridge. I suppose I just don't understand, that's all.'

Matt Logan watched her for a moment with his peaceful blue eyes, then he seemed to draw a very long, deep breath and shook his head slowly.

'No, I don't think I understand that, either,' he replied.

'No, I don't believe you!' Sophie Crompton cried, her eyes flooding with tears. 'There isn't any sick patient at Loxley Cross, and you know there isn't!'

Oliver threw her a furious look and saw her helplessly tucking strands of untidy fair hair behind her ears. He thought of Julia with her thick mane of chestnut hair falling forwards to brush him as they kissed, and his diaphragm contracted with pleasure, making him draw his breath sharply.

Then he saw his daughter watching him with her serious little face, and guilt made him turn away quickly, irrationally and unfairly angry with Sophie.

'I really don't know what's the matter with you,' he snarled, 'but I tell you this much, Sophie, if you continue to behave like this I shall seriously consider sending you to your parents for a while, because you're obviously not well!'

'I'll tell you what's the matter,' she sobbed, scrubbing at her face with her hands in a furious attempt to stem her tears. '*Julia Drake* is the matter! Everyone in the village is talking about it! They were all looking at me pityingly when I went into the shops this afternoon, or they stopped talking as I walked in, which was worse. It's not fair, Oliver, I've always tried to be a good wife to you, how can you treat me like this?'

He saw his daughter crouch down beside the fireplace, she seemed to be trying to protect herself against the hostility in the room, squeezing herself into a ball, her eyes big with fright. Oliver was painfully torn between his guilt and his passion for Julia, and at the same time frighteningly aware of what Sophie had just said. A ghostly echo of Julia's warning that morning on the terrace at Tremar jolted him, Surely he hadn't been mistaken about Mrs Collins? But if she hadn't been blabbing, who the hell had? No one else had seen anything – except that great, grizzly Scotsman!

All the same, he had told Julia he would be there tonight and he knew he couldn't stay away, for she was like some fabulous drug to which he was hopelessly addicted. He was consumed with passion and couldn't separate himself from his ghastly fascination with the humiliations and indignities she had suffered at Blackridge for so many years. The scars of the whip on her back and the white scar of her sterilization across her belly created in him an extraordinary obsession, and he was certain he would do almost anything to own her.

Now he looked unemotionally at Sophie, her face congested with tears, her hair hanging untidily about her head, and he was unable to feel the pity or sympathy he knew he should feel for her. He could only experience irrational anger at her behaviour. Swiftly he began gathering various items to put in his medical bag, tossing them in untidily which was completely foreign to his habit.

'For heaven's sake pull yourself together,' he hissed at her softly. 'Look what you're doing to Alice, you're frightening the life out of her. Now listen, I am going to Loxley Cross, I am *not* doing whatever it is you think I'm doing with Julia Drake, and if people in the village really are spreading malicious gossip then stand up to them, why don't you? Don't be such a wretched shrinking violet, Sophie, it is most unappealing in a woman of your age!'

As she stood before him almost incoherent with tears, clenching her fists in her rage and misery, he picked up Alice, briefly hugged and kissed her, told her to be a good girl for Mummy and headed for the door. Sophie fled after him into the black and white tiled hallway of Lamplighter House, sobbing hysterically.

For a second at the door he looked back and she was a pitiful sight, but it simply made him angry.

'I bet she's not a shrinking violet, is she!' she screamed at him furiously. 'Your damned Rhine maiden! A Valkyrie at least! Perhaps her father had it right, Oliver, perhaps she *should* have been locked away for immorality! She certainly doesn't seem to have lost her talent for it!'

He hardly knew what he did then and he had never been a violent man, but he went back across the black and white tiles like thunder and he was only really aware that he had slapped her when she squealed in pain. Without another word he turned on his heel and left the house.

Sobbing brokenly to herself the thin, fragile Sophie Crompton clutched her smarting face with her hand and leaned against the doorframe, sagging in her misery, as dark-haired little Alice watched in silence, her dark eyes wide with fright.

Julia, entirely unaware of his savage behaviour towards his wife, smiled at him as he entered the beautiful drawing-room which was subtly softened by the lengthening shadows, and as he approached her, slid her arms around his neck and kissed him.

'Do you want to take a walk before it gets dark?' she asked and he smiled at her.

'If you like.'

If she liked! Whatever she liked! He would follow her to hell if she asked him and he had already convinced himself that she felt the same way about him. Surely she saw him as her saviour, after all if it hadn't been for him she would have lived out the rest of her life and died in Blackridge. Besides, in these all too rare moments when they were alone together, she would look at him with deep, calm affection and for a brief period they would be the only two people in the world. Then he could convince himself that all his wild dreams would eventually come true.

They left the terrace and, hand in hand, wandered across the formal lawns towards the tennis-courts and the summer-house. Oliver had seen it from the house, but never been close enough to inspect it – and evidently neither had she since her return, because as they approached it he saw a slightly painful frown on her face. It was like a ruined beauty, standing there in the growing dusk – an old, old woman perhaps with nothing left but powerful memories.

'I bet it was wonderful once,' he whispered, reluctant somehow to disturb the silence of the dying evening and the dead past that the place stood for. 'And I bet it could tell some secrets, if it could talk.'

She smiled.

'Both the tennis-courts and the cricket pitch were wonderfully nurtured,' she murmured. 'It was like a sort of ritual. One of the gardeners used to add the final touches on a Friday, before there was a weekend party and then the chairs and rugs would be checked in the pavilion. . . .'

She closed her eyes and saw, in her child's-eye view, all those seemingly exquisite friends and relations of her parents. Beautiful women in white organdie dresses and picture hats, laid gracefully on the long, folding wicker-chairs, watching with languid interest as their men, in white flannels and striped blazers, batted tennis balls backwards and forwards to each other across the net. She heard the ping of the balls against the rackets and the friendly triumph of winning scores called out. Long, long-dead voices.

In the gathering darkness the summer-house – the pavilion, as it had always been called – crumbled quietly into decay. Brambles and weeds had grown up around the steps, covering and choking them. The door swung on its rusty hinges and there was not so much as a shard of glass in the window-frames. Deep inside, in the gloom, Julia could just make out what appeared to be the folding wicker-chairs, or at least what was left of the frames, anyway, and possibly a table or two, and the boxes with the pads would be there somewhere, but it was hard to look too deeply. She wanted to feel nothing, she certainly didn't want to feel sadness.

The boathouse had been different, that had been such a special place in her life. The pavilion had been fun for hide and seek, and often the children, local and visiting, had used it as a castle, or a prison, according to what fantasy game they were playing. It had annoyed them when suddenly the grown-ups had wanted to use it for its proper purpose and she remembered her father snarling at her mother once, because she and Alexander and the musketeers had chased straight across the tennis-courts, whooping at each other in battle, right in the middle of someone's game!

Julia turned and gazed at Oliver in the warm dusk. There was a tiny, bitter smile playing about her mouth and he very delicately touched her lips with his fingers.

'What's that for?' he asked, and she shrugged.

'I was remembering my father on the day we children crashed across the tennis-court in the middle of a game,' she replied softly. 'He told our mother we needed to be kept away from the village children because we were becoming savages. I think he thought we were going to catch something from them . . . And then he had me thrown into Blackridge amongst what he would have considered worse than the dregs of humanity. Strange man. Ah, well, I think I'll arrange with Matt Logan to have this place demolished and the tennis-courts and cricket pitch turned into something else. If there's going to be a war perhaps we could find a practical use for the ground.'

'Talking of your great, hairy Scotsman,' Oliver said edgily, suddenly remembering Sophie's hysterical outburst of an hour ago, 'it isn't possible he's been shooting his mouth off around the village is it?'

Julia stared at him in astonishment.

'Don't be ridiculous, he only arrived today!' she retorted. 'What on earth are you talking about?'

They were picking their way back across the weed-choked tennis-courts towards the terrace, which glowed in a friendly light from the drawing-room lamps. It was incredibly peaceful, no sound but a herring-gull mournfully calling above the cliffs.

He said, 'Well Sophie seems to think everyone was talking behind her back in the shops this afternoon, that the gossip in the village is buzzing with your name and mine.'

Julia pursed her lips sharply.

'Annie told me much the same thing,' she observed. 'Well it certainly didn't come from me and it can't have come from Mrs Collins either. The trouble is there are people about day and night around here, unless things have changed since I was a child. Probably some damn poacher saw your car outside, or saw you driving away or something. Look, I'm sorry, but I'm not going to be torn to shreds by them again, you're just going to have to be more discreet – and less frequent in your visits, too.'

Oliver felt as if he had been slapped in the face and his heart leapt in fright.

'You mean you don't want me to come here any more?' he whispered, and she gave him a long look.

'Did I say that?' she enquired calmly. 'I don't think I did. I think I said less frequent. Please, Oliver, we both have reputations to consider – and I did suggest you might be a little more considerate towards your wife this morning, too. Please don't try and push me into a corner because

I'll panic if you do. I'm free now and I don't want any more tight spaces, thank you. Now then, let's go and have a drink, and don't look so worried, I'm not driving you out of my life, you know.'

They were just about to mount the terrace steps together and the very last of the daylight was minutes away from being gone when there was a tiny noise behind them and they both turned quickly. Matt Logan had seemed to step out of empty air and when he saw them he smiled benignly.

'I've a mind to give a particular old poacher a bit of a fright tonight,' he said by way of explanation, but not in a tone of voice which suggested he thought he owed anybody one. 'A disgusting old baggage the lassie told me about this morning. She's a fine wee gel with a keen eye is young Annie. Good-night to you then.'

Julia smiled at him fondly.

'Good-night, Mr Logan,' she replied warmly, 'and if you catch him, tell him I'm considering reviving the old custom of chopping poachers hands off. That'll give him something to spout about in The Smugglers.'

The huge Scotsman melted away as softly as he had come and Julia leaned on the warm stone parapet, watching the place where he had been comfortably. After a moment Oliver leaned beside her and she felt his tenseness immediately.

'He's my estate manager, Oliver,' she said quietly. 'It's not in his interest to tell anyone what he's seen – or form an opinion about it, either. Please, take my word for it, he knows the rules and they bother him no more than they bother me. And please try to like him, because I promise you you're going to be seeing plenty of him in the future, all right?'

Half an hour later, when naked and exquisite she knelt astride his body on her huge bed and his need of her was almost frenzied, Oliver sourly wondered whether these were the only times when their class differences, which seemed to mean so much, could ever be pushed aside. And anyway, whom did they mean so damned much to? Him, if he was honest. She seemed to have slotted back into her place without the slightest trouble. She had a set of rules that were written in stone and with which she was perfectly at home. He felt inadequate and angry. He wanted to learn them, She didn't seem interested in teaching them to him. She, of course, had been here before.

'Don't you mind, then,' he asked, reaching up to touch her with soft, delicate fingers, 'that your grizzly must know, right now, what we're doing? Won't it make you feel vulnerable when next you see him?'

'He isn't thinking about it,' she replied calmly, 'and I wish you wouldn't either. For heaven's sake let it drop, will you?'

He sighed and softly cupped her breasts in his hands, stroking the nipples with his thumbs until they stood hard and proud and she wriggled with pleasure.

'I *long* to get out of this village,' he said unhappily, 'I truly do. I *hate* the country. You wait until I show you the sights of London, Julia, you'll be enthralled.'

'Mmm, quite possibly,' she answered, and then uttered a little gasp as his fingers whispered across her hard, naked stomach and found the warm darkness between her thighs, making her mewl softly and press down on his chest with her hands to lift her body and give him better access to his quarry.

She breathed, 'Oh . . . God . . .' and he penetrated her, pulling her down to take all of him into her warm depths. He bit his lips, making himself wait as long as he possibly could, watching, as she rode him, to see when she was ready. He brought her to the brink skilfully and quickly and as her body shuddered with fulfilment and she threw her head back crying out in her pleasure he was able, for just those few seconds, to think of nothing else but their delight in each other. Then they sank down, their bodies hot and deliciously satisfied.

'Why can't it always be like this?' he asked finally, as, satiated with pleasure, they settled into stillness and she slumped forward and seemed to hang above him, beautifully exhausted.

To his surprise she burst out laughing and looked at him with dancing eyes.

'Because the world would grind to a halt,' she replied simply. 'Oh, Oliver, stop looking for answers. Stop wanting everything to be different all the time. Be grateful for this and enjoy it while it lasts, you simply don't know what the future will bring. Blackridge taught me that.'

But he knew exactly what he wanted in his future and up until now he had happily gone along with the idea that he would get it, maybe even sooner rather than later. Now, as he watched her slide elegantly off the bed and go to the open window, then lean on the sill and gaze into the black night with a sort of wonderful contentment on her face, he had his first slight misgiving that, just maybe, she had other plans for her own future, and they didn't include him.

'Do you love me, Julia?' he asked and she turned to look at him.

She smiled a lovely, open, friendly smile but she did not give him the answer he wanted.

'It isn't an option at the moment, Oliver,' she replied gently. 'You are a married man with two beautiful children so let's not complicate things even more. We're wonderful lovers aren't we? Let's make that enough to be going on with.'

He felt his heart freeze as he read a thousand different messages into her words. He wanted to leap off the bed, to beg her, to tell her he would rather die than live without her but she cleverly anticipated him. She came to him swiftly and lay across him, pressing their bodies together warmly, and as her lips sought out his and her tongue flicked into the warmth of his mouth, he forced himself to abandon his fear. He would convince her somehow, he decided – he had to. He would make her love him as much as he loved her and then she would do whatever he wanted.

He had no concept whatever of the extraordinary will-power Julia had been obliged to maintain for twenty-three-and-a-half years to keep herself sane at Blackridge and absolutely no understanding at all that she would never be forced, by anybody, to do anything she didn't want to do ever again.

Chapter 11

Ten days after Matt Logan had started his job as estate manager at Tremar, he knocked on the front door at just after eight-thirty one morning and was somewhat reluctantly admitted by Mrs Collins.

'This is the second time you've come here this early in the morning, Mr Logan,' she said frostily, as he stepped into the hall. 'Miss Drake is having her breakfast, and I really can't say if she'll want to see you yet, I'm sure. If you'll kindly wait here, I'll ask.'

A moment later she returned from the morning-room and with silent disapproval threw the door open for him. He smiled his thanks and with quiet amusement watched her bristle away huffily.

Julia was sitting at a little table in the small, friendly, sunlit room drinking coffee and ploughing through her post. As he entered she looked up at him and offered him a lovely smile.

'Mr Logan!' she exclaimed, 'how nice. Do sit down and have a cup of coffee with me. Have some toast, too, why don't you? Mrs Collins always does so much, if I was to eat it all I'd be here till lunchtime.'

'Well, I wouldn't say no to a cup of coffee,' he replied, sitting himself down at the table opposite her, 'but I think I shouldnae eat your breakfast, not if I ever want yon housekeeper to let me in again.'

Julia raised her eyebrows in faint surprise and then shrugged.

'Oh, well, if you think not,' she said cheerfully. 'Annie would have helped herself without asking.' She rang a small, silver bell that stood beside her on the table and Mrs Collins entered a few seconds later. 'Would you be so kind as to bring an extra cup and saucer please, Mrs Collins?' she asked with brisk politeness. 'And a knife and plate as well, I think, in case Mr Logan would like some breakfast.'

As the large-bosomed woman backed her way out of the door and closed it very firmly behind her, Matt Logan looked up at his employer and they exchanged amused glances of understanding. Julia chuckled softly.

'Actually,' she said, 'she thoroughly disapproves of the fact that I won't eat my meals in solitary splendour at the dining-room table, but to be honest my blasted ancestors hung about the walls in there intimidate me so much I'd never eat *at all* if I was forced to use that room – and she'd make me sit there till it was all finished, too, if she thought she could get away with it.'

The great, bushy-bearded Scotsman shook with silent laughter and Julia knew he had conjured up the idea in his mind. It made her feel warm towards him; comfortable with him.

'You understand?' she asked, and he nodded.

'It was the way with the earl's children when we were bairns,' he replied. 'Their nanny would make them sit for hours at nursery meals, and a finer old witch you never could have found. We estate bairns would scatter whenever we saw her coming, all dressed in black and pushing a pram. The earl and countess were prolific breeders; nine children they had in all.'

'Lord!' Julia exclaimed. 'There's a huge estate somewhere near Bodmin where I believe the earl and countess had eight or nine children, all quite a bit older than Sandro and me if I remember. I wonder what happened to them all? Anyway, two were quite sufficient as far as my mother was concerned. Very tidy. An heir and a daughter – all problems solved. Sickening for them that it didn't quite work out that way, but there we are, aren't we.' She paused as Mrs Collins, with obvious stiff reluctance, laid a place before Matt Logan and then left the morning-room. 'So,' she continued brightly, 'what brings you to my door so early? Not that I'm complaining by the way, it's lovely to have company at breakfast time.'

Without the slightest sign of discomfort he allowed her to pour him a cup of coffee and helped himself to some toast and marmalade.

'I came to tell you that the scaffolding has arrived,' he said, munching his toast and raising his eyebrows in approval at the excellent, tangy, bitter marmalade, 'and they are even now in the throes of erecting it. Work should begin on the roof tomorrow.'

'But that's so quick!' Julia exclaimed. 'You're marvellous, how did you do it?'

He inclined his head and smiled at her.

'Mostly with the help of the "young" Mr Cruikshank if I'm honest,' he replied. 'He knows the area and the best companies. I put the problem to him a week ago and he came up with suitable names immediately. He's as worried about yon roof as you are. Mind you, it's going to take a good few months to right the damage, and cost a pretty penny, if I'm not mistaken.'

Julia shrugged.

'I've nothing else to spend my fortune on,' she said, 'except Home Farm, and I'm determined to bring that back into full production. And talking of "young" Mr Cruikshank, by the way, I've had a letter from him this morning. I asked him to find out some information for me on one Arthur Paynter from Rectory Farm, one time tenant farmer of the estate until my father showered goodies on him like free sweets for returning from France in 1918.' She lifted a carefully typed letter from beside her plate and passed it across the table. 'This is the result of Mr Cruikshank's digging.'

Matt Logan perused the letter carefully and frowned.

'Would this be the father of the wee lassie, Annie?' he asked, and Julia nodded. Disgustedly he uttered a sound deep in his throat. 'I have no stomach for a man who beats children,' he muttered. 'You canae put a shilling between the bruises on her arms and legs, I've noticed – and she didnae get them all from climbing trees, I know that.'

Julia raised her eyebrows.

'You should see her in the bath,' she retorted. 'I'm trying to find out if there's some way I can get her protected by law. Her mother loves her well enough, to be sure, but I get the impression she's as frightened of him as Annie is. What's more, he plans to send her away after Christmas to be some sort of maid-of-all-work to a family in Falmouth. Well I don't know about you, Mr Logan, but I've more than a mind to put a spoke in his wheel somewhere along the line, and I think we'll start by making life a bit difficult for him. Are you up for a spot of harassment?'

He grinned at her cheerfully.

'Miss Drake, I could try the patience of a saint if I had a mind to,' he replied. 'And I fear Mr Paynter is no saint. First of all I think I'll block the access across estate land here and there; places he's going to find it most annoying to get round. It's not gone unnoticed that your tenants and half the others in this village make free and easy with estate land they're not entitled to; in fact, I was told by one of your tenants yesterday that he had no intention of relinquishing the Home Farm land which he'd annexed without permission – until, that is I told him how much more rent he'd be obliged to pay.' Suddenly he frowned. 'You don't think mebbe the man Paynter might take his rage out on the child even worse though, do you? Because I'll no keep my temper if he does, I've proved I cannae do that.'

'If he does I'll take her away from him, bodily,' Julia declared angrily, 'and to hell with the legalities of it!'

'It would be nice if you could do that anyway,' Matt Logan observed, and abruptly the morning-room door clicked open very quietly and Annie poked her head round cautiously.

'Where did you come from?' Julia enquired and she grinned.

'Through the drawing-room. I crept in so *she* wouldn't see me, that Mrs Collins. She'm horrible, you know.'

Julia offered her a crooked grin and glanced at Matt.

'I've an idea Mr Logan and I feel much the same,' she replied, 'but you say so to anybody and I'll cut your wretched tongue out! Now come here and say good-morning properly.'

Annie put both arms around Julia's neck and wriggled her skinny little bottom on to her lap. 'Hullo,' she said with great affection, planting a hard kiss on her cheek, 'can I have some toast?'

Julia gave her a piece already buttered and spread with marmalade and cuddled her comfortably as she ate it. Looking across the body sprawled untidily on her knees at the big, quiet Scotsman sitting opposite her she offered him a glance of intimate understanding. She knew they both felt precisely the same about Annie; they were fond of her, she was vulnerable and they wanted to protect her, yet Matt Logan had known her exactly ten days.

Oliver was never going to be other than kind to Annie in passing because he knew that was what Julia wanted.

So could Matt Logan be fond of Minnie, too?

'Mr Logan,' she said quietly, handing Annie another slice of toast, 'there is one other thing I should very much like you to do within the next few days if you would, please. I should like you to buy me a car. You can drive, I trust?'

He nodded.

'Aye. I've driven since I was sixteen.'

Julia smiled.

'Then choose what you fancy,' she said, 'and I'll organize the money for you. I make a weekly trip of around thirty miles or so, every Thursday afternoon as it happens, and at the moment Dr Crompton takes me, but I really feel it's putting on him somewhat, it would be much more convenient to be able to go under my own steam. Is that all right?'

The morning sun sparkled in the warm, comfortable little morning-room, which was light and airy, with pale blue walls and light furniture. Matt Logan watched the woman and the child in their touching intimacy, and found it peaceful. He knew his employer was having an affair with the young doctor and he would not have questioned her choice or frowned on her behaviour because it was not his place, but he didn't like Oliver Crompton very much and he felt certain the young, ambitious, city-dweller's desire for Julia was not entirely altruistic.

Slowly, in his unemotional way, Matt Logan wondered if one day he would not only have to protect Annie Paynter from her father, but Julia Drake from Oliver Crompton as well.

And he knew he would do both those things with complete single-mindedness.

'I can have a car for the next time you wish to visit your friend in Blackridge, certainly,' he assured her calmly.

It took three days for Matt to catch Arthur Paynter trespassing on estate land and because Matt had taken to sitting quietly in The Smugglers for a while each evening, enjoying a pint and familiarizing himself with the natives, he knew who Arthur was perfectly well by sight. He had heard his drunken bluff and seen him lose his rag over a card-game already, and had soundlessly followed him home one night, so he knew precisely where Arthur was likely to trespass.

He wouldn't have needed to know him by sight, however, since Annie and the puppies were with him on the morning they happened across her father on a path across estate land which was a recognized short-cut to the pub, and which had been carefully blocked with barbed-wire and 'No Admittance' notices. The look on Annie's face said everything there was to say.

Arthur didn't see Matt to begin with, he was hidden by a clump of bushes. Annie saw Arthur, though, and froze in her tracks. She was wearing – on the heartfelt promise that she was only going to hold fence-posts for Matt and she wouldn't climb a tree in it – one of her new summer dresses and her white leather sandals of which she was so proud. She wore socks, too, something she had never possessed before and some white cotton knickers, Julia having bought her a dozen pairs upon discovering she didn't have any underclothes to her name at all. Her hair was brushed and held back from her face with a ribbon and she looked completely foreign to her father.

'Annie?' he exclaimed in some surprise as he saw her, and she uttered a muted sound of terror. Abruptly his face was cold with fury. 'Look at yer, you bleddy little bitch,' he snarled. 'Come here!'

His hand shot out and caught his daughter by the wrist. She screamed in fright but there was no escape once he had a grip on her, and he twisted her arm until she hung from it at such a strange angle it looked af if it would surely break, causing her to whimper in agony.

'You lying little *slut*,' he hissed into her petrified face. 'Where d'you get them clothes and them shoes? The mad bitch give them to you, didn't she?' He jerked her twisted arm making her scream, and raised his other hand to strike her. '*Didn't she*!' he spat, and was aware of a sound very close to him in the bushes.

Matt Logan stepped out, inches away from him.

'I wouldnae strike that lassie if you know what's good for you, man,' he said in a voice that even Annie thought was menacing. 'I *really* wouldn't. Now you just let her walk away or I swear you'll no be making it down to The Smugglers, you'll be needing to go to the hospital.'

Arthur certainly loosened his grip on Annie, but he didn't release her completely and he stood his ground.

'I seen you,' he observed quietly, 'in The Smugglers, sitting there quiet as you like, earwigging on conversations what ent none of your business. And come t'that, I've heard old Tranter bleating about you, an' all. What are you, mad bitch's bleddy gamekeeper? You'd be best off keeping an eye on *her*, she'm game enough, so I'm told, with that bleddy townie doctor.'

Matt took another small step towards him and Arthur backed up a pace.

'Estate manager,' he said, 'and for the last time will ye please let go of the lassie.'

Arthur eyed the terrified Annie thoughtfully. He really could afford to let her go, after all, she'd keep. She had to put in an appearance at Rectory Farm sometime and he'd thrash hell out of her when she did. He liked doing that, because hurting the child upset Gladys so much. He was about to give her a little push when lolloping into view with young enthusiasm came the two puppies, throwing themselves joyfully at Matt's boots.

Arthur's face darkened with fury as he gaped at the puppies in astonishment, and Matt made the mistake of taking his eyes off Annie for a few seconds to see what it was that had caused such rage to wash so abruptly over the man. Taken off-guard, he was not quick enough to prevent what happened next. Arthur whipped his daughter round to face him, almost breaking her arm in the process, and slapped her face with unbelievable savagery. Annie hit the ground with a thump, grunting as all the breath was knocked out of her.

'Jethro's bleddy puppies!' he snarled. 'You thieving little slut! I'll bleddy kill you for this,' and reaching for her hair he prepared to drag her up and slap her again.

Matt Logan recognized the emotion that flooded his body at that moment like an old friend. Through a mist of rage he could see quite clearly the small, overfurnished room in the Glasgow brothel, the little prostitute with her ruined, bloody face and the man with the knife sneering at her. It was probably only the presence of Annie that stopped him killing Arthur Paynter without a second thought.

He aimed a kick at the man that would most certainly have been fatal if it had caught him in the head. As it was it knocked him to the ground with astonishing force and sent him rolling in the dust, where he lay winded, watching in silence as with great tenderness Matt lifted Annie to her feet and held her protectively against him. As Arthur tried wildly to find his legs, Matt kicked him again, for good measure.

'I brought those puppies with me from Falmouth, Mr Paynter,' he said dangerously softly, as Arthur cowered in the dust in front of him, 'bought them from a farmer down there when I knew I was taking a new post. You see as manager I like to have ma own wee dogs to train. When they're grown I'll no be needing to chase you off the estate, they'll be doing the job for me. For now, however, you'd be wise to go back the way you came, if you'll not be wanting worse than you've already had – and if I should find the wee lassie here has *one more* bruise on her tomorrow than she has today, then I'll be coming after you, and that's a promise.'

'We'll see about that,' Arthur blustered, attempting to climb to his feet again and this time being permitted to do so. 'And we'll see about you blocking rights of way, an' all! Ever since she come home from the madhouse, that bitch up there has been causing trouble, and you can tell her that folks don't like it. She'm in for trouble with her airs and graces and her barbed-wire fences – you tell her!'

'Tell her yourself why don't you, Mr Paynter,' Matt replied evenly.

'Miss Drake asked me to tell you she's willing to grant you an interview any time you like, if you've a mind, so I'll tell her you'll be calling. Good-day to you then.' And still holding Annie against him he watched as Arthur stumbled back along the path he had come.

When he was out of sight Annie burst into tears, and the huge Scotsman lifted her in his arms, holding her warmly and fondly against him.

'You'll be all right,' he whispered. 'Come on, lassie, we'll go home to Tremar.'

He was still carrying her as they crossed the lawns to the terrace steps, and Julia came running out of the house to meet them.

'What happened?' she enquired sharply, and Matt told her. Immediately she pushed Annie's hair away with great care and they stared at her bruised face in disgust.

'Oh, for God's sake!' Julia exploded. 'What *is* the matter with the man!'

'He saw they puppies,' Annie whispered. 'He knows they's Jethro's – but it were nice of you to say they was yours, Mr Logan, only he don't believe it.'

Matt put his huge hands very gently on her skinny shoulders and leaning down, gazed into her face with his extraordinary blue eyes.

'Will he hurt you again when you go home tonight?' he asked and she grinned at him, resilient child that she was.

'Not after what you did,' she retorted cheerfully. 'He don't pick on my brothers 'cos they'm bigger than him; fact he don't pick on no one who's bigger than him. But you want to be careful, he's got a lot of friends; all them he drinks with in The Smugglers, for a start.'

'Yes, you do want to be careful,' Julia murmured, 'I don't want to find you in the wood somewhere with your head beaten in.'

Matt smiled at her warmly.

'Remember what I told you about me when we first met,' he said. 'It's no likely to be *my* head stove in. Tell me, can you no take the lassie to live with you and have done with it?'

Julia took Annie into her arms holding her protectively, stroking her unruly mane of red hair with trembling fingers.

'Don't think I haven't thought about it,' she replied, 'but he won't wear it, I know he won't. He'll have the authorities come up here and take her back and at the moment I haven't a leg to stand on. I'm frightened, too, that if I push him too far he'll wage a campaign against me and stop her coming here at all. At the moment he blusters and threatens but he seems too disinterested to actually make the effort to physically keep her away.'

Matt nodded and pursed his lips.

'Well you listen to me, little missy,' he said, 'you ken fine where Home Farm is, don't you?' Annie nodded and he touched her cheek with his fingers. 'Right then, *any* time you might be frightened, night or day, you'll find the key on a ledge above the front door. If I'm no there you lock yourself in and you wait for me. You promise me? And now, you stay here with Miss Drake for an hour or so and when I come back we'll do a wee bit more training with the puppies.'

Annie and Julia watched him descend the terrace steps, the puppies still close on his heels, and then, abruptly, Annie began to shiver. Her face was throbbing and she was very shocked.

'I think a little sleep might do you good, you know,' Julia whispered, gently brushing a couple of tears from the child's face. 'Come on, you can snuggle down in my bed for a while.'

Five minutes later, wearing just her little white pants, Annie climbed into Julia's huge bed and snuggled under the blankets. She felt very sleepy but she was reluctant to let Julia go, and her small hand was hot and sticky, Julia noticed.

'My pa done something to you once, didn't he?' she asked as Julia sat on the bed beside her, smoothing her hair on the pillow.

Julia inclined her head slightly.

'What makes you say that?' she asked and Annie looked slightly sheepish.

' 'Cos I heard Ma and Pa arguing over the footpaths,' she replied. 'Ma said, "After what you done to Julia, are you surprised she'm got it in for you?" and he told her if she didn't shut up he'd knock her bleeding head off. What did he do to you?' Her eyes suddenly widened. 'He didn't get you locked up in Blackridge, did he?'

Fishing in the dark and completely oblivious, she had stumbled straight into the truth, Julia thought ironically. Gently she bent and kissed the child's forehead.

'Your father was in France when I was locked up in Blackridge,' she answered. 'Now, go to sleep and then when you wake up the puppies will be back.'

Annie smiled at her, but as she got up to leave the child's hand tightened round hers sharply.

'What is it?' she asked softly, and Annie's eyes filled with tears.

'Don't let my pa send me to Falmouth after Christmas,' she said in a small, forlorn voice. 'Let me stay here with you. I could be your maid. I'd be ever so good and not break anything . . . but I don't want to go away!'

Julia stared at her for a few seconds, then a slow smile spread across her lips and she clapped her hands together very softly.

'Be *my* maid,' she repeated in slow, thoughtful delight. 'Of course you could! Well you couldn't, of course, but you haven't half given me an idea. Yes, young lady, I think you might just have solved your own problem. Now, go to sleep.'

Annie went home that night and returned the next morning without having set eyes on her father at all. Matt and Julia had wanted to go with her, but Annie had begged them not to interfere, saying that if they did it would just make things worse for her and Gladys. There seemed to be an indefatigable truth in that and so, reluctantly, they let her go alone. But something would have to be done, Julia decided, and probably rather quickly. She waited for Arthur to call on her. Puppies or no puppies, surely after being thrown off the estate and humiliated by Matt Logan he *must* call, she thought, but Arthur was either too frightened, or simply didn't really care, because two days passed and there was still no sign of him.

On the day of her usual trip to Blackridge, Oliver called in the morning to ask what time she would like to be collected, and as politely as she knew how she told him she didn't need him to take her any more.

'I have my own car now, Oliver,' she said, 'and Mr Logan will drive me.'

Oliver stared at her blankly. It was true he hated going to Blackridge and he found spending a couple of hours in Minnie's company each week quite wearing, but it was time spent with Julia, too, and now suddenly she didn't want him any more.

'But I always take you!' he exclaimed. 'Why don't you want to go with me?'

'It isn't a case of not wanting to,' she replied uncomfortably, wishing he would go away and not cause a scene, 'it's just that you have your practice to attend to and so forth, and I've got my own car now. It's what an estate manager is for, Oliver, to work for his employer.'

She saw his lip curl and the sharp of gleam of jealousy in his eyes.

'So you're quite prepared to let that bloody great Scotsman take you there and witness the humiliation you were subjected to for all those years?' he asked spitefully. 'That should sharpen up his respect, I'm sure!'

Julia was angry and it made her thoughtless.

'Oliver, Matt Logan spent five years in an asylum in Scotland when he came home from France in 1918,' she snapped. 'That's why "young" Mr Cruikshank chose him for me.'

The moment she'd said it she could have bitten her tongue off.

She saw a look of incredulous shock on Oliver's face as he gaped at her, and her heart sank. He wasn't going to let that one go by unchallenged.

'He *what*!' he exploded, rounding on her furiously. 'He spent five years in an asylum! Well I gave Cruikshank *some* credit for intelligence, but obviously I was wrong. He saddles you with a madman to make you feel at home. A first-class bit of management I call that! Now we can all sleep easy in our beds!'

Julia's mouth tightened. When he was in this sort of mood, Oliver was a boor. How was it possible, she wondered – not for the first time – that he could have been so sensitive and caring about her plight when he first met her and yet be so blunderingly callous where other people were concerned.

'It's been common practice for years,' she observed with biting sarcasm, 'to throw all the dregs of society in together, Oliver. Mr Cruikshank was just tidying up loose ends, probably!'

There was an explosive silence between them for a few seconds and abruptly she turned away from him, wanting to cry and determined not to let him see.

'So if it's all right with you then,' she muttered, 'I shall be going to Blackridge in my own car from now on.'

She felt him come up behind her and at once her body tingled with anticipation of his touch. Savagely, she thought, if only I could stop feeling like this I could put you in proportion. You're a mean-spirited bastard but you make me feel like a queen, and as his fingers whispered over her shoulders and his breath touched the back of her neck she gasped softly.

'Why did they put him in an asylum, Julia?' he asked gently, and at once she turned towards him, surrendering to his arms.

Even so, with the joy of his embrace, the truth in this particular case didn't seem like much of an option.

'Shell-shock, I imagine,' she lied, as he pressed his lips into the nape of her neck and made her squirm with delight. 'Wasn't it shell-shock with so many unfortunate men who came home shattered wrecks?' She waited for him to raise his head and then pressed her lips against his hungrily, sliding her arms around him. 'Please, my love,' she whispered, 'try to be on my side over this. Matt is a good man and it's far more sensible for him to drive me to Blackridge every week than you, don't you see that?'

His mouth became urgent and demanding against hers. He whispered, 'I want to make love to you,' and it was with reluctance that she slipped from his grasp.

'Not with Mrs Collins in the house, I think,' she replied with a smile. 'Come tonight, if you can. Please, Oliver, she knows you're here and anyway, Annie will be about in a minute. No, darling, don't – no more.'

'We've got to find a place for during the day, Julia,' he said, clenching his fists to thwart his desire to touch her again, 'somewhere where no one's likely to stumble over us. It's difficult for me to get away at night and I don't want any more rows with Sophie, but I can't bear to be away from you for so long.'

'Well, so far you haven't been away from me for any time at all,' she pointed out. 'But as it happens, I do have somewhere in mind. Sandro and I had a den in the attic where we used to play during the winter, when it was too cold to go outside. I'd forgotten all about it until Matt walked the dower attics to see that there was nothing stored there and then I remembered. Sandro and I reckoned it was above the bedrooms in the staff corridor in the main house, two floors above any family or guest-rooms; anyway, we used to make enough noise up there, and no one heard us. You reach it from the servants' staircase, so we'll go and look, shall we?'

'What, now?' he asked hopefully, and she laughed at him.

'No, later. I promise. Now go on, Oliver, go and do your rounds.' She kissed him swiftly. 'And no more getting angry, all right?'

He smiled at her gently and when his face was gentle he was extraordinarily good-looking. Was that what kept her tied to him so fiercely, she wondered.

'I can never stay angry with you, anyway,' he replied fondly. 'Goodbye then, till later.' And with her head slightly to one side she watched him leave with a little smile of satisfaction playing about her lips.

She was so lost in her quiet, warm thoughts that when a voice abruptly spoke right in her ear she actually yelped with surprise.

'I dunno why you bother with him,' Annie remarked candidly. 'Why don't you fall in love with Mr Logan? He's much nicer.'

'God almighty, I'll swing for you one of these days!' Julia exclaimed, clutching her hands to her chest. 'You really must learn not to creep up on people – and anyway, who says I'm in love with Dr Crompton?'

'Well you was kissing him,' the child observed. 'Isn't that why you kiss folk?'

'No, not necessarily,' Julia answered, trying to muster her dignity, 'and it's none of your business anyway. Besides, I kiss you, don't I?'

Annie nodded, smiling.

'And don't you love me?' she enquired.

Julia pulled a face at her.

'Yes!'

'Well there you are then,' Annie concluded triumphantly. 'Can I have something to eat? I'm starving.'

Julia grinned and sliding her arm around the child's shoulders she sauntered out on to the terrace with her. Matt, who had been doing his regular morning inspection of progress on the dower roof was coming round the side of the house with the puppies yapping happily at his feet and he waved when he saw them.

'Coffee?' Julia called out.

He nodded and a quarter of an hour later they were all sitting on the terrace wall drinking coffee and eating biscuits.

Julia thought, surely this is all I want, isn't it? I've got my beautiful home and my freedom, this adorable child whom I will keep no matter how hard I have to fight for her, this lovely bear of a man to watch over me and mine – and one day soon I shall have Minnie – so why do I want to complicate it all with Oliver? Because he reminds me . . . of that summer . . . of Arthur when he told me he loved me. . . .

'Annie?' she said, narrowing her eyes against the sun and gazing at the red-haired, green-eyed daughter of her lover – gazing, and remembering.

Annie turned towards her, frowning.

'What?' she asked, and Julia laughed softly and kissed her.

'Nothing,' she replied.

[illegible]

[illegible]

[illegible]

[illegible]

[illegible]

[illegible]

[illegible]

Chapter 12

Matt Logan stood on the gravel drive beside Julia and gazed up at the forbidding edifice that was Blackridge Asylum with narrowed eyes. Originally built as a workhouse in the long-distant past, the Victorians had, with their warped sense of values, vastly added to it, to turn it into a great human rubbish-bin, with a huge ornate clock-tower that cruelly chimed away the endless, hopeless crawl of life. Now, all red brick and tiny windows, it was a place of fear and shame.

'If you don't behave yourself, I'll have you put in Blackridge!' was the locals' variation on the bogyman with which to terrify their children into submission, and very few people ever admitted to knowing anyone who was a patient.

'Dear God what a place,' he observed thoughtfully. 'I thought mine was bad, but it was no as bad as this.'

'I can still remember,' she murmured with a small shiver, 'what it felt like that first day. I was so frightened. . . .' She frowned. 'I couldn't believe my parents had done it to me . . . I thought it was – an object lesson, you know? That they'd come for me a few hours later. . . .'

He touched her hand softly, a tiny gesture that was abruptly like pity, comfort and understanding all in one.

'And nobody came for twenty-three-and-a-half years,' he whispered. 'You must have been no more than a wee lassie. Unbelievable, such cruelty.'

Julia turned her eyes up to his big, placid face and smiled at him bitterly.

'It was always winter here; hopeless winter, even in summer,' she whispered, glancing at the clock-tower as it chimed mournfully, clanging its doleful bell across the empty moors. 'I was seventeen when I came and I don't even remember being twenty-five . . . Minnie will be frightened of you at first but she won't be when she comes to know you. Come on, let's go and find her.'

Miss Vincent came to the door to greet them and looked surprised to see Matt instead of Oliver. Julia explained the situation and then, from somewhere in the stinking interior, Minnie's voice could be heard along with her slightly clumsy, uncoordinated footfall on the tiled floor. She came running round the corner and towards the front door and seemed to come to a violent, stumbling halt at the sight of Matt, standing next to Julia on the doorstep.

'No,' she whispered, her eyes wide with fear. 'I don't like him, Julia. Make him go away!'

Julia held out her arms.

'Minnie,' she said softly, 'I wouldn't let anybody hurt you, you know that. Matt's a friend. A *real* friend. Come on, come and meet him,' she caught Minnie's hand and drew her forwards very slowly. 'Come on, he doesn't bite, I promise.'

Minnie wore her favourite summer dress – which simply didn't fit. One of her stockings was twisted because she was hopelessly inadequate with suspenders and she clutched a mismatched, empty blue handbag, because ladies who went out to tea always carried handbags. Flustered and untidy she stood on the steps in the sunshine staring up at Matt in terror, and he watched her benignly with his gentle eyes.

'Well you're a fine lassie and no mistake!' he observed. 'And I must be the luckiest Scotsman this side of the border, to be taking two such handsome ladies out to tea.'

Minnie's eyes began to lose some of their terror.

Slowly she asked, 'Are you Julia's friend?' and he smiled through his great, sandy beard.

'I am that.'

'So am I.'

'Aye. So if I'm Julia's friend, and you're Julia's friend, then we must be friends too, mustn't we? Would you like to ride next to me in the grand new car?'

Julia grinned and slid her arms around Minnie's neck, kissing her cheek.

'You can go in front if you like,' she said. 'You can choose where we go for tea, as well, if you want to. Your favourite place perhaps, where they have that lovely ice-cream?'

Matt put his hand out, to help her down the steps and to both Julia's and the Matron's astonishment Minnie put her hand firmly in his and let him lead her towards the car.

'If you could just spare me five minutes when you bring her back, Julia dear?' Miss Vincent said and waved to them as they turned the car in the drive.

It was a wonderfully relaxed afternoon. Matt and Julia sat in Minnie's favourite tea-shop and comfortably watched her spread ice-cream all round her mouth. They listened to her excited, childish prattle, they called each other by their Christian names without any embarrassment and Julia gazed in astonishment as Minnie warmed to the huge, gentle Matt to such a degree that she began to get coquettish with him.

He hardly seemed to fit in the tiny, doll-like tea-room; he was enormous at the little table, and how he managed to stay sitting on the chair Julia didn't even dare to contemplate, but all the time he twinkled merrily at Minnie and he reeled her in precisely as easily as he had reeled in Annie. By the time they were ready to leave she was almost leaning on him.

Maybe you've done it to me too! Julia thought, gazing at him in amazement. And perhaps I haven't noticed. Oh, Lord, I hope I don't flirt with you like that – but I'm sure I don't. Oh, but it *has* been nice this afternoon, you haven't made me feel uncomfortable once and I don't feel as if I have to rush it all the time, like I do with Oliver.

Back in the car Minnie chose to ride in the back with Julia and chattered continuously. Julia slipped her arm about her shoulders and held her with the same sort of gentle fondness she held Annie – but then Minnie and Annie were both children, only Minnie would never grow up. Minnie had already forgotten Julia's promise that they would one day live together at Tremar, in fact it was likely she had forgotten a lot about the years they had spent together at Blackridge; Minnie lived for now. Ilona Vincent said she was much happier and only talked these days about her trips out to tea, so it seemed to follow that when she was finally released into Julia's custody she would, in a fairly short time, forget about Blackridge altogether.

And if she did that, Julia thought enviously, then she was very lucky.

At the doors of Blackridge they gazed at each other and suddenly held hands tightly as they always did at the moment of parting, clinging to each other for comfort. Julia clung to Minnie because she genuinely loved her, Minnie clung to Julia as much out of habit as anything else, for her ability to love was as much impaired as everything else in her damaged brain, and she had learned to live without Julia now. But somewhere in her fog-shrouded past she vaguely remembered being forcibly removed from Julia and suffering pain, and that memory always surfaced as they came to say goodbye.

This parting, however, was noticeably different, for though Minnie hung on grimly to Julia, she kept turning her eyes to Matt who stood respectfully at a distance, watching in silence.

'Say goodbye to Matt, then,' Miss Vincent said quietly. 'Come on Minnie, there's a good girl. You'll see Julia again next week.'

Minnie let go of Julia's hands and reached out for Matt. He took her warmly in his arms and gave her a kiss on her cheek which made her giggle because his beard tickled.

'Goodbye, bonnie lassie,' he said softly, and still giggling with delight and touching her cheek with her fingers, Minnie hopped up the steps and disappeared into the building.

Ilona Vincent gave Matt Logan a very quick, approving glance and said to Julia, 'Do you want to come to my office for a few moments?'

Julia pressed her lips together and then nodded. She was still reluctant to cross the threshold, but each time it got a little easier, and besides, she didn't want Matt to see her fear – although as she glanced back at him and saw him smiling at her she did just wonder at herself. If she wasn't worried about Oliver knowing how she felt, she certainly shouldn't be worried about Matt Logan.

'The board are beginning to give a sympathetic ear to your request to have Minnie live with you at Tremar, my dear,' Miss Vincent said, offering Julia a seat in the office. 'They seem to think it should be done slowly; you take her for a day first and then possibly for a weekend, to see how she copes, and how you do. But I can't go any further with it for the moment, of course, until you confirm that you definitely do still want her. Your plans haven't changed at all?'

Julia stared at her in amazement.

'Of course not!' she exclaimed. 'What makes you ask?'

Ilona Vincent tapped her fingers thoughtfully on the edge of her desk. She seemed to be reluctant to look at Julia and she seemed to be choosing her words.

Eventually she replied with what seemed like undue care.

'Dr Crompton makes me ask, my dear. I am quite aware of his love for you, I have been ever since you left here. I think I'm aware of a certain fondness for him in you too, and I did just wonder whether, perhaps, you feel your future lies with him. If it does, well that's your decision, of course, but you cannot possibly take Minnie, he simply wouldn't wear it, I'm afraid.'

Julia put her fingers up to her mouth and began to pull at her lips. Her hand trembled, the other woman noticed.

'Have the rumours got this far?' she asked and Miss Vincent shook her head.

'I don't hear rumours, Julia,' she replied, 'I see what goes on before me, but I don't hear rumours. Unless I am much mistaken, Dr Crompton is a very ambitious young man and he wants to go to the top in his profession. He dreams of a consultancy in Harley Street one day, but he's going to need money to fund his dreams, and if you want me to be honest I think he hopes to raise that money from the sale of Tremar.'

Julia gaped at her.

'Tremar!' she echoed. 'You think Oliver is going to try and cheat me out of Tremar? Oh no, no, I'm sorry, he may not be very scrupulous, but yes, he does love me and he would never try and cheat me.'

Miss Vincent frowned.

'My dear girl, I don't for a moment think he will cheat you – out of anything,' she said calmly. 'I'm quite certain his plans are all open and above board, where you're concerned anyway. Where his wife and children are concerned is another matter, but that's beside the point. Only I really do think he believes you want what he wants, as much as he wants it and if you do plan to sell up and leave Cornwall with him, then I'm simply telling you you can't take Minnie with you.'

Julia looked steadily into the woman's eyes and her expression was firm, her gaze unwavering.

'Tremar is mine,' she said slowly. 'I hardly ever thought about it while I was here, because I would have gone mad if I had, but my love for Tremar is stronger than anything. When Oliver goes to London he will be going on his own, I assure you, I'm home at last and I *never* intend to leave again!'

The matron smiled gently and stood up, offering Julia her hand.

'Then I shall report favourably to the board,' she promised, 'but,' abruptly she glanced sideways at her beautiful ex-patient, 'your great big Scotsman, I hope he doesn't intend to leave, either.'

'That's up to him, I'm afraid,' Julia replied non-committally, but she realized as she walked towards the huge front door that she actually felt exactly the same.

On the drive Matt politely held the car door open for her.

'Miss Drake,' he said, and closed it behind her when she was seated.

She watched through the windscreen as he opened the great wrought-iron gates and then climbed into the driving-seat beside her, and a moment later watched again as he climbed out to close them. As always there was a great surge of relief within her. She was back on the outside again.

As the car nosed slowly down the lane towards the main road she said, 'You just called me Miss Drake as you opened the door for me, but all afternoon we've been calling each other by our Christian names.'

He nodded.

'Aye, I thought that was so as not to confuse the lassie.'

Julia smiled.

'What about confusing me?' she enquired and they glanced sideways at each other. 'Annie calls me Julia, so does Oliver. Only Mrs Collins calls me Miss Drake and I can't imagine I'll ever have any reason to change that, but we're – well we're sort of friends now, aren't we? I can't have Miss Drake, Monday to Sunday, and Julia, Thursday afternoons, it's much too complicated.'

'But you're my employer,' he pointed out, and she shrugged.

'My father called the estate manager in his day by his Christian name, I remember that quite clearly, he was called William. Oh, certainly William didn't call Papa by his, but then Papa was a stuffed shirt. Still, if it makes you happier to uphold the master/servant bit, we'll turn it into an order. From now on, Matt, you will call me Julia, is that clear?'

She saw him shake with silent laughter for a moment, then he glanced at her and his blue eyes were full of amusement.

'Very good, Julia,' he replied obediently.

Abruptly Julia did something that was entirely foreign to her habit. Placing her hand on his arm she squeezed very gently with her fingers.

'Thank you, Matt,' she said, 'for coming to Tremar. I hope you'll stay with me for always.'

'Well, as things are I can't think of any reason to leave, lass,' he replied and there followed a very comfortable silence between them.

Annie was sprawled on the sofa in the drawing-room reading a book when Julia got in at just before six. Mrs Collins, had long since left, but there was a delicious smell wafting up from the kitchen and Annie fairly leapt to her feet.

'I thought you was never coming home,' she declared. 'I'm starving!'

'You're always starving,' Julia retorted. 'Anyway, I've invited Matt to eat with us this evening, I thought it would be nice.'

Annie pulled a face.

'There won't be half enough!' she exclaimed. 'Mrs Po-face don't make enough just for us, there certainly ent going to be any for him!'

Julia frowned at her.

'Listen, missy,' she said, 'if I say Matt's eating with us, then he's eating with us and that's that. Now come in the kitchen and make yourself useful peeling some extra potatoes. Besides, Matt and I have been eating jam and cream this afternoon, so we'll not be as hungry as all that.'

Annie was quite happy to do as she was told and as she skipped across the room Julia realized with a start that she was growing at an alarming rate. They had only known each other six weeks, but it was as if her little body, having been kept short of food for so long and now finding itself well fed, was growing at twice the speed to make up for lost time. What was more, in the beginning the amount of food Mrs Collins had left each evening had seemed gargantuan and now, suddenly, she was complaining that it wasn't enough.

'That dress is going to be too short for you soon, you know,' she remarked, gazing fondly at the child. 'Annie, would you like to come to Blackridge one Thursday?'

Annie regarded her steadily.

'Will I be frightened?' she asked, and Julia shook her head sadly.

'Oh, no, I wouldn't let you go in. We only collect Minnie and take her out to tea, but you'll have to understand that Minnie is different from you. She chatters a lot and gets ice-cream around her mouth and she's very uncoordinated. If you laugh at her I will be truly very angry.'

'I wouldn't laugh at her!' Annie whispered indignantly, and abruptly Julia kissed her fondly.

'No, I don't believe you would,' she said gently. 'In fact I know you wouldn't, I'm sorry. Come on, potato time.'

It was a delightfully intimate dinner the three of them shared on the terrace in the warm evening air and there was plenty to go round, though Julia knew Annie wouldn't leave a scrap; she never did. Matt had brought the puppies and they played happily around everyone's feet during the meal. Then afterwards Matt and Annie did some training with them on the lawn and suddenly it was almost eight-thirty.

'I'll be walking across the headland to the harbour, lass,' Matt said to

Annie, 'would you care to walk that way with me tonight and then cut up home from there?'

Annie smiled at him brightly.

'That'd be nice,' she replied, and after they had said their goodbyes, and Matt had put the puppies in the stables, from where he would collect them on his way back to Home Farm, Julia sat on the terrace wall and watched them until they reached the far end of the orchard and disappeared from view. He was so big and gentle, this new extraordinary influence in her life, like a benign giant holding the hand of the little fourteen-year-old with her beautiful red hair and green eyes. She kept looking up at him and obviously he was telling her some story because once she uttered a peal of laughter that echoed back in the silence of the summer night. Julia closed her eyes in pleasure and listened to her heart, and there was no doubt it was so full these days it sang loudly enough to deafen her.

She went on sitting in the gathering darkness for another ten minutes or so, thinking about Matt and Annie and then about Minnie, idly making plans and enjoying the salt smell of the sea drifting in on the breeze. She was so lost in her delicious reverie that when a pair of hands very softly touched her shoulders she almost jumped out of her skin.

'Good God, Oliver!' she exclaimed. 'You almost gave me a heart attack!'

'Had you forgotten I was coming?' he enquired, and she smiled at him.

'No of course I hadn't,' she replied, 'I was just miles away. Did you get away without too much trouble?'

Oliver thought about Sophie's white face and thinly drawn mouth, about the lies he had told and the look in her eyes that told him she knew they were lies, and at once he dismissed it from his mind.

'Well I'm all right until about half past eleven,' he answered cheerfully and kissed her.

Julia slid off the wall.

'Then we hadn't better waste any time,' she observed and took his hand to go into the house with him, her body familiarly tingling with anticipation at the pleasure he would give her. But when, an hour or so later, she reached that sublime moment of bliss, the physical explosion of orgasm that was so exciting and so precious to her after so many years of sensory deprivation at Blackridge, it was Matt she thought of, she realized afterwards. She opened her eyes to look down at Oliver and she was completely bewildered.

Handsome, gentle and with eyes brimming with love, he gazed at her, and even as they touched in this extreme intimacy she felt herself taking another step back from him.

'He needs money to fund his dreams, and I think he hopes to raise it from the sale of Tremar,' Ilona Vincent said warningly in her head, and her body seemed to stiffen in protest. He wanted to take her away, to steal her home from under her, to mould her into something that slotted comfortably into the dream he planned, that she should pay for. Well she'd had dreams of her own once and she had certainly paid for them, it was not her turn to give again.

'Are you all right?' he asked, suddenly aware of her strange tenseness. 'You seem preoccupied tonight.'

Preoccupied! She smiled at him gently.

'I'm fine, Oliver' she replied. 'Don't be a doctor, just love me, we haven't a lot of time, remember.'

It was too complicated to make a decision now, she needed time to think. Lots of time. She had looked upon him for so long as her saviour that getting tough with him, refusing to do what he wanted had never seemed an option. She owed him her freedom, certainly, but did that mean she also owed him her life? She thought not. So start by learning to be strong, to resist him physically. She must teach herself that even if no one ever touched her again she had had this much and for that she should be grateful.

Start tomorrow, she thought distractedly, and drew her breath sharply as he touched her. Start tomorrow. . . .

If Julia had known at that moment what was happening to Annie it would have focused her mind very fast indeed.

It had been quite dark by the time Matt and Annie had reached the little harbour with its tiny inshore fishing boats bobbing about at anchor and the huge capstan on the slipway that was used to haul them up when needed. Matt was going on into The Smugglers and Annie would take the harbour road for half a mile or so and then cut across to Rectory Farm.

'You're sure you'll be all right on your own in the dark?' Matt asked her and she grinned at him.

' 'Course I will' she replied cheerfully. 'I done this hundreds of times.'

He bent his huge frame down and kissed her cheek.

'Then you run along home,' he said, 'and I'll be seeing you tomorrow. No loitering now!'

She laughed and began to trot along the dirt road, turning back to wave at him, The night was warm and still and Annie hummed to herself, not because she was frightened of the dark, but just to keep herself company.

Dinner on the terrace at Tremar had been lovely and she was deliciously full but she was always full these days. She thought about how she had crept in and out during the days when the old lady had still been alive and Julia still locked up in Blackridge. Who would have thought that far from losing her access to the library when things changed, she would have found someone to love, someone to love her in return and someone to feed her and give her presents. It was a big turn around in her young life, but because she saw things with that special optimism of youth she had no problems with it. She suffered none of the confusion Julia suffered over her relationship with Oliver, in fact as far as she was concerned everything was perfectly clear cut. Julia loved her and somehow she would manage to stop her father sending her to Falmouth after Christmas. After that she and Julia and Matt would live for evermore at Tremar, and safe there, she could see her mother when she chose and never see her father again.

She was happily developing this fantasy as she cut off the road to come across a couple of fields to Rectory Farm. Since her father had seen her in her new clothes on the day he had slapped her so viciously, she hadn't bothered to change back into her dirty old ones again. Now she went home in her new things every night and crossing the fields in her new, proper-fitting sandals was a great deal less hazardous than it had been in the ill-fitting boots. It was very dark and she was deeply lost in her thoughts. She simply did not see her father step out of the shadows into her path, she wasn't expecting him, so it had not occurred to her to look out for him and as he suddenly loomed before her she uttered a squeak of fear and stumbled to a halt in front of him.

'Well, well,' he whispered very softly, 'Annie, as I live and breathe – fancy meeting you here!'

The child fell back, gasping with fear. If he had been drunk she could have escaped from him, but he wasn't, and when he was sober he was much faster than she was. Quick as a flash his hand shot out and closed painfully around her upper arm, the fingers biting into her flesh.

'I'm talkin' to you, brat,' he spat, dragging her upwards, holding her at an angle that would dislocate her shoulder in an instant if she struggled. 'Too stuck up to talk to your pa nowadays, are you?'

'I ent done nothing Pa,' she bleated in terror, 'I ent. I ent done nothing.'

'Oh but you *have*,' he retorted, jerking her as he spoke and causing such a pain in her shoulder that she screamed. 'Look at you, with your white sandals and your pretty dress. So the rags I give you ent good enough no more, is that right? Well we'll see about that.'

He began to drag her in the direction of Rectory Farm as she sobbed and screamed in terror. When the noise became loud enough to attract attention he stopped in the darkness and slapped her to the ground.

'Shut up!' he spat, placing his boot on her chest as she lay on her back staring up at him in panic. 'Just shut up or as God is my witness I'll kill you right here and bury you where no one'll find you.' He bent down over her, grabbing a handful of her pretty dress to yank her to her feet again. 'Ent the same without your ugly Scotsman here to protect you, is it, you little bitch.'

It was more than ten painful minutes later that he hauled her into the kitchen at Rectory Farm. She was scratched and bruised and sobbing with fright, and Gladys turned desperately towards them as they came in.

Arthur picked her up bodily and dumped her on the table.

'Stand up!' he snarled and as she scrambled to her feet he fetched his big stick from the corner by the range. 'Now take them off!'

Sobbing almost incoherently Annie struggled to unbuckle her white sandals. Spitefully her father smacked the stick about her legs, not hard enough to leave obvious welts, but hard enough to make her cry out in agony.

'No, Arthur, no!' Gladys cried, but he ignored her.

'And the socks, and the frock,' he ordered.

The trembling child complied, eventually standing in just her white cotton pants, her legs stinging from the stick, her arms clutched about her vulnerable, naked little body. She wanted desperately to use the toilet and her fear was threatening to make her incontinent. Arthur swept the stick across her ankles and then smacked it sharply down on her toes. Annie wailed in pain, jumping up and down as her feet throbbed spitefully.

She sobbed, 'No, don't, don't,' and saw him draw back the stick again.

'Stop it!' Gladys sobbed, trying to wrestle the stick from him. 'Arthur, *don't* hurt her any more, it ent fair!'

Furiously he shoved her out of the way.

'Shut your mouth,' he snapped at her, and for pleasure swept the stick across the child's ankles again. With a broken little sob of despair, Annie bent her knees, squeezing her legs together, but it was too late, she simply couldn't hold it any longer.

A hot stream of liquid began to trickle down her legs and a few seconds later a little steaming pool began to spread around her naked feet.

'You dirty little bitch!' Arthur shouted. 'Get off that table!' and the palm of his hand caught the backs of her thighs with such force that the sound was deafening.

She screamed in agony and stumbling forward, toppled off the table on to the cold, greasy tiled floor, landing with a dreadful thud. Then, as she knelt sobbing and clutching herself in agony he wrenched the sopping wet, white pants from her body and threw them into the pile of clothes.

'Now get upstairs t'yer bed!' he roared, kicking her naked buttocks savagely with his boot. 'You dirty, filthy brat! And you,' he turned furiously to his terrified wife, 'put them clothes in a bag! Bleddy high and mighty bitch at Tremar gets them back tomorrow. I'll teach her who needs charity in this village!'

Annie stumbled away on her hands and knees in her haste to escape from her father, tripping and falling up the steep, dark stairs from the dog-smelling hallway. Her body stung and smarted and she was incoherent with terror. In her tiny little room, which was cold, cheerless and pitch dark, she threw herself on to the bed and wriggled down under the covers, putting her hands over her ears, begging, 'Keep him away, please, keep him away,' but listening, straining for the smallest sound that he might be coming up for a second helping.

Down in the kitchen Gladys miserably mopped up the puddle on the table and finding a brown paper bag rolled up the torn dress, wet pants and the white socks and sandals, pushing them down inside it.

'She ent got nothing else, Arthur,' she said quietly as she handed the bag to him. 'I ent seen her old things for a while now and she can't go naked.'

'She bleddy can,' he retorted spitefully, 'which means she'll have to stay up there until I say so – and don't you go to her neither, Gladys, unless you wants a hiding. She can stay there on her own!'

There was no point arguing that, because they both knew once he had gone out of the house Gladys would go to the child. The only reason she hadn't gone straight away was to keep him from getting any angrier.

He itched to go back upstairs and give her a proper hiding; he was feeling particularly savage at the moment and he was still smarting from the punishment Matt Logan had handed out to him a week ago, but it was that which stopped him. Tomorrow morning he would throw the bag of clothes and shoes at Julia Drake, which would almost certainly bring her to Rectory Farm in search of the child and if Annie was covered with bruises he very much doubted he would avoid the wrath of the Scotsman. Evidently Julia Drake had learned some valuable lessons from her years in Blackridge and one of them was to employ some muscle before throwing her weight around.

Well, he'd beat them somehow, he thought, he'd win the battle in the end. As soon as it was legally possible he would ship Annie out of Polwean as fast as he could and make sure that the Drake bitch and her foreign savage never found out where she was.

Furiously he slammed out of his stinking kitchen and set off for the second time towards The Smugglers. He knew perfectly well Gladys would already be upstairs comforting Annie and it made him feel impotently angry. His head hurt, bursting with his memories and his misery and he tramped sullenly through the warm night, nursing his hatred . . . remembering. . . .

Of course he'd known Julia was pregnant long before Alexander Drake died. Gladys's letter had reached him in France telling him that the Drakes had sent Julia away in disgrace, and for days he had waited in terror for Alexander to say something, until he realized that obviously no one had told him. That was the moment at which he had taken his first step on to his shameful path of cowardice. He could have confessed and Alexander might have managed to get some compassionate leave or something; he might have saved his sister. Instead Arthur had breathed a sigh of relief and said nothing.

His one act of heroism, carrying Alexander back from no man's land with a badly shot-up leg had been a sop to his conscience. He'd had a vague idea that when Alexander finally found out about Julia he just might forgive him because of it; only then Alexander had died. By that time the pit Arthur was digging for himself had already been over his head. So Alexander had died a hero and so had the twins. The only one who had not been remotely heroic had been him, and he had returned to a hero's welcome – offered by the Drakes. At that point his mouth had been sealed shut.

Only Gladys had kept reminding him, until he had learned to be violent in his cups and then she had stopped reminding him too.

But Annie. Annie had been sent as a punishment from God. Pretty, engaging, clever Annie; wasn't that how Julia's child would have been? God, he *hated* Annie, and *hated* Gladys for loving her. And now, to add to his trouble, Annie had found Julia.

Oh, but he'd stop it. Somehow, *somehow* he'd stop it!

Chapter 13

Julia was sitting in the morning-room with Matt Logan the following morning when Arthur arrived at Tremar. They were drinking coffee and discussing progress on the dower roof, and they were both slightly take aback when Mrs Collins came in to the room and announced in her 'important' voice: 'Mr Arthur Paynter to see you, Miss Drake.'

Matt Logan saw his employer's face drain of colour so abruptly that he thought for a second she was going to faint, then, just as he was preparing to put out his hands to catch her, she flushed an angry, unattractive red, and stood up very quickly.

'Show him into the drawing-room please, Mrs Collins,' she said in a tone Matt had never heard before, 'and tell him I'll be there directly.'

It was evident by the slightly curious expression on the housekeeper's face that she had also noticed Julia's strangeness.

She said, 'I can always tell him you're busy, if you'd rather not see him,' and Julia pressed her lips together tightly.

'I'll be there in a moment,' she snapped coldly. 'I have some business to finish with Mr Logan first. Thank you, Mrs Collins.'

Mrs Collins bustled out of the room and Matt Logan turned his eyes upon Julia. There was no curiosity in his expression however, he was calm and steady and faintly concerned.

'You seem a little unwell this morning,' he observed, 'would you rather that I saw Mr Paynter? No doubt he's come to complain about something concerning the wee lassie.'

Julia rubbed her hands distractedly across her face for a few seconds and then realizing how noticeably they were trembling, hastily dropped them into her lap.

'I – have to see him,' she finally replied. 'I've been expecting him as you know. It's just . . . there was never going to be a good time. So, now is as good as any, I suppose. Excuse me, Matt, I doubt this will take very long,' and without another word she left the room.

Arthur stood in the beautiful drawing-room clutching the brown paper-bag full of Annie's belongings. It was all of twenty years since the last time he had been in this room and he couldn't remember much about it, except that it had sported such splendid views from the windows. At that time, though, he had been facing Sir George Drake and his delicate, oddly cold, little wife. Sir George had offered a stiff, remote thank you, which had sounded more like a criticism, for Arthur's heroic act towards Alexander and explained that he was to receive a substantial reward. She, Lady Florence, had fingered her pearls and said nothing, but watched him with eyes that reminded him disturbingly of Julia.

Nowhere, that he could see, had there been a single photograph of their daughter, though there had once been many of both the children. Julia: who was locked in Blackridge because she had committed the sin of desire.

Abruptly the door opened and Arthur spun sharply back into the present. Julia strode into the room and for the first time since they had waved goodbye to each other on a railway platform twenty-four years ago, he saw her. She wore fashionably cut trousers and a cream georgette blouse that perfectly displayed her still beautiful body; her hair, though shorter was still the vibrant chestnut he remembered and her face, except that it was a quarter of a century older, was exactly the same: the face that had made his heart leap in his chest every time he saw it.

Her expression was as hard as nails.

'Hullo, Arthur,' she said eventually, when they had stood and stared at each other for what seemed like an age. 'At last. I thought you were never going to come and see me.'

He was most certainly not the god she remembered; in fact it was hard to equate this sour-looking, puffy-faced, unshaven, shabby creature with anyone she had ever known in her life, let alone the boy she had once worshipped in his resemblance to an exquisite bronze statue of Adonis. But wasn't *she* the one who had suffered inexpressible misery for so many years because he had been too afraid, or too callous, to admit what he had done?

Was it possible, then, that his guilt had brought him to this?

Abruptly she sank with extreme elegance into an armchair and waved her hand sharply towards the opposite chair.

'Please, do sit down,' she said coldly, 'and I don't want to hurry you but I have quite a busy schedule this morning – unless, of course, you've come to talk about old times.'

'I won't sit,' he replied primly, ' 'cos I ent staying. I just came to bring you these.' He threw the paper bag into her lap. 'My daughter don't need your charity, and I would be obliged if you would stay away from her!'

Julia opened the bag and emptied out the contents. The torn dress gave her heart a nervous tug, but the sopping wet pants made her draw her breath sharply.

'Where is she?' she demanded furiously, 'And why are these pants all wet?'

'She'm in her room,' he retorted, 'and that's where she'm going to have to stay, unless you feels like returning her proper clothes, 'cos we don't need fancy white sandals; boots is quite sufficient.'

Julia's nostrils flared with anger.

'Those boots were so small for her they were destroying her feet!' she snorted. 'And as for that disgusting, torn dress she always wore, well I tried washing it and it fell to bits! What have you done to her, Arthur? Have you beaten her? Because if you have I'll have the law on you!'

'You leave her alone,' he snarled at her. 'She'm not your daughter, Julia Drake, and you'm not having her.'

There was an explosive silence between them. Julia stared at him bitterly and to her extreme annoyance her eyes began to fill up with tears. She blinked swiftly to try and dispel them and they trickled down her cheeks so that she was obliged to wipe them away with her fingers and then rummage about in her pockets for a handkerchief to wipe her nose. Control was hard; she felt certain if she spoke her voice would shake but she was not going to let him walk away without some reference to their past. If nothing else, he was owed a reminder.

Eventually she whispered, 'We had a daughter, Arthur, did you know that?' and he turned his head away so that he didn't have to look at her.

His voice was cold and stony when he spoke.

'*You* had a daughter, Julia.'

'She was your child too.'

'So you say, she could've been anybody's.'

She stared at him in disbelief. *Surely* he hadn't been denying it all these years, that was too cruel.

'I was a virgin when you made love to me in the boathouse that first time,' she said softly, 'and you know perfectly well I was. I bled, for God's sake!' Abruptly she uttered a little sob. 'You said you loved me . . .' she pressed her fingers into her eyes, 'you told me that every time you lay with me. When you kissed me goodbye at the station you said always to remember that you loved me no matter what, and I did always remember; it was the only thing that kept me going! I built a shrine for you in my heart because I believed you'd died along with Sandro and the twins. You had to have died, otherwise you'd have come back for me, wouldn't you?'

His mouth tightened as she voiced his shame and his face twitched with anger but his eyes avoided her frantically. He wanted to leave about as badly as he'd ever wanted to do anything in his life, but he lacked the courage to simply walk away. Arthur had always lacked courage – except one notable time, and even that had been heroism spurred on by cowardice.

'I was going to war,' he finally replied harshly. 'I didn't want to die without knowing what it was all about! God almighty, Julia, I'd have said anything you wanted to hear 'cos I had a proper hot fancy for you, but you never thought as how we'd be wed, surely? Your father wouldn't never have worn that! Bleddy hell, he'd of had me thrashed if he'd ever a thought I'd bin fumbling around with his precious daughter! I'm sorry they tossed you into Blackridge, truly I am, but that weren't my fault!'

'No, but it was your fault I was there for *twenty-three-and-a-half years*!' she screamed, and abruptly he was obliged to look at her. Mesmerized he watched as her tormented soul glowed in her beautiful eyes, those eyes that had once looked into his and been like fathomless deep pools. Appalled he stared at her, as her suffering bit savagely into his tortured conscience, and then as he continued to watch, because he couldn't tear his eyes away, she pulled back, the suffering faded and died and in its place came cold, calculated anger.

Arthur would have been wise to have been frightened then. If he hadn't been so tormented himself, so permanently drink-sodden and vicious that he was no longer capable of recognizing emotion in other people, he might have realized in those few seconds that she had declared war on him. She wanted revenge and with the deathly coldness of one who has waited a long time for it, she planned to destroy him, piece by piece, as painfully as possible.

'I'll make a deal with you,' she said suddenly, in a voice that was sharp and businesslike. 'I find that I need a maid, I mean Mrs Collins does very well but there's too much for her to manage really, so I could do with a skivvy. Whatever that family in Falmouth is prepared to pay Annie after Christmas, I'll double it, if you let me have her. What's more, I'll pay you direct, after all she doesn't need any money of her own if she's living here with all found. What do you say?'

Exactly as she expected, he sneered at her nastily.

'You're not having her, Julia,' he replied triumphantly. 'She's mine, and I say what happens to her, and you're *not* having her!'

Julia shrugged lightly.

'Very well then, but until she's fifteen you can't send her anywhere,' she said, 'so Matt and I will be driving down to Rectory Farm in a minute to take her some fresh clothes and her shoes. If I find she's been badly beaten, or if you try to keep her naked and locked up in her room, I shall arrange with Dr Crompton to have the proper authorities notified and they'll take her away from you; and if they do, you won't get her back again after Christmas, it doesn't work like that. You can send her away once she's fifteen and I can't stop you, but until then she'll come here whenever she likes or you'll be sorry. Is that clear?'

Arthur Paynter's drink-reddened eyes gleamed maliciously as he watched her. He thought about some of the cruel things he had said about her recently in The Smugglers, the gleeful delight with which he kept alive the rumour of her affair with the young doctor, the implied suggestion that he knew what he was talking about from bitter experience. If he had ever stopped to ask himself he couldn't have truthfully said why he hated her so much, but even as he had loved her once with such a passion, he loathed her now. It was like two distinct sides of a coin and he had flipped this one over with a vengeance. He was angry, jealous, bitter and destroyed by guilt.

'Your day's coming Miss High and Mighty,' he snorted spitefully, turning away from her and striding to the door. 'You may think you're the lady here now, but your day's coming, I promise you!'

'Not nearly as fast as yours is,' Julia muttered as he banged out of the room, 'so keep looking over your shoulder.' And she went quickly in search of Matt.

'Annie's being kept a prisoner in her room,' she told him sharply. 'She's naked and at some time something was done to her to make her wet herself. Would you get the car out now, please, Matt, we're going to Rectory Farm.'

*

Gladys heard the car sweep into the yard outside the kitchen door and she didn't need to go and see who it was. She knew. She stood in her slum kitchen waiting, and her first sight of Julia in twenty-four years was as sharply defined as Arthur's had been an hour ago. Julia stood in the doorway for a moment, then without waiting to be invited, stepped into the room. The kitchen smelt unpleasant, it always smelt unpleasant, but unpleasant smells were nothing new to Julia and if she noticed she certainly gave no impression of it.

She faced her long-ago friend in silence for a moment, and the contrast between them was cruel.

Finally she spoke.

'Hullo, Gladys. I've come for Annie,' she said, and Gladys Paynter looked at her steadily.

They had last seen each other on the cliff-top above Tremar on Julia's seventeenth birthday, when Julia had been carrying Arthur's child. Now she wanted Gladys's child – in payment for the loss of her own, perhaps?

'She's all right, you know,' she murmured, 'and she's been fed this morning.'

Abruptly Julia's nostrils flared with anger.

'It's not enough!' she snapped. 'Why don't you protect her from him, Gladys?'

Gladys's mouth tightened sharply.

'Protect her!' she echoed. Her hand flew to her chin and with trembling fingers she pointed to a deep scar. 'See this?' She whipped back her hair, displaying a nasty scar across her hairline. 'And this?' She thrust out her arm; the burn scar was white and puckered. '*And this*? Them's just the scars that show, Julia! I've spent her whole *life* protecting her from him, feeding her when he wasn't around, loving her! I wanted her more than anything when she was born and the more she grew the more he hated her. It's been as much as I could do to stop him bleddy killing her!'

Julia stared at her, perplexed.

'But why does he hate her?' she asked. 'She's an adorable child.'

Gladys Paynter's plain, tired face twisted unhappily. For as long as she could remember her life had been bound up with Julia Drake. As a small, pudgy child she remembered her brothers regularly dumping her on Alexander's sister when they were supposed to be minding her themselves and she remembered stumbling along in the wake of the tall, lithe, daredevil Julia. But much worse, she remembered her seething jealousy when the handsome Arthur had become so ensnared in passion.

All Gladys had ever wanted was Arthur, and it shouldn't have been a dream beyond fulfilment. Julia Drake was from another world. It should have been just a brief summer when they had played and mildly flirted in that strange time between childhood and adulthood. Julia should have gone to London the following year, found a husband from her own kind and been for evermore just Julia, who came occasionally to Tremar and greeted them warmly when she did.

There shouldn't have been that looming threat of war, which had made her do something she surely wouldn't have done under normal circumstances. There shouldn't have been that unwanted baby and – dear God – if there had *had* to be all those things, how was it fair that of all those beautiful young men only Arthur had returned, changed beyond recognition, to punish Gladys for his crimes.

'He hates her because she reminds him of *you*!' she shouted passionately, and her eyes blazed with pain.

'Me?' Julia whispered, and Gladys began to sob.

'Every time he looks at her he remembers that his first child was a girl,' she wept. 'He remembers what he done; how he took everything your father offered, and said nothing! He thought when she died your mother would take her secret to the grave and he'd finally be free. And he thought if he could get rid of Annie he'd never have to think about it again. I knew, when I see'd her growing up how clever she was and I wanted to teach her, I wanted to make up for what I lost, but he won't allow us to have books in the house and he wouldn't never let me dress her in other than bits from the rag man's cart, so when she went to school they bullied her! Every day she grows more beautiful, like he was, and he punishes her more because he can't forget!'

Julia pursed her lips. That was all very well, but Gladys wasn't completely blameless.

'Well you knew what he'd done to me,' she pointed out quietly, 'but you were quick enough to marry him when he came home. Did you think you could forget too? And come to that, how did you know my child was a daughter? There's a few questions you need to answer, Gladys.'

Gladys put her rough, reddened hands up to her face and stared dully at her filthy kitchen. So many hopes and dreams; so much heart-break.

'Julia, I *loved* him!' She said wearily. 'That summer when all he did was moon about after you, I *worshipped* him! When you told me that day you was pregnant it tore my heart to pieces and then when he come home and asked to marry me – *I still bleddy loved him*! But you didn't understand, did you, any of you? What was I, in comparison to the rich and beautiful Julia Drake!'

Julia gaped at her. She felt a stab of guilt suddenly, remembering how completely single-minded she had been about Arthur. There hadn't been anyone else to talk about him to but Gladys and it had never occurred to her that Gladys loved him as well. Little, plain, dumpy, clever Gladys.

'I didn't know,' she whispered, and Gladys sneered bitterly.

'No, of course you didn't. I was just plain Gladys who smelt of fish all the time. Well I paid for getting what I wanted, didn't I? He's beaten me more times than I can remember. I've begged for food sometimes when the children was little, we was that hungry! And I has to produce a daughter who turns out to be as clever as me and as beautiful as yours would undoubtedly have been if she'd lived! So don't you talk to me about forgetting you, Julia, I ent forgotten you for one day of my wretched life!'

The two women stared at each other in silence in the stale-smelling kitchen as a pot boiled on the range, rattling its lid, and a mouse scratched in a corner. From outside the sun struggled to penetrate the greasy glass of the windows, filling the room with a light that seemed to make it groan under the weight of its own inadequacy, and now Julia planned to make Gladys's life even more difficult and poverty-stricken than it already was.

'Do you still love him?' she heard herself ask very quietly, and Gladys dissolved into tears again, sobbing into her grubby apron as if her heart would break.

'Love him?' she echoed at last, 'I loathe the sight of him. Every night I pray he'll be dead in the morning. We've all paid the price for what happened to you, Julia, all of us and Annie and me goes on paying, 'cos we don't have no choice! I wish I *hadn't* bleddy known your child was a girl, and I wish I'd never bleddy told him! He's punished me twice as much for that, and what happened to you weren't my fault!'

Impulsively Julia snatched the untidy, sobbing woman into her arms and hugged her tightly, clinging to her partly in comfort, but partly to give herself courage.

'Bear with me, Gladys,' she whispered. 'Stay on my side and somehow I'll make it better for you, I promise. I may have to make it worse for a while, but I won't let him go on ill-using you any longer than I have to and I definitely won't let him destroy Annie. She's going to have the opportunities you never had if I have to kill him to get them for her, and you have my solemn word on that.'

'Kill him by all means, if you want to,' Gladys replied bitterly, and broke from the embrace. 'Do us all a bleddy favour! Come on, I'll take you up to Annie, she'll be pleased to see you.'

Naked and vulnerable, her eyes red from weeping, Annie was standing at her bedroom window, gazing down into the yard, where she could obviously see Matt. It said much for her terror of her father that she hadn't opened the window and tried to call out to him. As she turned to see who was coming in the room, Julia caught sight briefly of the red and blue bruises on the backs of her legs where Arthur had smacked her so viciously the night before, then she was across the room and in Julia's arms.

Gladys watched from the doorway as Julia soothed the child and began to help her into clean white pants and another pretty dress. Surely this was the final irony, wasn't it? Arthur had not even noticed her all those years ago because of his love for Julia, and now the beautiful daughter she loved so much preferred to be with Julia as well.

After a moment she turned away and gazed at nothing in particular as in her heart she accepted the sacrifice she knew she must make. Annie could be anything she wanted to be with Julia Drake behind her – and Gladys wouldn't ever let them see her cry when one day they walked away together. For good.

Down in the kitchen again Annie briefly hugged her mother and then went out into the yard to be with Matt. Gladys and Julia saw him take her close in his arms, holding her protectively.

'I'm taking her with me now, Gladys,' Julia said quietly. 'If Arthur comes home and wants to know where she is, she's at Tremar.'

Gladys shook her head.

'Don't try and keep her up there, Julia,' she begged. 'He'll come and take her off you if you do, and that'll just be worse. It's only he's too bleddy lazy to make the effort at the moment, but you try making the rules, and he'll make her life a misery.'

'I won't try and keep her,' Julia replied, 'she'll be home tonight, I promise, but you tell him if she comes to me again bruised and battered, I'll have the law on him. And this much I promise you, Gladys, I will take her from him in the end, because I won't have him ruin her life. He ruined mine and obviously he's ruined yours as well, and he's not entitled to any more! We'll just see how long pride and sanctions take to make him come to his senses.'

Two mornings later at just after nine-thirty, 'young' Mr Cruikshank was shown into the morning-room at Tremar and greeted his client with polite, but obvious, delight. He was absurdly Victorian in his dress; seemed to have been left behind in another age, but Julia knew he was no fool, and as it happened she liked him a lot.

They shook hands warmly and he sat opposite her at the table. He said he would very much like some coffee and Mrs Collins was detailed to bring a fresh pot, then looking up at Julia steadily, he smiled.

'How was my choice of Matthew Logan as an estate manager, Miss Drake?' he enquired. 'Satisfactory?'

Julia smiled back.

'Oh, much more than that, Mr Cruikshank,' she replied. 'He's splendid, and absolutely marvellous at his job. As you can see from the windows the dower roof is well under way and he's arranging the redecoration of the whole house for me bit by bit; the decorators are already in upstairs. He's been around and introduced himself to all the tenants and he seems to think there will be no difficulty reviving the fortunes of Home Farm. Besides that he makes me feel very comfortably safe.'

The young, thin, prim Mr Cruikshank grinned at her – it was extraordinarily out of character!

'He certainly is a big chap!' he exclaimed. 'And he came with excellent references. Er – did he tell you anything about his past?'

Julia nodded.

'Everything about it.'

'And it doesn't worry you?'

'No more than mine worries him. We have a lot in common, Matt and I, as you well know, We've found a common bond here, too, in Annie Paynter, which is why I've asked you to call. Matt will be here in just a moment and I'd like to discuss Rectory Farm with him as well, if you don't mind, since any rules I make he'll have to enforce.'

Mr Cruikshank said he didn't mind waiting and continued to make mild small talk over a cup of coffee until Matt appeared at the door, coming in with the puppies at his heels. He shook hands with Mr Cruikshank as he took the third seat at the table.

To her astonishment, and with some admiration too, Julia noticed that although she and he had become really quite intimately friendly in the past weeks, not the slightest hint of that intimacy betrayed itself in front of the solicitor. Matt was politely formal with his employer to a degree that was quite unnerving.

Good Lord, she thought, if he did this to me without telling me why I'd be frantic. It feels as if he's displeased with me in some way, like it used to feel when a school friend was coldly formal and I knew I was in the doghouse. I'll have to watch it, or I'll be ingratiating myself.

'Well, to business then,' 'young' Mr Cruikshank said and took from a brown leather briefcase a variety of documents, yellowing and faded in places and obviously retrieved from some enormous dusty filing-system somewhere. 'After I received your call the morning before last, I talked at length to Father about it,' he said as he laid the paperwork on the table in front of him, 'because of course it was all formalized in the days when he was head of the firm. It's funny, you know, but he said he remembered it all very well because he hadn't approved at the time. Apparently he told Sir George that he shouldn't break up the estate, and if he felt he should reward Mr Paynter in some way for his services to Master Alexander, it certainly shouldn't be with swathes of woodland and life-long promises, as well as the farm.'

'Swathes of woodland?' Julia queried, and Mr Cruikshank hung some spectacles on his nose and flicked through the bewildering array of papers before him.

'He was given Rectory Farm, Swallows Wood and Fishers Way, which appears to be quite a wide belt of land adjoining the two sites. He was also granted free grazing rights to the two fields that back on to the Drake Arms, and the two fields that flank the road at the north end of the village. Added to that he was granted an annual income of one hundred pounds from Alexander Drake's estate; the Tremar estate buys all the timber from Swallows Wood and Fishers Way at a fixed price, for the Tremar Sawmills in Bodmin, and I understand now that he takes the Tremar apple harvest each year.' He looked up. 'And that is without the independent money he makes from his dairy herd and his sheep. If he was anything like a respectable farmer, Miss Drake, he would be very comfortable indeed.'

'Instead of which he lives in a slum, works his two lads half to death, beats his wife and cruelly ill-treats his wee lassie,' Matt Logan remarked bitterly. 'What a fine, upstanding citizen, is he not? My word that represents a fair quantity of alcohol passing through his liver!'

Julia drew her lips into a thin, sharp line.

'And exactly what can I do, legally, to stop this?' she enquired.

Mr Cruikshank perused his papers again, turning them over and neatly distributing them into piles.

'I see no reason why the estate should buy the timber at a fixed price,' he observed eventually. 'It should be sold on the open market with everyone else's timber – and it could be rejected by the sawmills. And obviously now you have an estate manager there won't be any question of his having the apple harvest any longer, of course.'

'And a hundred pounds a year from Sandro's estate?' she said. 'What estate, for Heaven's sake? Sandro died when he was twenty.'

'Young' Mr Cruikshank looked up at her sharply. He was like an intelligent crane, Julia, thought, very clever but very careful.

'You have an estate too, Miss Drake,' he replied quietly, 'apart from Tremar, that is. Your grandparents on your mother's side were very wealthy and they set up large trust funds for you and your brother when you were born. Your father was quite happy that they should do this, apparently it was a sort of family understanding. The money was invested and the necessary accounts were opened in your names. Your brother died without issue and without making a will, so control of it reverted to your father. You – er – well, it was expected that you also would die without issue, and anyway you were deemed mentally unfit to have any control of it, so that also reverted to your father.'

Julia's eyes flashed furiously.

'And he used part of it to pay for me to be kept a prisoner in Blackridge every year,' she spat. 'Not so much as a piece of clothing I could call my own, not a single, solitary luxury of any sort at all and *I* was paying with my *own* money! Jesus!' She got up with such violence that the puppies, sleeping at Matt's feet, jumped galvanically. 'I don't believe what's been done to me! He was my *father*! How can anyone treat their own flesh and blood in that way? Explain it to me, one of you, please!'

'Wee Annie . . .' Matt Logan muttered to no one in particular, carefully not looking at her. Abruptly she offered him a tight little smile.

'Thank you, Matt,' she murmured, returning to her chair. 'So, Mr Cruikshank, who now has control of Sandro's estate?'

He shrugged.

'Well technically you do,' he replied. 'You are the only survivor of the Drake family – the only one Cruikshank and Scattergood know about anyway, and so everything has fallen to you. When your mother asked for your release from Blackridge she was most particular about making a new will in your favour, and apart from certain small bequests, it was *all* to be left to you, without entail. All agreements made in the time of your father can now, I suppose, be legally broken. He made no provision for anything to continue after his death, not at the time anyway, and by the time he became ill the whole thing had long since been forgotten about. I doubt your mother even knew.'

Julia smiled triumphantly.

'Right then,' she said, 'I would like you to draw up some new legal papers for me please. All the money that was held in trust for Sandro is now to be held in trust for Annie Paynter, to be used as school fees and college fees when needed. Any money paid out to Arthur Paynter from the estate will cease forthwith, the Tremar Estate will no longer buy any timber from Swallows Wood and the apple crop is no longer available. He can keep the free grazing, it won't earn him anything, but if he feels the rest of the new restrictions will result in hardship for him and his family, Tremar would be perfectly willing to buy back Rectory Farm, at the current market price. However, if he chooses to sell but remain a tenant, he will immediately be subject to the rules all the other tenants abide by. There will be *no* special privileges, and I don't care a jot if he did save Sandro's life! Would you have that drafted into a letter please and sent to me. I should very much like it to be hand delivered.'

Cruikshank and Matt Logan glanced at each other very briefly and then looked at Julia. At the same moment it had struck them both that Julia's pathological hatred of Arthur Paynter was an abnormally violent reaction to his treatment of a child she had only known for a couple of months. It seemed as if she was allowing them to glimpse a wound so deep and so festering that it had eaten through to the bone. And in that instant they both instinctively knew the truth. Arthur Paynter was the reason Julia had been thrown into Blackridge.

Well, her father couldn't have known, Cruikshank thought as he began methodically to collect up his papers. Good Lord, poor old Sir George – miserable blighter that he was – the man who ruined his daughter and he rewarded him like a hero.

He carefully locked his briefcase and grasped the handle firmly, then took his leave of Matt. Julia walked with him to the front door and they stood together, looking at his black car on the drive, as the morning sun streamed in.

'That last time I saw Tremar, in 1915, it was a morning like this,' she whispered, 'only the sun was lower in the sky because it was winter. Every time I see it now I'm reminded of how much was stolen from me. Mr Cruikshank, Annie Paynter's father plans to have her shipped off to Falmouth after Christmas to be a housemaid. She'll be fifteen then and legally allowed to leave school, so apparently he can do it. Look into the legal implications of that for me, will you? See if there's anything that can be done to stop it.'

He smiled.

'I will,' he promised, 'and I'll have the other letter to you in a day or two. Goodbye, Miss Drake.'

She watched him go and then returned to Matt who was on the terrace with the puppies, apparently inspecting the fountain.

'They'll be starting on this next week,' he said, as she came out through the french windows, 'but I think they'll have to completely rebuild the basin, it looks badly cracked to me.'

Julia passed him, and leaned on the parapet, gazing intently across the lawns.

'You've guessed, haven't you?' she asked after a moment. 'I saw a certain look in your eyes. Do you condemn me?'

'What you might have done nigh on twenty-five years ago is no concern of mine, Julia,' he replied quietly, coming to lean beside her on the grey wall. 'But what you might be going to do as an act of revenge does concern me very much indeed. Remember, the likes of you and me are marked; singled out. Don't give anyone an opportunity to put you back into Blackridge for the rest of your life, whatever you do.'

Julia turned to look at him and they gazed at each other for a moment. His eyes were deep and penetrating and, absurdly, she wanted him to wrap her in his arms and hold her tight. To protect her.

'Keep an eye on me, Matt,' she said softly. 'I don't trust myself.'

'Oh, I'll be watching you, lass, I promise,' he replied.

Chapter I4

'Young' Mr Cruikshank rang later in the day to tell Julia it might take him a week or two to check all the legal implications of the letter, and to close any loopholes, pointing out that it needed to be absolutely watertight before it was delivered to Rectory Farm. Julia was happy enough. When you had spent as many years as she had in a situation where nothing happened at all, waiting a week or even a fortnight for something was singularly unimportant. Arthur would keep, and it was a long way to Christmas yet, so Annie was safe enough for the moment.

Annie was out of sight quite a lot of the time these days, Julia noticed, she seemed to want to divide her time equally between Julia and Matt. She was very anxious to help him with tasks at Home Farm and on the estate, and she seemed to want to impress him, which she actually did far more than he let on. She was far less inclined to have her nose stuck in a book than she had been, and Julia was quite happy about that. The child was fourteen and this was high summer, it was not a time to be shut in a stuffy library.

For Annie, life could not have been much better than it was during these halcyon days. Even having to go home to Rectory Farm every night was less frightening than it had been, because after Matt and Julia had come that morning to rescue her her father had seemed disinclined to come anywhere near her any more. She thought it might have been his fear of Matt; she knew, anyway, that he was frightened of Julia, though she didn't know why, but whatever it was she was greatly relieved to be able to creep in and out of her home in relative safety.

She asked Julia once if she could stay at Tremar and not have to go home at all, and Julia replied, 'If I get my way you will be able to, Annie, but for now I don't want to gave your father any weapons to use against us. You do understand, don't you?' Annie didn't understand, but she smiled and said she did, because that seemed to be what was expected of her.

Annie was growing up. When she had first picked the lock on the library door at Tremar she had been eleven years old and interested mostly in adventure stories, all of which she had devoured avidly. But the generations of Drakes who had added to the library had enjoyed diverse tastes in literature and at least one of them, in the not too distant past, had had a taste for somewhat erotic reading. When Annie had found these books she had dismissed them in the beginning, she had not been interested in love or sex. Now, when she thought Julia was busy somewhere else, she would occasionally snatch a look at them.

She found an illustrated book with a faintly Eastern-sounding name and, opening it, discovered on the frontispiece a drawing of a buxom-looking slave-girl with long, long black hair, standing beside a pool, completely naked, and wrapped in a heavy looking snake. She was dark-skinned with big, very red-tipped breasts and she held the snake's head close to her red mouth. A quick flick through the book, which was quite big and heavy, showed a number of other illustrations of Eastern-looking women in flimsy costumes with bare breasts and red mouths – and at least one gruesome story about human sacrifice. Annie decided she would like a more leisurely look at this book, somewhere in private, and so it was that she came to see something she definitely should not have seen and which she made sure she never let on about.

On her forays through the manor – and she never asked permission before she went nosing about – she had found a narrow staircase on the top floor which was boxed in but led to a large attic. It was a huge, lofty room with a small, square window which looked down on to the drive, and a floor littered with trunks and tea chests, old furniture and toys. Julia and Alexander's childhood was packed away up there, along with a wealth of very expensive, old-fashioned clothes and a couple of uniforms going back to their grandfather's time.

When Annie had first found the room, there were vague signs that once, probably many years ago, someone had had some sort of camp up there. Later, though, when she hadn't been there for a week or two and then scuttled up there one day in the rain to read in private, she found someone had made a bed in front of the window comprised of old mattresses and some pillows and blankets. And on a couple of occasions she made herself comfortable on it.

On a damp morning about ten days after the unpleasant incident with her father she sneaked into the library, took the book with the Eastern title and crept upstairs with it. Julia was in the morning-room working on some papers at the desk she had set up for herself in there; Matt wasn't anywhere about and Annie saw an opportunity for a few hours' reading without anyone knowing she was there. Settling down on the mattresses she began to leaf through the book – which was extremely grim in places and more than an hour flew by without her noticing.

When, abruptly, she heard footsteps on the attic stairs and quiet voices talking she almost jumped out of her skin. There was no way out, but she had no intention of being caught. She was where she shouldn't be, reading books she was sure Julia wouldn't approve of, and the only option open to her was to hide. So snatching up the book and hastily straightening the blankets on the makeshift bed, she scuttled away into the corner and took refuge behind a selection of tea chests. Crouching down, she peered through a gap and as she watched, she was astonished to see Julia and Oliver Crompton come across to the bed under the window.

Oliver took Julia in his arms and began to kiss her urgently, then, against her lips he murmured, 'I do find this exciting, you know, especially with Mrs Collins down there below us somewhere,' and he chuckled lasciviously.

Annie saw Julia stiffen, and turn from him slightly as she replied, 'How like a man. I really have no desire to play Russian roulette with my love-life – and I'm a great deal more frightened of Annie finding us than Mrs Collins – she doesn't even know this attic exists – but beggars can't be choosers, can they, Oliver?'

Annie put her hand over her mouth in a sort of horrified excitement, and in an agony of slow motion endeavoured to get a bit more comfortable without making a sound. In this she failed and saw Oliver turn his head sharply in her direction.

'I heard a noise,' he whispered, and Julia laughed at him softly.

'Of course you did, Oliver, we're in the attic,' she said. 'It creaks and groans up here all the time, at least it did when Sandro and I used to hide out up here. We used to spook each other sometimes with stories of ancestors who had crept up here to hide from the Roundheads and starved to death. Sandro said one of those old trunks has a spring lock on it and holds the bones of a long-ago lady who hid in it to protect herself and was never able to get it open again to get out. It's not true, of course, but it scared the hell out of me at the time.'

Oliver chuckled and kissed her again, his fingers busy with the buttons at the neck of her blouse.

'What a way to die,' he breathed, and the blouse fell away from her shoulders, whispering to the floor. Beneath it she wore a silk camisole and beneath that she was naked and as she put her hands to the waistband of her trousers, his hands cupped her breasts, stroking them softly with his fingers.

Annie's eyes opened wide in astonishment. From her hiding-place she could smell the strangely sweet, mingling smell of his cologne and Julia's perfume; it was a heady mixture. She could also see quite clearly, as Julia divested herself of the rest of her clothing, the thin, white scars on her back – but they didn't shock Annie like they had shocked Oliver. Annie had been beaten so many times in her young life that it didn't seem remarkable to her to find the scars of the whip on Julia's back.

When they were both naked they slid together on to the makeshift bed and began to make love. Annie was quite used to copulation, she had grown up on a farm and from the chickens upwards she had seen almost all the animals do it at some time. Copulation between animals was a strangely unemotional business. What was happening between Oliver and Julia however was entirely different, and not a lot like what she had gleaned from the books she had read either.

In the weak, rather grey light that filtered in through the attic window their bodies seemed to ripple and flow in their emotion. They were beautiful, both of them, firm and strong and their soft cries of pleasure were instinctive, almost abandoned. As she rose to her climax, Julia arched her back, thrusting upwards to meet him, and Oliver broke out in a thin sheen of sweat. They panted in their excitement, their mouths seeming almost to devour each other in their hunger, their hands clawing at each other's bodies. Annie stared in fascination as Julia's body suddenly shuddered violently and she uttered a deep cry of pleasure. A second later Oliver jerked, drew his breath in a couple of sobs and exhaled in a long, long sigh.

Slowly, contentedly, they relaxed and sank down, lying quiescent in each other's arms, all passion spent.

Julia whispered, 'Oh, God, that was good.'

But Annie, who had watched in complete, unembarrassed fascination, felt a sense of deep and savage resentment.

She didn't want it to be Oliver doing that to Julia. She wanted it to be

Matt!

After a moment or two Oliver rolled on his back and threw out his arm so that she could lie with her head against his shoulder. Julia lay on her side, her hand on his chest, her scarred back towards Annie. She kissed him and they smiled at each other, then a brief, slightly uncomfortable silence seemed to hang between them for a couple of moments, which eventually he broke.

'You never make me any promises, do you?' he observed quietly. 'You always tell me how good it was, but you never tell me you love me. Will you ever commit yourself to me, Julia?'

She sighed. She didn't want this conversation now. She wanted him, just once, to be grateful for what he had, not constantly searching for more.

'It isn't as simple as that, Oliver,' she replied, 'there are other people to be considered in this, not least Sophie and your children.' Abruptly she shifted her position slightly. 'And for me, there's Minnie and Annie. Minnie is not going to die in Blackridge, she was the only friend I had for almost twenty-four years and I owe it to her – and I have a vested interest in saving Annie, not just for her, for me too. I want her, she's mine by rights if you like, and I mean to have her. It means I simply can't make promises which I very well might not be able to keep.'

'You have a vested interest in getting your own back on her father, you mean?' he remarked, and she seemed to jerk slightly, giving him the idea that he'd said something wrong. He muttered 'Oops, tactless . . . I'm sorry.' And to his surprise she gave him a warm smile.

'No,' she said softly, 'not as tactless as you think. Arthur and Annie don't really go together, and yet, of course, they do. I'm not saying I wouldn't feel as affectionate towards the child if Arthur wasn't her father, or that I wouldn't feel so duty-bound to save her from him, but dear God I want my revenge. You've seen the scars on my back and you must be quite well aware of the pain I endured when they were put there. The man who did it to me didn't even bother to find out if I had a name, he called me an idiot and he said that whipping an idiot to teach it its place was like whipping a dog to train it! Well I don't know if Arthur whips his dogs, but I do know he beats his child and I know *exactly* the pain and fear she endures when he does it. The same fear and pain that I endured because of what he did to me in the beginning.'

'But taking Annie from Paynter won't punish him,' Oliver pointed out. 'He doesn't want the child.'

Julia smiled coldly.

'No, but he doesn't want me to have her, so I'm going to take her anyway,' she replied. 'And at the same time I'm going to ruin him. That's already under way: he receives a letter from me tomorrow which effectively cuts off half his income. He can have it back when he gives me Annie – all except the yearly payment from Sandro's estate. He can damn well whistle for that!'

Oliver brushed some strands of hair from her face as Annie watched, enthralled, through a tiny gap in the boxes.

'So you want to take her from him as an act of revenge, then?' he asked and Julia turned her head away from him and seemed to Annie to look directly at her for a moment, Annie closed her eyes and drew back. She knew Julia didn't know she was there and yet it seemed they gazed into each other's eyes, She waited, breathlessly, for the reply.

After a moment Julia said, 'No, Oliver. I want her because I love her.' And hard little Annie Paynter, who had learned years ago not to cry and only ever did it now when her father hurt her so much she had to, felt her eyes fill with tears and a great lump grow in her throat. So maybe after all she could have what she dreamed of, a home at Tremar with Julia and Matt – and she would work so hard to earn it, she promised God, as she crouched behind a box and her nose ran with her emotion. She'd be the best housemaid Julia had *ever* had, and when she wasn't dusting and polishing, she'd be at Home Farm helping Matt. Only please, please, let Julia stay for ever at Tremar!

Annie's dreams were way off beam.

Oliver Crompton raised himself on his elbow and looked down at Julia steadily as outside in the fresh air the last of the rain clouds had cleared away and the sun was flooding everything with warmth and light.

'You're never going to come to London with me, are you?' he asked softly, touching her face with his fingers. 'Admit it, you're not.'

Julia frowned at him.

'I didn't know you were going,' she replied truthfully, 'or was it a rhetorical question?'

He shook his head.

'Julia, there's a war coming,' he said. 'Oh, I know everybody talks about peace, but we all know there'll be war and there's no more we can do to stop it this time than we could last time. I'm selling up my practice and going back to London, maybe even before Christmas, I must make arrangements for Sophie and the children, get my affairs in order, do the things one has to do before one goes to war. I suppose I'd dreamed of coming home on leave and finding you waiting for me, but it isn't going to be like that, is it? Please tell me, it'll make things easier if I'm not kidding myself any longer.'

She felt a strange mixture of emotions. The idea of his going away to fight and perhaps never coming back, like Sandro, was painful, whilst the idea of not having him there any more, propping her up as he had done since he had first found her in Blackridge was quite frightening. Yet the idea of him no longer making demands on her which she simply could not fulfil was oddly comforting, He wouldn't be there to make love to her, certainly, but he wouldn't either be trying to manipulate her into being someone she didn't want to be.

'Well if there is going to be a war, Oliver,' she said carefully, trying to be tactful, 'I'm not sure I'd want to be sitting in the middle of London amidst the bombing waiting for you anyway.'

He chuckled ruefully.

'I wouldn't expect you to be in the middle of London, which you very well know,' he pointed out.

'But you wouldn't expect me to be at Tremar either, no doubt,' she murmured, 'and this is the only place I could ever want to be. We'll all have to do our bit, Oliver, and I can do mine right here. Matt tells me Home Farm will be back to full production in three to five years' time and reviving Home Farm means giving work to local people. Food will be a priority in a war and I want to go out there and grow some along with him. I could never sit around anywhere and do nothing whilst I desperately waited for you to come home on leave, you must understand that.'

'So you won't be coming with me?' He had begun to reach for his clothes, and clambering to his feet he started to get dressed. Julia did the same, which was a relief to Annie since she was beginning to feel seriously cramped behind her boxes.

'All right, no, I won't,' Julia answered. 'But I'll always be here, Oliver, if you want to see me – or is it all over between us now, because of what I've said?'

In the act of tying his tie he turned and gave her a gentle look, his head slightly on one side, then he reached for her mouth with his own and kissed her hungrily.

'What was the old music-hall joke?' he said. 'The show's not over till the fat lady sings? It won't be all over for me until the day I drive away from Polwean for the very last time and know I won't see you again.'

It would be, though, quite some time before he drove away from

Polwean for the very last time.

He went down and out into the sunshine and at once managed to push what she had said to him into the back of his mind. She said now she didn't want to leave, but when his practice was actually sold, well that would be different – when they were counting the days to saying goodbye. Oliver was very good at spinning off into day-dreams, it was easier than facing the truth. He loved her and his male vanity wouldn't allow him to believe she simply didn't love him in return.

Annie waited about an extra twenty minutes in the attic then slipped down through the house, went round the side of the dower and came back in by the terrace. Julia was in the morning-room sitting at her desk writing letters. As Annie opened the door cautiously and crept in she looked up and smiled.

'Oh there you are!' she exclaimed. 'I was beginning to wonder where on earth you'd got to. Have you been at Home Farm with Matt?'

Annie shook her head.

'Er – no,' she replied, 'I just . . . bin around, you know. I ent seen Matt today.'

Julia shrugged.

'No, I haven't, either,' she said, and got up from her desk. To her surprise Annie, in a fairly rare gesture of spontaneous affection encircled her with her arms and hugged her fiercely. 'Oh, thank you,' she beamed. 'What did I do to deserve that?'

Annie couldn't say, though she would have liked to. Instead she looked up into Julia's face and grinned.

'Can we do something, this afternoon?' she asked.

Julia shrugged.

'Well yes, if you can think of anything exciting. Oh I know, Wednesday afternoons those two poisonous old spinsters in the village shop sell ice-cream, don't they? How would you like to walk down to the village with me and buy some? In fact it's such a lovely afternoon, we could ask Mrs Collins to pack up some sandwiches and cake and we could go down to the bay for a picnic. How would that be?'

'Lovely,' Annie replied. 'Can Matt come with us?'

'Matt!' Julia stared at her. 'Well, not really. I mean – look, Annie, he's my estate manager, he's supposed to be working for me. I can't suddenly suggest he stops what he's doing and comes down to the bay for a picnic and a paddle, it's not the thing. You've got quite a crush on Matt, haven't you?'

Annie stared at her ruefully.

'No,' she answered with blunt truthfulness. 'But I wish you had!'

They set off after lunch, leaving Mrs Collins making egg sandwiches in the kitchen amid the smell of fresh baking, If she disapproved of the idea of taking cake and sandwiches to the beach, she knew better than to say so, but she muttered darkly about Julia's request to have a few extra sandwiches for later and forgo her normal big, cooked meal.

'One proper meal every day,' she muttered, 'I always says that's a must, but there you are, if you don't want nothing but sandwiches. . . .'

'Mrs Collins, I'm putting on simply pounds and pounds with all your lovely food,' Julia replied soothingly, 'it really won't do me any harm to go without once in a while, and Annie and I might stay late in the bay, it would be too awful if your lovely dinner was spoiled.'

Mrs Collins tightened her lips and banged away to take her cake from the oven and Julia and Annie grabbed the moment to slip quietly out of the kitchen.

'Oh Lord,' Julia whispered, as they crept down the corridor towards the front door, 'we're in the doghouse again,' and Annie burst out laughing.

From such an unpromising beginning the day was turning out to be simply splendid and Annie felt so proud walking down the long drive to the front gates and then on down the winding road to Polwean with Julia. The road was quite narrow and the hedgerows smelt deliciously fresh after the morning rain – and it really seemed quite hard to believe life wouldn't just go on for ever being this perfect.

'Will you stay at Tremar for ever and ever now?' she suddenly asked, mindful of the conversation she had had no business to overhear earlier in the day.

Julia turned to smile at her and her hair glinted in the sunshine. So did Annie's, that wonderful, rich red, the same extraordinarily beautiful hair she had looked down upon that day she had climbed the cliffs on her first afternoon home from school, and had seen Arthur and the twins gazing up at her, and wanted Arthur so badly.

'Well I can't see why not,' she replied. 'What makes you ask?'

'I was thinking of the doctor,' Annie muttered vaguely and Julia frowned at her.

'Why?'

' 'Cos I saw you kissing him that day. . . .'

'Annie, I'm not going anywhere with Oliver Crompton,' Julia said firmly, mindful now herself of the conversation earlier in the day – which she didn't know Annie had overheard. 'Tremar is my home and I waited nearly a quarter of a century to get it back, why should I want to leave it?'

Annie narrowed her green eyes against the brightness of the sun.

'Then I wish you'd tell me about you and my pa,' she murmured, 'cos he'm always banging on about you. I heard him telling Ma the other day that he was going to have you put back into Blackridge.'

Julia stopped and turned, putting her hands on the child's shoulders.

'He's never going to do that, Annie,' she promised, adding suddenly, with a tiny shiver, 'he'd have to die doing it!'

When they came to the green it was sparkling in the sunshine. The ivy-covered Drake Arms, the shady, leafy trees fringing the edge of the green itself, the church, warm grey in the sunshine.

Suddenly Annie said, 'You ever bin in there and seen that statue of your brother?' and Julia found her eyes drawn suddenly to the place where the mortal remains of her parents lay side by side.

She felt very slightly squeamish.

'I haven't had the courage yet,' she admitted.

Annie smiled at her.

'You ought to,' she murmured, 'its *ever* so beautiful. People comes from all over to see it, you know. We could go in now if you like, you'd have me for company then.'

Julia stared at her for a moment, then grinned and took her hand.

'Right, you're on,' she declared, and with firm footsteps they set off towards the lich-gate.

The church was cool but bright, the floor stained many colours with sunshine streaming in through a stained-glass window. Julia hadn't been in there since she was seventeen – the last time, she remembered, she had been alone, kneeling in terrified prayer, gazing up at a marble reredos of a benign-looking, splendid God, surrounded by his angels.

He might have looked benign and splendid, but he hadn't listened.

Or maybe she'd deserved her punishment. Her father had snarled at them once when they were children because one hot Sunday they hadn't wanted to go to church. They were Christians, he had pointed out severely, and anyway, it was their place to set an example to their tenants.

Christians! What sort of a Christian shut his daughter in a lunatic asylum because she was having a baby? What sort of a Christian refused to utter her name ever again, even though he knew she was still alive and probably suffering appalling abuse? What sort of example did *that* set the tenants? Jesus Christ had preached forgiveness of sins – but apparently her father had missed that.

Maybe that was the Sunday *he* didn't go, she thought wryly.

The statue of Alexander Drake was cold and ghostly white. He lay on his back with his ankles crossed and his eyes closed in sleep – or death? But the face was a shocking, remarkable likeness, perfectly sculpted and instantly recognizable. Julia drew her breath sharply and with a trembling hand reached out to touch his marble lips.

'Oh, Sandro . . .' she whispered, and her face crumpled as she groaned softly and rested her forehead against his marble curls, feeling the cold seeping through her skin. 'Dear God how could they have done this? How could they have borne to come in here week after week and look at it?'

Running her hand along the shiny, grey, Italian marble catafalque on which his exquisite six-foot effigy lay, she went slowly to the head and read the gold-lettered inscription.

'But you aren't *here*, are you?' she murmured, touching the cold, white face. 'No matter how much they spent, you're not here. I might get a sense of you, perhaps, if I was to go to Ypres and find you amongst your companions, but you're not here. Sandro, my darling, I miss you so much.'

'Is it like him, your brother?' Annie suddenly asked quietly, reminding Julia of her presence.

She smiled softly.

'Just like him. I don't know who did it, but it's brilliant.' She touched the lips of the statue once more and then turned away from him to look down the church. All around the walls there were other marble memorials to members of her family, ancestors from centuries ago. Some of them sported draped urns, or weeping angels, none of them were anything like the size of Alexander's monument, but they spoke volumes of belonging, of having a history. They and all they stood for were what she had been punished for.

'We used to have to come here every Sunday morning without fail,' she said to Annie as they gazed about them, 'and sit with ramrod straight backs in the family pew. The vicar back then was old and probably the most boring man in Christendom. He used to plough on through his sermon, with his false teeth rattling and clicking and he used to get so lost in the secondary thickets of his thoughts that he never actually made a single point, that I remember. God, it was awful!'

Annie grinned.

'I ent never bin to church,' she admitted cheerfully, 'but I like the vicar, he'm not a bad sort really.'

'No, you're right, he's not,' Julia agreed. 'He came to see me when I first came home and he was very pleasant. He seemed quite understanding actually and I don't think he ever expected me to start coming to church again. Oh, I've had enough of this, come on let's go and buy some ice-cream.'

Outside it was hot and sunny, warming their skins after the coolness of the church. Julia cast her eyes quickly in the direction of the family vault, tucked in the corner of the churchyard, so much bigger than everything else. It had an Albertine rose growing up the side of it, the pink flowers profuse and glowing in the sunshine.

'You'll be buried in there one day, won't you?' Annie asked, and she shook her head.

'Not on your nelly!' she retorted. 'But I shall come back to see Sandro sometimes, while I'm alive. Thank you for giving me the courage to come in.'

The bell above the door jangled harshly as Julia and Annie walked into Miss Penrose and Miss Hewlett's village shop. Inside it smelt predominantly of cheese. Miss Penrose was behind the scrubbed wooden counter, Miss Hewlett was on a step-ladder, lifting something down from a tall shelf. They were elderly ladies now, surprisingly elderly to Julia who had to hastily remind herself she hadn't seen them for almost twenty-four years.

Miss Penrose's eyes gleamed and she offered Julia a strangely ingratiating smile.

'Why, Julia Drake,' she observed, 'we thought you was never going to get round to visiting us, didn't we, Miss Hewlett? We said as how we couldn't believe you had developed airs and graces since you bin away, it just wouldn't be like you.'

Miss Hewlett climbed down from her step-ladder.

'Indeed no, Miss Penrose,' she replied, 'and didn't we say as how Julia was always in here with the village children, when her was a lass? Always ready to throw her penny in with the others and enjoy the share out. Alexander, too, God rest his soul.'

Julia could have thrown something at the pair of them, repulsive old spinsters that they were. She remembered quite well her mother's crisp dismissal of them, years ago when she had been small – and they had been relatively young: 'Viper-tongued and vulgar-minded!'

'Yes, well, I'm grown up now,' she said, quite unable to stop herself flattening her voice, 'and I don't do my own shopping these days. My word . . . ladies, you look just the same as you always did.'

'Well, we'll take that as a compliment,' observed Miss Hewlett, and worked her mouth in her strange fashion. Suddenly she turned her gimlet eye upon Annie and her neck seemed to stiffen. 'Can that be you, Annie Paynter!' she exclaimed sharply. 'All dressed up? What're you doing in here, might I ask? And where did you get them posh clothes?'

'Annie is in here with me.' Julia snapped officiously, 'and her dress and shoes came from me, too – if it's anybody else's business.'

Miss Penrose's mouth tightened at the rebuke, but it didn't keep her quiet.

'She's to be housemaid at Tremar then, is she?' she said. 'I had heard a rumour, though I wondered if it could possibly be true . . . I shall know then, shall I, when she's in here shopping for you?'

'Annie is not a housemaid at Tremar, Miss Penrose,' Julia replied with an entirely mirthless smile. 'Annie is my friend, and if I may say so, you shouldn't listen to rumours, they're so often wrong, I find. It's school-holiday time at the moment, so we're going to have a picnic in the bay this afternoon and we've come down to the village to buy some ice-cream.'

If either of the old women had been going to say anything else they were prevented from doing so by the sharp jangle of the shop bell. Julia turned and with a jolt she saw Sophie Crompton struggling in through the door with a push-chair. Sophie didn't see Julia until she was fully in the shop and when she did she seemed to fetch up short and her face flushed uncomfortably. Julia prayed that she wouldn't show her feelings in front of the old biddies.

To avoid any awkwardness she leapt in first.

'Mrs Crompton!' she exclaimed with a wide smile. 'How nice to see you. I haven't seen you for such a long time.'

'Miss Drake,' Sophie murmured, 'and Annie, if I'm not much mistaken. You look very smart, Annie.'

She turned automatically to draw little, dark-haired Alice towards her; it was a nervous sort of movement and she was tired-looking and untidy. She was also, Julia noted, extremely thin, the arms sticking out of her short-sleeved summer dress were like pale pink sticks.

Julia was anxious not to give either of the poisonous shopkeepers a chance to get a word in. Hastily she said, 'Mrs Crompton, Annie and I are going to the bay this afternoon for a picnic. Mrs Collins is making us all sorts of goodies and we thought we'd really spoil ourselves and have some ice-cream. Look, I've got a wonderful idea, why don't you and the children come with us? There'll be plenty of food, and you did promise you'd bring them down for a swim in the bay one day during the summer. Please say you will.'

Sophie Crompton felt like crying. The last thing she wanted to do was go and sit in the bay at Tremar with her husband's mistress. And she was his mistress, even if he wouldn't admit it, she was sure of that. He had as good as told her that when they left Polwean she and the children were going back to her parents, but at some point Julia would be waiting in London for him.

She muttered, 'I really don't think—' but Julia was determined to shut her up.

'Oh, please!' she exclaimed. 'I won't take no for an answer. Let's see who I can get on my side. Alice,' she bent down towards the pretty child, 'wouldn't you like to come to the bay this afternoon? Annie will be there and we could bring the puppies, probably.'

Alice turned her big, dark eyes up towards her mother and tugged at her hand.

'Please, mummy?' she begged, '*please*!'

Sophie felt trapped and miserable – but then, she thought bitterly, Oliver was always sniping at her for being a shrinking violet, so perhaps she should accept the invitation and perhaps she and Julia Drake could do some straight talking whilst they were about it. Unless of course the woman just wanted to gloat? Oh, dear God, please don't let that be the case – but what could she do, in front of these awful old women?

'Yes, well . . . thank you,' she finally murmured uncomfortably. 'It seems Alice is very keen on the idea, so we should be happy to accept your invitation.'

'Marvellous!' Julia cried, and turning to Miss Penrose and Miss Hewlett, who she knew had been hoping for a showdown, she said, 'Two large bricks of ice-cream, if you please, ladies and a packet of wafer biscuits, and would you be so kind as to wrap the ice-crean well in lots of newspaper, so that it doesn't melt on the way home? You're very kind.'

Outside the shop, as she stood with Sophie Crompton and her children in the sunshine she found herself still trying to keep the cheer in the conversation.

'Shall Annie and I go back to Tremar and collect the picnic and then wait for you?' she asked. 'Or would you like us to wait while you go back to Lamplighter House and collect the children's bathing things?'

Sophie Crompton stared at her resentfully.

'I don't want to have a picnic with you, Miss Drake,' she muttered unhappily, and Julia reached out and touched her arm softly.

'I know you don't,' she replied, 'and I don't blame you, but I do want to talk to you so badly. I – want to set some records straight, I think, because I don't think Oliver always tells you the truth, and I *had* to stop you saying too much in front of those two old witches. Believe me, Mrs Crompton, they are more trouble than pretty well everyone else in this village put together, they always have been.'

Abruptly Sophie smiled at her. It was a sad, somewhat wry smile.

'Oh, I know the things they say about me,' she said quietly, 'and I know when they're talking about me, too, because they always go quiet immediately when I walk into the shop. They look at me so pityingly, and I don't want their pity.'

'Which is just as well,' Julia murmured, 'because they haven't an ounce of genuine pity in them, either of them. My mother said they were viper-tongued and vulgar-minded and she was quite right. Come on, let's let them see us walk away together, it'll do them good.'

Sophie Crompton suddenly grinned.

'I'll nip in home and get the children's beach things,' she said, 'and then walk up to Tremar with you, if I may. Would you mind waiting, I promise I won't be long?'

She went into Lamplighter House with Alice, leaving the pushchair containing Edward outside with Annie and Julia. Annie had been very quiet for sometime, and it suddenly occurred to Julia that she was sulking.

'And what's up with you?' she asked. 'You have a face as long as a fiddle.'

Annie scowled at her.

'I suppose I have to splash in the water with Alice and *him*?' she pointed at the sleeping toddler in the pushchair, 'while you sit on a rug with her and talk all afternoon?'

Julia recognized a flash of jealousy. To Annie she was private property and only to be shared with Matt, and since Annie couldn't stand Oliver, it stood to reason she wasn't going to like Oliver's wife and children. Snarling at her was going to simply make things worse. Thinking swiftly, she came up with what seemed to be a sufficient sweetener.

'It's Thursday tomorrow,' she said casually, looking not at the child but at the door of Lamplighter House. 'I was thinking of asking you if you wanted to come to Blackridge with Matt and me.'

'*Really*?' Annie whispered, and Julia smiled at her.

'But only if you're nice to Alice and Edward this afternoon, of course.'

Annie glanced at her sideways.

'All right,' she offered, not very graciously, 'but you got to promise me.'

'Promise you what?' Julia demanded suspiciously, and Annie's green eyes seemed suddenly to gaze flintily into her soul.

'You got to promise you'm going to tell her same as you told me,' she said, her chin thrust out, 'that you'm staying at Tremar for ever!'

Chapter 15

It was ridiculous really: Oliver's two women sitting on a rug on the beach together, watching the children playing; the one he didn't want any more and the one who didn't want him. It kept going through Julia's head and she suspected it kept going through Sophie's as well. They were so different: thin, nervous, untidy Sophie, and lean, beautifully groomed Julia. But circumstances had thrown them together and suddenly, it seemed to Julia, they needed to stick together as an act of solidarity.

Julia had left a message with Mrs Collins when she collected the picnic that if she was to see Matt she was to ask him to bring the puppies down to the bay. After that, with both of them making heavy weather of non-comittal small talk, she and Sophie had walked through the grounds with Annie and the children until they had finally reached the shore and there, with it all to themselves, they had spread their rugs and settled down.

Annie was being very good indeed, considering she didn't really care for small children, and with her dress tucked into her knickers she was holding Edward's hands as he splashed clumsily about on the edge of the water and calling encouragement to Alice, who was making swimming movements in about six inches of water.

They were happy, they were thoroughly enjoying themselves, and for the first time for months, Sophie was free of complete responsibility for them. She took the pins out of her hair and let it fall like silky corn around her shoulders and even as she sat, her arms clasped around her knees, she began to visibly relax.

'We'll have to eat that ice-cream soon,' Julia said after a while, 'otherwise it'll all be melted. Shall I make up a wafer for everyone and then we can eat the sandwiches and cake later?'

Sophie nodded and smiled and watched as Julia began to prepare the ice-creams. Julia's hands were groomed now, her nails well manicured and all the blue staining from the material at Blackridge long gone, but she wore no jewellery other than one small, pearl ring on the little finger of her right hand, and twenty-three years of sewing, scrubbing floors, making beds and general heavy work had left their mark. Hers were not the hands of an idle lady.

'What was it like at Blackridge?' Sophie suddenly asked as she watched the progress of the ice-creams. 'Was it as awful as I think it must have been?'

Julia glanced up at her without rancour.

'Thank you for asking,' she replied quietly. 'Most people don't like to mention it, and I'm quite happy to talk about it. It was dreadful, like a prolonged nightmare. It's very hard to generalize and I don't want to bore you with the details, but suffice to say it was quite difficult to stay sane all those years.'

'Yes, I'll bet it was,' Sophie murmured, tucking her fly-away hair behind her ears as the breeze blew it across her face. 'When Oliver came home that first time after he'd seen you he could hardly talk about it he was so horrified. He was angry with your mother, too. He thought she should have done something sooner.'

Julia looked up at her quickly.

'Did he tell her he was angry with her?' she asked, and Sophie grinned.

'I don't think so. He was a bit scared of your mother, she was very sharp-tongued in her old age, you know.'

'She was sharp-tongued when she was young, as well,' Julia remarked, 'but she was hidebound by duty, and if my father said she wasn't ever to talk to me or think about me again, she obeyed without question. Well, if not without question entirely, without voicing the question, anyway.'

'What was your father like, Miss Drake?' Sophie asked with sudden genuine interest. 'I can't imagine any father doing what he did, you know, it seems so impossible to contemplate.'

Julia narrowed her eyes slightly and gazed into the distance, watching the sun sparkling on an azure-blue sea.

'He was very tall,' she murmured thoughtfully, 'Well over six foot and I can never remember him with any hair to speak of. His head was domed and his face was long and thin. He wore pince-nez balanced on the end of his long nose, they made him look dreadfully severe – and yet, he could laugh heartily if he wanted to, and did, regularly. He always wore expensive suits and beautifully coloured waistcoats, and he always had a white silk hanky in his breast-pocket and blew his nose on a black silk one . . . and I loved him, very much, until he betrayed me. I still can't really believe he did what he did to me, but the thought of him now almost chokes me – can you understand that?'

'Oh, God, yes,' Sophie whispered and to her own and Julia's amazement she spontaniously put her hand out and touched Julia's arm, very gently, with her fingers.

For a few seconds they held each other's gaze and it was as if there was a sudden and deep understanding between them, then Julia abruptly broke the spell.

'Children!' she called. 'Ice-creams! Come and get them before they melt.'

Annie and Alice took their ice-creams and went to sit on a rock to eat them, Edward stayed close to his mother since she had to help him with his. It was obvious to Julia that Alice was developing quite a little *schwärmerei* for Annie. She copied the way she sat and the way she ate her ice-cream, and she contrived to touch her at every opportunity. It was obvious, too, that Annie rather liked being the object of the child's adoration and was going out of her way to be patient and attentive.

Well, that won't do you any harm, Julia thought in high amusement, and since I think that's the way you've been feeling about me pretty well since the day you met me at least you've learned that as the adored object it's your job to be patient and attentive. You get on with it, my girl and leave me to extricate myself from Oliver.

When Edward had finally finished with his ice-cream there didn't seem to be an inch of him that wasn't sticky and Julia watched as Sophie patiently cleaned him up with a damp face-flannel. He looked at his little pink hands when she had finished with them and then held them up delightedly for everyone to see how clean they were, grinning all over his cherubic face. He had lovely, fair, curly hair that glinted in the sun and astonishingly sturdy little arms and legs – and he was Oliver's son.

Julia tried to examine her feelings as she remembered the white scar on her stomach which was her badge of childlessness. She remembered too, albeit hazily, expelling her half-grown baby from her body all those years ago; the smell of the room and the complete lack of warmth or concern from those around her. She looked at pretty, fragile Sophie Crompton and she thought, You never would have survived it, you would have died in that place, faded away as they systematically abused you. Oh dear, I *wish* you weren't married to Oliver, because he's much too selfish for someone like you, and all your married life he'll use you, but there's certainly nothing I can do about that.

A breeze blew across the bay, it ruffled Sophie's hair and seemed to make her look up suddenly. She rubbed her thin legs, as if she was abruptly cold and she looked directly into Julia's eyes. 'Do you think there's going to be a war, Miss Drake?' she asked.

Julia shrugged her shoulders.

'I don't see how we can avoid it,' she replied truthfully. 'That man Hitler's never going to stop at what it's been agreed he can have, no matter what promises he makes. Sooner or later he's going to want more and then he'll just march in and take it.'

'And what will you do?' Now there was no mistaking the hostility in Sophie's eyes; they were bright and uncomfortably penetrating.

At last, Julia thought, we've finally arrived at Oliver, thank goodness for that!

'I shall stay here and grow food, Mrs Crompton,' she replied firmly. 'Matt, my estate manager, is even now beginning the revival of the fortunes of Home Farm and I shall go out there with him and till the soil. It's the only thing I know how to do, and the only thing I want to do.'

'You don't plan to go to London, then?'

There was a pause, it was long and uncomfortable and abruptly Julia decided to lay all her cards face up on the table. She took a long, deep breath, checked briefly where Annie and Alice were and then licked her lips.

'Mrs Crompton,' she said, 'If I'm speaking out of turn then I'm sorry, but I don't think I am, I know what they're saying about Oliver and me all over the village and I've a shrewd idea Oliver is compounding the felony. He thinks he's in love with me, but the fact is I don't love him. I'm extremely grateful to him. He saved my life and you can't not be grateful to someone who does that, but I am never going to leave Tremar again, not for anyone. I waited more than half my lifetime to get back here and it means more to me than anything. He has spoken about selling his practice and returning to London, he says he wants to get his affairs in order before he goes to war, and I have told him, very firmly, that I won't be going with him.'

Sophie had looked away as Julia began to speak and to her horror she felt her eyes filling up with tears. To cry in front of this woman for whom her husband planned to desert her was humiliating. She opened her mouth to say something and nothing but a small sob came out, which was even more humiliating. Abruptly the tears overflowed and trickled down her cheeks.

'Damn!' she exclaimed, and fought to control herself grimly.

'You know, he doesn't really love me,' Julia murmured, being extremely careful not to look at her. 'He's in love with the tragedy of what I was, the idea of my life at Blackridge, the abuse I suffered. It's a grotesque fantasy and it has a kind of horrible fascination for him. You are his wife and the mother of his children, you're always there, so he treats you with contempt. If you were to leave him I think he'd be devastated, The fact is he doesn't deserve you.'

'He doesn't *want* me,' Sophie sobbed, quite unable to stem her tears. 'He thought he did when he married me, now he wants a Valkyrie, a Rhine maiden.'

'And I am neither of those things,' Julia replied quietly. 'I'm an embittered ex-inmate of a hideous asylum with plans of my own. For twenty-three-and-a-half years Minnie stood by me, loved me and relied on me and as soon as it can be arranged she will be coming to live with me. Annie is a clever, brutalized child who needs protecting from her horrible father and as soon as I've wrested control of her from him, she's going to school. My beautiful home is undergoing much needed restoration and Home Farm is virtually derelict but is going to be needed in the near future. I'm selfish, Mrs Crompton, I've been denied for more than half of my life, and from now on I'm going to have only what I want. My plans do *not* include Oliver.'

Sophie scrubbed her tears away roughly with her hands. If she'd been bolder, she thought, she might have pointed out that if Julia was planning so firmly to turn Oliver out of her life, now might be a good time to turn him out of her bed, but Sophie had been brought up in a strict middle-class home where sex was never even hinted at, let alone talked about, and 'affairs' were something other people had. The aristocracy, she had been taught, had the morals of alley cats; Julia was aristocracy and she had been locked away in the first place for being pregnant.

But Sophie Crompton had learned a valuable lesson from this afternoon that she had spent with Julia Drake. She might be bitterly jealous of her, but she couldn't help admiring her for her strength. She was –

eventually – going to send Oliver packing, and for once in his life he wasn't going to get his own way.

Sophie smiled at Julia and Julia was immediately aware that the tension between them was slightly eased. It was time to change the subject. The conversation could not progress further without deep embarrassment and it might never be raised again, but at least this thin, pretty, delicate waif had had the courage to come this far. She was not entirely the shrinking violet Oliver dismissed her for.

'I think we ought to have tea,' Julia said, 'the children must be starving hungry.'

So they sat on the rugs in the sunshine, the two women and the three pretty children, eating their picnic in comfortable companionship. When they had almost finished Matt came through the gate in the wall with the puppies and Alice watched, full of admiration, as Annie showed off how well trained they were. Matt drank some tea from one of the thermos flasks and in his tranquil way talked briefly to Julia about the day's progress at Home Farm. Sophie watched them.

She thought she couldn't be sure, because she had no experience of that sort of thing, but it seemed to her, from the way he looked at her, that Matt Logan was rather taken with Julia Drake.

It was very early the next morning, before eight o'clock, when Matt knocked at the kitchen door of Rectory Farm. Arthur Paynter opened the door to him and took an involuntary step backwards when he saw who was standing on his threshold, but Matt made no attempt to enter.

'I have a letter for you,' he said politely, handing the envelope which was carefully sealed with sealing-wax to Arthur. 'Miss Drake told me to tell you that should you have any queries about it she'll be pleased to see you at Tremar.' He half turned as if he was about to leave, then very slowly he turned back and bent close to Arthur. 'Oh, and by the by,' he said in a tone that was softly menacing, 'the lassie is going on a trip this afternoon, we're expecting her at the manor by mid-morning. If she doesn't arrive, or when she does she's showing signs of bruising, I'll be back, Mr Paynter, wanting an explanation. Do I make myself clear?'

Arthur sneered angrily; bloody Scotsman threatening him on his own doorstep. He knew what he'd like to do – if he didn't lack the courage.

In a sort of half-hearted gesture of defiance he thrust the letter back at Matt, squaring his jaw indignantly.

'I don't want no letter from the bitch up there,' he declared. 'Take it back and tell her I ent interested.'

Matt shrugged, but made no attempt to touch the letter.

'If you don't read it,' he said, 'you'll be wondering about the changes, Mr Paynter, because whether you know about them or not, they're going to happen. I should read it, if I were you. Good-morning.'

He crossed the filthy yard towards the car and Arthur slammed the door shut behind him. Furiously he tore open the letter, the paper on which it was typed was thick and creamy and at the bottom Julia's signature was flamboyant, but Arthur's reading skills were nothing like good enough for a letter in formal solicitor's language. Snarling with rage he threw it at Gladys.

'Read the bleddy thing!' he demanded.

It fluttered to the floor at Gladys's feet and she was obliged to bend down and pick it up. Very slowly she read it through, then, with an entirely impassive face she looked at her husband.

'If I were you, Arthur,' she said in a flat, emotionless voice, 'I'd give in and let Julia have Annie, because if you don't she'm apparently going to ruin us. This is an official letter, drawn up by a solicitor, notifying you of changes being undertaken by the new owner of Tremar, and as of now the hundred pounds a year you got from the old man is stopped, you don't get the apple crop n'more and the estate ent buying your timber. Apart from that, nothing's changing – 'cept she says she'll buy back Rectory Farm, if you fancy's selling.'

Arthur stared at his wife in astonishment.

'That's what it says on that bit of paper?' he whispered indignantly. Gladys nodded. 'But she can't do that.'

'I think you'll find she can. She inherited, remember.'

'But I was promised that money!'

'So you may have bin, but Sir George is dead now, and unless he left anything in his will to say it was yours, well it ent any longer.'

Arthur's nostrils flared with rage.

'And she can just *steal* it?' he demanded.

Gladys turned back to her cooking, to avoid having to look at him.

'She ent *stealing* anything,' she retorted. 'It's her bleddy money. For God's sake, Arthur, why are you so dog-in-the-manger about Annie? You don't want her, you hates the sight of her, and if you really minded about her being at Tremar you'd of took her away weeks ago. Fact is you'm taunting Julia with her, and you'm not going to win in the end.'

'Oh, I'll bleddy win,' he snarled. 'I'll take Annie from her come Christmas and she'm never going to see the child again. I'll make them *both* suffer, her and bleddy Annie. I ent having it, Gladys, I ent going to be made a fool of in me own home!'

'Well it won't be your home if you don't buck your ideas up,' Gladys Paynter retorted sourly, 'because I does the farm accounts if you remember. Jed and Jethro can't work no harder than they already do, I promise, and you'm about to be a hundred quid, plus the price of the timber short.'

Arthur suddenly had a vivid memory of Alexander Drake promising them once, that when he inherited Tremar he was going to give them all a farm of their own. Well, in a round about way he'd given Arthur his farm – and his sister was about to snatch it away again as an act of revenge.

He remembered those dreadful letters of Gladys's that had reached him on the battlefield in France. He had experienced a lurch of fear at that moment, and surely he should have felt sorrow? Julia was right, he had told her he loved her as she magically bared her beautiful body for him, but he'd said the words because he'd thought they were the right words. He hadn't loved her. He hadn't even known what the words really meant.

He glanced at his wife's back. Slovenly, untidy, plump and plain, she kept the house only just this side of a slum and when she looked at him at all it was with either fear or contempt. Dear God, he hadn't loved her either, and even young as she had been in 1918, she had run Julia a very poor second when she had offered him her body. But by then the constant pounding of the guns had shaken not just his nerves but his faith in life. He could still hear those guns, when he allowed himself to listen. He could still see blood and bits of human being scattered about in the glutinous mud. He could still smell that indescribable stink of decaying flesh and hear the shrieks and groans of the dying. The drink helped to keep it all at bay.

Abruptly the kitchen door opened and Annie came cautiously into the room. When she saw her father she stopped in her tracks and her eyes flickered with fear. It wasn't more than a few steps to the yard door, but she knew she'd never make it in time, he would head her off with ease. Arthur *itched* to hurt her.

'Come here to me,' he snarled at her and immediately he saw Annie's fear mirrored in Gladys's eyes.

Grabbing a handful of Annie's hair in his gnarled, dirty hand he twisted it sharply and yanked so that her head was forced backwards at an uncomfortable angle. Another yank and he could have broken her neck, he realized with satisfaction.

'You tell that bitch at Tremar,' he whispered softly into the child's agonized face, 'that she can do what the feck she likes to me: she'm not getting what she wants. You tell her we'd rather *starve* than give in to her.' Abruptly he smiled, very close to Annie's face. 'And you make the most of it, my girl, 'cos come t'other side of Christmas you ent *never* going to see her again. Now piss off out a my sight.'

He threw her away from him viciously and she was out of the door and into the yard as fast as her legs would carry her.

When she reached Tremar she was noticeably subdued. She kissed Julia in her usual way, but she only picked at her breakfast and Julia watched her suspiciously.

'What's the matter?' she asked. 'Has he hurt you Annie?'

Annie shook her head.

'No, just scared me a bit,' she replied as tears sprang into her eyes.

'Oh, Annie,' Julia said softly and drew the child down on to her knees, hugging her fondly. 'Was this because of the letter? Yes, of course it was. What did he say?'

Annie put her arms around Julia's neck and buried her face in her shoulder. She repeated precisely what Arthur had hissed into her face. She had no real understanding of what it meant, but she had a bad feeling about it.

'He's going to send me away after Christmas, isn't he?' she whispered, breathing in Julia's perfume and feeling her heart squeeze with the pain of loss. 'He's not going to let me stay here with you, is he?'

'No, he's *not* going to send you away,' Julia retorted fiercely. 'I'll stop him somehow, if it's the last thing I ever do. Come on, let's forget about him, we're supposed to be going out today, if you still want to go that is?'

Annie visibly brightened.

'What, to see Minnie?' she asked. ' 'Course I still wants to go I'm looking forward to it!'

Julia sighed and then kissed her swiftly.

'Well don't forget what I told you,' she said, 'you have to be especially patient with Minnie. Now, I'm about to walk over to Home Farm, do you want to come with me?'

To say the first meeting between Annie and Minnie was an unqualified success was an understatement. Julia had hoped they would like each other, that they might even find something in common, even though their levels of understanding were vastly different, but as they sat next to each other in the tea-shop, they were like a pair of naughty children together.

Even Matt, for whom Minnie had developed such a crush that she would go pink and giggle every time he spoke to her, suddenly found himself ignored. He and Julia were left to buy and pay for tea and then watch like a couple of outsiders whilst Minnie and Annie whispered and nudged each other and every so often spluttered with laughter over something that was not even remotely funny to Matt and Julia.

At one point, when they were on their second ice-creams and they suddenly exploded with laughter, Matt glanced at Julia and his eyes were veritably dancing with amusement.

'We might as well no be here,' he observed. 'Would ye care for a stroll around town whilst we leave these two here to get on with it?'

'Not likely!' Julia scowled. 'I wouldn't trust them further than I could throw them, either of them. I'm not sure who's supposed to be setting whom a good example, but neither of them seems any too anxious to take the initiative at the moment.'

Matt hastily swallowed a chuckle, then he caught the twitch of amusement at the corners of her mouth and his lips spread in a huge grin.

'Should we be threatening bed with no supper, d'you think?' he enquired, and watched her dissolve into laughter.

He knew her relief was paramount, that she had always feared there would be no rapport between Minnie and Annie and that suddenly she would be faced with a huge problem. He knew, too, that there had to be a certain ambivalence on her part to Minnie's reactions, first to himself and then to Annie. For almost twenty-four years Julia had loved and protected Minnie and had received single-minded love and devotion in return. Minnie was like a loyal dog, and for all that time she had had one mistress. Now, suddenly, her loyalty was wavering; because of her handicap she had forgotton the closeness they had once shared and she was choosing new favourites.

For the past three Thursdays she had elected to sit in the front of the car with Matt, today she wanted to be with Annie in the back and Julia was obliged to sit up front with him. It was easy enough to understand, but it was also easy to forget that Julia's perceptions were probably not like other people's. Certainly she was perfectly sane and normal, but almost a quarter of a century in an asylum could not have left her untouched.

As they left the tea-rooms Annie and Minnie linked arms and began to swagger along the pavement. They looked strange together, the pretty, spritely child with her bright green eyes and red hair and the middle-aged, uncoordinated woman with her confused eyes and grey hair. People turned and stared and then looked away swiftly, and Julia felt a sharp anger which made her press her lips tightly together.

Matt very gently took her arm and she looked at him with flashing eyes.

'What are they staring at do you imagine?' she hissed. 'Perhaps they think Minnie will infect her or something!'

'Hush,' he whispered soothingly, 'it doesn't matter what other people think, the lassies are happy, look at them, they don't see anyone else, only each other.'

Julia pressed close to him, finding his hugeness comforting. Her eyes were wretched as she glanced at him.

'I feel so responsible for them,' she murmured, 'and I want it all to be perfect. Why can't I just take them home to Tremar with me and let them play like this for ever?'

'Well you could take Minnie home to play for ever,' he replied, 'but Annie's got a life of promise ahead of her, remember. Are you a teeny bit jealous, Julia?'

Julia made a noise of protest in her throat.

'Jealous,' she echoed, 'of what?'

He shrugged slightly.

'When you first came home did you have anyone but Minnie on your mind? You told me once that on your first night back at Tremar all you could think of was growing old by your fireplace with Minnie in the chair opposite you.'

She pursed her lips and glanced at him swiftly from under her brows.

'Do you ever forget anything anyone tells you?' she enquired sourly, and he chuckled.

'No, not often, it's ma job not to forget. So, do you not want to answer my question?'

Julia watched Minnie and Annie striding along the pavement in front of her. They kept looking at each other and giggling and then putting on silly walks, but whilst Annie was graceful and really quite beautiful to watch, Minnie was heart-wrenchingly awkward and inadequate.

'Yes, I suppose . . .' Julia mumbled eventually. 'She was all mine for so long, she didn't have anyone else and she made me feel wanted. I didn't realize how easily she could fall in love – and I guess I wonder if she ever really loved me as much as I thought she did.'

Matt squeezed her arm very softly; it was astonishingly comforting.

'But in the end you'll be the one she sits across the fire from, won't you?' he said quietly. 'When young Annie has gone away to school and I'm at Home Farm. You know, it's about time you arranged to have the wee gel at Tremar for the weekend, whilst it's still the summer and young Annie's around to make her feel silly. Besides, there's going to be a war and she has to be living there with you before that, or they'll maybe decide no to let her come.'

They had fallen back a little from Minnie, and Annie and as they approached the car together Julia was suddenly penetratingly aware of Annie's eyes on them. Matt released her arm, they exchanged smiles and he began to unlock the doors.

'What are you staring at?' Julia demanded.

Annie grinned like a satisfied cat and briefly rubbed her bottom against the shiny back door of the car. It was a gesture of triumph. For a few seconds they were the only people in the world and Annie's message went sharply home.

Julia bent towards her and pressed her lips against the child's ear.

'Stop match-making!' she hissed. 'You're far too young, you precocious, presumptuous brat!'

She stepped back to pull open her door and to her horror she saw Annie mouth something at Minnie. It looked like 'she's going to marry him' and Minnie, who wouldn't have understood that, simply nodded vigorously and then began to giggle. She and Annie then made a great show of tumbling into the big, leather-smelling back seat and began to whisper and snigger together.

Julia looked steadily at Matt who was beside her in the driving-seat.

'I'm really very sorry about those two,' she observed, and he began to shake with laughter. A moment later she laughed as well and abruptly their hands touched.

It was gentle and unhurried and it was not an accident. It was something neither of them forgot either.

When they got back to Blackridge, Matt stopped the car on the drive in front of the great stone steps and, as was always the case, Julia sat for a moment transfixed, staring up at the huge, red-brick building. In the time it took her to gather her thoughts and step out of the car, Annie and Minnie were already on the steps and they were jumping up towards the front door, holding hands and grinning at each other.

The door was open and suddenly it seemed to Julia as if everything switched into a dreadful, dream-like slow-motion. Minnie and Annie reached the top step. Julia lurched forwards with her arms out and Minnie and Annie disappeared together into the building.

Julia felt all the colour drain from her face and she stumbled, tripped and fell on to her knees.

She screamed, 'Annie! *No*!' and Matt was beside her in an instant, lifting her to her feet. Her body was trembling all over and there were beads of sweat on her top lip. 'Get her out!' she sobbed, 'get her out!'

'It's all right,' Matt murmured soothingly, 'she'll no come to any harm, I promise you. I'll get her.'

He began to climb the steps and abruptly Ilona Vincent appeared on the doorstep with Annie beside her. They were smiling at each other and Minnie was just behind them.

'I appear to have one family member too many,' Miss Vincent said cheerfully,' I think this one belongs to you.'

Julia wiped her shaking hands across her face. She felt dreadfully sick so she had a good idea how she looked. She saw Annie's face cloud and at the same moment she saw a strange look of warning on the matron's face. Suddenly she knew that if she behaved badly she was going to spoil this moment and it was a very special moment. It was the moment when her dreadful old life and her wonderful new one came together and touched: blended, and, like the first snowdrops after winter, held the promise of renewal.

Taking a deep breath she went quietly up the steps, put her arm about Annie's shoulders and held out her hand to Minnie.

'Darling,' she said, 'if Matron says it's all right, how would you like to come home to Tremar with Annie and Matt and me after tea next Thursday and stay with us right through until Sunday afternoon?'

Minnie had no real idea of time, or of what she was being offered, she just saw Annie nod encouragement and joined in excitedly.

Miss Vincent frowned slightly.

'A whole weekend?' she murmured. 'I'm not sure, Julia, you may find she can't manage that long.'

'Well, we can bring her back if she becomes too agitated,' Julia offered, adding with a quick smile at Matt, 'not that I think she will, you should have seen the way these two have been behaving this afternoon. Frankly, I'm not sure they don't deserve a smacked bottom apiece, rather than a reward. So, will the board agree, do you think?'

The woman shook her head.

'I'm not asking the board,' she replied, 'I'm not telling anyone. I want to give Minnie every chance to get to know Tremar and settle there first and *then* we'll go to the board with it, as a *fait accompli.* I'll have her things packed for Thursday then.'

Julia smiled at her and then kissed Minnie fondly. For the first time ever Minnie didn't cling to her, instead she held out her arms like a child to Annie for a kiss, and with no apparent reluctance or embarrassment, Annie kissed her. After that she went to Matt for a kiss and then trotted off inside the building, leaving Julia staring sadly after her.

'It was bound to happen eventually,' Miss Vincent said, 'she's forgotten even her instinctive recall of her first parting from you. That's good. It might be hard for you, but it's good for her. She'll talk about Annie here for a whole week now, just the same as she's talked so much about Matt recently. Be happy for her, Julia.'

'I'm always happy for her,' Julia replied truthfully, 'and I'll always love her.'

Chapter 16

So Minnie was to come for a weekend, which meant Mrs Collins had to be carefully approached and, Julia supposed, the usual prejudices would have to be faced. It made her cross, the thought that she would have to justify her choice of guest, and she wondered wryly if the staff in her parents' time had ever disapproved of a guest invited to stay at the manor. Well, one thing was for sure, they never would have dared say so.

Uppermost in her mind, though, as she paced about her bedroom and wondered whether it might be easier to cut her losses and have Minnie sleep with her, was the problem of Oliver. He was like a rough strand in the smooth fabric of her life and all the time her fingers kept returning to touch it.

If only life could be simple; one dimensional. If only it were possible to take the physical pleasure he offered but with no emotion. If only she could send him happily on his way afterwards and be safe in the knowledge that nobody was being hurt. If only . . . if only. . . . If only, she knew from childhood, was an abominable waste of time.

Well, it was going to have to be resolved, and sooner rather than later. Oliver's hopes and dreams and Sophie's pain and suffering were emotions that crowded her life now and were spoiling her joy. Annie and Arthur had to be resolved too, but they were different, they were part of it all. Oliver and Sophie were trespassers and must be evicted.

As Mrs Collins came into the bedroom with fresh linen for the bed she looked faintly surprised to see Julia pacing about the room rather aimlessly and for a moment the two women looked at each other, each waiting for the other to make a comment.

Initially it was Julia who backed down and she was actually half-way to the door when she changed her mind, took a deep breath, and decided to face it. Turning back abruptly she called the housekeeper's attention. Knowing that her tone was crisp but unable to do anything about it, she politely informed her of Minnie's impending stay, and then, in a tense silence, waited for the suspicion and prejudice to surface.

Mrs Collins watched her for a moment, then carefully put the clean linen down on a chair, preparing to do the bed.

'She were with you at Blackridge, then?' she enquired. Julia nodded curtly. 'Good friend, was she?'

Julia frowned. This wasn't at all what she had expected.

'Well – yes, actually,' she murmured. 'In fact she was my life-long companion, for twenty-three-and-a-half years. I know what a name that place has, it makes people shudder even to think about it, but I'd like to explain something to you if you'll let me. It's important, because I don't want you to be afraid of Minnie and I most certainly don't want her to be afraid of you.'

Mrs Collins glanced at her and then shook out a snowy white sheet, deftly tucking it in at the corners of the bed. Julia thought: Well at least she seems prepared to listen.

'Blackridge is not an asylum for the criminally insane, you know,' she said. 'It's supposed to be a hospital. A lot of the people who spend their lives there have no real level of understanding at all, they don't know they're there and they don't care. More than half of them are so physically crippled as well that they can't walk, but the others, like Minnie, are there simply because they are not capable of coping for themselves in the outside world. Minnie was beaten by her drunken father. He hurt her so badly that he permanently damaged her brain. She is shy, frightened, and like a dog who has been ill-treated, she doesn't remember what was done to her, but she does know people can hurt you.'

'But she'll be all right here with you?' Mrs Collins asked.

Julia shrugged.

'Well I hope so, the plan is that she should come to live here with me one day. Her table manners aren't all that splendid, but I'm sure you'll forgive her that.'

'Don't sound to me that there's anything to *forgive*, Miss Drake,' the housekeeper said, pumping a pillow with her fists and tossing it to the head of the bed, 'she can't help being the way she is, can she, no more than my aunt could. I'm not sure, though – if you'll pardon me saying

– that she should be in a room on her own, p'raps? Maybe the first time we could move another bed in here with you? Don't want her needlessly frightened, do we, and it do creak a bit, this place.'

Julia gaped at her in astonishment.

'Mrs Collins, you're not telling me you had an aunt in Blackridge?' she whispered, and the woman shook her head vigorously.

'Oh, no, they never put her away, nor nothing. Well, my mother had that many brothers and sisters there were always someone to look after Auntie, but she spilled a good deal on the table at meal-times, I remember, and . . .' she suddenly glanced sideways at Julia, 'she did have another little problem. Night-times, if you understand me?'

Julia felt such a rush of relief that quite absurdly she could have kissed the woman. She offered her a smile that was probably warmer and more affectionate than any emotion she had ever shown her housekeeper before, and in return she received a look of great compassion.

'I've got a spare rubber sheet at home,' Mrs Collins said, 'I'll pop it up tomorrow for you – and if there should be any little accidents, well don't you go bothering yourself will you, dear, 'cos I can get that sorted quick as anything.'

'Oh, Mrs Collins, thank you!' Julia exclaimed. 'I was so *sure* you wouldn't understand. There's so much prejudice where handicapped people are concerned and round here any mention of Blackridge sends people rushing inside to lock their doors. Minnie is no more a raving lunatic than I am – in fact she's considerably less of one. And she and Annie adore each other.'

Mrs Collins had warmed to Annie over the past weeks – mainly because Julia had threatened Annie with the wrath of God if she waged war on the woman and Matt and Annie had recently got up a 'lets be sweet to Mrs Collins' campaign, which Julia found quite sickening, but which the housekeeper had completely fallen for. To begin with, after she had gone home in the evenings, if Matt and Annie started to mock her, Julia used to pretend to be annoyed. Now, knowing they were always careful, she let them get on with it and could sometimes even be induced to laugh.

'That don't surprise me none,' Mrs Collins observed, 'children is always better with they sort of folk. My aunt, she loved children. They got an affinity, somehow. 'Course I always thought young Annie were simple, like most people round here, till she started coming up here that is. You done Annie Paynter a great service, you know, Miss Drake.'

Julia thought of Annie and abruptly thought of Arthur. She thought of his savagery and his apparent determination that Annie's life should be as miserable as his own had been. From the window of the bedroom she gazed down across the formal lawns towards the sea, and shivered slightly.

'Dear God, I hope so,' she muttered to no one in particular.

Later that day, when Matt, Annie and Julia were sitting down to dinner, Julia prepared to tell them about her conversation with Mrs Collins. Matt ate at Tremar every night with his employer nowadays, it had been simpler than arranging a second housekeeper for Home Farm, and since he worked most days from dawn to dusk it had seemed singularly unfair that he should then be obliged to go home and prepare food for himself. It was an extraordinarily eccentric household over which she presided, Julia realized, and remembering some of the other aristocratic families with whom she had spent time as a child, she amused herself occasionally by wondering what they would make of Tremar now, had they been around to see it.

With Matt and Annie sitting either side of her and the puppies asleep under the table, Julia paused from piling slices of roast ham on to the plates and suddenly looked up at Matt. 'I've had an idea,' she said slowly, 'but you must promise to tell me immediately if it doesn't suit you. I was wondering whether you'd consider staying over the weekend, while Minnie's here?'

He took a plate from her, enjoying the delicious aroma of the honey-roasted meat and began to help himself to vegetables.

'In the house, you mean?' he asked, and she nodded. 'Are you expecting trouble then?'

Trouble. Julia hadn't even thought about it, Abruptly Annie let her fork fall rather hard on to her plate and Julia stared at her. She was looking frightened.

'If my pa finds out about Minnie being here,' she whispered, 'he'll throw a fit. He's itching for a fight with you and he'll use any excuse.'

'*Minnie?*' Julia exclaimed, and abruptly her nostrils flared. 'Oh, yes, of course, she's from Blackridge. I ought to have worked it out for myself, I was only talking to Mrs Collins about it this morning and I should have thought of it then. Oh, and by the way, before you two start, Mrs Collins had an aunt who was handicapped and she's been very understanding about Minnie, so lay off her, all right?'

Annie and Matt exchanged glances and Annie's eyes sparkled cruelly.

'Mrs Full-of-her-own-bleedin'-importance,' she scoffed, and Julia glared at her.

'Stop it,' she snorted. 'You know, I never should have taken you in, Annie Paynter. The first time I found you trespassing on my property I should have booted you over the wall the way you came! Now shut up and eat your dinner.'

Annie began happily to plough into her plate of food but suddenly Julia found she really wasn't very hungry.

'You don't really think there'll be any fuss, do you?' she asked, looking at Matt. 'I so want Minnie to have a lovely, trouble-free weekend.'

He smiled.

'Well I'll be happy to stay in the house with you,' he said in his calm and dignified way, which always made her feel so safe, 'and we'll take it I'm just here so the lassie can feel safe with familiar faces about her. It's a right shame young Annie can't stay as well, though I doubt you and I'd get much sleep with them giggling together all night!'

Julia grinned at him gratefully, but when they looked at Annie she was gazing forlornly at her dinner plate.

'If word gets to Pa,' she murmured, 'he'll lock me in my room and I won't be here at all. Oh, I *hope* no one tells him.'

But it was already too late to stop the news of Julia's visitor reaching the village, and all news in Polwean spread like wildfire. Always. Especially if it concerned Tremar.

Annie set off home at eight-thirty. Matt and Julia walked with her as far as the broken wall and watched her as she ran across the fields beyond, toward the back of the Drake Arms. It was the beginning of August now and considerably darker in the evenings than it had been when she had first come home in June, and as she and Matt walked companionably back towards Tremar, the terrace was flooded with light from the lamps in the drawing-room, which were already lit. They talked quietly about Minnie and the arrangements for her weekend, and Julia was feeling really quite delighted at the prospect of having Matt actually staying in the manor with them.

'Have a brandy with me, before you go back to Home Farm,' she invited as they neared the terrace, 'since you obviously don't intend to visit The Smugglers this evening.'

He smiled.

'I think I'll keep away from The Smugglers for the next few nights,' he said wisely. 'Mr Paynter seems to object to my presence whenever he sees me there, and it might be wise not to stir up trouble with him for a day or two.'

They climbed the terrace steps and Julia turned to look at him fondly.

'Oh, Matt,' she murmured warmly, 'thank you for being here – and thank God for 'young' Mr Cruikshank, too. I dread to think who I'd have finished up with as an estate manager if his father had still been in a position to choose for me. I mean, don't get me wrong, he's a nice enough old boy, but so *stuffy*, you wouldn't believe.'

Matt raised his bushy eyebrows at her comically.

'Well I'd no call 'young' Mr Cruikshank the life the soul of the party, exactly!' he exclaimed and they both burst out laughing.

The laughter died on Julia's lips abruptly as they reached the top of the steps. Oliver was standing on the terrace watching them and his expression was considerably less than jovial. She had found the courage to face Mrs Collins about Minnie that morning, and she truly wasn't certain she could find another dose of courage to face Oliver now.

'Oh, Oliver,' she said, completely unable to stop herself flattening her voice, 'hullo, I wasn't expecting you.'

'Evidently,' he replied icily. 'Is Mr Logan on his way home?'

Julia experienced a flash of anger.

'No,' she snorted 'he's coming in to have a drink. Do please join us if you haven't got to hurry away.'

'I'll maybe be on ma way, Julia,' Matt said quickly, with some idea of defusing the situation, 'the puppies could do with a run before bed anyway.'

Abruptly she was furious.

'No!' she snarled. 'I invited you to have a drink with me and you accepted! Now please, join me.'

Matt kept his face completely devoid of expression as he obediently followed her into the drawing-room with the puppies at his heels, but as he took the brandy she had poured for him and settled himself into an armchair he felt a pleasant surge of triumph. Julia was getting tired of the handsome, class-conscious young doctor, and if the strain of his company that she was evidently feeling now, had needed a helping hand along the way, the tea-party with his insignificant little wife and pretty children on the beach two days before would almost certainly have done the trick.

Matt didn't like Oliver Crompton, and whilst in the beginning the affair between him and Julia had only mildly disturbed him, he now felt quite selfishly possessive towards his employer. The likes of Julia Drake were not for Oliver Crompton. He was an ambitious social climber, but she was an extraordinary woman who even after almost a quarter of a century locked in a hell on earth, displayed to anyone who cared to see it that she had nothing whatever to prove. She was a lady, and she was far too good for him.

Matt drank his brandy slowly and when he finally rose to leave it was very noticeable that Julia went out on to the terrace to say good-night to him.

'And thank you,' she called after him, 'for accepting my invitation for next weekend, it'll be nice for both of us to have your company. See you tomorrow.'

Oliver leaned on the stone parapet of the terrace beside her, watching Matt disappearing into the darkness. He sort of hoped the other man might look back and see him, but he didn't, and after a moment he slipped his arm comfortably around Julia's waist. He was astonished when he felt her tense and pull quickly away.

'Shall we go in?' she suggested, and without waiting for an answer, walked away from him through the french windows.

'Why is he coming here for the weekend?' he enquired as he followed her into the softly lit room and closed the doors behind them. 'Home Farm sprung a leak has it, so he's got to live at Tremar? I shouldn't let him get too comfortable, he might not want to go home again.'

'Oh, I think he knows his place, Oliver,' she replied in a voice loaded with sarcasm. 'Minnie is coming to stay for the weekend actually, and since she thinks the world of Matt I thought it would be nice for her if he was here all the time. Familiar faces are important to Minnie. Would you like another drink?'

He smiled at her.

'No thank you, my darling,' he replied cheerfully, 'I haven't got long. I told Sophie I was going out for a drink, so she won't expect me to be longer than an hour or so.'

Julia sneered at him, and if he hadn't been so conceited he might have noticed.

'I see,' she said. 'You told Sophie you were popping out for a drink so that you could dash up here, enjoy a quick roll in my bed and then dash back to spend the evening being cosy with her? How romantic. Were you actually planning to take your clothes off or did you think you'd keep your shirt and socks on, to save time? Well, sorry, Oliver, but no thank you!'

Oliver gaped at her in astonishment.

'Julia,' he whispered. 'What on earth did I do to deserve that? I don't understand.'

'Don't you?' she spat, folding her arms tightly across her breasts, hugging herself almost as if she was cold. 'Well let me explain. I'm not a commodity, Oliver, I'm not a diverting change from what's on offer at home, and in case you've forgotten I made my position quite clear to you. I'm not leaving Tremar for you, I'm not going to London with you and I'm not preparing to be the new woman in your life!'

'But you told me I would still be welcome in your bed,' he pointed out, 'in fact, at the moment we discussed it I rather felt you were the one regretting that it might be all over!'

There was an indefatigable truth in that and Julia was forced to recognize it. She didn't want to look at him because her emotions were so at odds. When he touched her, when he lay naked beside her and whispered her name he made her feel wonderful. He always told her how beautiful she was and he said it with his eyes, not just with his lips. To send him away now probably meant the end of any physical love-life for her – who else would there be? Her life and her old age were planned around Tremar.

But seeing him standing there looking a mixture of hurt and anger brought immediately to her mind the picture of Sophie Crompton fighting to hide her tears and swallowing her humiliation as she came as near as her stilted upbringing allowed her, to begging for her husband back.

And it wasn't acceptable Julia decided. It was time to do the right thing. It must be dealt with right now – could not be put off any longer.

'I thought you always would be welcome in my bed, Oliver,' she said quietly, 'but I'm afraid I've changed my mind. Did Sophie tell you she and I and the children had a picnic together in the bay the day before yesterday?'

He frowned.

'Yes, of course,' he replied, 'it was very kind of you.'

'No, it wasn't kind of me at all. When she struggled into that shop with Alice and the push-chair I could see those foul old cats sharpening their claws with delight at the prospect of an afternoon of blood-letting. She didn't want to spend time with me, Oliver, but she's too nice to be downright rude and I pushed her into a corner. When we came to talk about you she wept. She cried in front of me and it was humiliating for her. She doesn't deserve to be treated like that!'

He narrowed his eyes at her.

'So what are you saying?' he asked, and Julia gritted her teeth to force herself to keep looking at him.

'I'm saying,' she answered quietly, 'in the only way I know how, that we won't be sharing my bed again. There's a big difference between Sophie and me, you know, and you seem to have missed it. She loves you. She really wants to go to London with you, in fact she'd follow you to the ends of the earth if you asked her. She is also a thoroughly nice woman and you and I have made a laughing-stock out of her! Well, I know exactly how it feels to be abused and I've done with abusing her. Now go home please, sit in your drawing-room with her and be grateful that for once in your life you won't have to lie. You popped out for a drink, and that was all you had – because if you think for one moment she really believes you're in the Drake Arms, you're more stupid than I took you for!'

Oliver stared at her with his mouth open. He couldn't believe what he was hearing and worse than that, he didn't want to believe it. He couldn't give her up, it was impossible.

'That's it?' he demanded indignantly. 'I don't want you any more so go away? Who do you think you are to walk over people like that, or have you decided your rough Scotsman is more exciting perhaps, so you don't need me any more?'

Julia returned his stare unflinchingly, smiling wryly at his reference to Matt.

'Actually,' she said softly, 'that's the one thing I haven't done to you, bedded someone else behind your back. As to who I think I am, I know exactly who I am and what's more I know *what* I am – and I'm not proud of it. Please go now, Oliver. If you feel there is any way we can stay friends then I should be delighted to see you from time to time, if not – well that's up to you, but please believe me I will never, ever forget that you saved my life and I will always remember you very fondly.'

A dozen cruel, spiteful retorts had flitted through Oliver's brain during her final little speech and she had cleverly left him no opportunity to use a single one of them. She had dismissed him as crisply as her mother used to do, but she had been so ladylike about it that there was simply nothing left to say.

Pressing his lips together he gazed at her for a final few seconds and then, because he couldn't resist it, he resorted to sarcasm.

'Would you prefer me to leave by the front door? Do the thing properly, since it's official?' he enquired.

She smiled at him like a duchess.

'Please yourself, Oliver,' she replied calmly, 'but if you decide to go via the terrace as usual, do be careful won't you, it's awfully dark out there.'

He banged the french window so hard on his way out that she was faintly surprised it didn't smash and for some seconds, as the breeze of his rapid departure still stirred in the room, she laughed out loud, then putting her hand over her mouth she burst into tears.

At Lamplighter House, a quarter of an hour later, Sophie looked up from her book in surprise as her husband strode into the room. She knew exactly where he had been going when he had lied about popping across to the Drake Arms, and her heart had wrenched as he had bent to kiss her absently on the cheek.

But it was less than an hour ago and already he was back, what was more he was very obviously in a foul temper. So Julia Drake had sent him packing – Oh, dear God, was that possible? She had promised two days ago that she had no intention of leaving Polwean with him when he had sold his practice, so had she decided in that case, to end it here and now? She must have done, God bless her.

Oh, thank you! Sophie thought. You are a lady after all.

Smiling fondly at him and carefully ignoring his furious expression, she put down her book, stood up, touched his hand softly and said, 'Hullo, darling, how nice to see you. Can I get you a drink, or a coffee perhaps?'

Oliver glared at her and suddenly he noticed that instead of her hair being carelessly pinned up at the back of her head as it normally was, it was loose and hanging soft and corn-coloured about her shoulders. He noticed, for perhaps the first time for months that she was really very pretty – and, to his astonishment, he noticed that she had tidied the room.

'Yes,' he said eventually, as the expression of rage and hurt began to fade from his face, 'let's have a coffee, I'll make it if you like, you go back to your book.'

Wisely she didn't push it.

'Well, thank you,' she replied and climbed back into her arm chair, tucking her legs underneath her.

As he went towards the kitchen door he suddenly stopped and turned back to her, watching her steadily for a moment. Then he said, 'You know, Sophie, your hair is much nicer if you leave it down, How would you like to go to a proper stylist, say in Bodmin, and have it cut and shaped? I'll pay, I don't mind.'

She smiled at him softly.

'I'd love to, darling,' she answered, 'thank you very much, that would be wonderful!'

And Sophie Crompton decided at that moment that she owed Julia Drake a favour. As it turned out she would get a chance to repay her much sooner than she thought.

Matt appeared at Tremar at breakfast-time the following morning and found his employer standing on the terrace carefully inspecting the work that was being done to the fountain. All the sludge had been cleaned out of the stone basin and the little lead statue had been boxed and was being stored in the stables.

Julia had never said anything about her mother's wedding-ring and it had never been found, Frankly she had felt sick at the idea of somebody having to sift through all that fetid muck to find a tiny gold ring which she had been careless enough to drop in there herself, and since she certainly had no emotional attachment to it she was quite happy to let it go.

She looked pale and rather intense, Matt thought, as he watched her walking round and round the basin, apparently lost in her inspection, and for a while he stood back and allowed her to finish what she was doing without disturbing her.

Finally she looked up at him. She was well aware that he had been standing there for sometime, but perversely had made him wait. His occasional flashes of rather subservient servant–mistress attitude grated on her nerves when they happened, and she knew perfectly well it was unfair because she *was* his employer, but the fact was it unnerved her, made her feel as if she had done something to incur his disapproval.

Eventually she snapped, 'Are you going to stand there watching me all day?' and abruptly turned away from him to go and lean on the stone parapet. After a moment she murmured, 'The fountain is coming on quite well really, isn't it?'

He came to stand beside her, leaning on the parapet as well. They didn't look at each other, they both stared across the lawns towards the sea, but Julia was sharply aware of him, of the difference in their heights and size. He smelt of tweed, it was a sort of warm smell. Comforting.

'I sent him away,' she mumbled bleakly. 'Last night, after you'd gone, I sent him back to his wife.'

'I'm so pleased,' he replied in his deep, calm voice, 'he wasnae good enough for you, lass. You're worth a lot more than a social-climbing, middle-class country doctor. Good riddance to him, I say.'

Julia turned her head slightly and frowned at him.

'That seems such a strange thing for you to say,' she observed, 'you seem as dismissive of his class as I understand my mother was. Does middle class offend you then?'

He smiled.

'Only when it strains to be something else. My father was a servant, born to a servant, we lived on a vast estate and my brothers and I roamed the woods with the earl's bairns, but we never forgot our place. We never expected to be treated as family.'

'I treat you as family!' Julia exclaimed. 'At least I thought I did.'

'Aye, but we *are* family, lassie,' he replied seriously, looking at her for the first time. 'Like I told you once before, we're marked, the likes of you and me. Yon doctor wants what your mother had; her aristocracy and her superiority, the supposed respect and admiration that goes with it. You and I have forfeited all that because of what we are. If you'd not spent half your life in an asylum do you think he'd have expected the favours he's received from you? Of course he wouldn't! He'd have grovelled for a word of thanks from you occasionally, and boasted at having you for a patient!'

She lowered her head, staring unhappily at her hands. Everything he said was quite true – which somehow made it worse.

'But he made me feel so good about myself,' she whispered. 'He made me feel. . . .'

Matt touched her very softly.

'Like a human being?'

'In the early years at Blackridge, before Matron came,' she murmured, 'there were a lot of male orderlies about the place and they were in the habit of helping themselves to what they wanted when no one was looking. After all, what else were female idiots good for, other than casual sexual encounters to pass the time?'

Abruptly she put her hands up to her face and suddenly she was remembering, not telling someone else any more. She could see a cruel, pock-marked face that she had struggled not to see for years now, smell a mingling, sour smell of unwashed hair and sweaty armpits . . . feel the terror of seeing him coming along the corridor towards her and knowing what he would do.

'There was one particular one,' she whispered, mostly to herself, 'he never even asked me if I had a name. . . .' Her voice became leaden with pain. 'He never took his trousers off, he just unbuttoned them and tugged his bits and pieces out with his hand, and then he'd push me up against the wall and yank my dress up around my waist. He called me girlie. He used to put his forearm across my throat and then . . . he'd whisper, "Don't wriggle, girlie, just stay still, nice and still" and he'd. . . .' Tears began to stream down her face as her breath caught in her throat and seemed to want to choke her. 'When he'd finished he used to rebutton his trousers with as much emotion as if he'd just urinated, and then he'd grin and pat my cheek.' She was shaking with sobs. ' "You won't tell, will you, girlie?" he'd say and then he'd laugh, " 'cos no one's going to believe you anyway, are they?" and he did it as often as he could get me alone, for years.'

Standing beside Matt she leaned on the stone parapet resting her head on her arms, running from eyes, nose and mouth in her misery as her sobs tore straight from her soul. It was a wretched, hopeless sorrow, an acknowledgement that there was never an escape from her memories; that now she might be beautiful, fresh, groomed, expensively clothed, but the humiliation was all still there, just under the surface.

Matt didn't look at her at all, but gathered her into his arms and held her tightly against his chest, letting her sob into him and holding her with firm, warm arms.

'I'm sorry lassie,' he whispered eventually, and after what seemed like ages, when she finally managed to regain control she turned, rubbed at her soaking face ineffectually with her hands and tried to twist her lips into a crooked smile.

'Yes, so am I,' she replied, 'I'd never meant to tell anyone that.' She drew a sharp, sobbing breath. 'And the irony of it is that Minnie doesn't remember any more, whilst I. . . .'

'Can never forget,' he murmured. 'It's so unfair. The arrival of yon matron ten years ago must have been a great relief.'

Julia wiped her face again, this time more successfully and leaned her back against the stone parapet, gazing up at Tremar. The dower was still encased in scaffolding, but the new roof was beginning to take shape and it was as if suddenly her beautiful house was coming alive again. Letting the sun warm her tear-streaked face she smiled and to her faint astonishment, held her hand out to him. He took it and held it gently in his great paw, and she realized that touching him was like a talisman in a way, something solid and comforting to hold on to.

'It was,' she replied eventually, 'but it took me a long time to notice. I'd cut myself off by then. I thought if I could go mad I could simply forget, but you know it's not that easy to go mad. I think I could have done in the beginning, during the first year, but after all that time life was so ordered there was nothing to go mad *for*, if you understand. God, that sounds daft!'

He chuckled and suddenly his deep blue eyes were sparkling at her.

'The likes of you and I don't go mad,' he said, 'we're too strong for that, too organized. When I killed that man in Glasgow and the fiscal said I'd suffered a flash of madness, a sudden loss of control with all the awful things I'd seen and endured in France I really wondered if that was true for a moment. But there was no madness, I knew precisely what I was doing. I killed him in cold blood, because he was asking for it – just as I could have killed Arthur Paynter that day when I saw him slap wee Annie!'

Julia looked steadily into his eyes. Though she felt much better, the hurt was still there in her soul, where it had always been and where, she was beginning to realize, it had been growing steadily since that first evening when she had discovered Arthur was still alive. When deeply buried moments of her suffering at Blackridge surfaced, as this last one had just done, her burning desire for revenge seemed to seer the edges of her consciousness and her pain became almost tangible.

'Arthur's mine, Matt,' she whispered, 'mine to kill, as I choose. But if I need your help, do I have it?'

'Of course you do, lass,' he replied immediately.

Chapter 17

The news of Minnie's visit to Tremar came from Mrs Collins in the beginning, and, sadly, she mentioned it only because she was delighted, both for Julia and for Minnie. Despite her funny ways, her tendency to bully and her occasional obvious disapproval of Julia's somewhat avant-garde lifestyle, she had become devoted to her employer in the months they had known each other, and she was very proud of her job at Tremar. She told Miss Penrose and Miss Hewlett in the village shop about Minnie's visit, because she was genuinely pleased that Julia was having a friend to stay. She was also, of course, quite used to her aunt and didn't see that it was at all out of the way for someone of less than average mental capacity to be visiting.

Miss Penrose and Miss Hewlett didn't see it like that and they were guaranteed to see to it that no one else in Polwean did either.

'A friend from Blackridge, you say?' Miss Penrose asked, glancing sharply at Miss Hewlett. 'A patient, you mean?'

Mrs Collins smiled cheerfully.

'That's right, Miss Drake says they was friends for years whilst she was a patient,' she replied. 'Apparently she and Mr Logan and young Annie Paynter takes her out to tea every Thursday afternoon.'

'Annie Paynter!' Miss Hewlett echoed. 'If you ask me she'm going to finish up as a patient in there herself, one of these days!'

Mrs Collins looked slightly ruffled.

'You got Annie wrong, you know,' she observed, 'she'm a very clever little girl, that one.'

'Well, clever enough to have taken you in, anyhow,' Miss Penrose remarked. 'You know, Mrs Collins, we've been in this shop for – oh, nigh on thirty years now, Miss Hewlett and I, and we don't miss much. She'm not right in the head, that Annie Paynter, same as Julia Drake. Oh, she'm nice enough, Julia is, but *we* knew her when she was a kiddie and she was always a bit odd. It didn't surprise us none that she finished up in Blackridge. I should be a bit careful about her having friends to stay from *that place* if I was you – and heaven alone knows what Arthur Paynter's going to say about it when he hears what's bin going on.'

Mrs Collins had always had her doubts about these two old spinsters, and now she knew why. They were very spiteful.

'Bearing in mind how little Mr Paynter seems to care for his daughter,' she retorted huffily, 'I can't see, myself, that it's any of his business! I don't know if you know it, but Miss Drake has completely reclothed that child, and out of her own pocket, too. What's more she'm taught her to read and write, and taught her lovely table manners. She were a little savage when she first used to come up the manor, but not any more!'

Miss Penrose and Miss Hewlett glanced at each other again. It was actually quite disconcerting when they did it and whilst it wouldn't be correct to say Mrs Collins was exactly frightened of them, like poor Sophie, she was certainly very wary of them. Sadly, she was not wary enough, or familiar enough with them to know better than to tell them anything at all.

' 'Course,' Miss Penrose said, 'Annie Paynter's not the only one who spends most of her time at Tremar is she, Mrs Collins? Seems to us that the good doctor's there a fair bit more often than he might be. Seems like that to Mrs Crompton, too, unless I'm much mistaken, sweet thing that she is with them two lovely children.'

Mrs Collins heard the warning bell sounding loudly in her head. Oliver Crompton had chosen her specially to be housekeeper at Tremar and she was not about to indulge in any form of character assassination of him with these two. Unfortunately her defence was indignation. Pushing her purchases firmly into her shopping basket she sniffed and turned towards the door.

'I'll not have a word said against the doctor, if you don't mind!' she declared, 'He's a very nice young man, and a very good doctor as well. Good afternoon!' And she marched out to the accompanying sound of the tinkling shop bell.

Miss Hewlett and Miss Penrose glanced at each other and smiled.

'Well, that's confirmed it, wouldn't you say, dear?' Miss Penrose enquired.

'Oh, quite definitely,' replied Miss Hewlett. 'If Julia Drake and that young man are up to no good, who's to know better than the housekeeper I'd like to know. And now she's filling the house full of mad people from Blackridge! Oh, her poor mother and father, they must be turning in their graves. Well all I can say is he's got a lot to answer for, that Oliver Crompton, he should have left her in Blackridge where she was safe; now for all us knows we'm all going to be murdered in our beds!'

Later in the day they happened to mention Julia's visitor to Mrs Pennard. Tom Pennard was a regular drinker in The Smugglers, and a drinking companion of Arthur Paynter's. Mrs Pennard went away from the shop with the idea that Julia Drake was filling Tremar full of raving lunatics, and she was furious and frightened when she told her husband.

On Thursday morning, before they went to Blackridge to collect Minnie, Annie thought she'd have a go at wheedling her way round her mother. Arthur and the twins had long since gone out on the farm and Annie and Gladys were alone in the gloomy, rank-smelling kitchen of the farmhouse. Gladys had given the child some breakfast and a big glass of milk, and as Annie obediently sat at the table to eat it, Gladys noticed that she didn't cram food into her mouth any longer, she ate slowly and politely.

'*Please* say I can stay over the weekend at the manor, Ma,' Annie begged, swallowing down her milk. 'I'll come home Mond'y, I promise.'

Gladys gazed at her daughter fondly. She was a completely changed child, from the frightened, skinny, dirty runt who had scuttled in and out like a starving animal a few short weeks ago. Of course, she was still very frightened of her father, and with good reason, but even that was tempered by the knowledge that she had a very large champion in Matt.

Gladys was delighted to see her so well and happy, even if it did mean she would one day lose her to Julia. She had her twins who were in every way the spit of her adored brothers, and she would always have them, she knew. It would be hard to lose Annie, but it would be tempered by the knowledge that the child would have the opportunity to fulfil her potential. The opportunity Gladys had never been offered.

'And if your pa finds out?' she said. 'Annie, you know what he'll do?'

'But I never see him anyway,' Annie pointed out. 'He don't know if I'm here or not most of the time. Oh *please*, Ma.'

As Gladys gazed at the child she realized that it might well be to their advantage to keep Julia sweet. Her sanctions were about to bite, since the first load of timber from Swallows Wood that was not going to be accepted at the Bodmin sawmills was due to come up in a few days' time. On the open market it was not going to fetch the price they automatically got from the estate, that was for sure. Then in October, the annual one hundred pounds from Alexander Drake's estate was not going to be forthcoming for the first time, and there was no doubt it was going to leave a sizeable hole in their finances.

Even if Arthur carried out his threat to send Annie into service after Christmas she wasn't going to be paid enough to make up the shortfall, besides which it was looking more and more as if there was going to be a war. So perhaps trying to find a compromise both Julia and Arthur could live with might turn out, in the long run, to be an advantage.

Gladys understood compromise, she understood most things, and she certainly understood that if things didn't change, by Christmas they were going to be very hard up indeed, but Arthur had become so paranoid, so blinded by his quite unreasonable loathing of Julia that if he wasn't careful he was going to lose everything.

Julia could well finish up with Annie *and* Rectory Farm, and if that happened, Gladys's life wouldn't be worth living.

'All right,' she said, 'I'll lie for you, but *please* be careful; he'll beat hell out of both of us; if he finds out, you know he will.'

Annie spontaneously hugged her mother and Gladys cupped her face in her hands and kissed her lovingly.

'Thanks, Ma,' Annie whispered. 'I'll see you on Mond'y.'

Annie had never spent a night away from home in her life and as she tore down the dirt road towards the harbour and vaulted one of Matt's newly installed fences, intended to keep the trespassers from taking a short cut across estate land, her heart sang so loudly in her ears, it almost deafened her.

She met Matt on her way through the copse, checking for signs of poachers. He was having some difficulty stopping the poaching; it had gone on for so many years that one or two of the regulars were thoroughly indignant at finding themselves barred from what they had looked upon as their rightful hunting ground, and they were waging a war against Matt.

They were learning, though, that he wasn't the easiest person in the world to wage war against, and that a lifetime of experience had taught him how to play them at their own game with consummate ease.

Annie raced up to him when she saw him, threw her arms around him and gave him a huge kiss.

'I can stay!' she cried excitedly. 'I can stay for the *whole* weekend!'

Matt gazed at her with his deep blue eyes.

'You got your father's permission?' he asked in surprise. 'How on earth did you manage that?'

Annie shrugged.

'Well no, but I got me ma's and that'll do for now,' she replied cheerfully and Matt, lifting his eyebrows thought, Aye until yon bastard finds out and exacts his revenge. I'll have to watch out for that.

Grinning he said, 'Well we best go and tell Julia straight away, hadn't we, so she can make up a room for you. And you watch it, missy, if you and yon lassie from Blackridge stay up giggling all night I'll have you digging potatoes tomorrow as a punishment.'

Julia was in the morning-room answering letters when Matt and Annie arrived. She had breakfasted early and was planning on having another brooding look at the room she had finally decided to set aside for Minnie. She still felt very uncertain about it. Minnie hadn't slept alone for so many years now that she undoubtedly couldn't remember ever having done so, but if she was to come to live at Tremar then she must get used to having a room of her own – and starting her off in Julia's room was almost certainly storing up troubles for later.

As they entered the morning-room Matt said, 'See what I found trespassing on the estate? And a more cut-throat ruffian you'd be pleased to find!'

Annie was almost snuggling against him and grinning from ear to ear. Julia leaned forward in a businesslike manner and rested her hands on her knees.

'Hmm,' she replied seriously, 'and this one is a persistent offender too, isn't it? I think we'll chop its hands off, Matt, teach the others a lesson.'

'Oh, I don't think so,' he replied. 'It claims it's staying the weekend, and since I feel in my bones it's going to behave abominably, it's going to be digging potatoes tomorrow which it won't be able to do with no hands!'

Annie's little body seemed suddenly to thrill with excitement. Her green eyes danced with delight and she threw herself at Julia joyfully.

'The whole weekend?' Julia echoed catching her fondly in her arms. 'Well I won't even ask how you got permission for that – only I bet it wasn't from your father. Do you own a nightdress?'

Annie shook her head.

'Never had one in me life. Can I borrow one of yours?'

Julia grinned.

'Well you could, but you'll need to put a knot in it somewhere. In case you hadn't noticed I'm about a foot taller than you. No, I think we'll have to buy you one this afternoon. In return you can do something for me, if you will?'

Annie looked as if she would be prepared to put the sun out if she was asked and Julia hugged her comfortably.

'Would you mind sharing a room with Minnie?' she asked. 'I'm really not that happy about her being on her own. I was thinking I might put her in with me, but I think she'd like it better if you had a bed in her room.'

Matt, who was still standing in the doorway made a noise of protest in the back of his throat.

'Them two, in together!' he exclaimed. 'Well, for sure you and I'll no get a wink of sleep! I think mebbe I'll take my bed and go and sleep in the dower!'

'Oh, there won't be any trouble, I assure you,' Julia replied, glancing at him with mock severity. '*One word* after ten o'clock and this one will be digging potatoes all night!'

As the car containing Matt, Annie, Julia and Minnie purred quietly into the village at just after four that afternoon, Sophie Crompton was in the village shop buying biscuits for the children. Miss Hewlett had been glancing restlessly through the window the whole time Sophie had been in the shop, and as the car went by she seemed to hiss, almost like a satisfied snake.

'Well there she goes, Miss Penrose,' she observed. 'Julia Drake and that friend of hers – and they got Annie Paynter in the car with them, as well!'

'Well I don't know, I'm sure,' replied Miss Penrose primly, adding to Sophie, 'I suppose your husband knows all about this visit?'

'What visit?' Sophie enquired, mystified.

The spinsters seemed to pounce, like a couple of hunting cats.

'Julia Drake is bringing folk back from Blackridge, to stay at Tremar!' Miss Hewlett exclaimed indignantly. 'From *Blackridge* if you ever did! Well I s'pose your husband wouldn't know, would he, else he'd have put a stop to it. But that Julia and that savage from up north she's got as a gamekeeper, well they behaves like they owns the place. He's put barbed wire across footpaths if you please, stopping folks going about their lawful business.'

Sophie Crompton regarded the two old women contemptuously, and struggled to keep it from her voice as she answered.

'Julia's friend will be Minnie,' she said, 'Oliver says she's a sweet lady; he knows her quite well, he used to take Julia to visit her every week, until Julia got her own car. As for Matt Logan, he's Julia's estate manager, actually, and I don't think you'll find he's blocked any rights of way, he's just trying to keep trespassers off the estate. She has a right to her own land, you know, ladies.'

'Well I'm surprised to hear you defending her, my dear,' Miss Penrose said with extraordinary venom, 'considering – what we knows about her. Still, it's commendably Christian of you, I'm sure. Isn't it, Miss Hewlett?'

'Commendably Christian,' Miss Hewlett agreed with a pitying look. 'Here,' she took up a penny bar of chocolate and pressed it into Sophie's hand, 'take a little treat for them lovely kiddies of yours.'

Sophie would have liked very much to throw the chocolate at her, but swallowing back her anger she took her purchases and left the shop, politely thanking the ladies for their gift.

She wanted to tell Oliver about Minnie, but he wasn't home and by the time he came home it had slipped her mind for the moment.

Minnie stood in the hallway at Tremar looking suddenly bewildered and frightened. All afternoon she had been giggling and whispering with Annie, safe and secure in her routine, but suddenly the routine had changed and she was thrown into a panic. Tremar's rich, dark hallway which to the others was a peaceful, tranquil place, was dark and threatening to Minnie.

'I want to go home,' she whispered. 'I don't like this place.'

Julia said quickly, 'Minnie, darling, this is a special place for you.' But Minnie backed away in a panic.

Annie grinned and saved the day.

'D'you want to see my room?' she asked, grabbing Minnie's hand and yanking her towards the stairs. 'I got this big room and there's two beds in it. You can share my room, if you like!'

Minnie hung back for a moment at the foot of the stairs, and as Matt and Julia watched, Annie touched her shoulder lightly.

'Race you!' she yelled, and at once Minnie was lumbering clumsily up behind her, Annie keeping only just in front and, touchingly, allowing her to ultimately win the race.

Julia turned to Matt, her eyes full of tears.

'She's a good child, isn't she?' she whispered, and her face crumpled.

Matt took her against him gently, wrapping her in his huge arms.

'She's a precious gift,' he replied softly.

When they had eaten an early dinner, which Mrs Collins had prepared with touching kindness, recognizing Minnie's difficulty with a knife and fork, the four of them elected to go for a walk in the grounds with the puppies.

Suddenly Minnie looked at Julia and abruptly her eyes lit up. It was very brief as the memory dawned, like a light switching on.

'Will there be daffodils, Julia?' she asked anxiously and Julia hugged her tightly.

'Fancy you remembering that,' she whispered. 'No, darling, it's summer now so there aren't any daffodils any more. Do you remember what flowers we look for in summer?'

Minnie frowned.

Ro . . .' she murmured, almost knitting her eyebrows together with the effort. 'Ro. . . ?'

'Ro . . . ses,' Julia said with a fond smile. 'That's right, and what colour are roses?'

'Yellow?'

'No, that's daffodils. Well, sometimes roses are yellow, but we learned that roses were red and pink, didn't we? Shall we see if we can find some?'

Matt had to help Minnie down the terrace steps; they were rough and uneven and her uncoordinated frame swayed dangerously as she forgot about holding on and threw her hands up in fright. Down on the lawn, however, she began to run about with Annie and the puppies again and for no real reason the party wandered in the direction of the derelict summer-house, forlorn beside the overgrown tennis-courts, and still waiting to be demolished.

It was a still, summer evening, with drunken bees lurching about in the warm air and herring-gulls calling mournfully above the cliffs. Every breath they drew seemed to be heavy with a heady mixture of perfumes and the peace was extraordinary. Beside and around the summer-house, roses grew in profusion. Once they had been the pride of much-tended flower beds, now they straggled wildly, but were bright and beautiful.

Matt took a small penknife out of his pocket and with great care selected three beautiful blooms, cut them, removed any thorns and handed one to each of his ladies with much gallantry.

Annie immediately pushed hers behind her right ear and taking Minnie's from her fingers did the same with it. Minnie seemed to contrast dreadfully with the bloom: her wrinkled, pasty-coloured skin was blunt and stark against the glorious pink smoothness of the rose. Annie had a bloom on her cheek as rich as her rose, she was young and full of the promise of life – and suddenly Julia realized, with a jolt against her heart, how beautiful she was, and how much like her father had been all those years ago, in that glorious summer before the war.

She turned her head swiftly to avoid looking at the child because of the pain of her memories, and abruptly Minnie seemed to pluck the emotion from the air and uncannily speak it out loud.

'Julia, you said he was still alive, the man who put you in here.' she said earnestly. 'You said you thought he was killed in the war and he wasn't, he was still alive.' And looking for approval at remembering, she peered closely into Julia's face.

Julia drew her breath sharply, and shivered with the irony of it. It had been the last time she and Minnie had sat by the shed at Blackridge, on her first visit after being released, and undoubtedly what had brought it to Minnie's mind were the circumstances but to hear her pain spoken out loud like that made her skin break out in goosebumps.

'Yes, darling, I did say that, didn't I?' she whispered, touching Minnie's earnest face with her fingers: 'And I was right, he is still alive, but that was a long time ago, you know. Weeks and weeks.'

'I thought it was yesterday,' Minnie said. 'I thought we were here yesterday . . .' She frowned and then turned to look at Annie. 'Can I hug one of the puppies?' she asked.

Annie scooped one up and held it for her and as they stood immersed in what they were doing, Matt took Julia's rose from her fingers and very gently pushed it behind her ear to match the others.

'It makes you look very beautiful,' he said gravely, and she laughed.

'I think I'm a bit old for roses behind my ear,' she replied, 'but thank you anyway. When they've gone to bed do you plan to go down to The Smugglers?'

'I should like to spend the evening sitting with you,' he answered with that remarkable knack he had of speaking the truth without embarrassment and with astonishing honesty. 'But you must say if that offends you.'

'I can't think of a single thing I'd like better,' she said, touching his hand gratefully.

It was extremely peaceful in the drawing-room at Tremar, when Annie and Minnie had gone to bed. The night was warm and dark, the lamps golden, throwing soft pools of light across the two occupants of the room who sat opposite each other in deep, comfortable armchairs and talked in tranquil voices, as the puppies slept between them on the carpet.

Less than a mile away in The Smugglers the hot air was thick with tobacco smoke and beer fumes, the pub door was open on to the slipway and moths flitted about in the light that streamed out into the summer night.

Tom Pennard and Arthur Paynter sat with three other swarthy-looking men, the earthy, sweatiness of their bodies adding to the potent mixture of smells in the tiny pub. They were drunk and they were angry.

'Filling the feckin' place with dangerous criminals from Blackridge,' Arthur snarled. 'Bleddy hell, there's children in this village, and we all stand to be murdered in our beds!'

'Well, my wife seemed t'think there was any number of them staying up there,' Tom Pennard said. 'Seems the old ladies from the shop told her. Bleddy scared out of their wits, they are.'

Miss Penrose and Miss Hewlett were unlikely to be frightened in the presence of the devil himself, and Arthur and Tom Pennard knew that perfectly well, but for Arthur Paynter this was a gift from God. Julia Drake had finally stepped over the mark. With any luck he might even get her put back in Blackridge for this and then she would be out of harm's way for evermore.

In a couple of rare sober moments recently, he had wondered if he might not have been wiser to have compromised with her, but the years of grinding, silent guilt had spawned a hatred that was like a beast within him. Every time the Drakes had been mentioned, every time they had made solicitous enquiries about his welfare, every bloody day of his life that Gladys had looked at him with reproach and contempt he had been forced to remember his cowardice. Then Annie had come along, and Gladys's voice saying, 'Julia 'ad a daughter; it died,' had echoed over and over in his head until he'd needed a drink to quiet it.

He knew he was wrong to dream of putting Julia back into Blackridge

– dear God, he didn't even want to try and imagine what twenty-three-and-a-half years of that must have been like, but, irrationally, he told himself that if only he could rid himself of her again then everything would go back to the way it was before. And now he was ready to join forces with anyone who would plot against her with him.

Looking round at the snarling faces of his companions at the pub table he took another large swig of beer and leaning back in the wooden settle, wiped his hand across his mouth thoughtfully.

'How many men d'you reckon you could get together between you?' he enquired.

The three discussed it briefly, then Tom Pennard answered, 'About twenty. There's plenty enough round here are thoroughly sick of the antics of that bleddy Scotsman; blocking paths we've used for years and threatening to take anyone he finds poaching to court!'

'Right then,' Arthur said triumphantly, 'we meet on the green at twelve o'clock tomorrow; gives plenty a time for anyone who wants to, to get in. Tell anyone who comes to bring a weapon: stave, pitchfork, whatever they fancies, and we'll march on Tremar. Twenty or so of us ought to be able to do a bit of damage, break windows and such like, and at the same time we can teach that feckin' Scotsman a lesson he won't soon forget! What d'you say?'

'I say we'll see you there at twelve tomorrow,' Tom Pennard replied, and eyed the other three. 'Right?'

'Feckin' right!' one of them answered gleefully, and went to the bar to buy some more beer.

Arthur Paynter was glowing with anticipation as he staggered back to Rectory Farm at closing time. Tomorrow he'd teach Julia Drake that she was much mistaken if she thought she could ruin him and he'd simply take it lying down. And depending on how rough it got, there was an outside chance that Scotsman who had kicked him in the dust in front of Annie would be seriously hurt. If he could be removed from Tremar, controlling Julia Drake after that would be easy.

As he lurched unsteadily into the kitchen, Gladys was sitting at the kitchen table doing some mending. She didn't bother to look up, she was quite used to him coming home in this state and she hated him twice as much when he was drunk as she did when he was sober.

Her two hard-working sons were already in bed and she thought briefly that if she could get Arthur into bed reasonably quickly she might be able to slip away and sleep in Annie's for once. At least it would be quiet. Arthur snored like a pig when he was as drunk as he obviously was tonight.

'Hello, my lovely Gladys,' he slurred, grinning at her, 'waiting up for me, was you?'

She still didn't look at him.

'Oh, get to bed, you drunken slob,' she retorted. 'Look at you, you can hardly stand up!'

He seemed suddenly to be suspiciously cheerful and Gladys supposed he had won some money gambling and then tossed it down his throat in beer form. On occasions such as these he would usually paw her clumsily when they were in bed, though if he could still actually do anything after so many years of drinking she would be surprised; there had been no coupling between them since Annie was born. In fact, it was hard to remember it at all now. She was about to sigh and put away her mending when he spoke to her again, and his words almost froze the blood in her veins.

'I'm not so drunk that I can't get bleddy Annie out a bed and tell her what I'm going to do to her precious bleddy Julia tomorrow,' he declared cheerfully. 'I'm not that feckin' drunk!'

Gladys leapt to her feet in alarm. It was a mistake.

She said, 'No!' and immediately he turned on her, his eyes wide and questioning.

'Why not?' he demanded suspiciously as his hand shot out and grabbed a handful of her hair. 'Why not, Gladys?'

She whimpered with pain as he twisted the hair in his fist, pulling so hard that it felt as if he was lifting her scalp.

'Why not, Gladys?' he repeated in a dangerously low voice. 'Because she bleddy well ent here, is she?'

'She'm asleep, Arthur,' she bleated, 'leave her be, please—'

'You lying *bitch*!' he snarled, and brought his other fist up into her face with an explosive punch.

She reeled away from him, crashing into the table, gasping for breath as blood ran from her nose and trickled unpleasantly into her mouth. Winded, and spitting blood, she backed away, struggling to put some distance between them and get close enough to the door to make an escape into the house. He wouldn't risk attacking her if she was near enough to the twins' room to rouse them from sleep; nowadays they didn't take too kindly to their father beating up their mother. But Arthur headed her off.

'She'm up at Tremar, ent she?' he whispered viciously, advancing on her, backing her into a corner where she was helpless. 'You tell me, Gladys, or so help me I'll break your useless neck!'

Gladys wiped her face with her hands, smearing blood all over the place. She sniffed and it ran down the back of her throat. Her face smarted from the savagery of his blow and she knew he would hit her again; she knew because she had endured countless beatings in her married life – but it didn't make them hurt any less.

'It were a treat for her,' she sobbed. 'She likes Julia's friend—'

'You said she could go?' he roared. 'After all I've said about her staying away from that place? This is *my* house, woman!' He slapped her savagely, 'And *I* say who does what here!' His hand came back with even more force. 'Well, when we've finished teaching bleddy Julia Drake a lesson tomorrow, I'll drag Annie back here by her hair, and when I gets her here, I'll bleddy *kill her*!'

Gladys was reeling, trying her best to roll with the punches to lessen their impact. Eventually she crouched down on her haunches, pressing herself into a corner trying to protect her head with her hands. She was covered in blood and her eyes were beginning to close, her body ached with blows to her ribs and her bottom lip was split, but it hadn't been as bad a beating as she had often received in the past, and she knew he would get bored in a minute, he always did once she was sufficiently cowed.

Finally, when the blows had lessened enough for her to speak, she tried, as was always her way, to take his mind off what he was doing. If he was angry enough at someone else it usually meant he would stop beating her.

'So what're you going t'do to Julia tomorrow, Arthur?' she asked in a small voice. 'I'm sure you'm going to tell me anyway.'

'There's going to be about twenty of us,' he replied triumphantly, leaning back against the table and viewing her bruised, blood-smeared face with satisfaction, 'and we're going to teach her a lesson she'm not going to forget easily. We're meeting on the green at midday and if I has my way we'll break every bleddy window in Tremar.' He folded his arms, smiling cheerfully. 'What's more I'm going to kill that feckin' Scotsman; it shouldn't be that difficult, with everything else that'll be going on. I'll teach Julia Drake to fill that house full of halfwits, and I'll teach her who's in charge in this village. We don't tug forelocks any longer round here, we help ourselves to what we wants.'

Gladys remained crouched in the corner listening to him, hoping he had begun to forget about her. She was in some pain, but after so many years she was pretty much desensitized to physical pain. Her ribs and her face would hurt for a day or two but if she was lucky he wouldn't hit her again whilst the bruises were healing. He certainly wouldn't say sorry, he never did that, so she had long since ceased to expect it. In the morning she could expect her sons to mutter darkly about their father's brutality, but they were unlikely to do any more than speak to him about it, and he would say sorry to them, and promise not to do it again, and that would be an end to it.

Far more seriously, she knew she had somehow got to stop what was going to happen tomorrow – the repercussions of a mob, led by Arthur, marching on Tremar and smashing the place up were too dreadful to think about.

Slowly, wincing slightly, she hauled herself to her feet and watched him nervously for a moment, as he perched on the edge of the kitchen table, gazing at her with drink-fuddled eyes.

'I'm going to bed now,' she announced and he shrugged.

Quietly she lifted the kitchen latch and let herself out into the dark, musty-smelling hallway.

Tomorrow she would have to be up betimes and walk to the village on the pretence of doing some shopping. She'd have to go to the doctor, he was likely to be the only person who could quell a riot – though how he might do it she didn't even dare think about.

Chapter 18

When Julia awoke in the morning she lay for a few seconds gazing at the ceiling and then remembered that Minnie and Annie were in the bedroom next door. She had not heard a sound all night, so apparently Minnie had slept peacefully and that was a good sign.

She thought she would creep in and see them in a while, but for a few moments she simply lay on her back in her big double bed thinking warmly about the evening before. She and Matt had stayed up talking until after midnight. She had told him things she felt sure she would never have told another living soul, and had an idea he had done the same with her.

At one point in the extraordinary evening she had hunted out the family photograph albums, which contained a faithful, year by year record of the young lives of the heir to Tremar and his sister. Somehow it didn't surprise her that her mother had never destroyed them, but she would have put money on it that she had never looked at them again once her son was dead and her daughter shut up in Blackridge. Two beautiful children growing with a new century – and ruined before the century was out of its teens.

As she and Matt had sat looking at the carefully labelled sepia photographs she had found to her astonishment that she could smile with the memories. Sandro, six and solemn, playing cricket with his father, neatly clad in a striped cap and blazer. She at eight, in starched and fussy white with a high collar, ridiculously large white hat, thick, black stockings and shoes, her hair carefully combed over her shoulders.

'Sunday best?' Matt asked, chuckling, and she wrinkled her nose.

'Absolutely *hateful*,' she replied. 'God, those clothes scratched *everywhere*!'

He grinned. 'Aye, but you were a beautiful child for all that.'

Why, she wondered as she wriggled comfortably in her big bed and enjoyed the memories, did it mean so much to her that he thought she had been a beautiful child?

Of the photographs just the last few had raised sharply painful memories, those taken during that remarkable summer of 1914. Sandro in cricket whites, grown up and handsome; so soon to be ripped to bits by careless bullets. She on the terrace in a skirt and blouse and a fashionable hat. The recent schoolgirl, soon to be débutante – but much sooner to be condemned to a living death. And then, on the very last page, three photographs which she had taken herself. Photographs that made her put trembling fingers up to her lips.

Sandro in his uniform and, below that, the three musketeers and their D'Artagnan in one photograph, and in the other, identical twin boys with a girl in a plain cotton dress, a straw hat and lots of curly brown hair.

Matt had touched both the pictures very softly with his fingers and finally pointed to the one of the four young men in uniform.

'Annie's father.'

Julia had touched the girl in the straw hat with equally soft fingers.

'And her mother.'

And suddenly Matt had been intensely close, his smell of tweed and sandalwood sharply defined. They had sat quite still, staring at the painful confusion of lives and emotions that seemed to shout from the photographs, and in some indefinable way he had touched her soul. He had soothed her pain without looking at her or touching her, but just by being there.

In the bright light of morning, as she stretched her arms above her head and listened to the ever-present herring-gulls calling above the cliffs of Tremar, she thought about Matt and felt extremely happy.

At last, climbing out of bed she pulled on a long-sleeved silk robe, tied it tightly at her waist, slid her feet into her slippers and went out into the corridor, dragging a brush through her thick chestnut hair as she went – and to her astonishment Matt was coming towards her from the direction of the stairs, carrying a vast ebony and silver tray with tea things on it that were completely dwarfed.

For a moment she stared at him, then she burst out laughing.

'Where on earth did you find that tray?' she asked. 'It's the thing they used to bring my mother's breakfast up on years ago, when I was little.'

'Well I'm right sorry for the wee lassie who had to carry it!' he retorted. 'But I couldn't find anything else. Where shall I put it?'

He was bathed and dressed and ready for the day, she noticed. Evidently it was not his habit ever to lie about in bed. For a few seconds she paused, wondering about the protocol, then, with a shrug, she threw caution to the wind.

'Take it into my room,' she replied, 'I'll be with you in a minute, I'm just going to check on the girls – they're suspiciously quiet for my liking.'

He disappeared from view and very softly she turned the handle of Minnie and Annie's room and pushed the door noiselessly open. The room was dim and quiet and her eyes took a second or two to adjust. Then Matt was at her shoulder and together they gazed at the two beds. Minnie's was empty. Annie's was full of both of them and they were both sound asleep.

Julia turned to look at him.

'She must have woken in the night,' she whispered, 'and Annie didn't even think to come and wake me. Oh, bless her heart, Matt.'

'You see,' he replied softly, 'everything is working out just fine.' And they crept away to have their tea.

Jed and Jethro Paynter stared angrily at their mother's battered face as they ploughed into enormous breakfasts. Arthur was late in bed nursing a hangover, but that was quite normal, the boys were always at work long before he was. This morning, though, Gladys was desperate to see the back of all of them, so that she could get into the village.

'What did he beat you for, Ma?' Jethro demanded and Gladys shrugged, bringing extra chunks of thick bacon to the table.

'He didn't beat me, silly boy, I had a fall, that's all.'

'A fall!' Jed echoed. 'Where from, the bleddy roof? He beat you, and one of these days I'm going to teach him a lesson about beating women.'

'Oh, don't antagonize him, please,' she begged. 'We had a row about Annie, that's all. Now please, boys, don't say owt to him, let it go, for my sake. All right?'

The boys glanced at each other – it was like a mirror image. Gladys bent her head between them and at considerable cost to her cut mouth, kissed each of them fondly.

'Well, one day,' Jed muttered, 'that's all – one day. . . .' And they went on with their breakfasts.

Arthur slouched downstairs at just before nine o'clock. He was dressed, but unshaven and he was a bit pasty-faced, but it didn't need a genius to see that he hadn't changed his mind about his march on Tremar.

He did open his eyes wide at the sight of Gladys's bruised face, but he didn't apologize, just sat himself down at the table and waited for his breakfast, which she took from the top of the range and put in front of him.

Two mouthfuls in he stopped and glared at her as he saw her gather up her shopping basket and purse.

'Where the hell are you going?' he asked.

'Up the village,' she replied, 'I won't be long but I got to do a bit of shopping.'

'What about your face?' he said, and she shrugged.

'I told the boys I fell,' she answered, 'they seemed happy enough with it, anyway, ent no business of anyone else's.'

Arthur grunted.

'Well, you mind you keep it that way,' he snorted and went back to his breakfast.

Sophie Crompton was tidying away toys in her draughty living-room and keeping one eye on the children in the garden when there was a knock on the side-door. She was surprised, because Oliver was taking the morning surgery and it was unusual for people to come to the house door when the surgery was open.

Swiftly tossing some wooden bricks into Edward's little cart she went to see who was calling. She looked pretty with the new hairstyle Oliver had given her as a present, and in the last few days she had taken to putting a little make-up on her pale skin. Oliver was being extraordinarily unselfish at the moment – for him – and she was much the better for it.

When she saw Gladys on the doorstep her mouth fell open in horror.

'Mrs Paynter,' she whispered. 'Look, you've come to the wrong door, the surgery entrance is at the front.'

'I don't want the surgery,' Gladys replied miserably, fingering her sore, swollen lip, which pained her every time she spoke. 'I've come to warn you, 'cos I can't think of anyone else who can do anything. Please, let me come in.'

'Well, of course,' Sophie replied stepping back immediately, 'come in and I'll make you a cup of tea – but I do think you should let Oliver look at you, you're terribly badly bruised. Did your husband do it?'

Gladys chuckled mirthlessly.

'Who else?' she retorted. 'This is Arthur's idea of fun when he's had too much to drink. But listen, it ent *nothing* in comparison with what he intends to do to Julia Drake this morning.'

Ten minutes later Sophie knocked on the surgery door and quietly let herself in. Oliver, who was with a patient, looked up.

'I'm sorry to disturb you,' she murmured, smiling her gentle smile at the woman with the child who were in consultation with the doctor and who had turned to look as she came in. 'I'm afraid there's a bit of an emergency, Oliver.'

Oliver didn't question her, Sophie was a very good doctor's wife and she would not have disturbed him if it hadn't been urgent.

'Can it wait a couple of minutes?' he asked, and she nodded.

'Of course, but when you've finished here,' she replied, 'speed really is of the essence.'

Five minutes later Oliver stood and stared in disgust at Gladys's battered face and then treated her with some balm as she retold her story.

When she had finished she said, 'Please don't treat me, Doctor, I've no money to pay you for treatment.'

Oliver pursed his lips sharply.

'There will be no charge for what little I can do for you, Mrs Paynter,' he assured her, 'besides, we're very grateful for your information. You will, of course, stay here with us for now, I hope.'

Gladys's eyes filled with fear and she clambered painfully to her feet. She hadn't bothered to mention the body blows she had taken last night, but her ribs were very painful and she was not looking forward to the walk home.

'Stay here!' she echoed. 'Dr Crompton, if Arthur finds out what I done, he'll kill me! No, I got to be home very shortly, and I can't have nothing more t'do with this. It's up to you now, and you *got* to stop it!'

When she had gone Oliver turned to look at Sophie. His face was white, and she knew he was frightened.

'So what are we going to do?' she asked, and he picked up the phone.

'Well first and foremost I must warn them at Tremar,' he replied, 'and I'll see if that grizzly bear of Julia's will come down to the village to try to head them off.'

She pressed her lips together and stared at him for a moment, then she said, 'You're not going up there then?'

Oliver shrugged his shoulders.

'What for?' he enquired. 'There's not a lot I can do up there, really, is there?'

Sophie felt what seemed to be a very ill-timed rush of relief and then chided herself for being selfish. She still found the need to defend Matt, though.

'Mr Logan is not a grizzly bear, Oliver,' she observed quietly, 'he's a very nice man, if you take the trouble to get to know him – and I have an idea he's very fond of Miss Drake, too.'

Julia broke the connection with Oliver and replaced the telephone receiver in the hall astonishingly calmly. She knew she must stay calm because there was simply no time to cope with a possible panic attack from Minnie, and she really didn't want Annie to know what her father was planning, but in truth she was quite sick with fright and absolutely furious. How dare Arthur stir up this sort of prejudice against her? Dear God, wasn't there *ever* going to be a moment when he'd done enough? She went first into the kitchen to see Mrs Collins.

'They'll not break any bleddy windows here!' the woman declared ferociously when Julia had told her what was about to happen. 'This'll be them two old witches in the village shop, you know, spreading lies and rumours – Oh, somebody ought to burn them at the stake!'

Julia couldn't have begun to tell her how touched she was at such loyalty, and was rather glad there wasn't any time for it.

Instead she said, 'I couldn't agree with you more, but for all that I don't want any heroics, Mrs Collins. I won't have you hurt on my behalf. What I'd like you to do, please, is collect Minnie and Annie, as calmly as you can, and take them across to Home Farm. Matt and I will deal with Mr Paynter and his cronies. Now I'll go and speak to the girls, they're still having breakfast, and then I'm off to find Matt.'

Minnie was making rather a mess with a bowl of porridge and Annie, who was downing quantities of toast and marmalade was surreptitiously helping out, mostly by using another spoon to shovel the spills back into the bowl.

'What's up?' she asked, frowning, as Julia burst rather clumsily into the morning-room, and Julia made a valiant effort to control her face.

'Nothing,' she replied lightly, 'I've got to dash out and find Matt, that's all. When you and Minnie have finished I wonder if you'd mind walking across to Home Farm with Mrs Collins.'

Annie knitted her brows suspiciously.

'What for?' she demanded. 'What's the matter? I'll go and find Matt for you.'

'No, I'll be quicker,' Julia answered, still trying to keep it light, 'er . . . there's something Mrs Collins has to, er . . . has to do over at Home Farm and she could use your help. Oh, for heaven's sake, Annie Paynter, stop asking questions and just do as you're asked! And you be nice to her, young lady, or I'll. . . .'

Annie grinned, her eyes sparkling wickedly.

'Yeah, you'll do what?'

'I'll make you learn a whole page of Latin translation. This afternoon. When the rest of us are going to the bay. And don't think I won't, you precocious brat! Now eat your toast, you dustbin.'

Annie cackled happily and Julia bent over Minnie, kissing her gently.

'Stay with Annie, darling,' she whispered, absently wiping some porridge from Minnie's withered cheek, 'and go with her and Mrs Collins. You'll be able to play with the puppies at Home Farm, so that'll be a treat, won't it?' And without another word she left the room and ran down the corridor to the drawing-room.

Two minutes later she was racing across the lawns to the orchard and the path through the rhododendrons that led eventually to Home Farm.

Arthur met Tom Pennard coming up from the bay at eleven-thirty. Tom was armed with a vicious-looking, heavy, metal spike, Arthur had a pitchfork. As they drew closer to the green others began to join them, mostly young farm workers who were fathers and had been given to understand that the guests staying at Tremar were extremely dangerous, particularly to children. They were young, strong and armed to the teeth, and the sight of them, coming finally on to the green at five minutes to twelve, was very frightening.

Miss Hewlett and Miss Penrose were pressed against their shop door excitedly watching, righteously congratulating themselves on having done their civic duty. But for all that, the door was locked: if there was going to be any trouble no one was going to be permitted to take refuge in *there.* What appeared to be a considerable number of the other inhabitants of Polwean were gathered in a group outside the Drake Arms and Sophie Crompton stood on her own at the gate of Lamplighter House.

Alone on the green, facing the oncoming rabble, stood Oliver and Matt. Oliver had no weapon of any kind. Matt carried the enormous stick he had brought with him to Tremar and from which he was very rarely parted. Oliver looked rather white. Matt looked perfectly calm. The sun shone brightly in a clear blue sky, the ivy over the front of the pub rustled in a gentle breeze and the clock on the solid, grey tower of the church struck twelve.

Arthur, Tom Pennard and their seventeen companions marched threateningly across the green and finally stopped, no more than two feet from Oliver and Matt. Arthur rested his pitchfork on the ground and leaned on it casually, and to his fury he saw what appeared to be a tiny smile of amusement playing about Matt's lips.

Savagely he narrowed his eyes.

'I should get out our way, if I were you, Doctor,' he observed menacingly, 'this ent no fight with you. It's *him* we'm after,' he pointed at Matt, 'and then when we've finished with him, we'm going on up the Manor to teach that Drake bitch a lesson she won't forget!'

'Oh, for heaven's sake!' Oliver retorted. 'This is ridiculous! What do you think this is, the Middle Ages? Go home, man, and take your friends with you, before you make utter fools of yourselves. You've got absolutely no grounds whatever to go storming up to Tremar, and you know that.'

'You'll no be allowed to, anyway,' Matt added calmly. 'You're no going past me, Arthur Paynter, so you might as well go back.'

Arthur's face became sharp and pinched as he remembered Matt kicking him into the dirt in front of Annie. Deep inside him he boiled with hatred.

'You!' he retorted, staring at Matt with glittering eyes. 'You think you'm going to stop me? I'm going to kill you, you feckin' foreign bastard!'

He took a step forward and at the same moment so did Oliver. There was a tiny, breathless pause and then, to everyone's astonishment, Arthur struck Oliver viciously across the side of the head with the pitchfork handle and knocked him to the ground.

There was a gasp of alarm from the little posse of farm workers, closely followed by an uneasy movement amongst them as they seemed to turn and look uncomfortably at each other and then fall back a pace or two. At that moment it struck Sophie Crompton that with the possible exception of Arthur Paynter and Tom Pennard, none of the others had actually expected, or really intended, to cause any damage at all. They had been whipped up into a frenzy by lies, and probably a pint or two of beer, but it had never occurred to them that they would really be expected to hurt anybody.

Yanking open the gate of Lamplighter House she strode across to where her husband lay stunned on the ground and planted herself between him and the men. Oliver was bleeding quite profusely from a cut on his ear and Matt had taken a step forward and was standing over him, almost guarding him it seemed but without taking his eyes off the rabble. Now all eyes were on Sophie, and she was astonishingly diminutive, her hands on her hips, her fly-away, corn-coloured hair blowing in the breeze, her feet firmly apart, facing a wall of huge, muscled farm workers.

'*That's enough*!' she roared furiously. 'Now stop it! All of you! I've never seen anything so pathetic in my life! A bunch of perfectly nice young men, armed to the teeth and preparing to march on a house full of women and smash windows. For goodness sake! I know most of your wives and children, you know, and I've an idea they would be horrified if they could see you now. Get back to your jobs, before this goes any further and gets really out of hand!'

A young man from somewhere in the group said, 'That's all very well, Missus, but we was told Tremar's full a mad people from Blackridge, and they was likely to attack our kiddies! Well we can't risk that!'

'Oh, for God's sake!' Sophie retorted contemptuously. 'Tell me, do you believe in Father Christmas as well? For your information there is *one* little middle-aged lady staying at Tremar. She's small and frightened and she has trouble using a knife and fork. Yes, she's a patient from Blackridge and do you know why she's there? Because when she was a child her father beat her so badly he damaged her brain! You know all about beating children, don't you, Mr Paynter? I've seen your little Annie with some very nasty bruises in the past. She's looking much better now though, since Julia Drake took her under her wing, isn't she!'

Arthur sneered at her.

'And what about the rest of it?' he demanded. 'Blocking paths, stopping folks going about their lawful business. And him,' he tossed his head towards Matt, 'attacking people for walking on a bit of land they bin walking on all their lives! She needs bringing down a peg, that bitch at Tremar – needs teaching a lesson, and she needs to be rid of *him* for a start!'

Sophie folded her arms and stared at Arthur, curling her lip as she did so.

'You have land, don't you Mr Paynter?' she asked. 'What would you do if you found somebody trespassing on it? More to the point, what would you do if you found somebody poaching on it? I've a *very* good idea. Julia Drake and her estate manager here are merely protecting her rights, because as the owner of Tremar she has a perfect right to keep anybody and everybody off her land. However, has it ever occurred to *any* of you who've been using unauthorized paths across it for years to simply go and *ask* her if she minds? No, of course it hasn't. The lady of the manor, she won't listen to us, that's what you think isn't it? Well you're wrong! She's a good woman and she's very fair, considering what's been done to her in her life! Listen to me, I'd like to tell you something very important, if you're prepared to listen.'

She was aware suddenly that Matt seemed to be of the opinion that she had the crowd under her control, and had put down his stick and was very carefully helping the shaken, bleeding Oliver to his feet. Swiftly she turned again to the sea of big faces before her, regarding them with extraordinary calm.

'Most of you were too young to remember Julia Drake being thrown into Blackridge,' she observed, 'not all of you, but most of you. Now I don't know what you were ever told; nothing, probably, until you heard she was coming home again, but for your information she is, and always has been, as sane as any of you. All she was ever guilty of was having a baby! Julia Drake was betrayed. She was betrayed by somebody in this village, somebody you all know quite well, I suspect. My husband found her, luckily, and rescued her, and all she wants now is to be left in peace. So put away your weapons, go home and get on with your lives, and leave her to get on with hers. All right?'

The group began to murmur between themselves, whispering to each other in low voices and Sophie took the opportunity to take a step closer to Arthur who still stood at the head of his now somewhat uncertain army.

'Mr Paynter,' she whispered very softly, 'would you like me to go on?

We could talk about a young girl being made pregnant, and a farm being accepted as a gift by a man who was really *not* entitled to it. We could talk about the same young girl being abandoned for almost a quarter of a century by the same young man, because he was too much of a coward to do anything to help her. Or shall I take Oliver home, shall Matt go back to Tremar and you and your friends go back to work? Which do you prefer? Either way it's all the same to me, I've got nothing to lose.'

Arthur glared at her furiously and knew he was beaten. They'd heard enough to decide them against marching on Tremar already, and to have Sophie Crompton spill out the rest was simply going to mean public humiliation for him. He turned to face his rabble of young men and to his further humiliation saw that three quarters of them had already turned away and were walking back across the green towards their homes.

Swinging back he snarled, 'You'll keep, you posh bitch!' And Sophie smiled.

'So will you, Mr Paynter,' she replied calmly, and pointing towards the pub added, 'look who's coming now.'

Across the green, looking very self-important in his well-brushed uniform and shiny buttons was the local policeman, He was a tall man, well into his fifties, and very good at handing out good hidings to local children caught scrumping apples. He would have had no idea of how to handle a riot, and Sophie realized it was more than possible he had recognized that some while ago, and chosen his time to put in an appearance with care.

'What's going on here then?' he enquired as Sophie found herself standing on the green with only Arthur, Tom Pennard, and Matt, who was still supporting the injured Oliver.

'Nothing at all, Constable,' she replied, 'my husband had a slight accident, that's all, so if you'll excuse me I'll go and attend to his wounds. Good-afternoon, gentlemen.'

At three-thirty that afternoon there was a second knock on Sophie Crompton's side door, but this time is wasn't Gladys Paynter. As she opened it she wasn't particularly surprised to see Julia Drake standing there, but it gave her a jolt under her diaphragm. It was going to be nice, she thought very briefly as she smiled and looked welcoming, when she and her family had finally gone back to London and she was no longer in danger of bumping into this beautiful obsession of her husband's.

'I came to say thank you,' Julia said quietly, 'I understand from Matt that you put yourself at some considerable risk on my behalf this morning.'

Sophie gazed at her jealously. She thought about the things she had said to the rabble a couple of hours ago and was vaguely annoyed with herself that she could boldly say and mean such things until actually faced with the woman herself – at which point she found it very hard to control her emotions.

She wanted to say, go away, I can only defend you if I don't have to see you. Instead she smiled and stepped back to invite her visitor in, saying as she did so, 'It was nothing, really. I did what I had to do. It was the right thing.'

Julia lifted her eyebrows quickly.

'All the same,' she replied, 'Matt said there were about twenty men and they were all armed. I dread to think what they'd have done to him, and Tremar, if you hadn't stopped them. He also told me Oliver was hurt, is he all right?'

'He's fine,' Sophie answered, 'well at least he will be in a day or two, at the moment his ear is very swollen and painful. He's been having a rest but I'll go and tell him you're here if you like.'

'No, please, you don't have to do that,' Julia whispered, 'it was you I came to see.'

The two women looked at each other steadily for a moment or two. Their paths had not crossed since the day they had picnicked in the bay, and this time they were on Sophie's territory. Sophie was looking very pretty with her new, flattering haircut and her delicately made-up face, and she was buoyed up with her newfound confidence. What she had actually done that morning had taken astonishing courage and she was just beginning to realize that. Suddenly she felt equal to the beautiful Julia.

'Please sit down,' she said with a smile, 'and I'll make some tea – it's my chance to repay you for the lovely picnic.'

Julia sat, and as Sophie went away to the kitchen she watched Alice through the french windows at the end of the long room, playing in the garden. The shiny-haired child was lovingly tucking her dolls into their pram. Julia would never see a child of her own play like that.

When Sophie came back she carried a tray with tea and cakes on it and began to pour for her guest with practised dignity. Handing Julia a cup and saucer she took her own and sat in an armchair opposite her.

'Do you think you'll have any further trouble, after this morning?' she asked politely.

Julia shrugged.

'I'll have trouble with Arthur Paynter for as long as we both live in the village,' she replied truthfully, 'and as neither of us is ever likely to leave, well, it's a stalemate, I'm afraid.'

Sophie smiled.

'But he'll never get the better of you, will he, Miss Drake?' she said and Julia glanced at her sharply.

Pressing her lips together she murmured, 'That sounded suspiciously like a criticism, Mrs Crompton.' And Sophie's face lit with warmth. Suddenly, astonishingly, she could say what she wanted to say, suddenly her repressed upbringing and her natural shyness seemed to fade away.

'Miss Drake,' she said quietly, 'I did what I did for you this morning because I'm very grateful to you. You sent Oliver away, didn't you, after that picnic we had on the beach? You told me you were not planning to share your life with him and the next time he came to see you, you sent him home. Thank you, for doing that.'

'So, it was one good turn deserves another, then?' Julia asked, knowing how much it would have cost Sophie to make a remark like that and silently applauding her for being brave enough to do it.

'Yes, I suppose you could put it like that,' Sophie answered. 'You did the right thing, so I had to as well. I don't know what you think of my relationship with Oliver . . .' she looked away quickly, staring at a spot on the carpet. 'Maybe you think I'm not the right person for him, I don't know. The fact is, however, I am his wife and the mother of his children and for better or for worse, I love him. He's putting his practice up for sale in the next few days and we hope to be gone from Polwean before Christmas.'

Julia watched her, watched what was the baring of an extremely private soul. She would have liked to say that, in her opinion, Oliver wasn't good enough for Sophie, but it was not her place.

Instead she said very quietly, 'I have no opinions on your relationship with your husband, Mrs Crompton, I just wish you the very best of luck when you move from here.' And at that moment Oliver came into the room.

As he saw Julia his heart leapt in his chest and then wrenched painfully, and he wondered if he would ever recover from the love of her.

She put down her cup and saucer and stood up quickly on his entrance and then was afraid she had made it uncomfortably obvious that she didn't want to be in the room with him.

'Oliver,' she murmured, 'I just came to say thank you, for this morning. As I said to your wife, I'm very grateful,' she stared at his face and winced slightly, 'and I'm very sorry that Arthur was so brutal with you.'

He put his hand gingerly up to his ear and didn't quite touch it. The side of his face was purple with bruising and the ear red, swollen and painful. It had taken some time to stop the bleeding.

He offered her a tight smile and said, 'Yes, well the mob did seem to have been somewhat misinformed. They'd been told you had a house full of raving lunatics enjoying a weekend break!'

'Oh, that will have been Arthur,' Julia replied. 'And those two poisonous old cats from the village shop. Mrs Collins told me they'd been doing their stuff. Anyway, if you're interested, Minnie's having a lovely weekend. She's sharing a room with Annie and – Matt's marvellous with her. On the strength of this I can't see it'll be long before she comes to Tremar to live.'

He wasn't interested. He didn't care about Minnie – dear God, but for Minnie, Julia might have left Tremar and gone to London with him. He knew he should smile and say how pleased he was and then, with great dignity, he should let her walk away but he couldn't resist one final, spiteful remark.

He said, 'I'll say this much for you, Julia, one way or another you seem to have managed to upset or irritate pretty well everyone in the village since you came home from Blackridge, haven't you?' and Sophie's eyes opened like saucers.

'*Oliver!*' she breathed, appalled.

Julia offered him a wry smile.

'Well perhaps not everyone,' she replied calmly, 'there do seem to be one or two people who'll still speak to me, I'm happy to say. Anyway, I won't take up any more of your time, as I said, I only came to say thank you, I'm really *very* grateful. And, when you've sold your practice, you will say goodbye before you leave, won't you?'

When Sophie came back from the door she glared at her husband angrily.

'How *could* you be so rude!' she exclaimed. 'Really, Oliver!'

Furiously he turned away, as it seemed to him, his very soul cried out for Julia and he wanted nothing more than to run out after her and fall on his knees in front of her.

'I just – want to get away from here,' he retorted. 'I want to go back to London and surround us with normal people again. They give me the creeps, the people in this village! Oh hell, I just want to be rid of her Sophie!'

Chapter 19

So the practice went up for sale and Oliver waited for a suitable buyer. He never went to Tremar and he never saw Julia – it was as if Tremar was in a different corner of the world from Polwean. August was beautiful, and people went on holiday, sunbathed, relaxed and waited with a kind of unreal dread for the war everyone thought was coming.

The builders finished at Tremar; the dower sported a fine new weatherproof roof. The fountain on the terrace came back to life and the fish that the little lead boy so lovingly cuddled spouted sparkling water from the rosette in its mouth, wetting the boy and making him dark and shiny, as Julia remembered him from childhood. She put lilies and goldfish in the basin and played the fountain every day.

Most of the inside of the house had been redecorated since her return from Blackridge and though the panelling still remained and her ancestors were still displayed on the walls, the paint was fresh, the bedrooms light and airy, all gloomy, flock wallpaper banished with the Victorian attitudes of the twelfth baronet and his wife.

There were, and it was quite noticeable, no pictures of Sir George and Lady Florence anywhere to be found.

Since taking on the job of estate manager, Matt had worked miracles, it seemed to Julia. Having had no proper care taken of it since before Sir George had died and particularly during the depression, when agriculture had been hit so hard, much of the estate had become blurred around the edges, there were boundary disputes between the tenants and between tenants and villagers. With maps, tact and firmness, Matt sorted them out and then had the necessary legal papers drawn up so that everyone knew exactly where they stood. And, finally, he was beginning to see the original pattern of Home Farm emerging and was able to make plans, with his employer, for its long-term future.

With long-neglected fields suddenly being called into service again, employment would become plentiful in the village, which warmed the locals to Julia Drake and her estate manager. Word went about that whatever she might have suffered in the intervening years, she was evidently determined to see Tremar back on its feet again, and that was fine by them.

In the meantime the farmhouse at Home Farm was being refurbished and Matt was living in the dower. It was a situation which Julia secretly rather liked. They spent many comfortable evenings together, and by the end of August she was beginning to wonder if it couldn't be made permanent – if she could find a tactful way to do it. The farmhouse could be let, in fact it could be divided up without too much trouble and let to more than one family, and to Julia it seemed proper that her estate manager should live in the dower.

The year began subtly to turn, the summer lingered briefly and then gave way to shorter, cooler days, the leaves took on the reds and browns of autumn, the lamps were lit much earlier in the evenings and Annie realized sadly that she would soon have to put away her summer dresses.

Julia said, 'Well, it doesn't matter, you've got some lovely new things that we've made for the winter.' But it did matter to Annie. Those summer dresses were the first real clothes she'd ever had. Seeing them washed and knowing that soon they would be stored away for the winter made her sad.

By next summer they'd be too small, she'd never wear them again – and anyway, by next summer there still didn't seem to be any way she was going to be other than a kitchen maid to a family she didn't know, living miles away from Tremar.

Julia saw the child beginning to grow sad and felt wretched and angry, but no matter how many sanctions she imposed upon Arthur, nor how much she knew they must be suffering from lack of money, he wouldn't give in. He was still determined she shouldn't have Annie, just as she was determined she should.

There was one last hope. In October, Arthur was due the hundred pounds from Alexander's estate, which he wasn't going to get. Finding himself a hundred pounds short with nothing to come from the Tremar apple harvest and only poor returns on his timber was surely going to make the final difference?

'Have patience,' Julia said gently to Annie, 'you haven't gone yet, there's still plenty of time.'

But Annie had made up her mind. If it came to Christmas and her father had still not given in, she was going to run away. It would break her heart to leave Matt and Julia but anything was better than becoming a kitchen maid. She never thought about where she'd go, though, that was too complicated.

Two events happened in the autumn, the first one, of national importance, came on the last day of September, as everyone was quietly making their preparations for the war that was surely upon them. Prime Minister Chamberlain came back from Munich waving a piece of paper and declaring 'Peace with honour!' and the world seemed to take a tentative step back from the brink. There were joyous scenes in London with the King and Queen appearing with Mr Chamberlain on the balcony at Buckingham Palace as the great crowd below them cheered frantically. But in only a short time, though everyone walked about smiling and saying 'peace!' it didn't feel as if anyone really meant it.

'It's still coming,' Matt muttered darkly, 'it's just no coming as fast as it was, that's all, you mark my words.'

And Julia did mark his words, and wondered, with a slight shiver, how she would have viewed all this if Oliver had never come to Blackridge to find her and she had still been there with no past, no future and only that day's lunch to look forward to. Another war – well, the repercussions for her personally couldn't be quite as bad as last time anyway. Whatever she might be in danger of, it wasn't getting pregnant.

The second event, two weeks later, touched only their immediate lives, for it was of absolutely no matter to anyone else. It was Julia's birthday. She was forty-one years old.

As it was to be a Saturday, she decided she would have a party; a tea-party, with just five guests. Annie and Matt, Minnie, Miss Vincent from Blackridge and Mrs Collins. Julia smiled wryly at herself when she went to formally invite her housekeeper – hadn't she once said she couldn't imagine ever sharing a social occasion with her? Prejudging, that's what she'd been guilty of, she who had prided herself on being above such a thing. She chided herself sharply, and particularly when she saw the look on Mrs Collins' face, for it was very obvious the woman was enormously touched.

'And we'll have all Minnie's favourites!' she declared happily. 'And some of Annie's too, of course.'

Julia chuckled.

'What about me?' she asked. 'It's my party!'

The housekeeper gave her a long sideways look.

'And was you allowed to choose what you wanted on your birthday when you was a little girl?' she enquired.

Julia inclined her head.

'Well now you come to mention it, no I wasn't,' she replied truthfully.

'Then nothing's changed, has it?' Mrs Collins declared, making her burst out laughing.

The Saturday before the party she took Annie with her and went shopping in town for some winter dresses for Minnie, a party outfit for Annie, since she'd never had anything shop-bought in her life, and a new dress for herself. She so rarely wore a dress that something really smart for her party seemed quite exciting – and it occurred to her that Matt had never seen her in anything other than trousers or practical skirts and blouses in all the time he'd known her – a thought she firmly squashed, reminding herself that she was buying a dress to suit herself, not anyone else.

Annie apparently didn't feel that way.

In numerous exclusive little dress shops she kept trundling in and out of the changing rooms with the most unsuitable choices: backless, slinky ball-gowns and the like, endlessly bleating about how much Matt would like this one or that one, until Julia could cheerfully have strangled her.

In the end they settled on a black afternoon dress in fine wool. There wasn't any doubt that it set Julia's lean body off to its best advantage – although she did remember her mother telling her at sixteen that she wouldn't be able to wear black after thirty. It was cut very slim and fitted like a glove and its only ornament was a wide black and white bow at the neck. To wear with it she bought herself a pair of very expensive, black high-heeled shoes – and she cared very much how Matt would think she looked, though she didn't say so to Annie.

For Annie she chose a little suit in pale green, with a slim jacket and pleated skirt and a cream georgette blouse to wear underneath it. It was probably too old for her, Julia thought, after all she was only fourteen, but she looked so well in it that it would have been criminal not to buy it. At the same time she bought her her first ever pair of stockings and a very grown-up pair of black, patent-leather shoes.

On the day of her birthday Julia awoke to a breezy, chilly, but bright October morning and stood for some time at her window, gazing out on to the leaf-strewn lawns. She hadn't celebrated her birthday since she was seventeen and the memories crossed the years sharply. That had been a nightmare day, hideous in its awfulness. She had known by then that she was pregnant and there had been no one to help her. Alone and facing the terror of it; counting the days until her condition was discovered.

Now, twenty-four years later, on a remarkably similar chilly morning, it was faintly ironic to remember her dread. No amount of fear could have prepared her for the punishment her parents had meted out. She didn't know exactly what she had expected, but it certainly hadn't been Blackridge asylum.

She had gone downstairs to breakfast alone, sorely missing Sandro. Her parents had given her a gold and pearl ring, the one she now wore on her little finger. Her hands had been smaller then and she had slipped it on to the third finger of her right hand and politely thanked them, these extraordinary, remote people to whom she belonged. Her mother, like an exquisite doll sitting there at one end of the table with her smooth face and smooth hair and attitude of slavish obedience. Her father with his familiar domed head and the pince-nez perched on his nose to aid his perusal of *The Times.* He had absently called her a fine young lady.

The same fine young lady he had tossed out of his life like yesterday's newspaper less than four months later.

The only other person who had given her a present that day was Gladys: a little, smooth piece of pink and white rock crystal pressed into her hand for luck. When, after her return from Blackridge, she had come upon her small trinket box stored carefully with her mother's jewellery, the ring and the piece of rock crystal had still been in it.

All those years her mother had faithfully kept – out of her father's view, of course – a little gold and pearl ring and a pink stone . . . and what? Brainwashed herself into believing the lie? My beloved dead daughter's pathetic remaining earthly possessions. Astonishing.

She had decided she was going to give Annie the ring, probably for Christmas.

When she was dressed and ready to face this first birthday for twenty-four years, she opened the trinket box to find her ring and saw the little stone nestling in folds of red velvet in the bottom of the box. Gathering it up she stared at it for a moment, then touched it to her lips, and slipped it into the pocket of her trousers.

The house was very quiet. She went down the stairs, across the hall and along the sunny passage towards the morning-room. The table was laid for three, Annie and Matt were joining her for breakfast, and she sat down to glance through her letters as she waited. Five minutes later they arrived, accompanied by the puppies, and Mrs Collins carried in a tray full of toast and creamy scrambled eggs, with a huge dish of mushrooms and lots of coffee.

'Oh, lord, how scrumptious,' Julia whispered, and was gently handed a prettily wrapped, soft parcel.

'Happy birthday, m'dear,' the housekeeper murmured and went out of the room with the empty tray.

'A present!' Julia said in genuine astonishment. 'And another,' said Annie, putting hers on top of the first one. 'And a third,' said Matt, placing his beside Annie's.

Julia burst into tears.

'I've never had a birthday like this,' she explained, and, quite overcome, uttered another couple of sobs and pressed her napkin to her face.

Annie and Matt sat on either side of her at the table and tactfully ignoring her, began to serve out the breakfast. Finally Julia wiped away a couple of tears with her fingers and grinned sheepishly.

'Sorry,' she muttered and began to eat.

Mrs Collins' present was a beautiful bleached-linen table runner, with some lovely drawn threadwork at either end, a very thoughtful present which Julia was proud to place on her dressing-table where it looked very fine.

Mrs Collins was as pleased as punch when she saw it there later in the morning.

Annie's present was six fine, white, lace-edged cotton handkerchiefs, upon each of which she had embroidered, in one corner, a pink rose and the letter 'J'. The embroidery was very carefully and lovingly done and Julia was so touched she almost started to cry again.

'They're wonderful, darling,' she whispered, kissing Annie fondly, 'but it looks to me as if you've spent every last ha'penny of the money you've been earning from Matt for doing jobs at Home Farm. You shouldn't have done that.'

'She didn't!' Matt retorted wryly, his eyes twinkling brightly, 'You remember on the first morning we met, yon lassie gave me some information on the local poachers, and decided on a favour as payment?' Julia nodded. 'Well she just called in the favour.'

Annie smiled complacently and Julia gazed fondly at Matt. Annie had had so many favours from Matt over the past months that he almost certainly hadn't owed her six expensive cotton hankies – and they all knew it.

Matt's present was a tiny, elegant gold wristwatch on an extremely dainty integral bracelet. When Julia saw it her mouth fell open and she almost dropped it in surprise.

'Matt,' she whispered, staring in astonishment at him. 'It's *beautiful*! But you shouldn't have.'

He smiled, watching her contentedly with his deep blue eyes.

'I've never seen you wearing a watch,' he observed, and she shrugged.

'I've never owned one,' she admitted. 'Oh, there are a couple of my mother's upstairs with the rest of her jewellery, but I wouldn't be seen dead wearing one of those. But this . . .' she gazed at it, held carefully in her trembling fingers, 'it's so lovely.'

Matt leaned forwards in his chair and kissed her cheek fondly.

'I've an idea this is the first birthday you've celebrated in a good few years,' he said, 'so there's a lot of catching up to do.' And he slid the watch on to her wrist snapping the catch closed with remarkable dexterity for a man with such huge hands.

Julia took up one of Annie's hankies and slipped it neatly under the little gold catch.

'There!' she exclaimed. 'Now I look like a proper lady' and she uttered a little snort of laughter.

Gladys cleared the table at Rectory Farm after giving breakfast to her three men. It wasn't much of a breakfast these days, lots of bread and potatoes but not much in the way of meat, the same as all their other meals. They rarely ate their own eggs now, they were needed to sell, along with rabbits snared on their land. Occasionally one of the boys would scrag an old chicken, one that had stopped laying, and there would be a pot of chicken stew for a couple of days, but it was eaten with a lot of potatoes and doled out with strict care, so that it lasted as long as possible.

Of course, life should have been easy for them with the gifts Sir George had showered on Arthur in 1919. No dues, no rent, no wages now the boys were grown up. They would have been quite wealthy by now, if the landlord at The Smugglers hadn't spent twenty years benefiting from the proceeds of Rectory Farm.

It didn't leave much room for Julia Drake's biting sanctions.

When the dishes had been rinsed and were standing on the draining-board, Gladys slipped on her coat and went out into the cold, dirty farmyard. The wind was bitter, just as it had been on this day twenty-four years ago. She went across the cliffs to Tremar, stopping for some moments at the top, on that stone bench where she and Julia had met and talked that morning. She looked out to sea at the brisk white horses whipped up by the sharp wind and remembered how they had gazed that day. How they had both wanted the same thing – the same man, to come striding up the path to meet them, or sail in on some fantasy boat, to bring home their hopes and dreams.

How nice it would have been, she thought bitterly, if he'd died, like all his companions. How cruel an empty promise had been that warrior's return.

An icy blast of wind made her shiver and abruptly she went on to Tremar. She climbed the broken bit of wall that was Annie's entrance and came out from the trees on to the formal lawns. And suddenly she was looking at Tremar for the first time for nigh on twenty years.

For the first time since that garden party when Sir George and Lady Florence Drake had welcomed home three pathetic survivors from the war to end all wars. Twenty long, miserable years.

Leaves blew about the orchard from the apple-trees, and the pavilion, which still hadn't been demolished, was a forlorn sight with the approach of winter. Gladys walked across the lawns until she stood twenty yards or so from the terrace, looking up at the house, and at that moment her courage failed her. She was ready to go back. She had nothing to say to Julia, nothing that hadn't already been said. She was stupid to have come and now it was time to go, but for a moment she gazed at the house as she allowed just a few of her precious childhood memories to creep back.

Julia had just finished making a great success of the fire in the drawing-room, fiddling about with it until it was blazing merrily up the chimney, and stood up to brush off her clothes, gazing out at the blustery day. The sight of Gladys, standing in the middle of the lawns gave her the shock of her life.

A moment later she had clicked open the french windows and was running down the terrace steps, sharply aware of the coldness of the wind.

'Gladys!' she cried in astonishment, 'how good to see you! Have you come looking for Annie? Come in and have a cup of coffee.'

Gladys felt her face flood with colour – of course she'd known Julia wouldn't spurn her. Julia had never been like that.

'Oh – no,' she muttered, 'I don't want to put you out none, I just thought I'd come and wish you happy birthday, seeing this must be the first one you've celebrated since. . . .'

Julia smiled gently, and fully recognized just how much courage Gladys must have had to find to do this.

'Dear Gladys,' she whispered, hugging her, 'that's so kind. *Please* come in. God, you're freezing!' She began to tug her gently towards the terrace steps. 'Come on, I really would like to chat, but this wind is cutting right through me.'

Gladys hadn't seen the inside of Tremar since she was a child. Even at that garden party the house itself had been firmly locked against outsiders. Locked and holding tight to itself its misery and loneliness.

The big drawing-room was not as she remembered it, except for its size – and even that wasn't as large as her childhood memories, but it was light and airy, and had a feeling of quiet contentment about it. It was not the terrifying, intimidating, ferocious-servant populated domain of the twelfth baronet and his wife. It was a home now – the place, ironically, her daughter looked upon as home.

And Gladys felt shabby and out of place amid such understated opulence.

When they were comfortably seated, and the coffee had been delivered, Julia put her hand into the pocket of her trousers and drew out the small, pink stone.

'Do you remember this?' she asked quietly, and Gladys gaped at it in amazement.

'Fancy you still having that!' she exclaimed. 'It's only a bit of rock crystal I picked up off the beach, and you kept it all these years!'

'Well, actually no, I didn't,' Julia replied, 'my mother did. I found my trinket box a couple of months ago and the stone was still in it. Ridiculous, frankly. What an odd woman she was, don't you think? She'd thrown me away, but she'd kept my possessions. Tell me, Gladys, after we talked that morning on the cliffs, did you write and tell Arthur that I was pregnant? Did he know before he came home? I'm sorry to do this, but there are questions that have simply never been answered, and I think you're the only one who could answer most of them.'

Gladys nodded, it was true and she knew it; odd, really, that the lady of the manor, and probably the lowliest of the local fishermen's daughters should between them hold so many secrets.

'Oh, yes,' she said quietly, 'I wrote straight away. I had to write to him in capitals, of course, 'cos you know he don't read well, but I told him, certainly. And I told him when your parents had you sent away, four months later. I thought he would a told your brother, but he didn't. He told me when he come home, he never said nothing.'

Julia walked slowly to the fire and absently warmed her hands. In the days leading up to this birthday things had seemed suddenly to be thrown into sharp relief in her mind, and a number of things she had found out since her return from Blackridge suddenly seemed not to make any sense.

'Well at least I know then that Sandro didn't fail me,' she murmured. 'I hadn't really thought about him knowing until recently and then I couldn't bear the idea that he might have done. For certain my parents wouldn't have told him – but dear God, I wish he'd had the time to come home on leave just once.'

Gladys smiled at her bitterly.

'And I wish Arthur'd bin killed with the rest of them,' she observed. 'I'd of swapped your brother for him, any day!'

Julia smiled at her quickly and then went to the french windows, staring broodily out at the chilly day as her mind, very unwillingly, skimmed through the pain of some of the twenty-three birthdays she had endured between this one and her seventeenth; the few that she could remember at all.

'Gladys,' she said, eventually, 'you told me once that Arthur hated Annie because she reminded him that his first child had been a daughter. How did you know I'd given birth to a little girl in Blackridge? You seem to be the only person in the village who does, apart from Arthur, of course. Even those two old witches in the shop don't know the truth, but you do – you always have done. How?'

Gladys remembered very clearly how she knew, for seeing Julia's mother, improperly dressed and reeling about on the cliffs weeping, one very cold morning, had been the first time she thought she'd realized that those remote people at the manor were real human beings, with real feelings. It had been very painful to watch.

'Well, actually, your mother told me,' she replied quietly and recounted the long ago meeting carefully. Frowning with her memories she said, 'She'd been clawing at herself, her face was bleeding in places.

She sobbed that she couldn't bear the pain, that the child had bin a girl and was born dead. "*My grandchild – I can't bear it*" she wailed, and sort of lurched away. I never seed her again, till that bleddy garden party, and she was heaven's frozen face by then. I waited till she were on her own and plucked up the courage to ask her about you. She just stared at me, like she ent never seen me before, and she says, "We don't acknowledge no one called Julia in this house", and she walked away; and I never saw nor spoke to her again the rest of her life.'

Julia's face crumpled and for a moment she put her head in her hands, then drawing a deep breath she looked up and tried to smile. It came out very crooked.

'Her *only* grandchild,' she whispered bitterly, 'but of course she chose for it to be like that. They must have had to give their permission for me to be sterilized, I suppose – or perhaps they didn't. Perhaps they never knew. They obviously wouldn't have cared. Thank you, Gladys, for telling me.'

Gladys pressed her lips together. And so now you want my Annie, she thought bitterly – and she wants you, just like he did that summer. She began to struggle up out of her chair and Julia was on her feet immediately. Spontaneously their hands touched and just for a second, gripped, warmly.

'Is it very hard for you at the moment?' Julia murmured, 'Are you suffering a lot? I never wanted you to suffer, only Arthur.'

Gladys shrugged.

'Well food ent exactly plentiful,' she replied truthfully, 'but we've had it this bad before a few times over the years, believe me. It's beginning to hurt, now we're having to manage without the hundred pounds, of course. I know, I does the farm accounts. Look, Julia, if you was to tell him he could have some things back, maybe . . . well, who knows, he might give in then, over Annie. He's bleddy determined at the moment. He says she's going to Falmouth no matter what!'

Julia shook her head.

'He's *got* to let me have her, Gladys,' she said fiercely, 'and one way or another he will, because dear God I'll *make* him! I *won't* have her wasted as a damn kitchen maid, she's much too clever for that! You tell him, if he gives me Annie I'll not only give him all his perks back, I'll even pay his debts.'

'What, even the hundred pounds you'll give him back?' Gladys asked doubtfully, and Julia winced.

'I don't know,' she whispered, 'I *can't* promise that. He betrayed Sandro, Gladys, and my brother would never have betrayed him. You of all people must understand that.'

Gladys Paynter nodded sadly.

'Yeah, Julia, I do,' she answered. 'I'll tell him what you've said. Give it a couple of weeks and . . .' she sighed deeply, 'I think you might get what you want, anyway. Thanks for the coffee, and I hope you have a nice party.'

'You could come if you wanted,' Julia suggested hopefully, and downtrodden, misused Gladys smiled wryly and pulled her threadbare coat around her tightly.

'I don't think so, thanks all the same,' she replied quietly.

Julia took Annie into her bedroom after lunch, when they went to change for the party, and carefully showed her how to wear a suspender belt and stockings, and check her seams were straight. Annie felt so grown up she was almost bursting, and as she slid her feet into her black, patent-leather shoes she actually sighed with pleasure.

Before the antique cheval-glass in the corner of the room they stood side by side, gazing at each other. Julia was breathtaking in her black dress and high-heeled shoes, her cheeks and lips softly pinked with rouge and lipstick, her watch on her wrist with one of Annie's hankies, delicately perfumed, tucked beneath the strap. Annie was every inch the young lady in her pale green suit, stockings and shiny shoes, her hair held back from her face with a black velvet band.

'Is that really me?' she asked at last, and Julia chuckled.

'I was wondering the same thing about me,' she replied truthfully. 'What a pair we are, Annie. Do you think we're in a dream and we'll wake up one day?'

'If this is a dream,' Annie declared, 'then I ent waking up for nobody. I like it too much!'

Minnie was also wearing one of her new winter dresses and like a small child she hopped about from foot to foot, itching to thrust her present into Julia's hands. The present, which was from Minnie and Miss Vincent – and Minnie had actually traced a rather shaky 'M' on the label – was a 'definitive de luxe edition' of *The Ingoldsby Legends*, illustrated by Arthur Rackham. Julia gasped with delight and held it with the reverence of an avid book collector. Annie drooled over it.

Miss Vincent smiled.

'You told me once your library was lacking *The Ingoldsby Legends* and you had never read them,' she said to Julia.

'Well it isn't now,' Julia replied, thanking her fondly, 'but I can assure you I won't get first go at them. Annie'll be sitting up all night reading them if I don't stop her! You must see my library after tea.'

'I'd like to see it all after tea,' the matron said, 'or anyway as much as possible.'

Tea was a splendid affair, Mrs Collins had done a remarkable job – and she joined them at the table without the slightest sign of embarrassment. Mrs Collins, Julia decided fondly, was getting used to the avant-garde household in which she worked.

They ate in the dining-room, surrounded by the Drake ancestors, dating back to Charles I's time, some of whom looked as if they had never laughed in their lives, and Minnie dropped trifle all over the tablecloth and crumbs all over the floor, much to the delight of the puppies.

There was a cake with pink and white icing and 'Happy Birthday' written on it, and Julia was sung to. She gazed at the people around her and she suddenly realized how very much she was enjoying this day and how much it meant to have a handful of people in the world to love.

After tea she took Miss Vincent on a tour of the house and the dower, walked very briefly with her on the terrace since it was very cold, and then took her to the library where together they chose the right spot on the shelves for her new book.

'Even I had no idea that your background was like this, Julia,' Ilona Vincent said quietly as she enjoyed the smell of varnish and old books and allowed her gaze to run through some of the titles on the rows of shelving. 'Dear God, Blackridge must have been such a nightmare.'

'Not after you came,' Julia replied truthfully. 'After all I was used to it by then and you improved things out of all proportion. It's good to be home though . . .' she drew a deep thoughtful breath, 'but it wouldn't be this good without Annie and Matt, I don't think, and Mrs Collins, in her way. I wanted it all to myself when I came home, but when all is said and done it's only a house and it doesn't love me back. When can I have Minnie?'

'Well before Christmas, my dear,' Miss Vincent said cheerfully, 'it should all be finalized in a few weeks. We've had to trace her family, of course, and we're just waiting on legal permission from them for you to take her to live with you, but they're hardly likely to refuse, I think.'

'No, hardly,' Julia retorted bitterly, 'she had one less visit than I did in all the years we were together. At least my mother came to see me once – I don't know if Minnie ever even had a mother. Thank you, by the way, for the way she looks today, you've obviously gone to some trouble.'

Miss Vincent smiled gently.

'And you, my dear, have gone to an enormous amount of trouble, if I may say so,' she observed. 'I had no idea you were so elegant. Your charming Matt can't take his eyes off you!'

Julia felt herself blush hotly and glared at the woman from under her brows.

'Oh, don't you start,' she muttered, 'Annie spends half her life matchmaking, it's most embarrassing!'

Ilona Vincent gazed at her steadily.

'Annie's not so very far off the mark, I should say,' she replied enigmatically.

Minnie went home with Miss Vincent at just after six o'clock; they gave Mrs. Collins a lift into the village. Annie, who stayed the night more often than she went home these days, went to bed, almost snoring on her feet, at half past nine. Julia, left alone with Matt, played dance records on the elegant, new, polished-walnut gramophone she had bought herself a week before – and she and Matt talked and danced, very intimately, until one in the morning.

It had been a truly wonderful birthday, she decided just before she closed her eyes to sleep, truly wonderful – and when she examined her feelings she realized, with a slight jolt, that they were romantic.

Chapter 20

It was a morning deep into November when the cat and mouse game Julia and Arthur had been playing since June finally came to an end. Julia was having breakfast with Matt, a daily event now that he lived in the dower, and an occasion on which they were sometimes, but not always joined by Annie. She wasn't around this morning, but if, as Julia suspected, she had been late out of bed and had breakfast at Rectory Farm, when she did finally come in at teatime she would be ravenous, despite having eaten lunch, which Julia paid for.

Annie was at school, much to her disgust. Julia had forced her back to the village school in September, explaining to her that if she was coming to live at Tremar after Christmas then she'd be going to a new school, and she'd better get used to going on a regular basis again. Besides, now she had a proper uniform, the correct shoes and a warm coat she no longer had to pretend she was stupid to gain sympathy. Instead, as far as Julia could gather, she was enjoying showing off. She wanted to be top at everything and with all her advantages she was experiencing no difficulty. Julia decided to let her get on with it, but she made it clear to her teacher that if there were any queries or difficulties, they were not to be addressed to Rectory Farm. If the headmaster thought it odd, Julia's uncanny knack of being imperious when it was needed prevented him asking any further.

Annie now slept at Rectory Farm during the week and at Tremar at weekends. It didn't mean anything, it was a sop to Arthur – and he paid little or no attention as to whether his daughter was at home or not, but it kept him from losing his temper too often. Matt also ensured Annie was safe when she was in her own home. Often of an evening, as he was leaving The Smugglers to walk home to Tremar, he would be seen to bend over Arthur and whisper something in his ear. Nobody ever knew what it was he said, but Annie was refreshingly free of bruises these days.

Julia had just finished her second cup of tea when Mrs Collins came into the room and announced primly, 'Mr Arthur Paynter would like to see you, Miss Drake.'

Arthur! Julia was momentarily caught off guard, though as she blinked at her housekeeper she told herself sharply that since she'd been expecting him for weeks now, she really shouldn't be so very surprised at his sudden arrival. But it was only the second time they had seen each other since her release from Blackridge in the spring, and since then, apart from his brutality to Annie, he had actually succeeded in whipping up enough bad feeling in Polwean to lead an abortive march against Tremar.

She muttered, 'Oh – er, yes . . .' and then abruptly pulled herself up. Last time, when Mrs Collins had announced his presence, she had almost fainted. This time she was determined to be perfectly calm.

'I'll see him in the drawing-room,' she said grandly, 'if you wouldn't mind asking him to wait, Mrs Collins.' And Mrs Collins bustled out importantly.

As she left the morning-room Julia put her hands together and pressed her fingers briefly against her lips, struggling to steady her nerves.

'Would you like me to come with you to see Paynter?' Matt asked, and smiling at him she shook her head.

'He won't even stay if he sees you,' she replied. 'Oh, fingers crossed, Matt, this is it. This is Arthur ready to capitulate.'

He was standing in the middle of the drawing-room clutching his cap in his hands, and for the second time Julia experienced a slight jolt of surprise at herself that she could *ever* have found him irresistible, for he smelt strongly of sweat and earth and his clothes were greasy. As she swept into the room she passed him with the briefest of acknowledgements and threw herself into a chair, then waved her hand imperiously towards him.

'Good-morning, Arthur,' she said grandly, 'please, do sit down.'

'I'll say what I has to say standing up, thank you,' he replied stiffly and she shrugged.

'Just as you please, but not too long about it if you don't mind. I'm rather busy this morning.'

Her aristocratic grandeur had exactly the desired effect, she saw that she had succeeded in making him both nervous and angry and his slack mouth twitched as he watched her resentfully. Julia stared back at him in the detached way she had watched her mother stare at people, when she was a child, 'as if they're only half there' she'd once observed to Sandro, making him snigger.

Arthur Paynter swallowed. He felt humiliated enough as it was and she was making him feel twice as bad – well she was going to get what she wanted, certainly, but he'd make her pay for it, so that should wipe the supercilious sneer off her face.

'I've come to see you about Rectory Farm,' he said, gritting his teeth and staring back at her. 'When you come back from Blackridge I had the idea you wanted it back – and that's fair enough. Like I told Gladys, we shouldn't expect you t'be as generous as your father and your brother; after all, you didn't have the same reasons, did you? Well, you said as how you'd pay the market value for it and if that's the case it's yours – for the right price. Be nice for you to get it back into the estate, I'm sure.'

Julia pressed her lips together thoughtfully, needing time to word her answer. She didn't want Rectory Farm, as well he knew, and she had to curb her temper against his cheap jibes.

Eventually, leaning back in her chair and comfortably crossing her legs she replied slowly, 'If you sell the farm to me, Arthur, you do realize you then become my tenant, don't you – provided you still want to stay there, of course? And as a tenant, the rent will be due on Lady Day, the same as it is from all my other tenants. If for any reason you can't pay the full amount come next Lady Day, then I reserve the right to evict you and your family – and you can take my word for it that's exactly what I'll do. You are clear about that, aren't you? Just so there's no misunderstanding.'

'I'll have the money next Lady Day,' he assured her, and she curled her lip.

'Quite possibly,' she said, 'but what about the year after? There's a war coming, so everyone believes. Do you remember what happened when the war came last time? Well, of course you do. Gladys's brothers went away and were killed – so what are you going to do if your boys decide to go away this time? There's no way you can run that farm on your own, not to make any money. Of course, if you let me have Annie you can keep the farm and I'll give you back most of your perks. I'll pay your debts too; it's a fair offer.'

Through his bloodshot eyes he watched her with contempt and Julia tried to equate this pathetic, drunken creature with the man she had loved so passionately twenty-four years ago. It was almost possible to believe it wasn't the same person, in fact, in a lot of ways it was easier.

'Annie's going to Falmouth after Christmas,' he said triumphantly. 'She'm going t'be a skivvy, 'cos that's what she's born to – and all you've done, Miss High and Mighty, is make it more difficult for her, 'cos you've let her believe she can be something else. Gladys thought she was better than folk around here, just 'cos she could read and write proper, well I soon put her in her place!'

'By using her as a punch bag,' Julia whispered disgustedly.

She got up and walked distractedly to the french windows, gazing out at the bleak November day. The wind was beginning to rise, hooting in the chimneys and shoving spitefully at the crumbling remains of the pavilion, and in her mind she had a very sharp picture of Gladys as a child, tucked in a corner of the library with her on a winter's day, and reading as avidly as Annie always did when she got her hands on a new book. The drawing-room was warm and beautiful, with an air of calm opulence and in the grate the huge fire settled comfortably with a crackle.

Taking a deep breath she turned to look at Arthur and found him still in the same position, as if he was in some way glued to that piece of floor.

'Who are this family in Falmouth that Annie's going to,' she asked at last, 'do they have a name?'

'Of course they do,' he replied, and told her. 'Your mother give me an introduction to them. Are you any the wiser?'

'Well, naturally,' she said, 'they're my mother's family. They're *my* relations, Arthur, God help me! You do understand, don't you, that whilst they may be prepared to give you some of her annual salary there will be a lot of things, like soap, toothpaste, ladies, items, and so forth, that she'll be expected to buy for herself, and out of the money they pay her? She'll be expected to buy her own clothes and shoes, too – other than her uniform, which she will only be expected to wear when she's working; and have money for her afternoon off. And they won't like it if she never leaves the house and lurks in her bedroom all the time, believe me! You don't really understand about servants, do you?'

He sneered.

'And you do, of course.'

'Well of course I do! I wasn't thrown out with the rubbish until you violated me, remember? I grew up with servants, so I know exactly what is expected of them. So, Arthur, looking a few years on, it's possible that one or both of your sons will be fighting a war, your daughter will either be a poorly paid kitchen maid, or doing war work – and I suspect it will probably be the latter – and you won't be able to find the rent for Rectory Farm. However, if you give me Annie instead of the farm, I'll give you five hundred pounds, I'll buy your timber, I'll open the paths across the estate that I've blocked to you and I'll pay your debts. Now that really is an offer, isn't it; quite enough to get you comfortably out of your difficulties, I should say? So how about it? Shall we now start to talk about what you've *really* come for?'

A gust of wind thumped irritably against the french windows, and looking out, Julia saw a spiral of dead leaves lift and swirl on the lawn beneath her. Matt was standing there doing nothing in particular and one of the puppies chased after the leaves excitedly. Matt was evidently waiting for Arthur to leave before he went to get on with his day's work – bless him. She raised her hand to him briefly and then turned once again to face Arthur.

'Well?' she asked.

He smiled at her unpleasantly, curling his lip with contempt. He looked coldly triumphant.

'So, fine words aside, what it comes down to is how much my daughter's worth?' he said nastily. 'You want t'buy mine because you can't have one of your own. Tell me, Lady Muck, would you pay more than you could afford for her? Or if I ups the price does she go to Falmouth anyway?'

Julia's nostrils flared with rage but she kept her temper admirably. Remaining aloof in the face of the enemy was one of the few worthwhile lessons she had learned from her tightly-laced, emotionless parents.

'Yes, I'm offering to buy Annie,' she replied calmly, 'but the price is not negotiable. I'm offering you five hundred pounds – that's a lot more than I'll give you for Rectory Farm. What's more, you keep the farm, which means you keep a roof over your head. If I buy Rectory Farm I'm not going to wait until the Lady Day comes when you can't pay the rent, you know, I'm going to have my legal representatives look into evicting you as soon as possible, for bad farming practices. I'd *love* to get you off my land once and for all! Five hundred pounds, Arthur,' she produced a pen and her cheque book from the pocket of the jacket she was wearing, 'that's more money than you've ever seen in your life. Five hundred pounds *and* I'll pay off your debts and allow you to keep your home. How can you refuse?'

He knew he must give in because he knew he couldn't afford not to, and anyway it was what he had come for. He'd had no more intention of selling her Rectory Farm than she'd had of buying it. His eyes gleamed as he looked at her cheque book.

'And what do you want for your five hundred pounds?' he enquired.

She shrugged.

'I want control of Annie, that's all, and I want an assurance from you that you won't interfere in her life. I don't want another thing from you Arthur – and you won't get another thing from me, either, so make sure you take care of the money, won't you? Shall I write the cheque now?'

He watched her as she opened the cheque book and rested it on a table near the window. He saw her scrawl her flamboyant signature and tear out the cheque and wave it about to dry the ink.

'If you give me a list of your debts and your creditors, I'll pay them individually,' she said, folding the cheque neatly in two and handing it to him, 'and after that I'm sure you won't mind, any more than I will, if we don't ever meet again. You ruined my life, Arthur.'

Arthur took the cheque, studied it for a few seconds and then slipped it into his pocket.

'You led me on, Julia,' he replied complacently, smiling at her. 'You don't really think I'd of laid a finger on you without you encouraging me, do you? I was a farm boy and you was a lady – or supposed to be. You couldn't wait to take your drawers off, and if you don't like what happened as a consequence, well you should a thought about it afore you done it. I don't blame myself for anything. Goodbye,' and turning on his heel he prepared to leave.

Boiling with rage, Julia rang for Mrs Collins to see him out. Then swinging round herself, she banged out through the french windows and ran wildly down the terrace steps where she uttered a scream of fury.

Matt was beside her almost immediately.

'Oh! I hate that man!' she shrieked. 'God! I wish he were *dead*!'

'But you got Annie?' he enquired.

Julia leaned against him, pressing her face into his chest for a few seconds and holding her breath until she was ready to burst, then, abruptly blowing out the breath she raised her face and smiled a smile of triumph.

'She's mine, Matt,' she whispered, 'she's here for the rest of her life and all for five hundred pounds. And I hope he drinks every penny of it and eventually his liver *bursts*!'

Matt touched her cheek with his fingers.

'That's better,' he said cheerfully, 'it doesnae suit you to be angry. Now go inside before you freeze to death and get ready to tell her when she comes home!'

When Annie came crashing in the short day was already beginning to close drearily towards evening, the sky was leaden and the wind rising with what seemed like the promise of an oncoming storm. She smelt of school – a sort of strange mixture of faintly stale children and floor polish – and she was so tall these days, Julia noticed, there seemed to be so much of her. Was it really only five months ago that she had been stunted and dirty with her hair full of straw and her skinny body covered in bruises? The only thing that was the same about Annie now were the bright green, excited eyes.

'Hullo!' she cried, throwing herself at Julia to hug her. 'I ent half hungry! That school lunch, you know, they don't give you nearly enough.'

'I don't think there's such a thing as enough for you,' Julia retorted, touching her rosy face fondly and feeling the chill of outside on her skin. 'I've got something very important to tell you, Annie Paynter.'

Annie's eyes sparkled.

'You and Matt's getting married!' she cried, and Julia glared at her.

'Annie!' she snapped warningly.

The child shrugged.

'Well I'm ever hopeful,' she said. 'So, if it ent that, what is it then?'

Julia told her. When she had finished she saw a tiny, unmistakable flame of hurt in the child's eyes and, understanding, offered her arms for comfort.

'It's what I want, of course,' Annie murmured, squeezing her body tightly against Julia's, hungry for the love that was offered, 'but it don't say much for a person, does it? To be sold for five hundred pounds.'

'My father paid for me to be taken away,' Julia pointed out quietly, 'and went on paying for me to be kept away for almost twenty-four years. We're two of a kind, Annie, which is what makes having each other so special. And at least your mother loves you, mine obviously didn't love me.'

Annie kissed her fiercely on the cheek, a passionate kiss of love which Julia recognized fully. They both suffered a great loneliness of spirit, and Julia wondered if perhaps they could only ever find the love they sought amongst their own kind.

Their own kind. She, and Annie . . . and Matt?

Matt came in at five-thirty as was usual in the now dark evenings, and his entrance was Annie's signal to finish the separate work that Julia set her and join them in the drawing-room for a chat before dinner.

Annie was wont to curl up on the settee beside him when he had washed and changed, and tell him all about her day. Like mother, father and daughter they would sit there enjoying quiet conversation for about half an hour and though no one had ever actually said so, there was a sort of tacit agreement between them that this was their favourite time of the day. This evening Annie leaned against him and Julia watched them comfortably.

They talked about a new school for her after Christmas, a school where she could take the exams she needed to go to university, and they talked about Christmas itself, about having a really special trip to Plymouth, perhaps, to see the shops decked out for Christmas, and making it a very special Christmas for Minnie.

Matt and Julia were both well aware that it would be a very special Christmas for Annie, too. Annie was going to be fifteen two days afterwards, and suddenly it was safe for her to be fifteen, no one was going to ship her away to a life of servitude.

For Julia the prospect of the approaching Christmas was so overwhelming that she couldn't talk about it to anybody at the moment.

They ate their dinner at six-thirty. There was a fair wind drumming up outside now and Tremar creaked a bit as it was buffeted about, but the noises were comforting, they made the house feel strong and safe. Julia remembered that when a gale had howled across the moors around Blackridge, screaming and raging in the darkness, somehow the place had felt like a dark, impenetrable dungeon. Tremar seemed to wrap them in warm arms, and Julia desired to do nothing more than curl up in front of the fire and read or indulge in tranquil conversation until it was bedtime but Annie obviously had other ideas.

She seemed to be wriggling uncomfortably on her chair at the table, as if she was desperate to say something, but didn't quite know how to, and eventually, as she finished her last mouthful of pudding, she pushed the chair back hastily and stood up.

'I got to go back to Rectory Farm,' she said abruptly.

Julia's eyes opened wide in alarm.

'What, to stay?' she whispered in disbelief, and Annie pulled a face at her.

'No, *'course* not!' she retorted, and then twisting her fingers together muttered, almost apologetically, 'but the thing is, see . . . well I bin making things, you know, in needlework class at school and that. They was surprise things for Christmas, so I took them home and hid them in my room at the farm, and now – well if my pa goes in there, and finds them he'll destroy them. I know he will.' Her face was suddenly sad. 'And I worked *ever* so hard at them. I *got* to go and get them.'

Julia smiled. In truth she felt a completely absurd sense of relief. For one dreadful moment she had thought Annie didn't want to stay at Tremar after all – though when she thought about that, it was even more absurd.

'Matt'll take you in the car,' she said, 'I'm sure he won't mind.'

'No, I'd rather go on the bike,' Annie replied, 'I – well I don't want Matt near the farm at all, 'cos if my pa happened to be there, it'd just make it worse. I know it's blowing a bit, but it ent raining and I won't be above an hour, or so. Besides, I'd *really* like t'say goodbye to my ma. I mean, I know I'll see her, and that, but I won't be living there no more, and I do love my ma.'

Julia frowned and bit her lip.

'Annie, it's so dark,' she murmured, and Annie chuckled.

'Julia, I bin running about this village in the dark most of me life!' she exclaimed. 'I'll be back by half eight or thereabouts, I promise.'

Matt gazed at her fondly with his lovely dark-blue eyes.

'Would you like me to go to The Smugglers and keep your father occupied?' he asked, smiling at her. 'It'd give you a chance to collect your things and have a wee chat with your mother in peace.'

'And how do you keep Arthur occupied, might I ask?' Julia enquired in astonishment. 'I can't believe he plays cards with you!'

Matt chuckled.

'I just sit with a pint of beer and watch him,' he replied. 'He gets *very* cross, but he'll no leave the pub before I do, it seems to be a matter of principle.'

Annie looked at him and grinned.

'Thanks, Matt,' she whispered and abruptly gave Julia a hasty kiss on the cheek. 'I'll be careful, I promise,' she said.

'Yes, you will,' Julia agreed firmly. 'And you won't be later than half past eight, otherwise I'll be worrying myself to a frazzle!'

The bicycle, which both Julia and Annie used, was a sturdy machine with a good lamp and a stout wicker-basket on the front. As Annie cycled along the road from the ornate stone gateposts of Tremar to the village, the wind tugged at her hair and blew sharp colour into her cheeks, but it was familiar and caused her no discomfort. As she came to the green, the windows in the houses on the far side twinkled with lights, and the Drake Arms was warmly bright, the sign swinging in the wind. Only about another fifteen minutes' ride – the worst bit being the rough road down to the farm – and she could warm her fingers a bit in front of the kitchen range.

It was certainly blowing up to a storm, spots of rain were beginning to blow into her face now and she thought she might be going to get a bit wet on the ride back – but then there would be cocoa in the drawing-room in front of the huge, crackling fire, and as much hot water as she wanted in the bath, and she was going to live there for ever and ever now, and her heart sang so loudly in her ears it drowned out the sound of the wind altogether.

In the yard the tin roof on the barn thumped in the wind. Annie put the bike in the porch to keep the saddle dry and turned the handle on the back door. As she pushed it open the familiar smell of stale dog, grease and general neglect assailed her nostrils, but it was steaming hot after the coldness of outside. She slid in quickly and closed the door behind her and her mother, sitting at the big, scrubbed table, surrounded by a pile of mending, looked up in surprise.

Too late Annie saw the look of surprise become one of serious alarm.

Too far into the room to be able to get out quickly enough she was abruptly aware of someone behind her.

Arthur was late setting out for The Smugglers this evening, and at the moment Annie had come cheerfully into the kitchen he had been behind the door pulling on his old mac, and now Annie stood between her parents, with nowhere to run. Arthur and Gladys had just had a serious row and Arthur was in a foul temper.

'Well, well!' he said triumphantly, 'If it ent our little lady, come to gloat. Come to offer us a bit of charity, has you – or has you just come for yer things? Well you're too late, girlie, 'cos I just put everything I found in your room in the stove over there. All your pretty bits of needle-work – made the fire burn a treat, they did!'

Annie felt her heart wrench with misery. She had worked so hard and so carefully on the things she had made and they had been lovingly chosen gifts for Julia, Matt and Minnie. Blindly and without thinking she rounded on her father furiously as the tears welled up in her eyes.

'I *hate* you!' she screamed at him. 'I *hate* you, you *pig*!'

The minute she'd said it she could have bitten her tongue off.

Arthur's fist seemed to come out of nowhere and exploded in her face with a burst of pain, knocking her savagely into the kitchen wall. Dazed and confused she reeled sideways and then lurched off balance as her hair was viciously yanked backwards and her father's big, calloused hand smashed across her mouth, crushing her lips against her teeth.

'I'll teach you to call me a pig, you foul-mouthed little *bitch*!' he shouted as he slammed her head against the wall again. 'I'll send you back up to her ladyship in bleddy *bits* I will!'

This time she went down and crouched on her haunches in a bewildered heap as blood began to pour from her nose. She put out her tongue to lick her lips and found them cut and bloodied, and sniffing because everything felt suddenly congested, caught a throat full of blood and coughed, spraying the whitewashed wall with spots of red.

Arthur reached out to grab her and haul her to her feet again. It was not the first assault of this kind she had endured, but she had never been punched quite so hard that she could remember and instinctively she flattened herself on the floor in terror. At once his boot smashed into her ribs and she screamed in agony, her body contracting upwards against the pain.

Gladys stared at her bloody, suffering daughter and a terrible rage rose in her like a tidal wave. Five hundred pounds he had sold her beloved child for, more money than he had ever seen in his life, but he still hadn't been able to resist a final act of spite. He had chuckled gleefully as he had burned her treasures and Gladys had hated him for it. Now, without any warning, she lost her temper. Leaping to her feet she snatched up her blunt, fat darning-needle from the table and drove it with all her might into his rump.

'Leave her alone!' she bellowed at him. 'You mindless bleddy bully! Leave her alone!'

Arthur roared in pain and stumbled backwards with his arms in the air as the needle plunged deep into his flesh. A second later he swung his fist round with the whole weight of his body behind it and caught Gladys across the side of the head. The force of the blow actually lifted her right off her feet and she smashed with terrible violence into the corner of the range, sliding to the floor in complete silence.

She appeared to be dead.

Aiming one last kick at the horrified Annie, Arthur flung open the kitchen door and strode off into the driving rain.

'And good feckin' riddance to the pair of you!' he screamed back as he disappeared from view.

Annie wiped her hands over her bloodied face and struggled to her feet. Her father's second kick had caught her in the hip and it was painful, as was her face, swelling now, her lips like unwieldy mounds of flesh, blocking the entrance to her mouth.

Gladys still lay where she had fallen and Annie limped across to her muttering thickly, 'Ma . . . Ma . . . *please,* Ma?'

Finally Gladys groaned and turned her head slightly and Annie gaped in horror, for the side of her mother's face which had hit the range was red and scorched with a jagged, deep cut above her eye that dripped blood. One of her arms seemed to be lying at an odd angle and as she tried to move she whimpered in agony.

'I'll get help,' Annie croaked. 'Don't – don't move, you'll be all right, Ma,' and whining with fear and pain she stumbled towards the door.

Outside it was lashing with rain and the wind was howling like a mad dog. Arthur had thrown the bicycle out into the middle of the yard and trembling and panting with exertion Annie retrieved it, righted it and hauled herself on to the saddle. Pedalling was agony, the kick to her hip had left an inflamed and painful bruise, but the rain washed the blood from her face and served to cool her swollen mouth somewhat, though the ride seemed to take for ever.

The village was deserted, which wasn't surprising in the teeth of such a storm, but there were lights on in the Drake Arms, and in Lamplighter House, as well. It only briefly crossed Annie's mind to go first to one and then to the other and both ideas she dismissed immediately. She wanted Julia. Only Julia. And after that she was beginning to form some rather vague idea in her mind that she wanted revenge. She didn't know it was possible to feel such hate, it even seemed to take away the biting cold. He had burned all her things, put them on the stove, all the things she had made with such care . . . and he had taken five hundred pounds in payment for her, *five hundred pounds* which he would drink and gamble while he continued to abuse and ill treat her mother. God, she *hated* him!

When at last she turned in through the gates at Tremar she was soaked to the skin and sobbing so hard that her tears blinded her vision even more than the rain. She dumped the bike on the drive and stumbled up to the front door, hammering on it desperately, then she propped her aching body against the ancient stone arch of the porch until she heard the door being unbolted, and fell through it into Julia's arms.

Julia drew a sharp, hissing breath.

'Oh, my God,' she whispered, as Annie clung to her sobbing incoherently, 'Annie, I'll ring for Oliver straight away—'

'No! *No*!' Annie sobbed desperately, 'you got to get the doctor to go to the farm. He tried to kill my ma!'

It took half an hour for Julia to get the whole story, during which time she stripped and changed the child, noting, with rising fury, the bruises to her ribs and hip as well as her savagely battered face. Oliver was dispatched to Rectory Farm to find Gladys, but when Julia wanted him to come to Tremar after that, Annie was insistent that he didn't. Then, dry and in clean clothes. Annie finally stopped crying, and sat, as she was told, in front of the drawing-room fire. Now, suddenly, there was an entirely different look in her eyes, one Julia had never seen before.

She drank some cocoa to warm her up, though it hurt her lips to press a cup against them, and when it was finished she went on sitting obediently before the fire, hunched and disconsolate. But as the minutes ticked by it seemed to Julia that far from beginning to relax, her attitude was one of tense indecision, An uncomfortable silence hung between them as they listened to the wind howling in the chimney, then Julia put out her hand gently and abruptly Annie backed away.

'Do you have a spare mac I can borrow, please?' she asked briskly, climbing hurriedly to her feet, 'I've made up me mind, I know what I has to do, I has to go out. I has to go to The Smugglers, 'cos I got to settle this once and for all.'

'The Smugglers!' Julia echoed. 'You can't do that! You'll never get there in this weather, and anyway, what can you do? Come on Annie, be sensible. Wait for Matt to come back and tomorrow we'll go to the police and make an official complaint against your father.'

'*Julia*!' Annie's face seemed to darken with passionate hate. 'I don't *want* to make an official complaint! Don't you understand? That five hundred pounds you give him was just a start! When it's gone he'll come back demanding more. He'll spread it about the village that you tried to *buy* me, and he took your money 'cos you'd do *anything* dishonest to get what you want! He's an evil, wicked man and I want him *dead* 'cos that's the only way we'm ever going to be free of him!'

'You want him dead? You mean you want to *kill* him?' Julia whispered, and Annie stared at her stonily.

'Don't you?' she demanded softly. 'I know what he done to you, I asked Ma and she told me. Twenty-three years in Blackridge 'cos he give you a baby and then wouldn't admit what he done. I'd want to kill him, if he'd done that to me.'

Julia felt herself blushing hotly.

'Your mother had no right to tell you,' she muttered and then became silent as the child stared deeply and unflinchingly into her eyes.

It was a look from which it was impossible to break away. Mercilessly stripping away Julia's still very thin veneer of normality, Annie found her tortured spirit beneath it and touched it with her own. Suddenly they both knew that a moment which would probably never come again had been handed to them and if they let it go by they would neither of them ever move on from their suffering.

It seemed to Julia that a frightening blackness, deep inside her, suddenly bubbled up to the surface, and with it came the enormous strength of hatred.

'All right,' she said calmly and quietly, 'there are spare boots and macs in the back kitchen, but we go together, and we go across the cliff-top, it's the only way we can be sure no one will see us.'

'And when we get there,' Annie said just as calmly, 'I'll go in and get him out. No one'll wonder at that, I've had to get him out The Smugglers dozens of times for one reason or another. And we don't have to worry about my brothers, 'cos they went to market up country this morning. They don't drive back when it's like this, they sleeps in the truck and comes back when its daylight. It's perfect!'

Perfect! They were standing in the drawing-room at Tremar amid one of the worst winter storms Julia had seen for a long time, planning a murder, and as they went calmly to the back kitchen to find macs and boots she realized in a completely detached way, that they were actually going to do it.

'When we get him outside, Annie,' she said, dragging on a pair of rubber boots and finding herself absurdly conscious of the smell of old boots and coats in the cold scullery, 'what then?'

'On a night like this?' Annie replied. 'We'm going to drown him. It's obvious.'

Chapter 21

They took an electric torch with them and went from the back door around the stables. The rain pounded them, the wind tore at their hair, it was viciously cold and the walk across the formal lawns towards the orchard and the pine copse in itself seemed like miles, without the prospect of trying to climb the cliff path.

Sheltered as they were in the dip that was the formal garden, the wind and rain were just about supportable. When they reached the copse the noise was so thunderous above them that they couldn't have spoken to each other even if they'd wanted to, and when they passed through the gate and began to climb the cliff path, they found they could barely stand up. The rain torrented down upon them, driving into their faces and turning the path beneath their feet to treacherous, slippery mud. The wind howled in their ears, punching at them like a prize fighter and they were obliged to cling to each other as they slid about helplessly.

If it had been an offshore wind, Julia realized, they would almost certainly have been killed, for they were quite unable to stay on the path and found themselves floundering about, crashing into obstacles, blinded by the rain, soaked to the skin and covered in mud.

It took the best part of an hour to reach the harbour and there the sound of the sea crashing on to the shore was deafening. Julia was seriously beginning to wonder whether Arthur would still be in The Smugglers – but then she wondered, too, why they hadn't met Matt on his way home and concluded that he must either be still there, hoping the storm would abate, or have taken an alternative route.

And if he had done that he would find Tremar empty and might very well call the police – and it was beginning to look as if this might not have been such a good idea after all.

The Smugglers Inn was only just discernible on the harbour wall, for its windows were so dirty and nicotine-encrusted that nothing much more than a faint glimmer of light filtered through them. As Julia and Annie came down the last bit of the path into the harbour, gulping their breath in agony and reeling about like drunks, the door to the pub abruptly opened. For the few seconds it took a couple of men to emerge, a dirty pool of light flooded the slipway, then they pulled the door to behind them and all was dark again. Annie pushed Julia back against the wall and they stood panting, as the two men turned and went up the harbour road, tugging their coat collars up about their ears.

'You stay here then!' Annie bawled. 'And be ready when he comes out!'

She went forward and Julia watched her push open the wooden pub door. Briefly, from inside she could hear a snatch of noise, carried to her on a gust of wind, then the door closed again and she was alone in the pouring rain and screaming wind, listening to the sound of the waves pounding the stones in the harbour.

The pub was hot and smelled of beer and tobacco. It was not as full as usual, because of the night, and Annie saw her father playing cards with Tom Pennard in a corner by the bay window. She also saw Matt, sitting at the opposite end of the room, and he saw her long before her father did.

All Matt's instincts sharpened immediately. No one else would know it, but he instantly recognizd the sodden, dripping mac she was wearing – and she hadn't gone out earlier wearing it. Briefly she turned to look at him and he noted her battered face. The bruising around her nose and eyes was blackening now, but her eyes were red-rimmed and he knew at once that the pounding rain had caused that.

So, bruised, battered and covered in mud, and wearing one of Julia's raincoats, she had obviously walked here from Tremar.

Why?

She went across to the table where her father sat. Arthur was very drunk and as she stood before him she adopted a cringing attitude, hunching her shoulders, looking frightened.

'You got to come, Pa,' she said, hopping from foot to foot, 'it's Ma – I think,' her face crumpled, 'I think she's *dead*, Pa.'

Arthur raised his arm and Annie backed away.

'Bugger off, you little bitch!' he snarled. 'Get out of my sight!'

Annie whimpered – it was a very convincing performance.

'Please, Pa, *please*,' she whispered in a sobbing voice. 'You *got* to come, you *got* to!'

Arthur rose unsteadily to his feet and Annie fell back very quickly. Matt rose to his feet, too, and stood quite still just watching.

'*Get out*!' Arthur roared and this time Tom Pennard touched him on the arm.

'Maybe you ought to go, mate,' he murmured quietly, 'I really think you better had.'

Arthur swore violently, rocking unsteadily on his feet, but by now the whole pub was watching the scene and he was just sober enough to recognize that striking Annie in front of everyone, when she was quite obviously already pretty badly battered, was not going to win him any friends.

'Oh, for hell's sake,' he muttered, 'all right then, you stupid child.' And he began to follow her towards the door.

Matt finished his drink and also began to make for the door, but Matt had an uncanny way of entering and leaving so quietly and with such a fluid movement that no one ever seemed to notice.

Annie opened the pub door and Arthur lurched out into the storm. Rain and wind instantly smacked him in the face, almost robbing him of breath, and leaving him briefly confused. Gasping for breath he staggered forwards and in the roaring darkness a figure suddenly loomed before him. Bewildered, he fetched up short.

'Hullo, Arthur,' Julia said softly, right into his face.

He tottered backwards, disorientated and suddenly rather frightened. He was sobering up quickly in the cold and wet and Julia Drake should definitely not be standing on the slipway outside the entrance to The Smugglers, not on a night like this.

'What're you doing here?' he asked, his words lost into the storm, 'you get away from me, you bitch.'

He came to a standstill right on the very edge of the harbour wall and she was still standing in front of him, threateningly close. He put up his hands in a futile gesture to ward her off and as the pub door opened again and briefly threw out a beam of light, he saw her smiling. Then the door closed, plunging the scene into darkness and her fist caught him right in the centre of his chest. With a startled scream of panic he stepped backwards into nothing and plunged down on to the stony beach.

Julia was on him in an instant, but the fall had been quite enough to sober him completely and Arthur Paynter knew he was fighting for his life. The pounding waves were only a couple of feet away, the spray soaked them, tasting thick and salty on their lips. In the darkness they were grappling and she was trying to beat him across the head with a sharp piece of rock, but he fought her with a strength born of terror. They slipped and slithered on the wickedly uneven stones, falling and rising but clinging to each other, both knowing that to let the other get free would be fatal, then another pair of feet landed close to them and another, huge, dark figure loomed up.

Arthur was wrenched away from Julia with a brief strangled exclamation. His feet scrabbled for purchase on the stones for the merest heartbeat and abruptly there was a crack, like a twig snapping underfoot in a wood. A huge wave burst on the beach, crashing over them and Julia, Matt and the dead Arthur were thrown against the harbour wall. Water filled Julia's nose and mouth, it was a disgusting feeling, and then it was running away and she was breathless and confused.

'Get up there with the lass!' Matt yelled above the hullabaloo as the wave retreated and Julia, winded, fought to see something – anything – in the darkness. 'Quick, woman! The tide's on the up!'

Weighed down with water and numb with cold, Julia did as she was told, lurching towards the edge of the slipway and then staggering up towards the black outline of the ancient pub with its dimly lit windows, finding the enormous capstan and hanging on to the icy-cold, wet metal grimly. Abruptly, from somewhere, Annie appeared and they clung to each other, stumbling about until they found a wall to lean against, then suddenly Matt was there.

He gathered them both into his arms.

'Can you walk?' he yelled above the roar into Julia's ear, and unable to speak at all she just nodded dumbly. 'Good, then stay close to me!' he shouted, and gathered Annie up in his arms as if she weighed no more than a puppy.

With one strong arm he held her close to him, her arms locked tightly around his neck. With his free hand he used his huge stick to haul himself up the almost liquid cliff path, keeping Julia always on the leeward side. He was like a giant against the violence of the storm, refusing to yield. Stumbling along in his wake, Julia's lungs eventually became so stretched that she slid to her knees, retching, and at once he stopped and stood over her, protecting her until she was able to stagger back to her feet again, sobbing wretchedly to herself. Then, at last, after it began to seem like the agony would go on for ever, they were coming down and there were thick bushes on the sea side of the path, offering protection.

They were at the gate to Tremar.

They went through and Julia leaned against it, gulping her breath, desperate for a rest, but Matt urged her on. The noise in the pine copse was excruciating, terrifying, then, suddenly, they were in the orchard and the fear was subsiding. Tremar was a black outline against the furious night sky. Julia sobbed with relief, she was so tired that she wanted nothing more than to lie down and close her eyes, but paramount was getting out of the wind and rain. It was wretched, tearing at their hands and faces like icy nails, and as they finally arrived at the back door it seemed like the door to heaven.

At last, stillness. Even in the cold, musty-smelling back-kitchen the peace was extraordinary. They left the heavy, wet macs and mud-encrusted boots in a pile and shivering and dripping went up the kitchen staircase to the drawing-room. They couldn't speak, any of them. Julia fell on her knees and with blue, trembling hands began to bank up the fire, Matt held the semi-conscious Annie close to the blaze and for perhaps five minutes they were transfixed; speechless, motionless. Then Annie groaned and Julia seemed to come to life.

'Get the lassie straight upstairs into a hot bath,' Matt said, 'and you'd better get in with her. I'll away to the kitchen and make some hot drinks.'

'Will you carry her up for me?' Julia asked, gazing at him dully, and nodding obediently he carried the child up through the semi-dark house and sat her on the edge of the bath as Julia switched on the taps and steam billowed up around them.

The bathroom window beat out an angry tattoo against the storm.

We were out in that! she thought stupidly, as she struggled to free Annie from her sopping wet clothes. We were out there . . . and we . . . killed him. We *killed* him!

She helped Annie into the huge bath and then stripping naked herself, climbed in opposite her and sat, feeling the heat of the water creeping into her freezing flesh, tingling life back into it almost painfully.

Speaking for the first time for ages, Annie muttered, 'That hurts.' and gingerly began to splash the hot water all over herself. Dumbly, almost stupidly, they stared at each other.

Eventually, soaped, clean and warm, Julia stepped out and wrapped herself in a towel, helped Annie out, and together they knelt on the hearthrug in her bedroom, in front of the gas fire which popped and hissed and was so absurdly familiar it was like an old friend. Silently she rubbed the child dry, then, almost zombie-like, she searched out night-clothes for them and fetched her black, Bakelite hair-dryer to dry their hair.

And still they didn't talk to each other. And finally there was nothing left to do.

Abruptly Annie sagged forwards and pressed herself against Julia's body as her bruise-blackened eyes brimmed with tears. The bridge of her nose was painfully swollen and her lips were a mess, not just cut and bruised but chapped as well now. Pressing her face against Julia's warm skin she very softly began to sob.

Julia felt a fierce, burning emotion. It was as if, in some almost shameful way, the aching, childless emptiness she had experienced for so many years filled abruptly like a fountain and spilled over, and touching this young body, so fiercely pressed against her, was exhilarating.

Her child. Her own.

'Oh, Annie,' she whispered.

'Can I sleep in your bed tonight?' Annie mumbled, and Julia kissed her.

'Of course you can,' she replied.

Matt had made Annie a posset – there seemed to be no end to his skills. He had gone through to the dower and changed into dry clothes and he brought her drink in a warm bowl, accompanied by the puppies lolloping at his heels.

Julia put her into bed, allowed the puppies to frolic about on the bedspread around her, and watched as she drank the posset, then, taking the empty bowl, let her cuddle the puppies for a few moments and then settled her down.

'Aren't you coming to bed?' she asked nervously, and Julia smiled.

'In half an hour, I'm just going downstairs to have a drink with Matt first. You'll be all right, Annie, you're quite safe, you know.'

Annie nodded and held out her arms for a kiss. Julia noticed that as Matt bent over her she hugged his neck fiercely and as he touched her bruised face with his huge hands, he was so delicate and gentle. Not like her father . . . Oh God! Whose dead body lay heaving about in the surf.

'Try to sleep, darling,' she murmured and taking the wide-awake, excited puppies, she and Matt crept away.

The fire in the drawing-room was blazing fiercely and the room was warm and tranquil. Outside, in that other, nightmare world they had inhabited only an hour or so ago the storm raged on pitilessly, but now what they had done was beginning to sink in. It wasn't a dream, it was real. And Arthur's body was going to be found in the morning, for the harbour at Polwean did not suck its flotsam out to sea, it tossed it up on the beach. Always.

Trembling slightly and clashing the decanter clumsily against the rim of the glasses, Julia poured two stiff brandies and brought them to the fireplace, where Matt sat gazing into the blaze, and the puppies rolled on the hearthrug.

'You'd best be up with the lassie,' he said, taking the drink from her. 'I'll lock up the house for you and then let myself through to the dower.'

'No,' she replied, 'we can't leave it like this, Matt, we simply can't.'

He didn't look at her, but seemed to examine the golden liquid in his glass with undue care.

'Leave what?' he enquired after a moment and she pressed her lips together tightly.

'You didn't have to do what you did,' she whispered, 'it wasn't your fight. You didn't even have to leave the pub when you did. Tomorrow, when Arthur's body's found it won't take Oliver two minutes to realize he didn't drown. He's lying out there in the surf with a broken neck, and where do you think Oliver's going to come looking for answers first? Why did you do it, Matt?'

The huge, sandy-haired, blue-eyed Scotsman shrugged his shoulders.

'You're my employer,' he said, 'it's my duty to protect you.'

Julia sucked in a shuddering breath, drained her brandy in a single gulp and put the glass down with some force.

'You want me to believe you did it because I'm your employer!' she exclaimed, rounding on him and clenching her shaking hands at her sides. 'Oh, rot, Matt! You'll have to do better than that, you really will!'

There was a tense, abrupt silence between them and the sound of the rain drumming against the windows made the puppies suddenly stir restlessly. One of them uttered a half-hearted single bark, then settled again in the warm and Matt raised his deep blue eyes to look at Julia.

She was tall and lean in her thin, pale blue silk robe, the contours of her body firmly outlined by the belt tied tightly at her waist. In the dim light there was a sort of spare gallantry about her, her eyes dark with tiredness, the beauty of her face picked out in sharp shadow. She stood directly in front of him and he could no longer keep his secret to himself.

'I love you, woman,' he whispered, 'and I'd do anything in the world to protect you.'

Julia fell on her knees at his feet and was immediately in his arms. They kissed passionately and with a fierce, biting hunger, abandoning all thought but their desire. He pulled the silk robe open and finding her naked beneath it, lifted her body towards him and then buried his face in the warm flesh of her breasts, kissing, and exploring with his tongue as she moaned in delight. If he had gone on to push her to the floor and take her, she knew she would not have put up the smallest resistance, but he didn't. Matt was too much of a gentleman for that. Panting, but with the first violent flush of their passion over, he held her close, pressing her head into his neck and they could both feel their hearts beating secretly together.

'Will you marry me?' he asked, and she lifted her face, to look at him.

'Of course I will,' she replied with a tiny chuckle. 'I thought you'd never ask!'

She kissed his lips once more, holding his face between her hands, then her head fell forwards slightly and two tears escaped her lashes and trickled down her cheeks.

'Do you think they'll let us get married, before they hang us?' she asked forlornly. 'Because they are going to hang us, Matt – or at least they'll hang you, which is worse. You won't get a second chance.'

He wiped away her tears with his thumbs, her whole face seemed to fit into his hands they were so big, and yet the touch of his fingers was like silk. He smiled as he spoke and his great voice was softly intimate, yet what he said was chilling.

'Aye, that's as mebbe,' he murmured, gazing into her eyes, 'but you still have to let me take the blame for it, Julia. You've got to think of Annie and Minnie first, their lives are depending on you now, and after all, I was the one who broke Paynter's neck, so I was the one who killed him. You may have been trying, but you weren't going to succeed, you know, he was much stronger than you and he'd sobered up right fast, I noticed. You didn't hurt him at all.'

'Only because you happened along,' she argued. 'I'd have won in the end, I'm sure I would. Oh, God, I *can't* let you take the blame, Matt, it isn't fair. Look, if I say I killed him probably all they'll do is throw me back into Blackridge, and I can live with that. But I won't let them hang you! I *won't*' Suddenly she dissolved into tears and began to rock too and fro in her misery. 'Tell me this is all just a bloody nightmare, Matt!' she sobbed. '*Please* say it is, *please* let me wake up.'

He held her in his arms and she smelt his lovely, tweedy smell. In one night, in just a few short hours, she had acknowledged the man she loved and wanted to spend the rest of her life with, and received the blessed gift of a daughter. One night, and in the morning it would all be gone.

Was this what it had all been about then? All those years in Blackridge and then the miracle of release, of coming back to Tremar, to this, her special corner of the world – all for one night?

Maybe she was supposed to be grateful. Maybe she was supposed to understand that a lot of people didn't even get one night. Dear God, but she wouldn't give it up without a fight!

She left Matt and the puppies in the drawing-room as the grandfather clock in the hall struck the hour of twelve, and as she went quietly up the dark staircase she knew he wouldn't go into the dower, that he would sit there in the armchair for the rest of the night.

And he would think of her, just as she would think of him.

Slipping out of her silk robe and into a night-dress she slid very carefully into bed beside Annie, hoping not to wake her, but immediately her body felt the heat of the bed and the child moved restlessly beside her, she knew she wasn't asleep. Reaching gently across she laid her hand on Annie's forehead, it was hot and sticky.

Annie was running a temperature.

Julia kissed her and at once Annie rolled against her. Her hand came to rest against Julia's chest and her palm was burning hot and very sweaty.

'Julia,' she whispered in the darkness. 'is my pa really dead, or did I dream it?'

'Oh, Annie, I'm sorry,' Julia replied quietly, 'I'm so sorry. Look, sweetheart, unless I'm much mistaken your father's body is going to have been found by first light and whoever finds him will send immediately for Oliver. He'll know as soon as he looks at him that he didn't drown, and my guess is he'll come here expecting some answers straight afterwards. You must tell him the truth, Annie, and you must tell the police the truth as well – but – if there was some way you could keep Matt out of it I'd be very grateful. If they think I killed Arthur, well they'll sling me back into Blackridge and that's not so bad, but if they think Matt did it, they'll hang him and I couldn't live with that.'

Annie wriggled beside her and rolled on to her back, her hair tumbling softly across Julia's face. Julia could sense that she was simply lying, staring up at the ceiling and she smoothed the abundance of curly red hair gently. Then Annie drew a sharp, deep breath.

'D'you love Matt?' she asked.

'Yes, I do, very much,' Julia replied truthfully. 'He's just asked me to marry him and I accepted. We wondered if they'd let us marry before they hanged us.'

'They'm not hanging either of you,' Annie declared softly, 'because I killed my pa. Leastways that's what I'm going to be telling the police. And since there weren't nobody else there 'cept you and Matt, then there ent nobody can argue with it.'

Julia reached out her arm swiftly and switched on the bedside lamp, then propping herself up on her elbow she stared down at Annie's battered and glowing face. Her green eyes were feverishly bright, her cheeks very flushed.

'You're not telling anybody any such thing!' she exclaimed. 'Annie, don't be ridiculous, you didn't kill your father! You're running a temperature, sweetheart, you don't know what you're saying. Things will look very different in the morning, I promise you.'

Annie closed her eyes.

'I'm so tired,' she whispered, 'but I'm so hot. Will you let me be your bridesmaid? I always wanted to be a bridesmaid and have a pretty pink dress.'

Julia muttered, 'There won't *be* a wedding.' but Annie groaned and twisted restlessly, throwing out her arms and legs to try and find some cool corner somewhere, and with a little sigh Julia crawled out of bed again.

For an hour she sat on the side of the bed, growing ever more chilly, until Annie was sleeping soundly and deeply and the high colour was beginning to fade, then pulling on her robe again she left the dim light on beside the bed and padded back downstairs, shivering.

Matt was dozing by the fire as the embers glowed. Julia threw on another couple of logs and then went to the french windows and looked out at the night. The air between the heavy curtains and the window was icy cold.

'The storm's going at last,' she said quietly, 'listen, the wind's dying down. I can't sleep with Annie, she's running a temperature and she's like a furnace, but at least she's sleeping now, anyway.' She came back to him and as he held out his arms, crawled on to his knee and cuddled into him gratefully, greedy for the warmth and comfort he offered. 'I'm so tired I can hardly keep my eyes open,' she whispered, 'and yet I want to stay awake all night with you. Don't let me sleep away our precious time together, Matt.'

'I won't,' he promised and kissed her, and he held her very close to him as she sank immediately into sleep, her face white as marble with fatigue and beautiful against his shoulder.

They awoke with bewildering abruptness to the sound of pounding on the front door. Julia slid off Matt's knee and lurched about stiffly, trying desperately to get her bearings and collect her thoughts. It was only dimly light, so it was obviously very early, before eight-thirty since Mrs Collins was not around yet.

The pounding came again with even more urgency, and she staggered towards the hall, pushing her thick chestnut hair back from her face. Seven minutes past eight the clock said.

Bruising her fingers, she struggled with the bolts on the front door and eventually managed to open it, finding herself immediately knocked backwards by a blast of freezing air. Protesting, she stood rubbing her fingers, her shoulders hunched, her heavily circled eyes gazing out from a pinched, white face, and to Oliver she was alarmingly reminiscent of that first time he had seen her at Blackridge. But that memory, with the knowledge of whose fault it was she had spent more than half her life there, filled him with foreboding. Uninvited he marched into the hall.

'Julia, where's Annie?' he demanded, closing the door behind him. 'Is she here?'

Julia hugged her arms close to her body; she was freezing and exhausted, but she still managed a touch of irony.

'Come in, Oliver, why don't you?' she said. 'Make yourself at home. Are you having trouble sleeping or something?'

'Where's Annie?' he persisted, and followed her as she turned away and slouched uncomfortably back to the drawing-room. Then he saw Matt. 'And what's *he* doing here at this time in the morning!'

'Oliver,' she said imperiously, turning to face him and folding her arms, hoping for a touch of grandeur, but seriously doubting she achieved it, 'Matt lives in the dower and is a farmer, so he gets up very early. Annie is asleep upstairs in bed and last night was running a temperature. I have been dragged from sleep by your persistent hammering on my door and the puppies are hoping for a walk any time now. There, that covers all of us, what else would you like to know?'

'Arthur Paynter is lying dead on the beach in the harbour, Julia,' Oliver said through clenched teeth, 'I've just come back from viewing the body.'

She smiled cheerfully.

'Oh, good,' she said, 'drown, did he?'

'No, and you know bloody well he didn't! Now what happened here last night?'

His face was white and pinched, she noticed, and not just with the cold, Oliver was very angry, and unless she was much mistaken, seriously frightened. So, he believed *she'd* killed Arthur? Well then, it shouldn't be too difficult to convince him that she had.

'We slept badly,' she replied facetiously, 'but I've already told you that. From what particular point would you like to know what happened here last night?'

She watched him lick his lips, a sign that he was uncomfortable. Matt had moved to stand behind her and she leaned against him, feeling absurdly comforted by his presence, and more determined than ever to keep him out of it.

'When you telephoned me last night,' Oliver said slowly, I went to Rectory Farm as you asked and I found Gladys Paynter, just as you said I would, still lying on the floor and badly hurt. I put her arm in a splint, stitched the cut on her head, treated her burns and helped her upstairs to bed. After that I came here to tell Annie what I'd done, and to my surprise I found Tremar empty. The lights were on and the back kitchen door was unlocked, but there was no one in the house. Then this morning I learned from the landlord at The Smugglers that Annie, very bruised and battered and soaked to the skin, was looking for her father at almost ten o'clock last night. Now I may be pretty dense about some things, Julia, but I'm not stupid enough to think you let her go across the cliffs alone in a storm like that! No one might have seen you, but you were certainly there with her!'

Julia smiled, it was a tight, bitter little smile and she watched him steadily.

'Are you saying then, that you think I killed Arthur, Oliver?' she asked.

His nostrils flared.

'Did you?'

At last, her confession time. She could keep the other two safe after all.

'Well what do you think?' she murmured. 'You were the one who rescued me from Blackridge. Twenty-three-and-a-half years I'd been there, amongst the mad and unwanted and Arthur had made no attempt to help me during all those years. Did you really think I was going to let him get away with it?'

Oliver Crompton swallowed uncomfortably. He didn't want this, it repelled him. He was still as obsessed with her as he had always been and the idea of sending her to the gallows was nightmarish. It would make *him* feel as if he had murdered *her*.

'Julia,' he said slowly, 'his neck's broken. How did you do that?'

'It wasn't difficult, he was drunk.'

'So how did you do it? Standing there on the slipway in all that wind and rain. Explain it to me please.'

'I pushed him, and when he toppled on to the beach I jumped on him and made sure he didn't get up.'

'Only he did,' Matt said slowly and calmly, speaking for the first time and at the same moment putting his hands very gently on her shoulders, 'and he not only got up, he attacked her. I broke his neck, Dr Crompton and I did it intentionally. I grabbed him round the neck and twisted his head, same way as you break an animal's neck.'

Oliver felt his face flush with relief. He suffered no squeamishness about sending Matt Logan to the gallows.

'So it was you, as I suspected,' he said, sneering very slightly, 'I knew all along it must have been. Why did you try and protect him, Julia? Is this some sort of aristocratic master–servant ritual that we less privileged know nothing about?'

Julia would have slapped him then, she had actually swung her arm back to do it when another voice, in the doorway, made them all turn sharply.

'They didn't either of them kill my pa! They'm just trying to protect me, and I'm *not* having it!' Annie declared ferociously, her damaged lips quivering as she spoke. 'I killed him, and I'm proud of it! When he come out the pub he was going to hit me, *yet again*, even after what you can see he done to me, and what he did to my ma! Oh, yes, Julia was there, 'cos she wouldn't let me go on me own, but I was the one what done for him, and I want everyone to know! For your information, she never even saw what happened!'

'Annie, sweetheart,' Julia murmured moving forwards quickly, 'come on, there's no need for this.'

'Oh, yes there bleddy is!' Annie shouted passionately. ' 'Cos *him*, bleddy doctor there, he wants to put you and Matt in prison, and I killed Pa! It were my right after all he done to me, and I did it!'

'I don't want to put anyone in prison, Annie,' Oliver lied, glancing very quickly at Matt, 'but I must know the truth. *How* did you kill your father?'

Annie's puffy eyes began to fill up with tears and her lips trembled. What she said bore no resemblance to what she could possibly remember, Julia knew, but she did wonder which bit of what she remembered could move her to tears so quickly.

'When he come out The Smugglers he was drunk as a lord,' she said, 'and it were blowing and raining something awful! It were so *bleddy* dark, that I couldn't see Julia no more, and I bashed into that *bleddy* capstan on the slipway twice! I thought my ma was dead and I wanted him to go home, to see what he'd done but he come at me in a rage so I pushed him, 'cos he scared me! I didn't know he was right on the edge of the harbour wall.' Suddenly her face crumpled and her bruised lips worked uncomfortably. She wiped her nose angrily on her sleeve and at last she wept, 'I heard this noise, like someone breaking a stick. I didn't think that he could be dead, but I was scared so I didn't say nothing, and then Matt come out the pub, and I told him Pa'd gone home, and we found Julia and he carried me home here, and. . . .'

Abruptly her body was racked with sobs and Julia gathered her up quickly, holding her close and rocking her backwards and forwards. Oliver stared at the three of them and Matt and Julia stared back at him. Well, certainly Annie had heard her father's neck break, she had described it perfectly, but as to whether she had done it, that was a different matter altogether.

'So all three of you say you did it, which means two of you must be lying,' he said, 'and I'm afraid my money's on your gamekeeper here. I'm sorry, Julia, but I shall have to return here later this morning with the police, you must understand that.'

She looked at him coldly.

'If you say so,' she replied, passing the still weeping Annie gently to Matt and pulling herself up to her full height. 'I'll see you out, then.'

She walked very calmly to the front door with him but as he put out his hand for the catch she touched his arm softly.

'Can't you let it go, Oliver?' she asked quietly.

He stared at her in astonishment.

'Let *what* go? He's got a broken neck Julia, he didn't drown! I can't issue a death certificate, it would be more than my life's worth.'

She pressed her lips together tightly and drew in a deep breath.

'Then can't you let Matt and me take Annie to the police this morning to make a statement? What have you got to lose? You saw what Arthur did to Gladys, you can see what he did to Annie first, and if you succeed in getting Matt and me charged with murder you're just destroying the child's life a bit more. She's got a chance now, an opportunity to go to school and then to university; to drag herself out of her meagre existence. She's got two people who want to be parents to her, the sort of parents every child deserves. You've sold your practice, I know you have, and in less than a month you'll be gone from here. You and I will probably never see each other again but you saved my life in the beginning. Are you really going to destroy me now because you simply can't forgive me for not being what you wanted?'

Oliver felt his heart wrench in his breast, he wanted to snatch her into his arms and kiss her and at the same time he wanted to beat her head in.

'Are you in love with *him*?' he asked, casting his eyes towards the drawing-room.

She smiled gently.

'He asked me to marry him last night,' she replied. 'I said I would.'

For a moment they stared at each other, then Oliver flung open the door.

'Oh, go to the police, the three of you,' he snarled, 'and say what you bloody well like!'

Chapter 22

The police came to Tremar at just before ten, long before Julia and Matt had a chance to take Annie into town. Julia didn't know what she expected, she had never had any experience of the police, but an inspector came, accompanied by a uniformed constable, and they both had charming manners.

Mrs Collins, who had known about Arthur's death before she arrived for work – such was the 'jungle drum' system in Polwean – showed them into the drawing-room, and Julia noticed that she was very protective of her brood and faintly disapproving of strange men with big feet tramping all over the manor.

The statement they gave the police was word for word the story they had told Oliver, and just as untruthful. Annie swore that neither Matt nor Julia had seen her father fall, or heard anything, which wasn't surprising in such a storm, and she had been too frightened to say anything. Matt and Julia didn't contradict her.

'So when did you know Mr Paynter was dead?' the inspector asked, and Julia smiled at him politely.

'This morning, when Dr Crompton came looking for Annie.'

Annie's bruises had been ripening all night and she was showing signs of being feverish again. As the two policemen gazed at her they were both frankly disgusted. Each of them was a married man with children of his own, and that a father should leave his daughter looking like Annie looked was appalling. They had seen Gladys, too, and they were both privately of the opinion that a man who could do that to the women in his family was probably better off dead.

There were no charges to answer that they could see. Certainly the landlord of The Smugglers, and Tom Pennard, had confirmed that the child had come looking for her father in the storm, but neither of them could say for sure when Matt Logan had left. In fact, the landlord seemed to think he'd still been there for some time after Annie and her father had departed, so if he'd set off home and caught up with the two women on the way, well, he wouldn't have been any the wiser.

In the half-hour they spent with Annie they liked the fact that the girl seemed very attached to and at home with the obviously charming owner of Tremar. They drank coffee with Julia and Matt, they admired the puppies, they wished Annie luck and they left.

They said they were unlikely to be back, that it was obvious Arthur had died as a result of an unfortunate, freak accident.

When Mrs Collins had seen them off the premises she came back to the drawing-room and observed to Julia that she and Annie looked as if they could do with a damn good sleep.

Julia smiled at her fondly.

'I certainly think Annie could do with one,' she replied, 'but I have something I must do first. Annie, will you be good and go to bed or do I have to go through the "if you're well enough to stay up you're well enough to go to school" routine?'

Annie smiled through her bruised lips, but her face was flushed and she looked dreadful.

'I can't wait to go to bed,' she admitted frankly, 'I got a terrible headache.' Suddenly she reached out and touched Julia again. 'But I can stay in your bed, can't I?' she asked.

Julia kissed her, cupping her face in her hands fondly.

'Of course you can,' she said, 'and I'm sure Mrs Collins will look in on you now and then to see if you're all right. Matt and I will be back by lunchtime.'

As she and Matt, with the dogs at their heels, set out across the formal lawns of Tremar it was the most extraordinarily beautiful day. The sky was brilliant blue with hardly a cloud to be seen and though it was quite as cold as it had been the night before, it was hard to believe the nightmare of the storm had really happened. Like something unreal, half remembered in the back of the mind.

But more than Arthur had passed away in the raging tempest. The first thing they saw as they went towards the orchard was that at sometime during the night the pavilion had finally been demolished. Bits of it were scattered over what had once been the tennis-courts; the remains of the roof was stuck in a hedge.

Gone, and with it beautiful, hazy memories of a vanished life.

'All that rage and turmoil last night seems to have done quite a lot of clearing out of the old life, doesn't it?' she remarked, watching her breath rise in white wisps from her lips and float away into the china blue sky. 'First Arthur, now the pavilion.'

Matt took her hand, holding it tightly clasped in his.

'Even more than that,' he replied, 'when I took the pups out early, we walked down to the bay. The boathouse has gone too. There's bits of it all over the beach and up the cliff path.' He glanced at her. 'D'you think yon doctor will hold his tongue, or will he want to make an issue out of Paynter's death?'

'I think he'll hold his tongue,' she murmured, 'but I think he'll go away from here sadly disillusioned. You know, Matt, when he first found me at Blackridge he honestly did what he did for purely altruistic reasons. Miss Vincent told me he was determined to get justice for me. It was just such a pity for him that he had to fall in love with me – and a pity for me, too, I think. When he's in love he's utterly selfish, he wants everything his own way.'

'I don't want you ever to be anything other than you are, my sweet Julia,' Matt said suddenly, stopping and taking her into his arms to kiss her. 'Do you think you can manage that?'

'I think I can have a jolly good try,' she answered with a grin. 'Tell me, did you mean it when you asked me to marry you last night, or was it just that we were on the verge of an abyss? I would understand if this morning things look a bit different.'

He squeezed her warmly against him, rubbing his cheek against her hair as the bitter cold nipped sharply at their faces and fingers, and they could feel each other's warm breath.

'As a matter of fact,' he replied eventually, 'things do look very different this morning. Last night I was expecting to be hanged, today I'm planning my wedding. I thought, mebbe, we could do the deed a couple of weeks before Christmas, with the lassies as bridesmaids. I have a fancy to have a good woman to wake up next to on Christmas morning.'

Julia pressed her cold lips briefly against his.

'I think I could accommodate that,' she said with a chuckle.

They reached Annie's bit of broken wall and found that the little spinney of trees which had grown up around it over the years was somewhat depleted this morning. Julia supposed there would be damage all over the area and she was right. They came upon many uprooted and damaged trees as they made their way to Rectory Farm, and as they crossed the stile at the side of the Drake Arms, they saw the sign had gone. What was left of it was leaning drunkenly against the churchyard wall.

'I'll replace that,' she said, 'as a wedding gift. We'll have a new sign there with the family coat of arms, and perhaps some brass lamps. Do you realize the Drake name will be gone from Tremar by Christmas? How strange, after so many centuries!'

The farmyard at Rectory Farm was in a sorry state; most of the barn had been demolished and there had been some damage to the farmhouse roof, as well. Julia viewed the devastation in silence for a moment or two, then pressed her lips together.

'I'd like to see Gladys on my own if you don't mind, my love,' she said, glancing at Matt. 'Maybe you could do a quick assessment of the damage here? I'll want to pay for it.'

He smiled and nodded and she went away from him to the kitchen door, knocking only briefly and entering without waiting. Gladys was sitting in a threadbare armchair by the range. Jed and Jethro were either side of her like matching bookends; black-suited, sombre and, so it seemed to Julia, more bewildered than grieving.

Gladys looked dreadful. Her face was burned, bruised and dreadfully swollen, her eye closed, the cut above it covered by a bandage. Her right arm had been carefully splinted and was supported by a sling; her other hand held the damaged one protectively.

'Hullo, Julia,' she said very quietly, 'I was expecting you. How's Annie?'

'Sleeping,' Julia replied coming to the range and putting out her hands towards it, grateful for its warmth. 'She's got a slight temperature, but she'll be fine. She's not nearly as badly hurt as you are.'

Gladys shrugged and watched Julia with dull, lifeless eyes.

'Doctor patched me up very comfortably last night,' she said, 'thanks to you. It were good of you to send him. He said he wanted to come back this afternoon, but I told him not to. Doctors is a luxury we can't afford.'

'I'll pay Oliver's bill,' Julia answered immediately, 'and I insist he comes here as often as he thinks necessary. Gladys, could I talk to you alone, do you think?'

Gladys smiled, but it was no more than a meaningless movement of her facial muscles. She reached up her good hand to whichever of her sons was standing on her left and he bent towards her gently. They were so much alike, Julia thought, that she would never be able to tell the difference between them – but then she'd been hard pushed to it to tell the difference between Gladys's brothers, all those years ago.

'Be good boys and let me talk to Miss Drake on me own,' she murmured. 'One of you might look out yer pa's suit; give it a good brushing and airing afore we bury him in it.'

The two boys bent and kissed their mother and then went through into the house together. Julia wondered at the logic of airing and brushing a suit they were about to consign to earthy darkness for evermore, but she wouldn't have been rude enough to say so. Gladys invited her to pull up a chair and they sat opposite each other in the grimy, smelly kitchen.

'Gladys, did Arthur tell you about the five hundred pounds I gave him yesterday morning?' Julia asked.

Gladys nodded, her face seemed grey, but it had to be with pain, not grief, surely, Julia thought.

'He made a big song and dance about it,' she replied bitterly, 'said he had you right where he wanted you and he'd be able to get money off you for evermore, 'cos you'd do anything to keep your hands on Annie, but you'd also do anything to keep the village from knowing. The cheque's in the front room, you can have it back now, he was going to put it in the bank this morning.'

'The money's yours to keep, Gladys,' Julia said quietly. 'I also told Arthur I'd pay his debts, so I'll need a list of his creditors at sometime. Can you afford to bury him?' Gladys shook her head and suddenly her lips trembled, Julia touched her, softly. 'I'll arrange his funeral then, you don't have to tell a soul if you don't want to – and Matt is doing a quick assessment of the damage outside at the moment, because obviously I'll pay for that.'

Suddenly Gladys's head came up and she stared at Julia with a look of bitter resentment on her face.

'Why would you do that, Julia?' she demanded. 'Pay his debts, pay to bury him, pay for all the repairs that wouldn't be needed if he'd done the proper maintenance in the first place? You don't have to *buy* Annie from *me*, you know, I've only ever wanted the best for her – and that's all I wants from you, a promise that you will do the best. When I see'd him burning her things last evening, lovely little bits of sewing that she'd done in school – well I felt like killing him then!'

'Yes, but I *did* kill him, Gladys,' Julia murmured.

Gladys gaped at her.

'*You* did?' she exclaimed. 'Well that weren't as how I heard it. The police told me he was so bleddy pissed when he come out The Smugglers last night, that Annie give him a shove and he fell off the wall and broke his neck! After what he'd done to her I'm not surprised she shoved him!'

'That was what Annie told the police,' Julia said quietly, 'only it wasn't true. I was quite prepared to tell them what happened, but she wouldn't let me. I shoved Arthur off the harbour wall and then I made sure he didn't get back up again. I'm telling you, Gladys, because you're the one person who has the right to know. And if you insist I should, I'll go to the police immediately and confess.'

There was a long pause and the kitchen was very quiet, Somewhere, in another part of the house, Julia heard one of the twins going up the stairs with a heavy step, then, abruptly, Gladys uttered a bitter little chuckle.

'If I had any money, Julia,' she observed, 'I'd give you a bleddy medal!' She broke off and her lips began to quiver as her eyes filled with tears. 'But I still say it were partly your fault he were like he was. Oh, you paid for your sin, by God, you paid, but . . . but maybe he wouldn't have bin quite so bitter an' twisted if it hadn't bin for you. You gave him a taste of the life he could never have, and when he lay with you he dreamed dreams, same as you did. Difference was they was only dreams to you, whatever you thinks now, but he thought if he could have you, he could have the rest of it and all!'

It was probably quite true, but it wasn't something Julia could think about sensibly. Any logical thoughts she might have had about Arthur were tainted by her memories of Blackridge, and the blame was black and white in her mind. It would always be so – but the past was the past. The future was Matt. She reached across and touched Gladys's hand.

'I'm sorry,' she whispered, squeezing softly with her fingers, and after a moment, Gladys returned the pressure of the touch.

'Take care of Annie for me,' she said, 'and take her with my blessing, Julia. Give her the opportunities I never had, please. I'd love to be proud of her, even if only from a distance.'

'Oh, she's going to university, Gladys,' Julia promised and then, climbing to her feet she bent and kissed the woman fondly on the cheek, 'but she will always be *your* daughter, I promise, she'll never want to forget that. I'll go now, but in a day or two we'll make arrangements for the funeral – and please, grant me a favour? Let me help the twins restore Rectory Farm to the way it was in Arthur's parents' time. I owe you that, whatever you think.'

They buried Arthur a week later. It was a bleak, November day with relentless sleet dropping from the sky and a merciless wind tossing it into the mourners' faces. Annie went with Matt and Julia, but she stood beside her mother in the church, with Julia on the other side of her, and she hugged Gladys very close.

There were not many in attendance, and some that were, like Miss Penrose and Miss Hewlett, were, in Julia's opinion, most certainly not there in sorrow. As she entered in the procession behind the coffin, with Annie and her mother and the twins, she saw the spiteful old spinsters nudge each other and glance in her direction.

'And Julia Drake!' exclaimed Miss Penrose in the shop that same afternoon, 'Walking in as bold as you like with the chief mourners! 'Course we always said as how Arthur Paynter had some sort of hold over the Drakes. I mean, giving him that farm and all, when he come home after the war. And now young Annie living there at Tremar. Oh, it'd be interesting to know what *that's* all about!'

But they never would know.

And in the fading light of the cold, miserable afternoon, just the sexton remained in the graveyard, shovelling cold, wet earth into Arthur's grave.

Julia had buried him as close to her parents as she had been able to get. It was tidier, she decided, to have all the people she never wanted to visit in the same corner.

Just over two weeks before Christmas, Matt and Julia were married in the village church. In the weeks between Arthur's death and the wedding, Annie and Julia worked tirelessly at the sewing machine and Annie had her dearest wish: a bridesmaid's dress – it was not pink, however.

During those weeks, too, Minnie left Blackridge for good and came to live at Tremar. She brought nothing with her but the clothes Julia had given her and she came from the only place she could ever remember being in her life. But she came to spend her remaining years surrounded by love and comfort, and she was as excited as Annie at the prospect of being a bridesmaid.

'You – you don't mind,' Julia asked Matt carefully, 'about Minnie? I mean, not everyone would find it easy to live with her all the time. She can be quite demanding.'

Matt hugged her fondly.

'Julia, I would not have asked you to marry me if I'd not been absolutely happy with the life I know we'll lead,' he replied honestly. 'I knew about Minnie and Annie long before I asked you to be my wife, and I don't want to change anything, any more than you do.'

Julia gazed at him. Daily, now, there would be a moment, sometimes more than one when she would experience a small start of surprise at finding herself so much in love. She would come upon him unexpectedly somewhere and her heart would squeeze with delight, or they would sit together through a long winter evening, not always talking, but absolutely contented in each other's company. Often she would curl up against him on the sofa and sometimes they would get really romantic and dance to music from the gramophone, but there was no repeat of that one very brief and frantic physical encounter on the night of the storm.

Matt was not prepared to ask her to grace his bed before she was legally his wife and Julia, touched by such gentlemanly consideration, was quite happy to wait.

Flouting convention to the limit – which was always Julia's wont – she asked Ilona Vincent to give her away at the wedding, 'Since,' she pointed out fondly, 'you were the nearest thing I had to a parent for years.' And Miss Vincent, who was no stickler for convention either, was delighted to accept. It was going to be a very small, select wedding with only a handful of invited guests – but almost the entire village was going to be in church for the ceremony.

That much tradition, Julia was happy to follow, and on the day of the wedding she laid on free beer at The Smugglers and the Drake Arms and provided a spread in both public houses of astonishingly generous proportions: quantities of food, sweet and savoury, laid out on huge dishes. Once it had been what Polwean had expected when a Drake from Tremar was married. Now, there was not a single inhabitant left who remembered such an occasion – the last marriage had been the twelfth baronet and the pretty, dainty Florence from Falmouth – but nevertheless, everyone seemed to know about the tradition.

Their invited guests were Gladys and the twins, Miss Vincent, Mr and Mrs Collins, for Mr Collins was providing the wedding car, 'young' Mr Cruikshank, Andy, Matt's youngest brother who was to be his best man, and was coming all the way from Scotland for the occasion, and Oliver and Sophie, who had delayed their move from Polwean especially.

Oliver hadn't wanted to go, he had initially thrown the invitation in the rubbish bin. It was Sophie who had quietly insisted they attend. Sophie wanted more than anything to watch for herself the beautiful Julia commit herself for life, before God, to somebody else.

The day of the wedding dawned cold but satisfyingly bright. Miss Vincent, Minnie, Annie and Julia were up at first light. Matt and his brother, Julia suspected, had already been up for an hour or more, and probably done the usual rounds with the dogs in the dark, but since Matt was the bridegroom, he was absolutely forbidden to step from the dower into the house on pain of death.

Andy Logan had arrived two days before and Julia had found him as charming as his older brother, but that hadn't surprised her much. Matt's manners were so beautiful, she couldn't believe any member of his family would be any different. Andy had looked at Julia, raised his eyebrows and very gallantly kissed her hand.

The appreciation in his glance had said it all.

Annie and Minnie had long dresses of rich, green velvet with little, green matching hats. They wore cream kid gloves and carried cream leather prayer-books – and of course Annie looked spellbinding. The clever thing was that Minnie also looked eye-catching, Julia had chosen carefully and wisely. And when Annie, with Minnie beside her, stood and looked at both of them in the full length glass, she understood immediately why Julia had refused to let her have a pink dress. Minnie would have looked uncomfortable and sad in pink.

Each girl wore a single string of pearls; Matt's present to the bridesmaids. Annie would treasure that string of pearls for the whole of her life.

Julia's dress was cream lace lined with heavy silk, cut very slim to accentuate her lovely figure. It was free of ornament or frills and she wore no jewellery other than her diamond engagement ring. On her head she wore a wide-brimmed, cream silk hat at a fashionable angle, and she carried a heavy bouquet of red roses – which had been expensive and hard to come by, two weeks before Christmas.

She looked so exquisite that as Ilona Vincent stepped back to check the final effect before they left for the church, she actually caught her breath sharply, and stared at Julia in faint bewilderment for a moment.

'Can you really be . . . the same person?' she eventually asked softly.

Julia smiled.

'As that middle-aged creature who was drifting into death at Blackridge, less than a year ago?' she replied. 'The same skin and bone covering, yes, but not the same person, I don't think. Today I don't feel hatred towards anybody, not my parents, not Arthur Paynter, not anyone. Because of everything that's happened I have Matt and that wouldn't be the case if anything at all had happened differently. Oh, I'm not saying I'll always feel like this, and I'm not about to regularly put flowers on their graves, but today I'm at peace with them and myself.'

Ilona Vincent smiled and gathered up her gloves and handbag.

'You're an inspiration, Julia,' she said quietly, 'and what you've achieved is remarkable. Hold that to you always. What you've done in the last few months I suspect would be beyond the reach of most people, and now you've even succeeded in putting your bitterness behind you. I hope you and Matt will be *very* happy.'

'I don't think there's much doubt of that,' Julia answered confidently.

As she entered the packed church and the organ struck up to announce her arrival, Matt and his brother stepped up to the altar and then Matt turned to greet his bride. It was the first time they had seen each other and they were both absolutely enchanted. Matt wore full Highland dress, as did his brother, and he looked magnificent. His astonishing height and huge frame were splendid in kilt, white shirt with lace collar and cuffs and black velvet jacket, and the heavy plaid he wore across his shoulder was held in place with a fabulous silver and amethyst brooch.

As she took her place beside him she looked up into his face and grinned.

'Are you real?' she whispered, and he uttered a low chuckle.

'Well you don't look so bad yourself,' he replied.

Gazing at each other they made their vows in clear, ringing voices. When they were pronounced to be man and wife they kissed fondly and then took their little party away to the vestry to sign the register. Emerging at last to the familiar wedding march, and perhaps fully conscious for the first time that the church was positively stuffed with people, they went slowly up the centre aisle towards the door, pausing, before they left the building, at the serene marble monument to Alexander Drake.

Julia took a rose from her bouquet and laid it on the crossed, marble hands with great affection.

Oliver Crompton watched her and was suddenly reminded of the day of Lady Florence's funeral; of Miss Higgins laying her flowers on Alexander's breast and talking about Julia being wilful. He had just begun to love her then, was rushing as many times a week as he dared to Truro to see her, and delighting in the looks of admiration and wonder she gave him as he took her to new places, bought her lovely things, taught her about the world.

His heart wrenched in his chest and in jealous anger he turned away, a gesture Sophie didn't miss. Julia kissed her brother's likeness very gently and then she and Matt emerged into the winter sunshine, as the bells in the church tower pealed out in the cold, still air.

Most of the villagers stood around the outside watching as photographs were taken of the couple; it was likely quite a lot of them had never seen a camera and were fascinated by the procedure. It didn't take all that long, which was just as well because Julia was beginning to be extremely cold, then Mr Collins arrived in the wedding car and Matt handed his new wife into the back to many cheers and shouts of good wishes.

All the other members of the wedding party were handed into their various cars and in the end only Oliver and Sophie were left, walking across the green to Lamplighter House to collect their car, and watching scores of villagers pushing their way into the Drake Arms.

'I'm told she's laid on enormous spreads in there and The Smugglers,' Sophie remarked, 'and the drink is free for the rest of the day. There'll be a few thick heads in the morning. They made a beautiful couple, didn't you think, Oliver?'

Oliver glared at her as he fished in his pocket for his car keys.

'They're a pair of killers, Sophie,' he replied, 'who, to save their miserable necks, have put the blame on a child!'

Sophie sighed.

'Oh, *Oliver*!' she exclaimed wearily. 'That isn't how I heard it, you know, and it certainly isn't what Annie told the police. For God's sake, do you think anybody actually *misses* Arthur Paynter? So I'm told, Julia has paid off all his debts, footed the bill for the repairs to the farm and given Gladys and her twins a large sum of money. What's more, she apparently bought them all new clothes for the wedding, *and* she's sending Annie to St Margaret's Academy after Christmas. That's the most expensive private girl's school in Cornwall! Would it have been so much better for everybody if she'd been hanged, or thrown back into Blackridge?'

Oliver opened the car door for his wife and looked down at her briefly as she made herself comfortable.

'You're just like everybody else, aren't you?' he remarked. 'You think she's so wonderful. So perfect!'

'No, Oliver,' she replied very quietly, '*you're* the one who can't get over her.'

Lunch was salmon mousse followed by roast pheasant and then many and various delicious sweets. The centrepiece of the occasion was a magnificent, three-tier wedding-cake, exquisitely decorated with sparkling white icing and sporting a single red rose in a tiny silver vase on the top. It was Mr and Mrs Collins' wedding present to the couple and when Julia had first seen it she had very nearly burst into tears. Of course, traditionally the top tier should have been carefully wrapped in tissue paper and stored in a cool, dark place to await the christening of the first-born. But there would be no children of this union.

Julia had decided to send the large bottom tier to Blackridge for Miss Vincent to distribute as she thought fit.

The wedding party sat in the austere dining-room at Tremar, surrounded by the Drake ancestors, and somehow managed to create an atmosphere that was relaxed and genial. Minnie dropped jelly and trifle everywhere as usual, but Annie was getting so adept at spooning it back into her plate these days that nobody really noticed. 'Young' Mr Cruikshank sat between Jed and Jethro and, amazingly, they seemed to get on famously. Gladys sat next to Sophie Crompton, and Oliver found himself next to Ilona Vincent, who spotted his gloomy mood immediately. She didn't try to jolly him out of it, that wasn't her way, but she did try to offer him some advice.

It might have made him feel better if he'd listened.

As the afternoon wore on and the cold day outside was beginning to show signs of fading into evening, Julia slipped upstairs and changed out of her wedding-dress. Miss Vincent had offered to stay at Tremar for four days, to give Matt and Julia a chance of a short honeymoon, and they were going to spend it at an expensive hotel on Plymouth Hoe. It would take them a couple of hours or more to drive to Plymouth and they knew they must be leaving soon, if they were to be in time for dinner.

As she came down in her black dress, the one she had bought for her birthday, she saw Matt and Andy putting the cases into the car and she went into the drawing-room to say goodbye to their guests.

Sophie Crompton was right by the door. Julia had been watching her on and off all afternoon. She was dressed in pale blue and there was a kind of delightful freshness about her, but very noticeable was the calm confidence which she displayed these days. It was the first time they had been able to speak to each other without anyone else hearing, and Sophie put out her hand to stay Julia briefly in the doorway.

'Mrs Logan, thank you so much for inviting us today,' she said quietly, 'and I really do want to wish you all the luck in the world. I know we'll probably never meet again, but I'll never forget you.'

Julia gave her a sideways glance.

'I'm rather afraid to ask what that means,' she murmured with a smile. 'Mrs Crompton, I hurt you, I know, and if you can believe me, I'm terribly sorry. Perhaps you could find it in your heart to give me the benefit of the doubt and put it down to my shocking lack of experience? I wish you luck, too, I hope you and Oliver will be very happy in your new life, and I hope Oliver achieves his Harley Street practice one day.'

'I just hope he learns to live without you, one day,' Sophie replied, and then, taking a sip of champagne, offered Julia the friendliest smile she had ever managed. 'But thank you, for your apology, and thank you, too, for teaching me to stick up for myself. I shall probably have to do it again, one day, and next time I'll know how to start, won't I?'

And you, Julia thought, have had a spot too much champagne, but well done anyway, for having the courage to say your piece.

She moved into the room and was aware suddenly of Oliver standing alone by the french windows. He had been watching her short exchange with Sophie and he was still watching her, but as she caught his eye he instantly looked away.

Deliberately she crossed the room to speak to him.

'Aren't you going to wish me luck, Oliver?' she asked quietly, and he glared at her sourly.

'Luck!' he echoed. 'I think you've had all the luck you're entitled to recently, don't you? You and that great hulk of a husband of yours are lucky you're not both languishing in prison cells waiting to be hanged.'

She nodded, gazing out through the window at the darkening day and the little fountain playing over the lead boy and his fish.

'Would that have made it easier for you?' she murmured. 'Would you sooner have seen me hanged, or back in Blackridge, than let me have a life I wanted for myself? I couldn't *be* what you wanted, Oliver, and if I'd tried to be it would have destroyed both of us in the end.'

'You *were* what I wanted,' he persisted, 'until that Scotsman came on the scene. Dear God, we loved each other, we couldn't leave each other alone! Admit that when you lived in Truro, before you came back here, you couldn't wait for me to call!'

Julia studied his handsome face for a moment, then she shook her head sadly.

'You were the man who saved my life,' she said, 'you took me from a living death and you gave me freedom. You courted me gallantly, you steered me through the maze of modern life and you taught me to live again, but I never did love you, not in the way you wanted. I won't forget you, I promise, but I – I can't bear to think you're going away hating me.'

Oliver abruptly drained the glass he held in his hand and half turned away from her. Matt had come into the room and was watching them, but there was no jealousy or anxiety on his face, he was just politely waiting for them to finish their conversation. And *he* was the one Oliver hated!

'You got away with murder, Julia,' he observed with a mirthless little chuckle, 'now go away on your honeymoon and if it means so much to you to hear me say it, then I wish you luck in the rest of your life. But do me one small favour, would you, forget about me as soon as you can? You can be sure I'm going to do my best to forget you!'

Slowly and with great dignity she walked away from him.

She kissed Annie and Minnie and made them promise to be good for Miss Vincent and Andy, who was staying for a couple of weeks before returning to Scotland. She hugged Mrs Collins tearfully, and thanked her profusely for all she had done, for the wedding breakfast had been a truly magnificent feast, and then she and Matt took their leave of the rest of their guests.

In the car it was cold and they had a long journey ahead of them, but at last they were alone.

They passed close to Blackridge on their way towards the Devon border, but it was dark and Julia never saw it. Matt smelt of tweed and sandalwood soap, the sharp mixture of fragrances filled the car and Julia realized that those smells had become so familiar and safe in recent months that for evermore they would make her feel calm wherever she might encounter them. He was huge and protective in the seat beside her and she was brimming with love for him.

They dined late, overlooking the black water and twinkling lights in Plymouth Sound and they went to bed at eleven o'clock, tired, but contented.

And now, at last, Matt prepared to make love with her. Naked for him for the first time she let him see her scars.

He whispered, 'The whip!' as he saw the thin white stripes on her back, and he tightened his mouth in disgust, but he didn't ask her to spoil her wedding night by voicing her dark memories.

'Are they ugly?' she asked, 'I've never really been able to see them properly.'

He chuckled softly and touched her in such a way as to make her tingle and gasp with pleasure.

'There's nothing that's ugly about you, woman,' he replied, 'not a damn thing inside or out, and you'd have a right and a reason to be ugly, if you had a mind to be.'

Julia looked up at him.

'I have ugly memories,' she said, 'and they make me think ugly thoughts sometimes. I wasn't kind to Sophie Crompton and – there's Arthur of course.'

Matt kissed her for a long time.

'I said you weren't ugly,' he answered eventually. 'I didn't say you were a saint!' He bent his head to her and heard her mewl softly in delight. 'But I suppose you might make it to saint yet, of course!' he added and he laughed against her skin, his warm breath so sensuous that she shivered.

Now, wanting no more conversation but the fulfilment of what he had waited such a long time for he pushed her back on to the crisp, white pillows and laid his body across her.

She breathed, 'Oh, yes . . .' very softly, and he took her.

Matt was a big man, but his lovemaking was so gentle that Julia found only the greatest delight in accommodating him. He would not have hurt her for the world, and in time to come she would discover again and again what a remarkably gentle man he was. Now, though, with simple joy they loved each other, and their pleasure was mutual and passionate.

When at last they lay in each others arms, exhausted, but fulfilled and content, Julia suddenly turned her head to look at him and smiled into his deep blue eyes.

'Matt,' she said, 'if it was all for this, then it was all worth it.'

He touched her face very softly with his fingers.

'It wasn't all for this,' he replied, 'not for either of us. This is the bonus we've been granted for surviving the rest.'

'Then I'd happily survive it again for such a bonus,' she observed, and he kissed her.

'Me too,' he agreed. 'Welcome to our first day of married life, Mrs Logan.'

Oliver and Sophie Crompton left Polwean two days later and, taking the same route as Matt and Julia had taken, passed close by Blackridge on their way. Oliver stared at the huge, ornate clock-tower that seemed to dominate the surrounding landscape and his heart was so full of pain and rage that he couldn't have spoken even if he'd wanted to.

Sophie said nothing until the clock-tower was completely out of sight, then she turned to look at him and murmured, 'Oliver, no matter how bad you feel, please don't wish you'd never found her in the first place, will you?'

'I don't wish that,' he lied. 'I don't wish that at all! I just don't think she and that loutish Scotsman should be allowed to get away with murder!'

Sophie smiled bitterly.

'That's not the issue, Oliver,' she said quietly, 'and you know it isn't. You're obsessed with her and you simply cannot understand why she doesn't feel the same about you. Well, I very much doubt that we shall ever see them again, so the sooner you learn to live without her, the easier it's going to be, but I do hope one day you might come to understand her feelings a little bit better. For your own sake.'

Oliver would come to understand. In the not very distant future he was to be given a powerful and painful insight into hopelessness, and Sophie was wrong, too, when she doubted that she would ever see Julia again. The Cromptons' lives were destined to be bound up for a long time with the woman he had rescued from Blackridge asylum. Now, however, they drove through Plymouth, which brought them very close to Julia, and drove on, which took them many miles away.

Two days later Julia and Matt left the city and drove back to Tremar and the day after that they resumed their lives on the estate. Nothing really changed at all, except that they now shared a bedroom.

They celebrated Christmas lavishly; lots of holly and mistletoe and a huge Christmas tree. The manor looked splendid. Two days later it was Annie's fifteenth birthday, and Julia gave her the little gold and pearl ring. She threw a party for her, too; a party which, for both of them – and for Gladys – celebrated their freedom. And so the happy week rolled on to New Year's Eve.

At twelve midnight, Julia, Matt and Annie stood in the drawing-room at Tremar and drank a toast to the first day of 1939. In a chair close to the fire, Minnie snored comfortably with the dogs at her feet. It was, for Julia, a moment of perfection, just the people she loved most in the world there in the room with her.

'Twenty-four years,' she whispered, 'since the last time I could wonder what the next year would hold, Now, no matter what happens it will be an adventure.'

'For both of us,' Annie agreed fondly, kissing her and then hugging Matt.

They didn't really think about war as they enjoyed each other's company; it wasn't appropriate, but beyond them, and beyond their control the world spun towards change.

Soon nothing would ever be quite the same again, but many times they would look back to their first summer together, and many times they would talk about it, with love.